The

TOYMAKER'S
APPRENTICE

ALSO BY
SHERRI L. SMITH

Orleans
Flygirl

SHERRI L. SMITH

G. P. Putnam's Sons
An Imprint of Penguin Group (USA)

G. P. PUTNAM'S SONS
Published by the Penguin Group
Penguin Group (USA) LLC
375 Hudson Street
New York, NY 10014

USA | Canada | UK | Ireland | Australia
New Zealand | India | South Africa | China
penguin.com
A Penguin Random House Company

Library of Congress Cataloging-in-Publication Data
Smith, Sherri L.
The toymaker's apprentice / Sherri L. Smith.
pages cm
Summary: Journeyman toymaker Stefan Drosselmeyer is recruited by his mysterious
cousin, Christian, to find a mythical nut that will save Boldavia's princess and his own
kidnapped father from a fanatical Mouse Queen and her seven-headed Mouse Prince,
who have sworn to destroy the Drosselmeyer family.
[1. Fairy tales. 2. Adventure and adventurers—Fiction. 3. Toy making—Fiction.
4. Apprentices—Fiction. 5. Princesses—Fiction. 6. Kidnapping—Fiction.] I. Hoffmann,
E. T. A. (Ernst Theodor Amadeus), 1776–1822. Nussknacker und Mauskönig. II. Title.
PZ8.S4132Toy 2015
[Fic]—dc23
2014045980

Printed in the United States of America.
ISBN 978-0-399-25295-2
1 3 5 7 9 10 8 6 4 2
Design by Annie Ericsson.
Text set in Carre Noir Std.

For my brother, Derek,
who distracted our piano teacher
while I read Hoffmann's wonderful book.

BOOK I

The Toymaker's Apprentice

IT WAS A DREARY DAY for the time of year in Nuremberg. Gray clouds hung low over the peaked roofs of townhome and hall. The cobblestoned streets seeped with drizzled rain. A little gray dove leapt into the air from a great oak tree that stood in the graveyard. From his perch in the limbs of the tree, Stefan Drosselmeyer watched as the bird flew over hundred-year-old graves, and the newer crypts adorned with weeping angels and family names.

A thin line of mourners followed the coffin in a sad parade through the cemetery gates and into the mossy rows of the dead. In the distance, two gentlemen on horseback, clad in the same black as mourners, regarded the scene from a nearby rise.

A hitch developed in the smooth strokes of the dove's wing-beats and it faltered. Stefan frowned as the wings froze and the bird glided back toward his tree, where he snatched it from the sky. One of the men on horseback looked up, revealing an eye patch and a single bright blue eye.

Stefan scooched farther back into the shelter of the tree. He bit his lip, turning the dove over in his hands. Up close, the bird looked less like a dove and more like a child's approximation of a bird. A solid shape, no feathers, and only a dark spot of paint for the eye. He had just completed his apprenticeship as a toy-maker and was proud of his bird. His father, who also happened to be his master toymaker, was the old-school sort who thought toys should only move when lifted. But Stefan was more interested in the modern trend toward automation. He brushed a shock of damp hair out of his eyes and frowned at the damaged wings. The paint had failed to seal the joints completely, and rain had gotten in, swelling the wood.

In the graveyard beneath his tree, the procession had come to a stop before a low black crypt. He could hear the priest droning on, the sound of his father in tears.

"Where is he?" a sharp-nosed woman whispered. Stefan's absence had been noticed.

"He's just a child," a plump woman murmured. "The church service was more than enough."

It *had* been more than enough, Stefan agreed. The gloomy cathedral, soot blackened, candles barely bright enough to see by. And his mother, cold and pale in the narrow coffin.

His father had insisted on building the casket himself, a tribute to his beloved wife. He wished to be alone with only his tools, not his son. Left to his own devices, Stefan had decided to make the dove.

Murmured condolences covered the gossip of the two women. Stefan examined the wooden bird. When wound by the pegged tail feather piece, the wings would crank to a point of tension and then, with the tail cocked just so—the bird would take flight. Light wooden wings beating a frantic blur. A favorable wind could keep the dove aloft for minutes at a time.

But today the wind blew strange. He stuffed the bird into the pocket of his redingote and pulled out a sketchbook. The wool coat was too big for him, and too heavy for the weather, but it was his only black coat. He'd grow into it, his mother had said. For now, it kept out the worst of the rain.

He jotted down a few thoughts in his notebook beside a sketch of the bird device. Below, he could hear the priest's blessings come to an end. He risked a glance down at the gathering. The door to the crypt stood open, black as night, blacker than the lacquered coffin. Above the lintel, a name was carved deep into the stone: *Drosselmeyer*.

With a slide of wet leaves, Stefan dropped out of the far side of the tree and hopped the fence, his coat snagging briefly on the rusty iron bars. He dragged himself free without looking back. A tear in the wool would be more easily mended than a tear in his heart, and that was what would happen if he watched them roll his mother into her grave.

Don't look back, he told himself. His hair was in his eyes again, the same blue-green eyes as his mother's, the same dark blond hair. He pushed the locks brusquely out of his way. "Never look back," he said through clenched teeth, and walked out into the gray world. His boots clattered onto the cobblestones, gaining in tempo as he broke into a run.

ON THE HILL overlooking the graveyard, the men on their strange black horses shifted. No breath rose from the nostrils of their stone-still mounts. The men shook their reins, and with a soft click of gears, the horses followed Stefan into the street.

THE CAT AND THE RAT faced off in the alleyway. The tom was less mangy than the rat would have liked. He preferred his predators old and toothless. The rat was not as fat as the cat would have preferred. He liked a nice plump snack, but this rat was one of those rangy fortune hunters who had fallen on hard times.

They eyed each other in the night. The rat's nose twitched, long whiskers glistening with the damp of the wharfside cobblestones. He rose to his full height, an impressive seven inches, and spoke.

"I should warn you," he said in perfect Catish, "I am quite the dab-hand at this." On the last word, he pulled his rapier from its sheath. Slender and wicked, the sharp blade (which he liked to call "Viper's Sting") flashed brightly, a vicious slice of moonlight in the depths of the shadows.

The cat raised a whiskered brow. Most rodents spoke a few words of Catish—mainly phrases such as "spare me," "please," and "mercy." Although that last one was a mistranslation. There was no word for mercy in the cat tongue, only "swiftly."

Ernst Listz was the sort of rat who knew the difference, the sort that could converse in more languages, both Man and Animal, than the average river rat, or even the exceptional one. Indeed, few scholars, rodent or human, spoke the tongues of other species. For, though they lived side by side, rarely did they try to understand each other. The cat might consider him an extra-special meal as a result, but Ernst would make sure it was hard won.

Suddenly, the cat made a sound that needed no interpretation: he chuckled and grinned, revealing two rows of very compelling argument. Each ivory tooth was as long and sharp as Ernst's little blade.

The rat set himself *en garde*, his sword at the ready, and waited for his opponent to strike.

The cat flattened his ears.

Ernst twisted the sword in his paw and smashed it into the cat's bared fangs with a quick snap.

The cat blinked, startled, even as his forepaw shot out.

Ernst dropped to the ground in that peculiar way only rats can. He whipped his hard pink tail around, poking the cat in the eye.

The cat hissed and struck, snagging the tip of Ernst's tail.

"Ha, Sir Rat! I have you now," the cat purred, his open eye gleaming green in the dark. The offended eye remained closed. Until Ernst pricked it with the tip of his sword.

"Do you?"

The cat winced. They formed a circle, linked tail to claw and eye to sword.

"*Détente?*" Ernst proposed. The scales were in perfect balance—neither cat nor rat had the upper hand—but for how long? More than one tomcat had willingly surrendered an eye for dinner. But, like a rat's tail, once lost, the eye would not grow back. The fight was a draw.

The cat sighed. "Well played, friend Rat. Fortunately, it does not suit my purposes to eat you at this time."

Ernst nodded, but his sword did not waver.

"Well then, I bid you on your way, Sir Tom. May our paths lie ever in opposite directions."

The cat appreciated the sentiment and chuckled again, a deep throaty sound called a "purr" by those human wretches who kept cats in high regard. Ernst held back a sneer.

By unspoken agreement, each released the other and took two paces back.

"Adieu," said the cat, displaying an unusual knowledge of a human tongue. Like cats and rodents, Man and Animal lived side by side in companionable ignorance. The only thing more rare than a cat who spoke Human was a man who spoke Catish, or any of the other languages of the Animal Kingdoms. But of course, these wharf cats came from all over and ate scraps at the tables of the world. Like rats had done once, long ago. Ernst relaxed his stance as the feline turned slowly and slipped into the night, his tail whipping silently in his wake.

And then Ernst collapsed against the cobblestones and breathed deeply, never mind the muck and the smell. The sweetest breaths always came immediately on the heels of cheated death. He could have hurt the brute with Viper's Sting, certainly, but with that mouth full of fangs, it was more like a battle of one against thirty. Odds even an adventurer like Ernst would rather avoid.

After a moment, his heart slowed enough for him to take stock. These alleys were likely crawling with cats waiting to take advantage of newly docked ships, and of the dull-witted rats who had spent too much time at sea, unsteady on their legs, out of practice in avoidance and combat.

Ernst sheathed his sword, inspected his tail—dimpled, but not cut, by those claws—and smoothed down his fur. Likely the tom had passed him up so easily because he was already full, dining on those very sea rats.

No one I know, of course, Ernst comforted himself. He might have acquaintances and kin in Paris, London, even Munich. But he was new to Vienna. If he disappeared here, no one would notice. But he was a Listz, from a long illustrious line of rodents, born of better times, destined for greatness. Or at least betterness. A hot meal, a soft bed, and an appreciative audience would be a start. Clean clothes would be better, but . . . Ernst sighed, retrieved his satchel from the gutter, and slung the strap across his shoulder. He stretched his long back, dropped to all fours, and scurried the rest of the way to the Underwall, a tavern near the water where he had heard a rat might find work. Someone with his talent for languages and etiquette, his understanding of human culture, could surely find a way to put a meal in his belly and the night on the far side of a sturdy door.

It was time to sing for his supper.

3

BY THE TIME you read this note I will be gone . . .

Stefan hesitated for the hundredth time. Writing a letter was almost as hard as telling his father to his face: Stefan was running away.

"Not running," Stefan corrected himself. "Just leaving. It's time." But he didn't sound as convinced as he had been earlier.

The fact was, he had served out his time in his father's toy shop. Every toymaker with three years' apprenticing graduated to the status of journeyman. Yes, he might have stayed to work in Nuremberg if his mother were still alive . . . But scarlet fever did not care for his plans one whit. Now, the "journey" part of "journeyman" called to him. Seven years to see the world. Seven years to put between him and the little stone crypt at the end of the graveyard.

In France, there was a toymaker who built lifelike dolls called automatons. Nightingales that sang operas, dogs that chased balls. In England, they were making life-size clockwork people!

A tremor of excitement ran through him. His father thought he was too young to leave home, but the world was waiting. Besides, home didn't feel like home anymore.

Stefan finished his note and left it on his father's workbench, clearing a space among the wood shavings and dolls' legs. He hesitated, touching the smooth edge of the sign his father had been carving before his mother fell ill.

Drosselmeyer and Son, it read in flowing letters, flanked by the raised images of a wooden soldier and a toy horse. Stefan swallowed hard and turned the sign over before the guilt in his belly could change his mind. The smooth white paper stood out starkly; his own blocky writing simply read, "Father."

Stefan stooped to gather his tools. He placed his awl, knife, chisel, and sanding cloth into a piece of leather fitted with pockets for each, then rolled it up. He scanned the shop—two benches, one old and stained with years of varnish and paint, the other newer and built to accommodate a young boy. He had outgrown the bench last year. And now, he realized he had outgrown the shop as well. They looked smaller, these rooms that had once been his entire world. The workshop to the left, the storefront with its counter and display shelves cluttered with wooden soldiers, sewn dolls, and the occasional porcelain-faced angel. The living room in the back with the trestle dining table and cozy hearth. His parents' room. The loft where he slept. The guest room, where his mother had . . .

His stomach turned and for a moment he feared he was going to be sick. The place was too small, he decided. His father might even be glad of the extra room once he was gone. That was a lie, he knew, but it helped him take the next step. He shouldered his bag, stuffing his tools deep inside. The world was darker now that his mother was gone. If he stayed any longer, it would go completely black.

"Don't look back," he reminded himself, and reached for the door.

Someone knocked. The door flew open, bounced off Stefan's boot, and slammed shut again.

"Ow!" Stefan said.

"Hello?" The knock was repeated, this time from the safety of the jamb. Stefan gingerly opened the door.

"We're closed," he said.

Two men stood before him dressed in black. One tall and lean with white-blond hair and an eye patch. The other dark-skinned, his hair kept hidden beneath a cleverly wrapped turban.

"Oh, hello, dear boy! We aren't customers," the white-haired man said. "We're family."

Stefan eyed the pale man and his dark companion dubiously. It seemed unlikely he was related to an albino or a Moor. "You were at the cemetery," he realized.

"And you were in the oak tree," the man said. He bowed by way of introduction. "Christian Elias Drosselmeyer at your service."

"Samir abd al-Malik," said the swarthy man with a similar bow.

"Cousin to the toymaker, your master, Zacharias," Christian Drosselmeyer said. "May we come in?"

"My master . . . ?" Stefan couldn't see a resemblance. This man was thin and pale, where his father was plump, broad chested and dark haired. Besides, the only family he had was at the graveyard. "I'm sorry, but I was just stepping out."

The self-proclaimed Drosselmeyer looked him over. Stefan wanted to hide his reddened eyes, and the huge bag hanging over his shoulder. He pressed his lips into a thin line and hoped the men would leave. Instead, they brushed past him, crowding into the workshop. Stefan's protests fell on deaf ears.

"Samir, what do you think? Is he 'just stepping out'?"

The Moor remained silent.

"Running away from your apprenticeship while the master is at a funeral!" Christian clucked his tongue. "I can't believe it's all that bad. Zacharias is the best man I know."

Stefan's face grew hot. "I'm not running away. I'm—"

"Stepping out, yes, yes," Christian interrupted.

Now Stefan really *did* want to run away. He tried to step around the unwanted visitors.

"Whose funeral?" Christian asked. "We passed by but didn't want to intrude."

Stefan's jaw stiffened. To these men, the procession in the graveyard was nothing more than a curiosity. To Stefan, it was the end of the world.

"My mother," he said, jaws clenched to bite back his grief.

"Your—" Christian paled and collapsed against the door frame. "Elise? My dear, sweet Elise . . . ?" His single eye grew bright with tears. "You're not the shop boy, you're her son. My little cousin, Stefan." He faltered for a moment. "I . . . I am so very sorry for your loss. What happened?"

Stefan's own eyes begin to sting. He tried to swallow the lump in his throat. "Scarlet fever. Really, I must ask you to step aside. I have a coach to catch," he insisted, racing against his grief.

"Of course," Christian said, his voice softened in sympathy. "You were just stepping out."

Stefan shoved past, afraid he would burst into tears in front of these strangers. His bag swept the workbench, and the half-finished sign, *Drosselmeyer and Son*, slapped to the ground with a clatter. The letter to his father drifted to the floor beside it.

11

All eyes were on the sign now. Stefan grimaced, wishing he could sink into the earth and disappear.

The dark man grunted. "Running out seems more like it. A family trait, I suppose."

Stefan gasped, surprised by the man's bluntness. He scrambled to pick up the fallen note, and shoved it into his pocket to hide his embarrassment. Christian bent beside him and picked up the sign. "On the day of his mother's funeral, too."

Stefan sputtered, embarrassment turning into anger. But with whom was he angry—them, or himself?

"Quite heartless," Christian murmured. Dusting off the sign with a gloved hand, he placed it back on the workbench, upside down once again. "Or, perhaps the boy feels too much?" He stepped back, clicking the heels of his black boots together. "Don't let us keep you. We'll just wait inside for your father and explain when he gets here. Unless, of course, you left a note." He scanned Stefan's reddening face. "Ah, you *did* leave a note. You're not cruel, then. Just restless, eh? I was the same at your age."

"You can't just stay here," Stefan said.

"Why not? You're leaving. It's nothing to you anymore."

Not true, Stefan realized as this infuriating man sat on the stool before one of the workbenches—*his* workbench! The one his father had built just for him when he could barely see over the top of it. His chest swelled at the offense. If only his tongue would untie itself long enough for him to respond.

"Your mother was a wonderful woman, Stefan," Christian said suddenly. "You must miss her terribly."

Stefan blinked away more tears. "I'm trying not to look back," he said stoically.

"We all try," Christian replied. "Now, before you're off, would you be so kind as to help my man with our luggage?" He indicated the open doorway.

Stefan gave up. He left his own bag by the door and stepped outside to find Samir closing the latch on one of two large black suitcases. Leather saddlebags lay against the side of the house. The horses were nowhere to be seen. At least he wouldn't have to play stableboy, too.

"Charmed you, has he?" Samir asked.

"More like confused and surprised," Stefan said. "But not charmed."

"Then you would be the first. I see he has managed to keep you from leaving?"

"I'm just here to help with the bags. I still have manners. And you have odd ones, for a valet."

Samir raised an eyebrow. "Valet?" He shook his head and broke into a white-toothed grin. "I'm no manservant."

Stefan flushed. "My apologies. He called you his 'man.' You are friends?"

"No," Samir replied. "I am his jailer." He tossed the saddlebags effortlessly to Stefan, who staggered under their weight.

"His jailer . . . ?"

The Persian or Moor or whatever he was stepped back, bowed deeply, and said, "Samir abd al-Malik, formerly of Arabia, Royal Astrologer of Boldavia and royally appointed jailer of the criminal Christian Elias Drosselmeyer, formerly of Boldavia, formerly of Nuremberg, at your service."

"Criminal?" Stefan repeated. Something tickled the back of his mind. He *had* heard of a cousin in royal service somewhere to the east, but not one that was also a criminal. "Isn't he a royal clockmaker?"

"Indeed," Samir said.

"But . . . if he's done something wrong, why isn't he in jail?"

"All the world's a prison when you are not free to choose your own road," Samir said obliquely.

Stefan shook his head. "I don't understand. Is he a thief?" The Arab remained silent, so Stefan's mind filled in the blanks. "He's a thief, and he's alone in my house!"

Stefan raced for the shop door and threw it wide, banging it against the wall.

"Aha!" he said, leaping out of the way as the door bounced back and slammed shut behind him. Across the shop, Christian closed the door to the bedrooms, unruffled.

"Aha, yourself," he said calmly.

Stefan blinked. The man seemed quite composed for a thief caught in the act. "What have you taken?" Stefan demanded.

Before Christian could answer, the front door burst open again.

"Herr Abd al . . . Samir," Stefan called, "contain your prison—"

But it wasn't Samir standing in the doorway. It was his father.

Home from the graveyard, his mourning clothes still damp with drizzle, Zacharias Elias Drosselmeyer stared back at his son. And then he saw the man with the white hair.

"Christian?" he said. "You came!" And he collapsed into the open arms of the criminal who shared his name.

IT WAS A ROUGH PLACE, this Underwall. Like most rodent taverns, it was nestled beneath the cellars of an ancient Man-built edifice. A sign swinging from an iron bracket above the doors marked the human building as an inn. A much smaller sign hung low to the ground, depicting a hole in a wall—indicating the entrance for a different crowd.

Inside, wharf rats and a few scraggle-coated mice huddled around low tables, drying their fur by the chimney that ran down from the ovens in the human kitchen overhead, heating the room to an almost intolerable degree.

Ernst stretched luxuriously in the welcome heat, cracking his knuckles and neck. It was good to be out of the cold. Gossip rose and fell around him. His sharp ears flickered back and forth, getting a feel for his audience. News of the richest crops, which ships were leaving soon, the latest sites of human battles—Men were always going to war. Armies made for good pickings, but troops and artillery were a plague to the field mice who lived beneath them.

He heard rumblings of some nonsense about a mouse up-rising in a place on the Black Sea. That would be crushed soon enough, Ernst thought, and the rest of the gossipers seemed to agree. He detected a wistfulness from a few of the rodents. It would be a quiet night.

Brushing his whiskers into shape, he sidled up to the bar and presented himself to the proprietor.

"Good evening, Master Barkeep. I am Ernst Listz, at your service," he said with a slight bow.

The old mouse looked him up and down. "At my service? What are you, then? A bard? A scribe?"

Ernst preened his whiskers. "Which do you have most need of tonight?"

The barkeep looked around the room. A few tired mice were finishing their meals; some were already rising to head home. In the darkest corners, wharf rats hunkered down over hard crusts.

"We could use a bit of song," the barkeep decided. He was a stout little mouse, more muscle than fat. "Nothing rowdy, though. Don't like the look of them sailors." He nodded toward the rats. Ernst did not take offense. He didn't care for the look of them either.

The mouse gave Ernst a considering look. "Tell you what, sing a song or two to get them in their cups, and do what letter writing there is, and there's a meal in it for you."

"Plus my writing fees," Ernst added.

"Aye, plus whatever you can glean from these stingy vermin. There's a table there with reasonable light."

Ernst thanked the mouse and made his way to the table by the fireplace. There, he set down his satchel, brushed the last of the night's dampness from his fur, and moved to stand beside the fire. No one seemed to notice this newcomer silhouetted against the flames. The murmur of gossip continued, the saying

16

of farewells, the rustling of coats. Ernst smiled. The mention of the mouse uprising had inspired him. Orange flames lit his hoary fur, glinting silver and copper in the warm light as he cleared his throat and began to sing.

I travel the long way home
Although it leads nowhere
O'er track and field and stone
Through cold and bitter air
Still I go on
Through field and farm
To where my darlings lie
T'was only the weight of bitter Fate
I lived while they did die

Soft at first, his voice rose until it seemed to fill the room, silencing tables, mice pausing halfway to their feet. Ernst sang in a sweet, clear tenor, the ballad of Hameln town. It was a song every rodent knew, of the death of the rats in the hamlet that had once been their kingdom. Mouselings learned it in the nursery, a cautionary tale to never stray too far into the realm of Men. Every rodent, beast, and blade of grass had its place, and nature kept the balance, no matter how cruel or kind. Rats knew the tale from late nights at family gatherings, when the old ones got in their cups and longed for the lost days of yore. Every mouse and rat in Underwall knew this folk song like the beat of his own heart.

But not the way Ernst sang it.

The tune he followed was as old as the hills, raw and sad, weirdly familiar yet strange. He added verses long forgotten by other rodents, words that gave voice to the cruelty of Hameln. His was the original song, the melody of a time long past. It thrummed deep and rose high, tugging at ancient memories. The wharf rats were the first to rise to their feet to join him, adding their baritones to the old tune.

When Ernst reached the chorus, every mouse, rat, and mole in the bar joined in, singing the simple verses alongside his heartbreaking melody.

Hameln town is a long way down, a long way down.

The walls hummed in resonance until the last note faded away to bittersweet silence.

Before the fire, Ernst bowed his head.

No one spoke. In the corner, someone sobbed.

The rats raised their claws to the barkeep and a plump mouse maid rushed a tray of tankards to their table in the corner. Mice that had been about to leave sat down again and ordered a round for their fellows. Better to be among friends than alone in the cold night just now. Soon the buzz of conversation returned, but it was soft with nostalgia.

Pleased, Ernst took his seat, ears twitching at the snippets of conversation. There was talk of another uprising in the east of France, where a war amongst Men had caused damage. Some mice argued in favor of pressing back against the driving force that was Man. Rodent populations tended to grow whenever there was a human war, since shooting each other made them forget to set traps for mice. And then there was the Black Death. Bubonic plague always brought rich days for the rodent kingdom. When all the humans were sick and afraid, rats and mice could run rampant through the streets.

Ernst shook his head at the dreamy nostalgia in the speakers' voices. Every rat worth his salt knew a plague would sweep whole villages of men away, and leave no one to fill the larders or till the fields. No, he thought, now was not the time for plagues or uprisings. Famine always followed. And Ernst, for one, did not intend to starve.

He opened his satchel and pulled out the wares of his second trade—a sheaf of paper, an inkwell, some quills. But before he could attract his first customer, the barkeep approached.

"Put that away for now," the stout mouse said gruffly, shoving a warm bowl of seed and nut porridge with a bit of cheese across the table. "You've earned a hot meal, I think. And a glass or two. Rare form," he said.

He waved away Ernst's thanks and hurried back to the bar, where the tears in his eyes would be less noticeable.

Ernst ate his meal with less relish than he had intended. The ballad of Hameln town was effective, to be sure, but even he was not immune to the sorrow it conjured. He had been a wanderer for most of his life. The thought of a homeland, no matter how long ago, affected him deeply. But the road was his lot in life. To hope for something more was like building a castle on a cloud.

Nursing a headache and a growing sense of melancholia, Ernst finished his meal and the first glass of beer. Then he rearranged his papers and ink on the table, signaling that the scribe was open for business.

His first customer of the night was a love-sick sailor hoping to win his sweetheart back with a poem. Ernst rolled his eyes as he took down the would-be poet's composition.

Many rats spoke a minimum of two languages (not including Mouseish or Volean or Mole—Rattish was the root from which they all sprang). But few could write, and even fewer could manage it in another tongue. And so, acting as scribe for the riffraff of Vienna, he earned himself a sip of ale and a place to sleep the night. The melancholy of his song soon lifted as he went about his letters and gossip.

He wrote three apologies to worried mothers from wayward sons, an inquiry to a distant relative for a city mouse looking to move back to the country, one will, and three birth announcements (those were the most tedious—so many babies, such long names!).

The scents of wet rodent and ink filled the room as he wrote and chatted with the sailing rats and dock scavengers that were regulars whenever their ships had come in. Scribes and information rats such as Ernst were expected in these parts of town, just as a storyteller might be, or a bard with songs to sing. The barkeep seemed pleased that Ernst could offer all of the above.

The room was cozy enough, and the supper had been filling. He even bartered for a lovely fish and beetle custard for dessert. Ernst would write until his wrist grew tired. Another day's honest work for the rat. Tomorrow would bring its own worries, but for now, he felt very fine indeed.

Until the piebald mouse stepped up, anyway.

5

EVERYTHING HAD GONE WRONG. Stefan should have been miles away by now. He edged toward the door and reached for his duffel, not sure if he should make a run for it or simply hide the bag, when his father released Christian and caught Stefan's eye.

"Yes, put their things in the little bedroom, Stefan, thank you. We've scrubbed and aired it quite well . . ." He faltered. "But . . . of course, take my room. I'll—"

"Father, no," Stefan interrupted. He couldn't believe he would be willing to sleep in his mother's deathbed.

The gorge rose in Stefan's throat. He left the bags and stepped outside into the street, where the rain could hide his tears until he had them under control. He squeezed his eyes shut.

"You'll catch your death out here, child, dressed like that," a woman said in a sugary voice. Stefan kept his eyes closed. Talking to Christian had been a mistake. One he would not repeat with whoever this newcomer was.

"Come inside, Stefan," another voice said. Someone tugged at his shirtsleeve.

Stefan opened his eyes to find the local mourning committee, a collection of five widows and spinsters, all looking for a husband. Stefan had heard rumors of their ability to quickly find guildsmiths in mourning—in one fell swoop their children could gain both a father and an apprenticeship. Stefan's mother used to laugh when she saw them. The Wild Hunt, she'd called them, after the Welsh tale of gods that hunted the souls of men.

If the women in front of him had their way, his father would be remarried within the year. Stefan refused to be a pawn in that arrangement. He didn't want a new mother, just time to properly mourn the one he'd lost.

"I'm fine, Mrs. Waldbaum." He plucked his sleeve from her grasp and gave the women a slight bow. Mrs. Waldbaum was an apple-cheeked older woman with three children, two of them boys just about apprenticing age. Behind her, Drusilla Prue, a dour stick of a woman who had never married, stood with a basket on her arm. The rest of the committee looked much the same. Plump or thin, short or tall, they were all draped head to toe in black gowns, overcoats and bonnets, with baskets of food and drink on their arms, and a feverish gleam in their eyes.

"I've brought knockwursts fresh from the butcher," Miss Prue said proudly, "and a bottle of my elderflower cordial. It will settle your father's stomach. Grief causes such indigestion!" She forced her pinched face into an expression of sympathy. "You poor, dear boy," she cooed. Coming from her, the sound was as jarring as hearing a stork meow.

Stefan made no move to open the door.

Finally, Mrs. Waldbaum brushed him aside. "I'll just let your father know I'm here . . . that *we* are here, all of us, in his time of need." She bustled through the door, the rest of the Wild Hunt following in a rustle of skirts and coats.

Stefan waited outside a moment longer. It *was* cold today. His arms were goose-pimpled and his nose had gotten chilly.

22

Dragging his feet, he followed the ladies inside just in time to hear Mrs. Waldbaum screech, "Oh! A Moor! In your very house! How unexpected!"

Stefan bit his lip to keep from smiling. Laughing, even at the startled Mrs. Waldbaum, felt disrespectful to his mourning. The thought of more people patting his head and cooing over him was even worse. He escaped up the ladder to his sleeping loft. Pulling on a too-small coat from last year that hadn't made it into his duffel bag, he clambered through the trapdoor in the roof and left the murmur of the adults behind.

The rooftop of his father's shop was pitched to keep snow from piling up dangerously in winter, but if you sat with your knees to your chest, you could perch comfortably for hours. It had been his mother's favorite spot, and now it was his.

Before him, slate and shingled roofs stretched to the horizon like a sea of frozen waves dotted with church steeples. The drizzle had stopped and the sun shone pearl-like above the town's distant clock tower. Stefan's jaw unclenched and sorrow flooded in.

His mother was dead and buried. And he had failed to leave before his father came home. Stefan had watched him age years in the past few days since her death. To have to look him in the eye and tell him the last of his family was leaving—Stefan could never do that.

And so, the future stretched out before him as monotonous as the rooftop sea. He had outgrown the rooms downstairs. Next, he would outgrow the city, and then, like a dog chained too long to a house, he would grow until the shackles cut into his ankle and crippled him for life. Painful, yes, but the hurt he would cause his father by leaving would be far worse. Stefan sighed. He would stay in Nuremberg and help his father. He would fend off the Wild Hunt for at least a year, until his father could decide for himself if he wanted to marry again.

The thought made him queasy. But he would feel differently in a year, he hoped. In fact, if his father remarried one of those nosy women with children of her own, then maybe Stefan would be free to leave.

"One year," Stefan said out loud.

There was a rustle as the trapdoor opened. A shock of white-blond hair emerged. His criminal cousin climbed out onto the roof like a spider emerging from a crack in the wall. The likeness made Stefan's skin crawl. No one had ever invaded his sanctuary before.

"Ah. I knew you'd be up here," Christian said, arranging himself into a sitting position next to Stefan. "This was Elise's favorite escape, and that flock of biddies deserved a good escaping from." He smiled easily, folding his long legs to his chest and leaning back on his palms. "I've missed this city," he said.

"Why are you here?" Stefan asked. His father had been delighted to see this stranger, leaving Stefan even more alone in his misery.

"It's a long story and I'd rather not tell it twice. I think the ladies will be leaving soon and they've left a nice spread for supper. Come down and I'll tell you both over a glass of elderflower cordial."

"No," Stefan said. "Not why are you here in Nuremberg. Why are you here *now*?"

His skin prickled at his own rudeness, but he didn't care.

Mysterious criminals with eye patches and royal jailers didn't get to just show up and have polite conversations on other people's rooftops. Stefan stiffened his jaw. "You turn up and act as though you're part of the family. My father seems to adore you. But I've never even heard of you, apart from a few stories about 'our cousin at the royal court' of wherever. If you knew my mother well enough to sit on this roof with her, then where were you when she got sick?"

Christian's easy manner grew solemn. "I loved your mother, Stefan. Had I known she was unwell, I assure you I would have come."

"But why have you stayed away all these years?"

Christian's mouth twisted in consternation. "Have you ever wanted to impress someone? I mean, really show them that you've done well?"

"Yes," Stefan said. Every apprentice strove to impress his master. That his master also happened to be his father made it both better and worse. There were days he thought his father was too hard on him, and days he was too easy. Stefan often wondered if his work was as good as his father sometimes said, or as bad. The only way to be sure was to always do better.

"Then you'll understand," Christian said. "I wanted to impress your parents. Zacharias is one of the best toymakers in the city, and your mother was the best woman I've ever known. I was a bit big for my britches when I left. It's hard to come home in chains. Especially to the people you admire the most."

"But you're here now," Stefan said.

"Precisely. As the clockmaker said to the clock, better late than never."

25

"And you're not in chains, exactly," Stefan noted. "If you're a criminal, why aren't you in prison?"

Christian smiled wistfully. "Like I said, it's a long story."

Everything was a long story when it came to adults. They muttered and murmured to each other all the time, but rarely shared any of the conversation. It was a wonder Stefan ever heard anything of use.

"Where is Boldavia? Or is that a long story, too?" he asked.

"As a matter of fact, it is," Christian replied.

Stefan rolled his eyes.

"You know, you won't remember this, but I used to visit Nuremberg every year at Christmas," Christian said. "The last time, you must have been five or six. Elise was very proud of you. You had just learned how to count to a hundred. And you wouldn't stop doing it. She said you might make a good clocksmith someday. You know . . . because of the numbers."

Stefan shrugged. "I don't remember that." Which wasn't exactly true. He remembered the counting, and his mother calling him "regular as a clock." The image of her smiling down at him rose from a place buried deep inside him. His stomach ached, missing her. But he didn't remember Christian being there.

"You're right, of course. I'm a stranger to you and I haven't been around," Christian said, echoing his thoughts. "We shall have to get to know each other. If you are willing."

They sat in awkward silence, watching the sun make a fiery path across the tiled sea.

"I lost my own mother when I was less than half your age," Christian said quietly.

Stefan's stomach curdled. He would not wish such a thing on anyone, especially someone so young.

"But I was lucky, as far as orphans go. I have a foster family, here in Nuremberg. Good people. Better than I deserve."

Stefan faced his cousin in surprise. "But what about your father?" For their differences, Zacharias would never send Stefan to be raised by strangers. The thought brought another twinge of guilt for wanting to leave.

Christian shrugged eloquently. "I don't remember my father. It was always just my mother, me, and a name. Drosselmeyer." He smiled sadly. "I've had to make of it what I could. With mixed results."

Stefan swallowed the lump in his throat. "I'm sorry."

"Don't be. You have enough loss of your own to deal with. And mine's an old sorrow." He clapped a hand on Stefan's leg. "It makes us who we are."

Stefan nodded, though he didn't quite understand. If sadness shaped people, how was there ever joy in the world? It was the sort of conversation he would have had with his mother, sitting on this very rooftop with the promise of hot chocolate waiting in the kitchen below. A new wave of grief, cold and sharp as ice, splashed through him. He reached for a distraction to keep him afloat.

"Tell me something about my mother," he said.

Christian shifted on his perch. "I'll tell you three things. One, she loved Mozart—"

"I know that. I do, too." Stefan recalled the afternoon concerts his mother would take him to at the university. They would sneak pieces of candy from her pocket while the music students played. To Stefan, Mozart was the sound of happiness.

Christian held up a gloved finger. "Ah, but she loved Mozart so much that she wanted to name you Wolfgang in his honor."

"Wolfgang!" Stefan blurted. The only Wolfgang he knew was a snooty boy who couldn't play a triangle, let alone a piano, but still insisted on calling himself "Maestro."

"Fortunately, your father changed her mind. Still, as long as she carried you, she referred to you as 'Wolfie.'"

Stefan pursed his lips. "What if I'd been a girl?"

"Brunhilde, of course," Christian said. "A solid German name."

Stefan held back a snort. He refused to laugh but, strangely, he felt a bit lighter. As if the story held some of his mother's glow. "All right. That was one."

"Two. Your mother loved pickles and won a pickle-eating contest at Oktoberfest one year. That was the day your father decided he wanted to marry her."

"That's not true. I know this story," Stefan protested. "He fell in love when he saw her *making* pickles for the fair."

"Ah, so they've whitewashed it," Christian said. "Maybe Elise didn't want you to know her full pickle-eating capacity. I believe it was twenty-seven in all. And they were very large."

Now Stefan was struggling in earnest not to laugh. "She never touched a pickle in all my life. Said they made her ill!"

"And they did, after that day. Somewhere between the end of the contest and a very upset stomach, your mother managed to charm my cousin completely. She was quite a woman, Elise."

"Yes," Stefan agreed. This time, he didn't try to hide his smile.

Remembering his mother felt a thousand times better than mourning her.

Again they sat together in silence. But this time, it was more companionable.

"You said you'd tell me three things," Stefan said eventually.

"Ah yes, the third is this. Every morning at precisely four a.m., your mother would wake up and look in on you sleeping."

Stefan felt a spark of surprise. She used to brush his hair back and kiss him on the forehead. Even if he didn't wake up, somehow he knew she was there.

"How do you know that?" he asked. "Did she tell you?"

Christian winked. "Clockmaker's secret. Anything to do with time . . ." He tapped the side of his nose. "It's part of my craft."

Against all odds, Stefan laughed. It was less horrible than he'd expected, sharing this spot with an uninvited guest. He remembered what Samir had said: "Charmed you, has he?"

It appeared that he had.

"Now tell me, why are you leaving?" his cousin asked.

The subject had changed, and so had his tone. He hadn't said "running away," Stefan noticed. Christian was no longer judging him.

"Unless, of course, you'd rather explain it to your father over dinner?" his cousin said slyly.

Stefan blanched. "No, I was just . . . I've completed my apprenticeship. I was always supposed to leave home afterward and find a new master to journey with."

"And have you found a position?" Christian asked.

Every toymaker in Nuremberg followed the same path— apprenticed to a master toymaker, three years in their shop, and then seven years at home or abroad as a journeyman before creating a masterpiece and joining the guild as a master themselves.

"Not yet. I had a list . . . I was writing letters of inquiry when Mother got sick. And now, I just want to see what's out there."

"Well, I'm afraid the West is no place for a young man alone just now," Christian advised. "Napoleon is once again in exile, but until the Congress of Vienna is settled, the chance of misadventure is grave. Highwaymen are bad enough. Add a few hungry armies and their deserters, not to mention anarchists, loyalists, and opportunists, and the roads between here and France become much too dangerous for even the experienced traveler."

"So, no Paris, no England," Stefan said, absorbing this information. It was the first time someone had spoken to him about his journeyship like an adult. If only this conversation brought better news. "I had hoped to see the automatons made for the king of France, and the tin clockwork androids of Henri Maillard in London."

"And you will, in another year or three. But the courts of kings are always tricky places," Christian said. "It would be wise to get a bit more road beneath your feet before facing them."

"Then what should I do?" Stefan asked, afraid his uncertainty would make him sound too young, as his father believed.

"Well, if I were you, I'd secure a berth with a master for, say, the next three years. Get your footing, and then move on to France and England. Ours is an old family name, Stefan. Surely your father's connections can find you such a place."

Stefan shook his head somberly. This had been a bone of

contention with his father for the past few months. "Father is a carver. He believes in simple toys. 'Real' toys, he calls them, made of wood, a bit of porcelain and glass. When it comes to movement, joint work is as far as he's willing to go."

"And you?" his cousin prompted.

"Clockwork," Stefan gushed enthusiastically. "It's the future of toymaking. Windups and moving dolls. I've read all about them, studied the drawings. I'm trying to make one, but Father doesn't approve. He says such toys are for royals and we're 'humble toysmiths.' That even our wealthiest customers are too practical to squander money on a 'passing fashion.'"

His cousin chuckled.

"No insult to my father," Stefan said quickly. "But we could do so much more."

"Then why not switch trades and join the clockmakers' guild?"

"I'm the son of a toymaker," Stefan said. "I was *born* to make toys."

"I see your point," Christian agreed. Folding his hands behind his head, he looked as relaxed as Stefan was agitated. "Well, you could always apprentice again."

"And live with kids half my age?" Stefan cringed at the thought. Apprentices often slept in the shop with their work. The boys he knew complained of having to bunk with sniffly, homesick first-years who couldn't tell a chisel from an awl. Stefan had been lucky to apprentice alone. "That's not what I had in mind."

"Perhaps a clockmaster outside of Nuremberg, then?" Christian persisted. "One who wouldn't mind taking on a well-read young man with some wood-carving skills who can count. The sort of situation that allows for travel, excitement, and even an introduction or two to royalty."

Stefan laughed gloomily. "Sounds perfect. Where do I sign?"

"No signature required, just a handshake." Christian held out his gloved hand.

Stefan stared at it. After a moment, Christian removed the glove. "Sorry. There. What do you say, cousin? Want to be journeyman to the Royal Clockmaker of Boldavia?"

A surge of relief crashed through him. A royal appointment! Or, at least, as close to it as a journeyman could get. It wasn't Paris or London, but it was a start. He couldn't believe his luck.

Then doubt set in, like a worm gnawing through a frosted cake. Cousin or not, Christian was a criminal he knew very little about.

Stefan studied the clockmaker's face before asking, "What do you suppose my mother would say?"

"She'd tell you, 'Wolfie, say yes.'"

And, somehow—with the exception of "Wolfie"—Stefan knew that it was true.

He grasped the offered hand in his own. "When do I start?"

"Today, of course," his cousin said, and moved to climb back inside. Stefan gripped his hand harder.

"Wait! I mean, thank you. But . . . are you sure?"

"Of course I'm sure. Travel with us and I'll teach you. Not much in the way of room and board on the road, but you'll receive the same accommodations as myself and Samir. And your own chambers in Boldavia, once a few matters are settled there. Might I have my hand back now?"

"But, how can a clockmaker teach a toymaker?"

"Presumably we're both speaking German?" Christian gently reclaimed his hand and reapplied his glove. "Besides which, I *am* the Boldavian guild. I say what is and isn't to be done. Remember that, Stefan."

There was a hard glow in Christian's eye that made Stefan's mouth go dry. He recalled Samir's words.

"But . . . you're a criminal," Stefan said hoarsely. "An outlaw."

"Does that frighten you?"

Stefan suddenly wanted to look away, to not be tied to this strange man. But his longing outweighed his caution. "No," he said. "It doesn't."

"Ah. Then you *do* have much to learn. Give it time, Stefan. Truth be told, I sometimes scare myself! Any other reservations?"

Stefan's stomach slumped. "My father. He needs me here."

"What every father needs is a son with a future." Christian pursed his lips in thought. Stefan could only guess at the calculations going on inside that head. Then the pale forehead cleared. "I shall have to convince him that I need you more. Now, let's get in from the cold and have some of that food those ghoulish ladies brought."

He flipped open the trapdoor and scuttled inside, pausing to take a final look at the view.

"Nuremberg," Christian said, with a smile.

This new cousin was undeniably strange, but interesting all the same.

He caught Stefan's eye one last time. "I see Elise in you, young man. This is going to be fun."

6

ERNST DID NOT turn around. He sniffed the air, catching the distinct scents of river water and powdered lavender. This was a mouse that had traveled in diverse circles.

"Please, have a seat," he told the shadow at his elbow. The slightest movement, and the shadow sat across from him, resolving into a scarred mouse of middle years with an old cloak that did nothing to conceal the fact that he was a piebald.

Ernst resisted the urge to recoil. Piebalds were the lowest of the low in the rat world. Usually slow to move and slower to think. The Piper's Children, they were called. But a rat of business could not afford to choose his customers. Even if they were piebalds.

"Well met, good sir. And how may I assist you this evening?" He twisted his wrist in a circle, prepared to write yet another love note, another map to a hidden wheel of cheese.

The piebald twitched a whisker and gave Ernst an acknowledging nod. "Well done," he said in a gruff voice that had seen more than a few winters. "Not many know the full verse of Hameln town."

Ernst nodded. "Not many mice, perhaps, but every rat knows the tale through and through." Once upon a time, rats had ruled Rodentia. Smarter, stronger, and superior to common mice in every way, it was rats who brought the great plagues that laid humans low. Man slipped a few rungs down the ladder of dominance when the rats were on the rise.

But Hameln . . . Hameln had shown all of Rodentia, down to the smallest shrew, that rats were mere vermin after all. Such a fall leaves a bitter taste, even generations later. Ernst smacked his tongue against the roof of his mouth, and reached for his cup.

From within his coat, the piebald withdrew two wheat stalks that looked as sweet as the day they were cut.

Ernst's mouth watered. Too much time in cities had deprived him of such luxuries.

The piebald offered him a golden stalk.

"I hate to chew alone," he said, placing a crisp shoot comfortably between his back teeth. Chewing slowly, he surveyed the room.

Ernst accepted with sincere thanks. He slid the stalk between his teeth and nibbled ever so slightly. A sweet rush of nutty sap tickled his tongue and he sighed. "Like country sunshine," he said.

"Indeed."

The two chewed in silence for a moment, warming themselves by the heat of the chimney. And then the piebald spoke.

"You are a rodent of languages?" he asked.

Ernst shrugged. "Most. Not Chinese, nor Russian," he admitted regretfully. "Some things are best left to the squirrels."

The piebald laughed. "And the rapier?" He glanced at where the slender blade was concealed beneath Ernst's coat. This mouse was a soldier, then. Only a trained weapons master would have noticed the gleam of silver in the dim light.

"Recently used to persuade a cat to turn the other cheek," Ernst boasted.

The piebald pulled the wheat stalk from his jaws and grinned. "Very good. We've had our eye on you, Herr Listz."

"We?" Ernst asked, scanning the room for compatriots.

The piebald merely smiled. "Suffice it to say you've been noticed—here in Vienna, and in Hamburg, Munich, Düsseldorf. A rat from a good, if impoverished, brood. Classical education, etiquette, swordsmanship. You've made an impression."

Normally, Ernst would have preened at such a compliment. Instead, his fur crawled. Being watched! By piebalds, no less!

If the mouse in front of him realized how disturbed he was, he gave no sign. Instead, the piebald said, "I have a proposition for you."

The rat watched the piebald reach into his coat, fascinated by the way the firelight made the black and white markings on the mouse's face dance like sunlight and shade.

"You've heard of Boldavia? And the ambitions of our queen?"

Who hasn't? Ernst thought with a nod. It had been the talk of the tavern. But what did a suicidal bunch of mice matter to him?

"Do you know where it is?" the piebald asked, dropping a small sack on the table.

Distracted by the promise of payment, Ernst had to think a moment. He sifted through the gossip he'd heard. "On the Black Sea. A mighty mousedom, as I understand it." A provincial backwater was more like it. Remote and stupid, he presumed, if the lesson of the Piper had taught them nothing.

"We're soon to have need of a royal tutor," the piebald explained. "My mice have heard about you."

"Good things?" Ernst wondered aloud. Despite his misgivings, a spark fluttered in his chest, like a match sputtering but not yet catching light.

"The right things," the piebald said.

"Thank you." Ernst inclined his head.

"Are you interested?"

The match inside him caught fire. A roaring inferno of relief. Ernst tried to play it calm, but he was already reaching for the sack. A royal commission, life in a palace once again. Music. Refinement. Food, clean clothes, and a warm bed . . .

Or coddling a brood of royal brats in whatever drafty pile of rocks country mice called a castle. A hopeless uprising against the humans, defeat, embarrassment, and possibly death.

But he could always leave before it came to that. Let the mice have their revolution. He'd take the commission and run.

"I accept."

"Well, not so fast. The seed in that sack will get you to Boldavia. What's between your ears will get you past the Queen. Be prepared. She's a sharp one and wants only the best for her mouselings."

Ernst bowed, even though he was still seated at the table. "I shall endeavor to do my best, sir. I shall give her my all."

The piebald smiled.

"Pretty manners. You'll do very well at court. Just make sure the Queen likes you first. In my experience, compliments never hurt." At long last, he offered a mottled paw. "They call me Snitter."

Ernst accepted, noting the calluses on his benefactor's paw. "A pleasure to meet you," he said. His eyes were on the piebald, but he was talking to the sack of seed.

7

STEFAN'S STOMACH WAS uneasy from Frau Waldbaum's potato casserole and Frau Kirche's sour cherry pie. He had eaten twice his fill in order to hide his nerves. They had been downstairs for over an hour now, but it was poor manners to talk business or question guests until they had dined, and Christian had yet to raise the subject of his offer. Now that the meal was over, Stefan's nerves returned. He drowsed near the fire while his strange cousin and his father pulled their chairs close together at the hearth. The astrologer, Samir, sat in the shadows, keeping his own counsel and an eye on his prisoner.

"Stefan, you look as though you could use some of this cordial," his father said. "It does my heart good to see you eat so well, but I fear you are out of practice."

Stefan straightened up, embarrassed. He dragged himself out of his chair. "If you think so," he said. "Would anyone else . . . ?"

He went to the cupboard to find a mug. If Miss Prue's potion would do the trick, he was more than willing to try it out.

A mouse scurried inside the dark reaches of the cabinet, startling him wider awake. He'd have to place traps in the morning. With a sigh, he shut the cupboard and poured himself a draught of elderflower cordial.

"You have both been very patient," his cousin said as he regained his chair. "So I will tell you what brings me—us"—he nodded toward Samir—"to Nuremberg."

Stefan's heart jumped into his throat. He forced himself to take a sip of the elderflower concoction. It was herbal, sweet and light. And it did absolutely nothing to quell his anxiety.

"Stefan, stop fidgeting," his father said. "Your cousin is speaking."

Stefan muttered an apology and turned away, his eyes growing damp. His father's tone was clear—he was upset with Stefan for skipping the funeral. In truth, Stefan was disappointed in himself. Shame heated his cheeks. He turned back to the fire and caught his father's eye. His heart thudded in his ears. And then his father's face softened with a look that was almost as good as a hug. He understood.

The hand that had been squeezing Stefan's stomach relaxed.

Christian nodded, as if gathering his thoughts, and began again.

"The king has sent me on a quest. We've ridden a long, hard way these past seven years," he said wearily. "Finally, I convinced Samir it was time for me to come home, if only for a little while. There are people in the city who might help us. But mostly I've been missing Nuremberg."

"There's not another city like her," Stefan's father said. "And of course, we're glad to have you back. I only wish it had been sooner. For Elise's sake."

Stefan was swamped by another swell of grief. His mother was dead. He couldn't possibly leave his father, not when the house was so newly empty.

Suddenly, the mouse from the cupboard skittered across the floor. Stefan yanked off a slipper to hurl at it, but Christian's glove struck first, stunning the little pest and knocking it over.

"Catch it, quickly!" Christian bellowed.

Zacharias scrambled up from his chair. Stefan and Christian lunged toward the mouse. The poor creature scurried along the wall, searching for a crack to escape through, squealing the whole while.

"Don't let him get away!" Christian cried.

Stefan grabbed a bowl from the table and dropped to his knees in an attempt to trap the mouse inside. Only now did he have the sense to wonder, why make such a fuss over a mouse?

"Samir, now!" The clockmaker had the mouse cornered. It began to scream, a horrible shrill sound. Samir slammed a boot on the ground by its head and the mouse fell into a stunned silence. Christian scooped it into his gloved hand.

"Quickly, a box," he said calmly. Stefan's father grabbed an empty cocoa canister and handed it to Christian, who stuffed the mouse inside.

It started screaming again, the shrill sound taking on form. Stefan realized that it was speaking. In *German*.

"You are too late, Clockmaker, too late! The Queen is with child. Our time is at hand!" Still screaming, the mouse struggled from the canister and drove its sharp teeth into Christian's glove.

Christian threw the mouse to the floor. Instantly, it hopped up and ran away.

Stefan stared at the crack in the floorboards through which the mouse had disappeared. "What the devil was that?"

His father had turned ashen gray. "Stefan, watch your language. Your cousin's been bitten. Get a bandage."

"It's all right," Christian said. "The glove took the brunt of it." He held up the injured hand where his skin showed through the black leather. "I'm no tailor, but I think it will live."

"What *was* that?" Stefan repeated, careful not to swear. His skin still prickled with the sound of those unnaturally high words.

"A spy," Christian said darkly.

"But, it spoke!" Stefan exclaimed. He looked wildly to his father who, though ruffled, seemed less than surprised. "What's going on?" he asked.

Stefan's father looked chagrined. "Son, there is more to this world than apprentices know. Even a master toymaker such as myself has mostly only heard of, and rarely seen, these things." He turned to the scowling clockmaker. "Christian, this has nothing to do with toys."

"But it doesn't make sense," Christian muttered to himself. "We are no closer to our goal than we were seven years ago." He scratched his chin. A look passed between him and Samir. "Sit down," Christian said. "I'll tell you all I can."

With more than one backward glance for more mice, Stefan and his father sat down again at the table. Spreading his fingers wide, Christian began.

"Several months' ride from here is the small kingdom of Boldavia. Rich and important by virtue of its location, Boldavia is an island nation at the crossroads between Europe, Asia Minor, and the Ottoman Empire, which leads on into Africa and points south. Seven years ago, the King of Boldavia had not a care in the world, but for his one joy and heartache, his daughter, Pirlipat . . ."

PRINCESS PIRLIPAT WAS CRYING. That was nothing unusual. Pirlipat was always crying. It was a sound that had soaked into the very stones of the castle, shrill, angry, and unending. The queen wrung her hands. She had guests arriving and her famous pudding to oversee, but her darling little Pirly-teeth was screeching to wake the dead.

"Imebella, isn't there something we can do?" her husband, the king, asked. They had proven poor parents from the start. Pirlipat was three years old and had spent much of that time screaming her head off.

"Lovekins, you know I have to be in the kitchen with the chefs. Isn't there anyone to rock the cradle? She seems to like that."

The cradle in question sat on the dais in the main audience chamber, next to the thrones of the king and queen. Usually the castle was quieter if Pirlipat was kept in the nursery (which was really a dungeon, the queen knew, but "nursery" sounded nicer, especially when speaking of a place for one's child), but with guests arriving, the royal family was expected to make a full presentation of itself.

"No, there is not anyone to rock the cradle. The musicians are making music, the soldiers are soldiering, and the ladies-in-waiting are . . . waiting, I suspect. Besides, the royal crib is too big for them to rock. And I can't very well do it. I'm the king!"

"Of course, dear," she said, patting his arm. King Pirliwig was a very large man with reddish hair and even redder cheeks. When he got angry, the queen was always afraid he'd be mistaken for a beet and planted in the royal garden. So she did her best to quiet him by reminding him that there'd be some of his favorite pudding soon, if only he'd let her go to the kitchens instead of worrying about rocking Pirlipat into silence.

Eventually, the violinist gave up violining to rock the child, leaving the rest of the quartet much the poorer for it, although at last their music could be heard.

The guests arrived and, as long as one of the musicians stopped playing to rock the cradle, the royal banquet went on uninterrupted.

But eventually even the royal musicians grew weary, their bowing arms cramped and unable to play, what with all of the alternate music-making and cradle-rocking. Once again, much to Queen Imebella's dismay, Pirlipat began to wail.

"Somebody, do something!" the king bellowed, at his wits' end, the queen knew. Otherwise he'd have never admitted to not being able to handle a small child.

Nobody moved.

And then a chair pushed back from the table and a remarkable-looking young man rose, tall and thin as a scarecrow with a shock of fair white-blond hair. He looked pallid and mysterious in his black suit. The young man made his way to the royal crib and paced around it three times, deep in thought.

"Darling, is it safe?" the queen whispered to her husband.

"Yes, my dear, I'm sure it will be quite all right," he whispered back, although he couldn't know for certain.

After a long moment, the young man gestured to the musicians for their instruments. Smashing a viola on the floor, he proceeded to rig the most amazing system of hoists and pulleys strung to-gether with violin string, at the center of which he put the musi-cians' metronome.

The room was utterly silent (except for Pirlipat's screaming). Queen Imebella held her breath.

The young man surveyed his handiwork. And then, with a daintily gloved hand, he pushed the crib, one gentle rocking motion, and stepped back.

The crib rocked to. Inside, Pirlipat made a hiccupping noise, as if swallowing the rest of her scream. The crib rocked fro. And to, and fro, and to, with the same steady, reliable motions of the metronome.

"Perpetual rocking machine," the young man said with a shrug, and in the utter silence that followed, he returned to his place at the table.

"But . . . but . . ." Queen Imebella sputtered, tears welling in her eyes. She tugged her husband's sleeve, too overcome to speak more clearly.

"What is your name, young man?" her husband bellowed. "How do you come to be here?"

Queen Imebella was quite taken with the way the young man rose and bowed to the king. "Christian Drosselmeyer, formerly of Nuremberg. I am a clockmaker, and most glad to be of service."

The king looked at the queen, then rose to greet him. "Of service you shall be! From now on, Christian Drosselmeyer, most trusted friend of the Kingdom of Boldavia, you shall be Our Clockmaker and forever be held in our highest royal esteem."

"AND THAT'S HOW I BECAME the Royal Clockmaker of Boldavia," Christian said.

"I had become Royal Astrologer in much the same way,"

Samir added. "The king and queen are quite practical people and only hire staff when there is a reason to do so."

Stefan frowned. "Then why didn't they hire a royal crib rocker? Or just make a lighter crib?" It seemed so obvious to him. For the first time, he wondered if cleverness was a requirement for being a king.

"Perhaps the royal family is not as smart as you," Christian said with an amused smile. "In any event, they suffered until I showed up, and then they hired me. And I lived rather happily in Boldavia for almost three years, until tragedy struck.

"Mice had been a problem in Boldavia for as long as anyone could remember, which is to say at least since Pirlipat stopped crying and they could begin to notice other nuisances.

"You see, Boldavia is an island nation that rests in the mouth of a river. The bedrock it sits on is granite riddled with caverns carved by wind coming off the sea. An easy place for rodents to hide, and so there was already mouse trouble in the royal kitchens, but it was tolerable. Cats are illegal in Boldavia due to the king's allergies. Still, the problem might have been managed with traps and poisons, but toward the end of my third year as Royal Clockmaker, I made a mistake . . ."

"What sort of mistake?" Stefan asked.

For the first time that day, Christian seemed at a loss for words.

"Hubris," Samir rumbled, his deep voice rising from the shadows. "Our wonderful clockmaker forgot about his duty and chose, instead, to make himself great."

Christian paled, looking younger than Stefan had guessed

him to be. "Do you know why I left Nuremberg? Too many master clocksmiths, not enough work to appeal to my grand ideas. I left to make my fortune. I didn't want to build university clocks and mantelpieces. I wanted something bigger. I wanted to make *art*."

Stefan knew what that was like. He didn't want to spend his own life making toy soldiers and wooden swords. He had big ideas, too. But Christian didn't look triumphant.

"It was to be my masterpiece. My greatest creation." A ghost of a smile crossed his lips and vanished.

"It was Christmastime, and the king had demanded a grand amusement for his little girl. I strove to give it to him. An Advent calendar on the scale of nothing that had ever been done before. You say you like automatons, Stefan? This would have held a city of them. Twenty-five tremendous caverns, which already existed in the bedrock beneath the kingdom. I would have carved them out, shaped them, and filled them with such wonders, more amazing than anything Boldavia or Nuremberg had ever seen."

His face fell. "I dug too deep, with no regard for the kingdom below. There had been a balance between mice and men; the rock was their truce. Until I broke it. With chisels and hammers, I destroyed their homes. And the inconceivable happened. The mice had been digging from the other side, seeking to expand their territory. When I cracked the rock, I set them free. They rose from the depths, their numbers more than triple those of the people living on the island. The Queen of Mice demanded counsel with King Pirliwig. A kingdom for a kingdom, she said. A fair share in ruling the country, above and below."

"But mice are dumb animals," Stefan said. The thought of mouse royalty was ridiculous. "How could the king blame you? That's like being blamed for a thunderstorm."

"Spoken like a true apprentice," Christian said. The words stung, but it was Christian who winced. "A master clockmaker should have known better. I'd studied the animal kingdoms the way you've read up on automatons. I knew of mice and their ambition. But reading and understanding are two different things. I chose to do what I wanted, rather than consider the consequences."

He gave Stefan a look and shrugged. Stefan knew he'd done the same thing by planning to run away without speaking to his father.

"And now you're a criminal in the eyes of Boldavia?" Stefan's stomach sank.

"If only it had ended there," Christian said. "Of course King Pirliwig refused her. He was the sovereign ruler of the realm and would remain so until the end of his days, at which point Pirlipat and her future husband would take his place.

"But the Queen of Mice would not have it. If he wouldn't share his kingdom, then she'd take it from him. Her own heirs would rule. So she attacked the young princess, who was by now a pert young lady of six, and bit her on the leg.

"If she had been a regular run-of-the-mill pest, we might have treated the wound with a good wash and a bit of honey to keep it from festering. But royalty is different. Like the queen bee who may sting again and again and not die, the bite of a royal mouse is designed not to deter, but to destroy. Part wound, part curse—it taints the blood with vile intent. The venom in that bite took terrible effect. It deformed the princess, poisoning her into a shrunken little manikin seeming for all the world to be carved out of rough wood."

Stefan's stomach turned. It was a horrible death.

"I was arrested and set to be executed. And *that* is why I am the most dangerous criminal in Boldavia," Christian said with a sad smile. In the corner, Samir grunted, as if satisfied with this honest confession.

"Because you killed their princess," Stefan breathed.

"What? Oh, no. She lives . . . well, lives with difficulty, but she does draw breath and is alive."

"Mein Gott!" Stefan's father exclaimed. "A living doll?"

"And an ugly one at that," Christian confirmed. "As you can imagine, the king and queen were beside themselves with terror. Pirlipat remains in good health despite the affliction but, so cursed, she can never hope to marry, rule with dignity, or provide an heir of her own. A monarch's wealth is in his or her children. You must have a successor to succeed."

"Not only in monarchies," Stefan's father said. Stefan cringed. *Drosselmeyer and Son* was a sign that could have hung over their shop for generations, if only he had chosen to stay at home.

"Samir and the Royal Physicians were assigned the duty of finding a cure. Fortunately for me, Samir discovered what the others could not. The cure is the meat of a nut called a *krakatook*. It has curious properties, is exceedingly rare and, according to the stars, I am destined to find it. At first, the king refused to let me go. Instead, he sent his men out in search of the nut. Every young man in Boldavia followed suit. But, when the *krakatook* was not readily found, the king commuted my sentence on one condition—I must find the nut. And then I'll be set free. Samir was assigned to be both my jailer and astrological guide. We have searched for seven years, but have yet to find a single nut.

"In the meantime, the mice have not stopped watching us. If we find the cure, the king will no longer fear the Queen of Mice, and he will surely hunt and destroy her. Until then, he cowers in his castle while the mice run roughshod all over Boldavia."

It all sounded like a fairy tale. Talking mice, human kings, and animal queens. Stefan wouldn't have believed it had he not heard the words of the mouse spy.

"What can we do to help?" Stefan's father asked. This was the father he loved—sensible and brave.

"Thank you, Zacharias," Christian said with feeling. "We've searched the world for the nut—France, England, Asia, Russia, the Ottoman Empire, Arabia. Why not Nuremberg?"

"We'll begin immediately," Zacharias announced, half-rising from his seat.

"Actually," Christian said slowly, "I've recently taken on a journeyman. I think this would be a wonderful opportunity for him to show his worth."

Stefan almost choked on his elderflower cordial.

"Truly, Christian?" his father asked. "Who is the lucky fellow?"

"I believe you know him. It's your son."

Zacharias's eyebrows flew into his hairline. He turned to Stefan, who had the decency to blush six shades of red.

"Father," he began.

"My boy?" Tears dimmed his eyes for a moment and he

49

touched the wedding ring on his finger. The sight stabbed Stefan to the core. The ring's twin lay with his mother in her grave. Guilt crushed his chest. He could not breathe.

And then, his father smiled.

"Well done, Stefan!" he bellowed, pulling him into a bear hug. "You could do far worse than your cousin Christian. And you'll discover far more than I could ever hope to show you as a wood-carver."

"You're a wonderful toymaker," Stefan said hoarsely. He hugged his father tight. When last they had been so close, his mother had been part of the embrace. "*You* are wonderful." He cleared his throat of tears and looked up. "Do I really have your blessing?"

His father looked down at him, and Stefan suddenly felt very small. *Say no*, he silently wished. He'd stay if his father needed him, and it would be all right. He'd make it so.

"You have it," his father said. Stefan's cheeks were wet, but he grinned. They turned to Christian, who seemed very pleased with himself.

"It's settled, then. For now, we all need sleep. And in the morning, *you*, my dear boy, will begin your work as a journeyman."

8

SNITTER WAITED. That was the bulk of his job, waiting. Yes, there was intrigue and travel, and there had been more than a few battles in his day. But mostly—in the antechambers of the Queen, or the bow of a ship, or the back alleys of some cold, damp city—he stood on his hind paws and waited.

Blackspaw was late. The moon's pale face was turning gray with the coming dawn. Nuremberg was far, even by the underground riverways. Perhaps the messengers had been waylaid by weasels or an impatient snake. It was a rough business, transporting intel. Another half hour and he would have to leave without his lieutenant.

There was a rustle of paper and leaves. Snitter angled his ears to better catch the sound. Scurrying. The clittering of nails on cobblestone—he would have to tell the young mouse to trim them. Long claws might be useful in battle, or fashionable in court, but in the world of spies, they were simply an alarm.

Snitter resisted the urge to call out to the lad. Softer paws were afoot. The rat at the inn had already had one run-in with a cat, they didn't need another.

A small piebald rounded the corner out of breath, shaking with exhaustion. The camouflaging gray dust had washed off in the gutters, exposing his mottled white fur and black paws. On seeing his superior, the bedraggled young mouse snapped to attention and saluted.

Snitter waved the salute away and uncorked a small flask. "Steady, son. Refresh yourself and report."

Blackspaw shook his head, out of breath, and wiped the sweat from his brow, his dark paw like a smudge of dirt on his creamy forehead. The young mouse bowed and Snitter could tell by the tip of his whiskers and the droop of his tail that something had gone amiss.

"Flicker was seen?"

Blackspaw thrust a sooty note into his captain's paw. Snitter cursed under his breath. Flicker had been chosen for his size and speed. His very name came from his ability to appear as no more than a flicker in the corner of the eye.

Blackspaw's shoulders drooped. "Caught and questioned, sir. But he escaped!" he added quickly. "He told them nothing!"

Blackspaw and Flicker were littermates. Of course he would defend his brother. But they were also zealots—members of the Queen's guard because they believed in her mad ideas, the dominion of Mouse over Man. Snitter doubted the boy would have kept his mouth shut. No, he would have spouted venom and contempt like prophecy.

Snitter sighed and took a swig from the flask. That was the trouble with mice these days—rushing headlong into trouble, announcing themselves at every turn. Blackspaw was no different from their Queen. Snitter was born of a quieter breed. The sort of mouse associated with churches and timidity. *That* was a position of power: being ignored. Then a mouse could do anything he fancied. "There is a reason why mice squeak and the wind roars," Snitter's grandmother used to say. "Who are we to replace the wind?"

He remembered the day the thunder came and split open the roof of their world. There was no fate worse for a mouse than exposure.

But the Queen had other ideas. Seven years ago, almost to the day, she laid the Boldavian princess low, striding across the throne room floor slowly, deliberately. It had seemed like an age passed as she climbed the stairs to the royal crib. The king and queen stood by, their furless faces stricken dumb at the boldness of this tiny rodent. The Queen of Mice had smiled at them, a cat's smile of wicked teeth and venom, and slithered into the blankets where the princess slept. They'd moved to save her, but too late, too slow. Sharp teeth and a tender limb. A scream that shook the air.

Snitter had thought his heart would stop, he who was meant to guard the Queen. But she emerged from the sheets unscathed. Dabbing at her snout with a lace handkerchief, she smiled again, this time a mouse's smile, no teeth, just sweetness.

She pointed at the stricken princess. The girl had already begun to shrivel and petrify. "One bite, and this," she'd said in the difficult language of Men. "Two bites, and dead."

Queen Imebella sobbed, the king gasped.

At that moment, the royal clockmaker entered the room with a net.

"Do not!" the Mouse Queen cried. "Or two bites! See?" She bared those teeth again.

The king nodded. He would not risk what life his child had left. The man called Drosselmeyer dropped his net and the Queen of Mice grinned.

"Boldavia. Is. Mine." The first human words she'd ever

learned. The servants said she had been practicing them since the day the earth broke open. She was an old breed. The languages of Men did not come easy to her. But she'd taken the time to learn the speech of a conqueror.

She'd leapt from the crib and whisked out of the throne room, ushering in a new age for mice. Where generations of mousekin had lived quietly under the flagstones of Boldavia—wintering beneath the castle, summering in the fields—the new Queen would have sun and summer all year round.

And, for a short time, she did.

But then came the reprisals. Traps and cats and a slaughter like mousekind had never seen. All because of that blasted clockmaker, Drosselmeyer.

The rat's song shivered across Snitter's memory. Seven years had passed since those dark days, but there was no song for Boldavia. The Queen had yet to finish the verse. She would take the world of Men and squeeze the juice from it like a blackberry.

A pretty idea, Snitter admitted, but an impossible one. Fields need to be sown to reap wheat. Mice were not farmers any more than cats were men. Chase them away and who would sow the fields? Who would make the cheese? When the castles and cottages were all in ruins, only then would the Queen see the folly of her ways.

Until then, Snitter would remain her faithful servant. She would not be the first monarch he'd seen brought to ruin, nor the last. And if, by some mad twist of luck, she succeeded? Well then, he'd have earned his endless summer, after all.

"Back to Boldavia with you," he said to Blackspaw now. "Tell the Queen I've found her tutor. Ernst Listz. You travel together at first light. I'll arrange to babysit the clockmaker as long as he's in Nuremberg."

Seven years they had carried this duty, watching the clockmaker, reporting his movements. The eighth year would be no different, nor the ninth, should Snitter live that long. The nut the clockmaker sought was a fable. It did not exist, or he would have found it by now. The Queen could have her babes in peace. The tutor would train them to be heroes and, fate willing she had boys, a King would be named. The battle for Boldavia's castle would continue under the banner of the son.

"I shall find him at once," Blackspaw said, seemingly recovered from both his bad news and the journey. Snitter twitched his tail in annoyance. The boy was too stupid to be tired.

"You'll find him at the Golden Note Hotel by the opera," he told the lad. The young mouse's eyes widened. It was an extravagant choice for a rat who, only hours before, had been singing for his supper. "I'm counting on you to deliver him safely to the Queen."

"Never fear, sir." With a swish of his tail, Blackspaw disappeared into the night.

Snitter sighed and made his own way into the darkness. One thing life had taught him—fear was the first step on the road to wisdom. A lesson some mice never lived long enough to learn.

9

ALL THE GUILDHOUSES of Nuremberg lined a single street like embassies of foreign lands. The bakers' guild, the carpenters' guild, the silversmiths', ironsmiths', and coopers' guilds, the toymakers', and of course, the clockmakers' guild. Like a box of chocolates, from the outside each building looked the same—a tall, thin, multistoried townhouse that shared thick walls with its neighbors. Only when you became a member could you see the varied treasures and secrets hidden inside.

Stefan and Christian stumped up the stairs of the clockmakers' guild—distinguished from its fellows by a simple clock set in the peak of its roof, black hands on a white face, and the words *Tempus Fugit* carved into the stone lintel over the front door: *Time Flees.*

They entered a high-ceilinged foyer where a clerk looked up from his ledgers. He attempted to stop them with his basilisk gaze. His expression suggested he'd just eaten a lemon while smelling an old boot.

Christian broke into a wide smile, introduced himself as Master Clockmaker to the Royal Court of Boldavia, and demanded the ledger for Stefan to sign.

Stefan Zacharias Drosselmeyer, he wrote, *journeyman first year in the service of Christian Drosselmeyer*, et cetera, et cetera. His hand shook as he drew the final line with the clerk's ridiculously large quill pen. He was no longer just his father's son.

He was a journeyman now. A smile quirked the corner of his mouth. He hoped his mother would be proud.

Stefan watched as the clerk peered through narrow pince-nez glasses at his handiwork, rolled a blotter across the ink, and put the ledger away.

"Welcome," he said finally, and smiled as if he'd been forced to. In truth, he only had eyes for Christian, of whom he seemed to deeply disapprove.

"Now, a quick tour and we'll be on our way," Christian announced. He saluted the clerk with a little wave and produced a small key from a chain in his vest pocket. "A master key, quite literally. Given only to those who reach the highest order of master," he told Stefan. It was an unimpressive little key for all that. Christian inserted it into a small hole in the wall, unlocking a door that seemed to be nothing more than wood paneling. And they entered into the guildhouse proper.

"Did you know him?" Stefan asked, once they were out of the clerk's sight.

"Hmm? No, he must be new. But my reputation precedes me. I'm afraid they don't like me much here," Christian said. "I left in quite a huff years ago and it appears I've not been entirely forgiven."

They were in a narrow cloakroom with another hidden door in the far wall. Christian inserted his key, then turned and caught Stefan with his single-eyed gaze. "You've heard the phrase 'too many cooks in the kitchen'? Well, there were too many clockmakers in Nuremberg. I built my masterpiece, but they would not accept it."

"Was it another Advent clock?"

"No, something far smaller. A wristwatch."

"I've heard of those. British, aren't they? Wearable clocks for women that look like bracelets." He had only ever seen pocket watches, himself. In workshops, anything on the wrist could be dangerous if it snagged on a tool.

"Correct. Wristwatches do already exist. So, what do you think would make mine a masterpiece?" Christian asked.

Uh-oh, Stefan realized. This was a test. They had stopped in the antechamber. Stefan stared at the hanging coats and chewed his bottom lip.

"I suppose it would be easier to see. You wouldn't have to open your coat and jacket to get to it."

"Yes?"

"But . . . well, wouldn't winding something so tiny be a chore? And all that movement would jostle the mechanism. The gears would shift too much."

"Unless?"

Stefan bit his lip.

"Use every fault to your advantage," Christian advised. "That's how the best inventions succeed."

Stefan pictured a clock strapped to his wrist, the way his arm swung back and forth as he walked. Like a pendulum. Like clockwork. Like—

"A self-winding watch!" he exclaimed.

"Excellent!" Christian grinned. "You've a good head for visualization."

"But, that's brilliant!" Stefan cried. "A watch like that could keep almost perfect time!"

"Yes. Good news for the wearer, but . . ." Again, Christian gave him an expectant look.

"But . . ." Stefan's mind raced. If clocks kept perfect time, they would never need to be set or recalibrated. "Who needs a clockmaker with a perfect watch?"

"Precisely. Clockmakers would lose customers. The guild did not approve—of the work, or the maker."

But Stefan did. It was an amazing idea. "So what did you do?"

"I took my clockworks, and I left."

Christian unlocked the second door and led the way into the heart of the guildhouse.

It was a neck-craning, ear-assaulting experience. A thousand clocks lined the walls. Clocks of gold, and clocks run by water that dripped clear liquid into cups shaped like lily pads. There were grandfather clocks set in casings of rare and fragrant wood, small clocks on long shelves like never-ending fireplace mantels, formed of porcelain figurines and rustic cuckoos.

Stefan had never seen so many beautiful timepieces in his life. He passed a glass case of pocket watches, each gleaming in brass, silver, or gold. There were clocks with precious stones encrusted into each numeral. There were some of such odd shapes that they did not appear to be clocks at all—one that was merely a series of lines on the wall, with a narrow window cut into the opposite side of the hall. A small sign declared it some sort of sundial—it marked time by how many of the lines were covered in shadow. Most remarkable of all, each clock kept the exact time so that, when they ticked, it was a resonant sound that vibrated the building. *The striking of the hour must be deafening,* Stefan thought. His chest expanded with each tick, filling him with the most remarkable sense of rightness. And these were just timepieces. With carpentry and a little ingenuity, imagine what more he could do.

"Welcome to the clockmakers' guild," Christian said, leading the way through the gallery and up a banistered stair. "Ignore the clocks in this room. They're mostly rubbish. But there is something I want to show you."

"Rubbish?" Stefan highly doubted that, but he rushed to keep up with his long-legged cousin.

"Not rubbish, I suppose, but nothing you haven't seen before—hands, numbers. The same as you'll find at any street fair or decent shop. But this . . ." Christian said as Stefan gained the top step. "*This* is extraordinary."

At the back of a long white room, empty of all other timepieces, sat a glass case with a box inside. Stefan peered through the glass.

"It looks like a pile of gears," he said at last. Indeed, it seemed to be a drawer of spare clock parts arranged in a vaguely circular pattern, piles of golden gears and cogs stacked on top of each other, as if a child had tried to create a sunflower from the discarded pieces.

"Look again," Christian said. "There is a design to the madness."

Stefan leaned closer until his breath fogged up the glass. "It's a clock," he realized.

"Built in 1606 by a Benedictine monk."

"But . . ." There were no hands or numbers to count off the hours. As Stefan watched the gleaming wheels of gold, some of the larger gears moved slowly. It was like spying on an ant colony from far above. "What does it do?"

"Nothing. This is just a replica. Would you like to know how it works?"

Stefan tore his eyes away from the remarkable device. "Yes, I would."

Christian seemed pleased. "Excellent. Now, for your first assignment." He turned and led the way downstairs again.

Stefan pulled his notebook from his pocket, torn between wanting to sketch the curious clock and needing to take notes for his first duty as journeyman.

"I have people to see," Christian explained as they clattered through the hidden doors and out past the sour-faced clerk.

"Your foster family?"

"Among others. You'll be on your own for the rest of the day. See what you can find."

Stefan blinked, once again hurrying to keep up. "Find? Find what?" he asked, gaining the sidewalk once more, pencil at the ready.

Christian turned around and smiled. "The *krakatook*, of course."

HE'D STARTED OUT methodically enough. From morning until noon, he visited the nut sellers themselves, and the warehouses where imports were brought in by the wagonload. From there, he'd eaten his way through a dozen bakeries, ordering hazelnut tortes and walnut pfeffernüsse, always asking to see the baker's store of nutmeats. But he'd had seventeen pieces of cake so far, and no sign of the *krakatook*.

He visited physicians and herbalists, all manner of people who used nuts—stationers who used crushed shells of raw walnuts to make brown ink, apothecaries that ground nut shells into powders fine as ash for polishing faces, boots, and silver. He even climbed a few trees looking for the elusive *krakatook*.

But Christian had hunted for seven years with no success. How was Stefan supposed to do better in a single day? The difficulty was this—no one knew what a *krakatook* looked like. The very nature of the nut was that each one was different. It was said to resemble an almond, a walnut, and occasionally a hazelnut, but never a cashew (which Stefan learned wasn't really a nut at all). That much, at least, Christian and Samir had divined from their research. Yet Samir assured them they would know one when they found it. Stefan hoped that was true, and that he hadn't already eaten it.

At his wits' end, he headed toward the botanical garden.

The entire length and width of Nuremberg was littered with gardens, large and small. Horticulture had been the pride of the city since the 1500s. Stefan could spend his entire journeyship searching in people's courtyards and fields for the nut. But the Nuremberg Botanical Garden had existed for almost two hundred years in one form or another. Surely they would have at least *heard* of the *krakatook*. Maybe the groundskeepers at the garden would have some advice for him.

The botanical garden was a patch of paradise on earth. A vast expanse of greenery, from shrubs to trees to flowers, stretched out in rows as far as the eye could see. Walled in by the city, it seemed a secret place, although it was open to anyone. His mother had taken him here when he was very young. Aside from a game of hide-and-seek that had been mostly one-sided, the place had not made much of an impression on him. Now, however, it could have been the Amazon, that great jungle in the New World that seemed to laugh at Portuguese explorers and swallow them whole.

He avoided the outdoor planting beds and found the greenhouse, a pretty structure of whitewashed metal and soaring windows that held tropical plants. He stepped inside and was met with humidity and the scent of exotic flowers. Wandering the winding path through the center of the greenhouse, he followed the sound of a spade and rake until he discovered the source—a groundskeeper kneeling in the dirt. The little man looked up as Stefan approached.

"Hoy there, young sir! Pleasant day, isn't she?"

"Yes, very pleasant. As are your gardens," Stefan replied. When asking for help, it never hurt to start with a compliment, particularly one that was true.

The old man grinned. "If you're here to meet with your young lady, I believe you'll find her by the tulips."

"What? Oh, no, I'm not meeting anyone. I was looking for you, in fact." The heat rose in Stefan's cheeks at the very thought of a girl waiting for *him*. The only girls Stefan knew were under the age of eight and pining for his father's dolls.

"That's a pity," the old man said. "She's an easier sight on the eyes than me." Stefan helped the man rise to his feet and waited while he dusted off his hopelessly stained trousers. "All right, then. What can I do for you?"

"I'm looking for a nut."

"Oh, nut trees and bushes are down to the left, the last

corner lot. We had to separate them from the other plants so they wouldn't sprout their seeds all over tarnation."

The man nodded and turned back to his plants.

"Actually, I'm looking for something rare. It's been impossible to find. It's called a *krakatook*?"

"A *krakatook*!" The man broke into an even wider grin, and his shining white teeth became almost menacing. Stefan took an involuntary step backward.

"You might as well be looking for a mermaid! The *krakatook*. I haven't heard that one in years. It's fool's gold, young man."

"But you *have* heard of it," Stefan said, relieved. He couldn't stand returning home a complete failure on his first day, even if he had been given an impossible task.

"Sure, I have," the gardener said. "A mystical nut from the Far East. Marco Polo wrote about it in his diaries."

Stefan was staggered. The nut was real!

"But it doesn't exist," the man continued, "or we'd have one by now. Someone's playing a prank on you, I'm afraid." The gardener gave him a considering look. "Are you newly apprenticed?"

"No, I'm a journeyman," Stefan said. *But for how long?* he wondered. The man gave him a dubious look.

"A new master, then. Yep, those fellers are always pulling some new boy's leg. I'm afraid they've firmly yanked yours. Speaking of which, these weeds won't pull themselves, so if you'll excuse me."

Stefan let the gardener return to his work. "A prank," he muttered.

It wasn't unheard of. Journeymen played jokes on apprentices all the time. His own father had pulled one or two over on him—telling Stefan that sea horses were shaped like the letter "C," leading to an entire mobile of ridiculously shaped creatures that had his father bent over with laughter. Or when he was given a strange piece of wood to carve a cup from, only to discover upon drinking from it that the soft wood had in fact been very hard soap. He'd gotten a foam mustache for his troubles.

"A rare nut," he said. "And I fell for it."

Christian's whole fairy tale had been exactly that. So had the journeyship, no doubt. Christian and his father were just putting him in his place. That whole story about the princess and Boldavia—all just to show Stefan he belonged at home with his father and not off on an adventure. His neck flashed hot beneath his collar. He felt a headache coming on. They were probably relaxing in some biergarten having a good laugh. Well, maybe not laughing—he couldn't imagine his father would ever do that. Still, he felt like a fool.

He reached the end of the greenhouse and stopped in front of the doors, resisting the urge to bang his head against them. Through the glass he could see a field of tulips, red-and-white striped flowers nodding sleepily in the breeze.

Tulips had been his mother's favorite. There had been a vase of yellow ones by her bed when she died.

Without warning, tears rolled down his cheeks.

"If it's rare, it won't be here," said an amused voice. Stefan turned on his heel, wiping furiously at his eyes, but they would not stay dry.

"What makes you think so?" he asked in a gruff voice, addressing the row of plants behind him. *Rubber trees*, the sign said, exotic-looking things with trunks like twisted vines.

A pair of eyes peered at him from behind the large, shining leaves. They belonged to a girl seated on a low bench with a bit of embroidery in her lap.

She held up a piece of linen. "What do you think? I'm meant to be embroidering these in the parlor, but I hate sitting inside on a day like this. Not that this isn't inside, but it's peaceful and green. Will this do?" She handed him the linen. It was a small handkerchief embroidered with a pale blue "S" and small dark blue flowers.

"It's . . . it's very nice," Stefan said awkwardly.

"Thank you. Have a seat." She patted the bench beside her. Stefan sat.

"I really think it's rather rough," she continued. "Feel that on your cheek." She took the handkerchief from him and wiped his eyes.

"It's . . . fine," he managed to say. She had taken him by surprise. He couldn't think.

"Maybe for a boy. It's a bit too coarse for my taste. And I've mangled the embroidery at the bottom."

"It's an 'S'," Stefan said. "That's my initial."

"Ah, well, then, it's yours. It was a practice run anyway." She thrust the handkerchief back into his hand and picked up her embroidery. Stefan took a moment to clean his face and wipe his nose. He should have been embarrassed, caught crying in front of a stranger, and a girl no less. But she didn't seem to care. In fact, she appeared so absorbed in her needlework that she didn't notice him staring at her.

Her lips were wide, and her eyes large and brown. Her hair was braided into two shining chestnut plaits that hung low over her ears, and she wore a neat day dress of red and white with an apron over it. Skeins of embroidery thread stuffed the apron pockets.

"Pardon me," he said. "I thought I was alone."

"As did I," she replied. "But that's been remedied. Why don't you tell me about this rare nut?"

Stefan had no better plans now that his quest had been disproved, so he settled in beside her and watched her needle dipping in and out of the cloth in her hands.

"I think I've been played for a fool," he said.

"An apprentice's prank, like Arno said," she surmised, with a tilt of her head toward the sound of the old groundskeeper's raking.

"I'm a journeyman toymaker, er, clocksmith. My new master's led me on a merry chase."

She looked at him skeptically. "Which is it, toys, or clocks? They don't let you do both, do they?"

Stefan blushed. "No. I suppose not . . . not in Nuremberg. I'm journeyed out of country, actually. A kingdom far away." He attempted a rakish grin.

The girl smiled. "Now who's telling fairy tales?"

"It's true! I'm leaving town just as soon as I find—"

"The rare and mythical nut," she concluded, puncturing Stefan's pride.

"Well, yes."

The girl patted him sympathetically on the leg and gathered her materials. "I have to be getting home. We young ladies must leave all the adventuring to men, or so my mother insists. But look—" She checked the label for the tree beside them. "*Ficus elastica.* That's an India rubber plant, which means I've got as far as Bombay today." She quirked a smile. "As for your nut, if it exists and it's truly rare, why not try the Natural History Society. They collect the oddest things."

"The Natural . . . I've never heard of them."

"Not many people have," she said, rising from the bench. "They're eccentrics. They only speak to each other. For vegetation, see Professor Blume. He's the foremost authority on botany in all of Nuremberg. Recently returned from a trip around the globe."

It was Stefan's turn to be dubious. "How do you know all of this?"

"Because I can read," she said. "And I read anything I can find. Professor Blume's in all the gardening journals. He's been to Amazonia and Indochina, Oceania, and even the Arctic, where plants only bloom a few days a year. Ask Arno, he collects all of his journals. He can tell you where to go."

Stefan sighed. "My cousin's been looking for a *krakatook* for seven years. Maybe the joke has been played on all of us." It was a terrible thought. Maybe Samir had lied, and this goose chase was Christian's punishment for angering the king of Boldavia. The whole story began to unravel until he wondered if any of it had been true.

The girl gave him a mischievous smile as she brushed past. "Even better when you inexplicably show up *with* one. Tell Professor Blume about the prank. He was a boy once. He's sure to play along."

"That's brilliant. Thank you." He rose to his feet and gave her a quick bow. "My name is Stefan." His heart fluttered oddly in his chest, like a moth.

"Pleased to meet you, Stefan," she said, and dropped a quick curtsy. "I'm sorry, but I must go."

"Where can I find you?" he asked.

She took a step back.

Stefan blushed. "I mean, to return your handkerchief . . . of course." He mentally kicked himself. He was being too forward, but he could not stop himself. This girl was someone he wanted to know.

"Oh. No, it's yours. If you truly are going abroad, take it with you. Imagine, my handiwork visiting places I will never see. Maybe you'll take it to India someday! Good-bye, Stefan. And good luck!"

She exited in a whirl of skirts, the red-and-white pattern of her dress blending into the field of tulips as she hurried out of sight.

Stefan watched her go. Something about the girl reminded him of his mother. They had the same twinkle in their eye. Looking at the gardens, the sight of tulips no longer made him sad. He would like to see her again. Tell her how the prank played out. Maybe take her to a café for cakes.

He smiled to himself, and immediately moaned. He had forgotten to ask her name.

10

ERNST SIGHED AND SANK deeper into the bathing bowl, the tips of his claws poking up from the lavender-scented bubbles. He'd been inspired by the piebald Snitter's powdered scent and left the docks for better climes. At the Golden Note, a luxury hotel in the walls of the massive Imperial and Royal Court Theatre, he could bathe in warm water and hear the symphony wafting up through the pipes and cracks in his hidden room. Perhaps the music of Mozart or Beethoven would be played tonight. Ernst wriggled his toes and sighed. For the next three hours, this was the life.

The knot in his shoulder from the skirmish with the alley cat had finally eased in the hot water and he was just beginning to doze off, when there came an awful pounding at the door.

"Open up! Open up!" a male voice demanded.

"Probably my escort," Ernst decided, settling back into the tub, preferring the continued pounding over leaving the warmth of the water. Once he answered that door, this little retreat would be over and his duties would begin. Who knew when he'd get another bath like this one?

Just one minute more . . .

He settled a washcloth over his eyes and began humming along with the orchestra tuning below.

A key turned in the lock and the door to Ernst's bedroom burst open.

The rat sighed and pulled himself out of the tub. Wrapping a plush robe around his thin frame, he dried his feet on the mat with a little dancing step.

"I told you he wouldn't be here," he heard a mouse say disdainfully. "You can't trust a rat." The speaker was a young piebald with a mottled face and black paws. He was venting his anger on the small gray mouse that served as night manager of the hotel. The manager held his back straight, but his whiskers quivered nervously. "They're all thieves and cheats," the piebald continued.

"Really?" Ernst asked dryly.

The gray mouse balked and lost his composure, cowering like a meadow mouse in the face of an owl. To his credit, he recovered quickly, preening his short whiskers, and lifted his chin as if he had never doubted the integrity of his guest. "Forgive the intrusion, Herr Listz," he began, only to be interrupted by the piebald, who refused to quail.

"Yes, they are," he said. "Only a rat would waste a month's wages on one night of . . ." He took in the opulent suite. "'When the seed runs out, so does the rat,' as they say. The name is Blackspaw. My commander sent me to guide you." The way he said "guide" sounded an awful lot like "guard" to Ernst. "We leave at dawn. I'll be outside."

"Keeping me honest, eh?" Ernst chuckled. He leaned against the doorway nonchalantly. Let the mouse think he was a wastrel. He could use it to his advantage. "I should think a soldier such as yourself would trust the judgment of his commander implicitly." Ernst sucked his teeth and studied his newly trimmed claws. "We had such a nice rapport, Snitter and I, and he was so kind to offer Her Majesty's tutor a guide to Boldavia. I suppose he'll be very disappointed when I make my report. What will the Queen think, I wonder."

At last, the piebald was shaken. He bristled and shrank as the air left his puffed-out chest. "Ah . . . ah . . . apologies, Herr Listz. Clearly you are a gentlerat of . . . uncommon breeding. I was . . . merely concerned for our . . . ah . . ." The piebald realized he was flailing and, with a concerted effort, stopped.

"I shall be in the hallway. We leave at dawn." He clicked his heels and retreated.

The manager wrung his paws together apologetically. "Herr Listz, is there anything I can bring you?"

"More hot water, please," the rat said. He sauntered over to his sack of seed and pulled another portion out to tip the night manager. "And a blanket for my guide out there. Or cover him with something pretty so he doesn't frighten the guests."

The manager smiled and removed himself with a bow.

A few minutes later, three white mice appeared with freshly boiled kettles. They silently reheated Ernst's bath and left. He sank back into the tub with a sigh.

Despite the variety of Rodentia, when it came down to it, there really were only two types of rodents in this world: squirrels and rats. Squirrels were chipper little fools who believed they'd live forever, so they spent all their time gathering nuts, storing them away for that bright future. Anyone with that blithering outlook was a squirrel. Including that impudent little piebald—so certain of tomorrow that he'd rather wait than live today. But rats appreciated the brevity of life. Death was around every corner for rodents without a bushy tail—rat and mouse, vole, mole, and shrew. But only rats lived for the moment (as did, perhaps, a criminal vole or two). The rest were squirrels by nature, if not form. Even mice were mostly squirrels at heart. Timid and hopeful, diligently thinking of winter even in the spring. But why save for tomorrow what you could spend today? Especially if each day could be your last.

Ernst Listz was a rat. Which was why he had willingly spent more than half his bag of seed on wine, a bath, a second dinner, and a very soft bed. If it meant sneaking on board a barge headed down the river the next day rather than purchasing proper accommodations (carved out in the bulkhead of one of the more luxurious boats), so be it. He would gladly sleep beneath a coil of rope in exchange for this one night of being clean, safe, and well fed.

Ernst wriggled his toes in the steaming water, the last of his aches and pains easing away. He dismissed all thought of the morning to come, and the state of the kingdom at the end of his dangerous journey. For now, it was a hot bath and a full belly. In short, it was heaven.

11

"CLARA," STEFAN SAID to himself, committing the sound to memory. Arno the groundskeeper had been forthcoming with directions to Professor Blume's house, and with a name for the girl in the red-and-white dress.

Clara. A perfect name, thought Stefan as he passed through the professor's front garden. It sounded like a bell.

The professor's front lawn was impressively laid out in beds of flowers and herbs, and rows of carefully trimmed trees. It mimicked the botanical gardens in miniature.

Stefan was admitted through the front door by a dour servant who left him in a large entryway filled with enough plants and flowers to rival Arno's greenhouse.

Stefan paused to peer closely at a side table covered in miniature trees planted in ceramic trays. There was a red-leaf maple tree that stood no more than twelve inches high. Despite their tiny size, they appeared to be fully grown. It was breathtaking. He imagined the sorts of figurines his father might carve to decorate the trays. A small picnic scene would charm many of the ladies who came to the shop.

He was alone in the hall, so he pulled out his sketchbook to draw a quick design. The scene unfolded beneath his pencil, a tiny sheltering maple and a girl in a full skirt and tulip-shaped apron sitting beneath the tree. The fact that she looked exactly like Clara escaped him entirely.

Stefan startled when a voice spoke close to his ear.

"Bonsai," the gruff voice said. "Japanese technique. Some of those trees are a hundred years old."

Stefan looked up to see Professor Blume, a man shaped like a large turnip with a velvet housecoat over his shirtwaist, vest, and slippers. He appeared to be in his early sixties, with wiry gray hair sticking out from beneath a small fez of burgundy velvet that complemented the pattern in his robe. Spidery red veins blossomed across his bulbous nose.

He smiled at Stefan and held out a hand. Stefan hastily pocketed his notebook and shook hands with a slight bow.

"Welcome, Herr Drosselmeyer, was it? Come to my study. We can discuss your interests over a cup of tea. My own brew, actually, grown on one of my plantations in Ceylon. Have you been? Fascinating part of the world, Ceylon. Humid as a hothouse, but the vegetation! Theologians are still out on the subject, but I do believe it might be the original Paradise."

Stefan followed the professor into his study. Conservatory was more like it. Yes, there were bookcases, a desk, and two very comfortable-looking armchairs, but they were woven from rattan and bamboo instead of the tufted leather that usually graced a gentleman's den. And where one might expect tapestries or wood-paneled walls stood vines and potted plants, seedling trays, and all manner of vases filled to the top with exotic flowers.

"Have a seat, my boy. I'll ring for tea. Now, what is this about a nut?"

Stefan settled into one of the chairs. Professor Blume sat opposite him. The humid room had turned the older man's face an alarming shade of red, but he showed no sign of discomfort. Stefan, on the other hand, began to feel both sweaty and foolish.

"Sir, I apologize for bothering you. It's just that . . . well, I've recently become journeyman to a new master and he's set me on a task. To find a nut called a *krakatook*."

"A *krakatook!*" Professor Blume exclaimed. He pulled a damp-looking handkerchief out of his robe pocket and mopped his forehead.

Stefan winced. "I know, a fool's errand," he said quickly. "And I have been a fool. But I had hoped . . . It was suggested to me that I might turn the tables with your help. Is there any chance you have a nut in your possession that I might pass off as the *krakatook*? Something unusual that my master wouldn't have seen before? I'd like to surprise him with it. And I'd return it to you, of course . . ." He faltered.

The professor was struggling to rise from his chair.

Stefan jumped to his feet first. "I understand if you want to throw me out. Don't get up. I'm leaving."

"The devil you are, my lad! What do you know about Chinese mythology?"

Stefan blinked. "What?"

"The Chinese! Celestials! Much like the Greek gods and their ambrosia, the Chinese gods maintained their immortality by eating peaches from a certain tree in the gardens of heaven on Mount Kunlun. That wall hanging there is a representation."

Stefan rose to admire the finely woven tapestry that hung hidden behind the fronds of a palm tree. It depicted a stylized mountain wreathed in clouds. At the base of the mountain, farmers toiled in the fields, while at the crown, a shining city of pagodas rose above the clouds, a tree at its center. He could just make out the small fruits on its limbs. It reminded him of the view from the roof of his house.

The professor continued. "Got that one off a monk in Nepal. They wear yellow and red robes over there. Far cry from a Benedictine, wouldn't you say? Where was I? Ah, yes. According to legend, the *krakatook* is not really a nut, you see, but the stone of the peach of immortality. Peach stones have medicinal value in China, good for a variety of ills—stagnant blood, allergies, and the like. But the stone of the peach of *immortality* has extraordinary properties—great wisdom and longevity among them. It's a cure-all, like so many magic talismans waved about by heathens in the night. And, like magic, it's all balderdash. You can't exactly eat a peach stone, after all."

"Yes you can," Stefan said. "If you crack it open, there's a soft seed inside, shaped like an almond."

"Aha! Those are called bitter almonds, and they're poisonous."

Stefan frowned. He'd eaten the seed inside a peach when he was little and lived to tell the tale. He said as much.

The professor waved his hand in annoyance, the tassel on his fez bouncing.

"It would take bitter almonds by the pound to kill you. And all the mythological hocus-pocus—longevity and medicinal traits—all as fake as the Feejee mermaid. I've been to China and I've never seen any gods living on mountaintops eating peaches. But mystical or not, the *krakatook* is real."

Stefan's eyebrows rose. "What makes you say so?"

"Because I have one," he said. "Upstairs. Would you like to

see it? What now? Are you choking? Overcome with joy, no doubt. Hold on, I'll see about that tea."

Professor Blume grinned conspiratorially and scuttled from the room, slippers slapping the oriental carpets, his fez tassel bouncing from side to side like an excited dog's tail.

Stefan recovered his composure and sat down. *Eccentric*, Clara had said. That didn't even begin to describe his host.

The slap-slap of slippers soon returned, accompanied by an out-of-breath professor. Stefan jumped to his feet again.

"Still here? Good, good. Sit down." He beamed at Stefan, a small casket clutched in his pudgy hands.

"Here you are, young fellow. The *krakatook*, fresh and hard as the day I first bought it off a merchant in Istanbul who did not know what he had. Of course, I didn't either, or I wouldn't have bought it, I suppose." He thrust the casket into Stefan's bewildered hands and sat down abruptly to catch his breath. The rattan protested with a scrunch, but held. "Well, don't just gawp at the thing. Open it!"

Stefan examined the box. It was a small chest of tooled silver, no bigger than his hand. He flipped open the latch.

There, on a bed of blue velvet, sat an ordinary nut.

"It's a walnut."

"No, it only looks like a walnut. Turn it over."

On the reverse of the nut, there was a word carved into the surface of the shell in flowing golden script: *Krakatook*.

"It's still a walnut," Stefan said. "It's just been gilded or engraved."

"But *how*?" asked the professor, brandishing a finger in the air.

"How what?" Stefan was lost. Professor Blume was clearly batty.

"How was it engraved? Everyone who knows anything about the *krakatook* knows the name is a corruption of 'crack a tooth!' The surface is impervious to tooth or blade, mallet or sledge-hammer. Rather convenient for a mystical nut, wouldn't you say?"

"But sir, there's no such thing—"

"As a *krakatook*, I know, I know," the professor said. "But there it is, hard as a young man's head. I broke a tooth trying to prise it open once. But it was no good. Give it here."

Stefan handed the nut over. He would be polite and try to leave as soon as possible. But for now, he had to humor the madman.

"Give me that casket, too. You've felt it, eh? Heavy. Solid silver with a bit of lead in the hinges. Now." He placed the nut on a marble-topped side table, holding it carefully in place with his finger and thumb.

The tea never came, Stefan thought.

And then the professor slammed the silver casket down onto the nut with all his might.

The casket rebounded into the air, yanking the professor's arm with it.

Stefan shouted in surprise, raising his hands to block the shards of flying shell. But there weren't any. "Mein Gott!" he exclaimed.

The *krakatook* sat quietly on the table.

"Unshatterable!" the professor pronounced.

He smiled and tossed the nut back to Stefan. "Useless as a snack and, if it has any of those mythical medicinal qualities, well, short of sucking on it like a candy, I don't know how it would be of much use."

Stefan turned the nut in his hands. "Impossible!"

The professor rubbed his arm. "It gives the bones quite a shake. Ah, here comes that tea, just in time. Sit, my boy, and recover. You've had quite a shock. Like finding a narwhal horn in the woods, I should think. Startling discovery indeed."

Stefan had no idea what the professor was talking about now, but he willingly sat and drank his tea, slowly recovering his nerves.

"So . . . this nut," he began to say.

"It's yours, take it. I'm a botanist. If I can't crack it to study it, nor plant it to grow more, then it's no use to me except as a parlor trick. It's not as if I have a line of celestial mystics asking after it. And I could do without all the squirrels it draws into the attic. Must protect my specimens, you know. Can't have rodents gnawing at my trees."

Stefan looked around the room. There had been no sign of squirrels, or talking mice for that matter. As far as he knew, the professor was playing another parlor trick on him.

"Thank you, Professor Blume. I'll mention your bonsai trees to my father. They would make perfect dioramas."

"Indeed they would," the professor said brightly. "Well then, you can see yourself out. Dioramas . . ." he muttered to himself, and turned to gaze at his plants.

A bemused Stefan found himself once again on the doorstep of the professor's peculiar house, the *krakatook* inside its casket stuffed deep into the pocket of his coat. It had been a strange day. He turned his feet gladly toward home.

12

"ZACHARIAS ELIAS DROSSELMEYER?" the flamboyant man in a red feathered hat inquired at the door.

"Yes, at your service," Zacharias said, buttoning his coat. "But I'm afraid I'm running out. Errands, deliveries." Christian and his strange friend and even Stefan were out on their bizarre quest, but he had a business to run. "Perhaps we could set an appointment?"

"I'm afraid not," the man said. "Your son has been injured. Some sort of run-in with a cart and horse. If you'll accept my carriage, I can take you to him."

A shock of cold fear pierced Zacharias from heart to stomach. Elise was gone, and now this? He grabbed his hat, a modest brown felt thing that he crushed in his hands rather than put on his head.

"I'll just . . . lock up." He fumbled his keys, closing the shop. "Oh, I should leave a note for . . . I have family . . . visiting."

The scarlet man gently took the keys from him. "Calm yourself, sir. Your hands are shaking. Climb aboard my carriage. I'll leave a note on your behalf." He smiled kindly. "All will be well. Sit in back. And remember, prayers are welcome."

Shaken—*prayers? Was it as bad as that?*—Zacharias did as he was bidden.

The carriage was harnessed to an old nag, and both had seen better days. Not so glamorous as their owner. The windows were curtained in sackcloth where one might have expected velvet, and the seats were stuffed with scratchy straw that poked Zacharias in the legs when he sat down. But he barely noticed. His mind was already racing through the streets of Nuremberg toward his son.

"Is it far?" Zacharias asked, sticking his head out the window of the carriage as the man emerged from the shop.

"Not far. Here." He reached into his coat pocket and produced a flask. "Some brandy will settle your nerves." He poured a draught into the cap and offered it to Zacharias.

The toymaker hesitated, then drank. It burned its way down his throat and he coughed.

"And one for luck," the man said gently, pouring another. This one Zacharias took without hesitation. It seemed to work. A moment later, he was sitting back, his breathing steady. The hat fell, forgotten, into his lap.

It should have struck him as odd, he thought later, when the man in scarlet jumped into the coachman's seat on top of the carriage, rather than joining Zacharias inside. Surely such a grandly dressed gentleman would have a driver.

"Thank you," Zacharias said, his words dissolving into a yawn.

The carriage lurched forward in a clatter of hooves, throwing his head back, then forward to rest on his gently snoring chest. He was quite unconscious when they left the city of Nuremberg far behind.

13

BLACKSPAW DEPOSITED ERNST at the foot of the quay.

The rat was exhausted. It had been an exhilarating trip down the River Danube, but he could have done without the underground route they'd taken. Their haste had deprived him of long days lounging on deck in the sun. But now he was here.

The Kingdom of Boldavia was an impressive sight—seven long docks jutting out from a series of porous caves at the base of the island. The castle itself towered atop the sheer mass of rock, a thousand feet above. In between, a second row of caves ringed the island, larger and squared off in a way that suggested Man, rather than nature, had shaped them. The view from there must be magnificent.

Ernst could hear the teeming kingdom of mice, weaving their way through the rock cells above. So the rumors about the uprising were true. The question was, were the men fighting back?

Ernst shivered. The quay was impressive, but it would have been more so if the Mouse Queen had bothered with a dinghy, or even a raft—some way of conveying guests from ship to shore without them having to swim.

Once safely back on land, Ernst gathered himself and shook for all he was worth, nose to tail. A splatter of water hit the gray stones around him and left his fur reasonably dry. With a sigh, he unbundled his clothes from their oilcloth wrapping and dressed himself with all the dignity a damp, travel-worn rat of middle years could muster.

Blackspaw watched from the rocks below. "This is the servants' entrance," the mouse said. "I must report to my sergeant. I trust you can find your way the last few yards?" Blackspaw sneered. He'd made his opinion clear every step of the trip downriver—he did not approve of a rat teaching the royal heir any more than he'd approve of an alley cat brought in to serve as a wet nurse.

What a rat had ever done to him (other than be taller, better looking, and much better educated), Ernst could not guess. He was glad to be rid of the little nuisance, and hoped that the other Boldavians would prove more agreeable.

"Young sir, I may be a stranger to Boldavia, but I know my way around a royal court." Fully clothed in his best blue silks, Ernst hoisted the last of his bundled wardrobe and bowed to the piebald. "Would that I could say it's been a pleasure," he added.

Blackspaw snorted. "Likewise," he said, and scurried away.

The trip, of course, had been anything but pleasant. From that first early morning departure, with the angry little mouse pacing in front of his hotel room, to the wet dash aboard a southbound barge. The meager fare. The dull company—really, who wants to hear about the dreams of a mouse soldier who has traveled much but seen little beyond his own ego? True, there had been a particularly good sausage procured in Romania. Aside from that, the travel had been like cold oatmeal— lumpy, bland, and best thrown out. Still, Ernst had arrived, alive and relatively well. A hot bath, a decent meal, and some minor repairs to his clothes were all that was needed. And then, once he secured the Queen's approval, he'd look forward to as royal a feast as Boldavia could muster and a new wardrobe befitting a royal tutor.

He glanced around the rocks, taking in the dark water and pale, distant sky. Boldavia smelled of pork fat and flowers. A promising perfume, he decided as he entered the servants' tunnel.

Halfway up the curving stone corridor, he heard someone scurrying toward him. Ernst took a moment to straighten his whiskers, crack his spine, and relax.

A young mouse, this one gray as a winter morning, came skidding up to him.

"Sir! Do I have the pleasure of addressing Ernst Listz the rat?"

"Certainly. Good afternoon."

"Wonderful, wonderful!" the mouse squeaked. "I am Fleet-foot. I'm to convey you to the Queen."

"Perhaps I could have a moment to refresh myself?" Ernst ventured.

The little mouse had already taken his bag and was scurrying away. "She don't like to be kept waiting, sir. Please. This way. She's in the audience chamber already. Blackspaw was meant to get you here this morning."

Ernst spat a curse at his nasty piebald escort. Trying to ruin his chances at getting the job, eh? Not likely. With a snap of his tail, Ernst picked up the pace and made all haste to meet his new Queen.

14

STEFAN CAME HOME to a house in disarray. The furniture had been overturned, the shop had been ransacked, and Christian was standing in the middle of the living room, his head in his hands. The astrologer Samir was nowhere to be seen.

For a brief moment, he thought perhaps Christian had proven himself a thief after all. Then his cousin turned and the look on his face told a different story.

"What's happened? Where is my father?"

Christian shook his head. "Gone. Taken."

"Taken? What is this? One of your jokes?"

"Would that it were," Christian said. "We found the place like this. Samir went to search for him. I wanted to wait for you. I'm so sorry, Stefan. The mice have him."

Stefan stared. "The mice? Do you know how ridiculous that sounds? You're not just a criminal, you're a liar. I can't believe anything you say. The *krakatook*? Seven years? Princesses, talking mice? You're either wicked or mad. What have you done with my father?"

In answer, Christian pointed to a scrap of paper on the table.

In very small, precise writing, there was a note:

To the criminal Drosselmeyer,
Stay away, or the Toymaker dies.

The accusation and the smudged paw print at the edge of the paper gave proof to Christian's story. He was a criminal to both mice and men. "What did you do to make them hate you this much?" Stefan asked.

"Only my duty. When the mice first emerged from the tunnels under Boldavia, I tried to send them back into their caves—with traps and other means—to chase them out of the kingdom. And it worked, at first. We killed . . . *I* killed mice by the hundreds. But, for every one we saw, there were a dozen more in the walls. They rallied and . . . I've told you the rest."

Stefan collapsed onto the bench beside the table, stung with a hundred needle points of fear. "Mice did this?"

His cousin picked up an overturned chair. "More likely men working for mice. An anonymous sack of gold will buy much in this world."

He grasped Stefan by the wrist. "We will find him," he promised.

Stefan nodded. His father, taken, his mother, dead. What was left for him now?

His free hand drifted to his coat pocket and brushed against the embroidered handkerchief there. It brought him a small bit of comfort. This piece of linen came from a world where mice were just dumb animals, and parents didn't disappear.

He felt the casket in his pocket and pulled it out with a sigh. "I almost forgot. This is for you," he said, and opened the box.

Christian froze, as if seeing the face of Medusa.

"Mein Gott!" he breathed.

"I—" Stefan began.

His cousin swiftly pressed a finger to his lips and eyed the upended room. Christian gripped Stefan's shoulder and looked him in the eye. He did not speak, but mouthed the words: *No. One. Must. Know.*

Releasing Stefan, he swiftly flipped his eye patch up and secreted the *krakatook* in the void left by his missing eye. Stefan blanched but, given the circumstances, it was a better hiding place than his pocket.

Christian smiled as he readjusted the patch. "Samir!" he bellowed. "We have work to do!"

There was a scraping sound overhead, and the Arab appeared in Stefan's sleeping loft. "What in the seven hells do you think I'm doing?" the astrologer said.

"I thought you were out looking for my father," Stefan exclaimed angrily.

Samir raised the small brass telescope in his hand. "There is more than one way to seek a man."

"The stars? That's ridiculous. You should be out on the streets looking for him. We all should!"

"This is a spyglass, Stefan, for streets, not stars," the astrologer said calmly. "We can cover more area from high ground than wandering these mazes you call roads." He turned to Christian, ignoring Stefan's outburst. "No disturbances, no ripples to indicate a wave of rodents. If he is with them, they are underground or they have already left the city."

"If I hadn't been running around like a fool eating cakes all day trying to *help* you, I could have stopped this from happening!" Stefan cried, his shock replaced by panic.

An expression flickered across Christian's face. Was it guilt?

"Perhaps," he said. "Or maybe both of you would have been taken. What matters is what we do next."

Stefan deflated. He was yelling at Samir and Christian when he wanted to yell at himself. He was good at losing parents, it seemed.

"Will he be okay?"

"Dear boy, he's worth more to them alive than dead."

"As what—a hostage? Why? As far as they know, you're further away from finding the nut than ever."

Christian gave him a warning glance.

Samir quirked an eyebrow, and a look passed between the astrologer and the clockmaker.

Christian nodded slightly. "Time to pack, Samir," he said.

Samir broke into a grin. And then he began to sing. It wasn't a song Stefan knew, but Samir belted it with gusto as he moved about the shop, straightening the mess.

If only Stefan's life could be tidied so easily. "I'm going to the city guard," he announced. They had men at the gates around Nuremberg. They should be able to tell him if his father had left the city. He reached for the front door; Christian's gloved hand held it firmly shut.

"You will do no such thing."

"I will do *something*. Something more than singing and cleaning house. He's my father. Maybe that means nothing to you, but—" He broke off, unable to continue. He couldn't stand to think of this place as home without his mother. With his father gone, too . . . There'd be time for guilt and blame later. For now, he had to act.

"What will you tell them?" Christian asked, easing off the door. "'My father has gone missing'? Not a rarity after the death of a spouse. They'll assume he'll turn up in a biergarten somewhere. 'He's not at home and the place is a wreck.' No woman has been here to keep it tidy, they'll tell you, and give you their condolences for your loss. Say, 'He's been taken by mice!' and they'll lock you up, Stefan. They'll think you're mad."

Every word Christian said was true. The city guard would not, *could not* believe his story. His whole life had gone topsy-turvy since his cousin came to town. No, even earlier, since his mother got sick. The world no longer made sense. In a way, Christian and his crazy stories fit perfectly into this new scheme of things.

"Well then," Stefan asked. "Am I? Mad?"

His cousin placed a hand on his shoulder. "No. You are a journeyman clockmaker. And now you will learn what that means.

"Come, Stefan. It's time to introduce you to the true power behind our guild. The Brotherhood of Prometheus."

15

"OH, HOW THE MIGHTY have fallen." Ernst Listz gazed imperiously across the royal throne room of the mice of Boldavia, giving his usual speech with all the gravitas he could manage given his damp fur.

The Court of the Queen of Mice shifted uneasily, listening to their guest.

Peasants, Ernst thought. For all that this was a royal court and the Boldavian mice seemed to have secured more of a foothold in the city than he'd believed possible, they were still bumpkins compared to the old splendors of Ratdom. They could use a history lesson or two.

Ernst knew he cut a fine enough figure before the court—his waistcoat and tails might have been slightly out of date, the sky-blue silk faded, but his fur was groomed and his tail still firm. To such country mice he must look quite fashionable. Amused at the thought, he took a slow breath, and resumed his oration.

"Before the Fall, we were royalty, three tail lengths from the skirts of the Rat King himself. We feasted on the finest cheeses in the royal cellars of Bavaria, sipped deeply of the wines found there. We feared no man, or beast. We were the rulers of the Underearth. If only we had been satisfied to remain so. But the world of Men above was rich, and we climbed too far."

He cast a warning eye at the gathered faces. Was anyone listening? How many knew that their ascent into the human kingdom could not last? A few traps, a few hungry cats, and all of this would be gone in an instant. He decided to put the weight of prophecy into his speech.

"What I know of that golden age is only what I've heard at family gatherings or in the old histories. I read them quite often. They remind me that what I saw as Paradise was only the fading light of a truly glorious age. The age before Hameln town and the Cursed One whose name must only be whispered . . . *the Piper*."

A gasp ran through the room. Ernst preened his whiskers, pleased. Even here, in the backwater court of the Mouse Queen, they had not forgotten the devastation of Hameln.

Ernst puffed up and lowered his voice to a confidential stage whisper for effect. "Humans called him Pied, for the piebald outfit he wore." He scanned the room, noting the piebald mice in the crowd. There were too many to offend, so he added to his description. "Gaily colored, they say, like a jester—black and white, yes, but also red, green, yellow, and blue. Leggings, tunic, cap, and feather, each of a different hue. A jolly figure, no doubt, if not for his cold, dark heart."

Here, he paused dramatically.

"For that reason, and for the serpent-tongued pipe he played, all of ratkind call him Black. The Black Piper of Hameln, bane to the Kingdoms of Rodentia."

A silence followed. Even the Mouse Queen seemed upset by the thought. Her whiskers twitched nervously, but her eyes remained calculating. Ernst waved his paw lightly in the air.

"But that was long ago, many generations by rat standards. For a while, my family used unwitting humans to buy and sell what treasures they had hoarded over the years—grain and cheese purchased with pearls and golden buttons, those sundry riches a diligent rodent might find, lost and forgotten by Man. Sadly, such wealth can only last so long.

"Mine is a gentleman's trade. I act as a liaison between worlds. Animal or Man, if you desire to learn of either, you can come to me. Ernst Listz, Procurator, Tutor, and Scholar Extraordinaire. At your service, Your Majesty."

The gray Queen squinted at him from her throne, a makeshift affair shaped out of tin and wire, fitted with a cushion of velvet and grass. She was no longer young, early middle seasons perhaps. One husband lost already. Probably to the traps, Ernst thought, though he'd heard whispers of darker dealings. Such rumors often turned out to be unfounded, usually planted by the subject to make themselves appear more dangerous than they really were. In this case, the Queen was said to be a witch. Leave it to country mice to be superstitious.

Ernst sucked his teeth, taking in the full length of the Queen's purple brocade gown. She was heavily pregnant and appeared huge and lumpy, even beneath the elaborate dress. At least it was tailored—not the pilfered doll clothes most mice seemed to get away with these days. But she seemed common to the rat. All in all, not much of a witch, or a figurehead.

Ernst ran a paw delicately across his black whiskers.

The Queen sat silently, studying him. *What is she waiting for?* Ernst wondered.

As if in answer, there was a commotion at the back of the hall that turned everyone's head, except for the Queen, who continued to gaze at the rat with a satisfied look.

A small, neat-looking piebald in nondescript clothes approached the throne. With an imperceptible nod, the Queen allowed him to come closer, and the piebald whispered something into her ear. The mouse court truly was a different place. Here, the piebalds seemed to be the Queen's right hand. *Spies*, Ernst thought, with distaste. But it was clever. What decent rodent would ever give a scruffy piebald a second thought?

With a wave of her hand, the Queen dismissed her agent. Her eye fell once again on Ernst, and he straightened under her gaze.

When she spoke, her throaty voice belied her size. Her accent spoke of old royalty. "Thee speak of Hameln, rat? A true failure—for your kind."

"For all rodents, madam." Ernst favored the Queen with a gracious bow.

"For rats!" the Queen said sharply, her paw squeezed into a fist. "We mice have not failed! You see the city above, the world around? Mine! Thee speak of the Piper, the scourge of ratkind. Dost thee know naught of the enemy of mice?"

"Beg pardon, Your Majesty?"

"Yes, 'beg,'" she scowled. "This, we mice no longer do. We fight. We rule. We thrive!"

Ernst was at a loss. Was the old bag insane? "But, surely the legend of the Piper tells us—" The Queen cut him short with a huffed wheeze that he realized was a laugh.

"They send me an educated rat," she said to her court. "But what does he know of suffering and survival?" Her laughter grew and the audience shifted nervously, unsure of the appropriate response.

Ernst stiffened. He'd made his way through palaces and

hovels for many a season. He would not be insulted by this little upstart. But then again, the first meal a true survivor swallows is his pride. He looked up at the Queen, innocence and confusion painted on his face.

"Your Piper, Sir Rat, was so very long ago. A tale to scare younglings, yes? Oldlings, too, perhaps?" The Queen waved her paw as if clearing the air. Her black eyes glittered, all humor gone. "A tale of defeat."

"Apologies, Your Majesty. I did not mean to offend," Ernst replied with a fluid bow. Not just a simple country mouse, this one. At least not one easily impressed. He held himself in that position, nose to floor, until the Queen spoke again.

"Thee speak to me of the Pied Piper to frighten me? The Queen of Boldavia?" She snorted. "We have fought and died in our own time beneath the heel of Man. Your Piper is but a fable. Our villain is real."

Ernst slowly stood erect, but kept his eyes downcast in a show of obedience. The Queen liked that, he could tell.

Toe the line with this one, Ernst. Ego is the way in. "Forgive me, my Queen, if I speak out of ignorance. Your kingdom is mighty. The very fields lay down their wheat for you. What ill can plague you that you have not yet conquered?"

The Queen preened before her court, drawing her whiskers through her small paws. "Drosselmeyer."

"And what is a Drosselmeyer?" Ernst asked. A shudder rippled through the crowd of mice at his back.

The Queen grew very still. "He is the Scourge of Mousekind. Maker of Traps. Killer of Broods. Whole families, gone. Bloodlines, gone. Hope, gone."

Ernst's mouth grew dry. They may have been a backwater kingdom with country ways, but bloodlines ended? Even in the darkest of days, they were mice. That was impossible.

"But we are many, Your Majesty," he ventured.

"And he is but one," she said, raising a sharp claw. "And yet . . ." She looked across the chamber and signaled for the little gray that had led Ernst here. The mouse bowed deeply to his Queen.

"Fleetfoot," she said, "bring him to the device." The Queen gave Ernst a considering look. "Business between us is well desired. You speak the tongues of mankind? The ones in Allemandes, Deutschlandes?" she asked. The unfamiliar names stuttered off her tongue like pebbles from her throat.

Ernst dabbed his nose with a lace kerchief, yellowed with age. "Of course. I speak German, French, and Italian." Boldavian was but a version of German, and every worthwhile rat spoke at least two other tongues. But the lady before him was not a rat.

"Good," she purred. "Now go. Learn of the enemy, Drosselmeyer, that you may teach us how to defeat him. And perhaps thee shall be tutor to our royal heirs." She patted her stomach. "Kings, they will be. Among mice and men. Kings to be feared."

Ernst sighed inwardly. Not the ideal situation. Being nursemaid was one thing, but another entirely when the mother was mad. Fortunately, mouse children grew quickly. At most, he would be stuck here for half a year or so. And being at court, even a country mouse court, was better than living on the streets.

Ernst bowed deeply. "Until the joyous event, then, my lady."

The Mouse Queen merely laughed as her attendant led him away.

16

CHRISTIAN FLEW THROUGH the streets of Nuremberg, Stefan close on his heels. They passed the flower market, bakeries, printing houses, and the guildhouses of carpenters, toymakers, leathersmiths, goldsmiths, and—

"Wait!" Stefan cried. "That was the toymakers' guild. I have to report this to them."

"They can't help us," his cousin said. "This is beyond them, I assure you."

Stefan grit his teeth. "I was a toymaker before I agreed to be your journeyman. What sort of apprentice would I be if I didn't follow the rules?"

Christian sighed. "You're right. You must do what you think best. I'll wait outside."

Stefan ran up the front steps to the guildhall and through the front door. The motto of the guild was painted in gold leaf on the ceiling above the double-high foyer: *Feinste arbeit, glücklichste spiel—Finest work, happiest play.*

Stefan raced down the hallway past glass cases, each containing the best examples of their craft. Rows of tin and wooden soldiers, clusters of porcelain dolls with muslin cloth bodies, tiny zoos, and fairy-tale castles—all a colorful smear as he rushed past. His eyes were watering by the time he reached the guildmaster's office at the back of the hall. The walk past this grandeur used to impress him, but now it was a waste of time.

"Herr Grüel!" Stefan called out, knocking on the massive oak door and thrusting it open.

Inside, a tiny man with a swirl of graying red hair looked up from a chart on the table. "Yes?" he said.

"Herr Grüel, forgive me, but it's urgent. My father—"

"I'll tell you what's urgent," Herr Grüel said, coming around the side of the desk. "The layout of this year's Kindlesmarkt. Do you know we've had twenty-two applications from Munich, of all places? Munich! Why don't they have their own fair, I say?"

"Sir," Stefan interrupted. "Please. My father has been kidnapped!"

Herr Grüel gave a sly smile. He shook a long finger and laid it aside his nose knowingly. "Ah, he's sent you to make excuses, eh? He was supposed to be here today to help me. 'It will be fine, Hans,' he says. 'We'll make room for everyone,' he says. Nuremberg is a great city, it's true, but do we have to let in every random peddler that applies?"

"Sir, you're not listening. My father has been *kidnapped*! By *mice*!"

The guildmaster continued to smile knowingly, then took in Stefan's flushed face, damp with sweat from his run, and seemed to register the fear in his voice. The smile slid from his face and he turned a surprising shade of white. "Heavens, my boy. We've heard of this! Journeymen on the road gone missing, turning up a day later with strange stories of whispered orders for impossible things. It's like a fairy story. They awake in a strange place, are given a task, and when they fail, they awake again in a field somewhere, miles from whence they started. Could this have happened to your father?"

Stefan slapped his forehead, yanking at his hair. He'd heard rumors of these disappearances, too. At the time, they'd sounded like tales to scare apprentices on the verge of journeying. Even if they'd been true, he would never have imagined they could be engineered by mice.

Stefan was aghast. "This is real? Why didn't you warn the guild?"

"Of what?" Grüel asked, looking ashamed. He tugged at his ginger hair. "The ravings of a toymaker or two who'd had too much ale? It's only now you say it that I give any credence to it at all! Zacharias is missing? It's never been a master toymaker before. Always journeymen and apprentices—rather easily led astray, I'd supposed. But a master?"

He sat down on his desk, upending the inkpot over his carefully laid-out plans for the market. Ink ran onto the floor, unheeded.

"What are you going to do about it?"

"Me?" Stefan exclaimed. "You're the guildmaster!"

"Aye, but my duties are clerical in nature—trade, organizing fairs, judging applicants, and the like. I deal with paperwork, not missing people."

This was the mighty toymakers' guild? One might as well be unguilded. Random peddlers, indeed.

"Then, who do I turn to?" Stefan asked. "The city guard?"

"Perhaps . . . Or perhaps he'll turn up again, in a day or two, with a headache and nothing more, like the others." The guildmaster shrugged weakly. "Impossible tasks often remain impossible."

Stefan took a breath to bring his temper under control.

Christian had warned him, and he'd wasted enough time now. Hopefully his new guildhome could offer more help.

Stefan met Christian outside and told him of the other kidnappings. "Maybe they'll release him," he said, hoping against hope.

"Not likely," Christian replied. "Certainly not if they know he's a Drosselmeyer."

Stefan's heart skipped a beat. The criminal Drosselmeyer had single-handedly turned their entire family into the enemies of mice.

They reached the guildhall with its simple clock face and engraved lintel. This time the motto made Stefan go cold—*Time Flees*. They needed to save his father, and quickly. He turned to go up the stairs and nearly tripped over his own feet when Christian continued hurrying down the block.

"But . . . that's the clockmakers' guild," Stefan called. "Where are you going?"

"The guildhouse is a formal meeting place, Stefan. Display cases, offices, lodging rooms. Useless, really. Now, pay attention and keep up; you need to hear this."

Stefan raced to catch up.

"Yes, that was the guildhouse and if, say, you were going to ask for a raise or a better spot at the Christmas market, that would be the place to go. However, we don't want to speak to clerks and doormen, do we? We want to speak to the real power."

"The real power?" Stefan repeated. They rounded the corner at the end of the block. "The brotherhood you mentioned. They're not in the guildhouse?"

"When Napoleon was emperor of France, where would you find him?"

"In . . . France?" Stefan guessed.

"No! Not in Paris, nor Versailles, cooling his heels in a Louis Quatorze chair. He was at the head of his army, Stefan! Fighting for his crown!"

Of course, Stefan knew this. It had been in every newspaper, and was a common topic of dinner conversation. Napoleon Bonaparte, the little general, a Corsican who had made his name at the head of the French army and taken the crown. The world had only recently turned against him, taking back both crown and country. Now the former Emperor of France could indeed be found cooling his heels on the island of Elba.

"But we're clockmakers," Stefan said, stumbling over a curb as they turned a corner into an alley behind the guildhouses. "And this is Nuremberg. There is no war."

Christian turned and pinned Stefan with his single-eyed stare. "There is *always* a war somewhere. Remember that, too."

They came to a sudden stop in front of a plain black door. Above them, the building rose three stories high. The façade tapered at the roof to form a stair-step pattern, like a jigsaw puzzle against the evening sky. A golden clock face was set into the triangular space where the roof began.

"This is the back of the clockmakers' guildhouse," Stefan realized.

"The servants' entrance, to be precise." Once again, Christian produced his small master key and unlocked the door. "You recall that there are different types of toymakers."

Stefan nodded. "Wood-carvers, doll makers, automatonists—yes."

"There are toys," Christian said, opening the door. "And then there are *toys*."

A staircase leading off a narrow, dimly lit hallway greeted them, along with the nearby sounds of the guildhouse kitchens preparing meals for the clockmasters in residence. Sauerbraten and roasting potatoes. Stefan's mouth watered.

"I suppose," he said.

"Well then, you'll understand me when I say that there are clocks, and then there are *clocks*. Out front is the clockmakers' guild. But this is the way to the Brotherhood of Prometheus."

Stefan stared into the dark passageway. "And what do pantries have to do with the Greek Titan that gave us fire?"

Christian smiled. "Fire. Light. The ability to create and destroy. So many gifts wrapped in one burning package." He held up his little master key. "Remember what I said. This key goes to masters of the highest order. That order is the Brotherhood."

"Is it some sort of club? Like the Freemasons?" Stefan asked. There were several levels of master in the toymakers' guild, but it had more to do with position and wealth than anything else, as far as he knew.

"The Masons are stonecutters who got into politics," Christian said dismissively. "We're above that. We're *behind* it. Prometheus gave us fire. Fire gave Man the ability to rule the world. Clocks are the tools by which we do it, and the Brotherhood of Prometheus is the hand that winds the clocks. The rest of the guild is just . . . keeping time."

Stefan stifled a sigh. It was guild-speak, the same bravado

every trade spouted about their own importance—toymakers were the bastions of childhood and joy, carpenters sheltered the world, ironmongers worked the bones of the earth, et cetera. There were rumors of secret societies within the guilds, the highest orders of master craftsmen. It was like any other club. After all, who didn't want mysteries and a hidden clubhouse?

"This way," Christian said, and they hurried down the hall, past storage rooms and closets to a solid wooden door. Stefan reached for the knob.

"No, this one." Christian turned to the last door on the right. The one labeled "Custodian."

"We're here to see the janitor? That's your Napoleon?"

Christian gave Stefan a hard look. "Another rule to live by, Stefan. Keep your eyes open and your mouth closed."

He opened the door and led Stefan inside.

A sudden light flared as Christian struck a match, holding it to a small lamp that sat on a shelf inside the door. He trimmed the wick and Stefan got his first look at the room they were in.

It was a broom closet. Barely large enough for two people. Lined with mops, brooms, and a rather large bucket that forced Stefan and Christian to stand uncomfortably close together.

Christian shut the door behind them, turned the doorknob, and pressed the lock.

The closet shuddered. A whirring sound rose up around them and the room shook.

"What the—!" Stefan hissed. "Are we . . . moving?"

Christian grinned. "Impressive, isn't it? Pulleys and counterweights. We call it a 'descending chamber.'"

"Descending to where?" Stefan asked, suddenly noticing a

chill in the air. They were moving underground, beneath the streets. He could not say how he knew it, perhaps the sinking feeling in his stomach, or a sense of weight over his head. "Does it go up again?"

"Does it what?"

"You called it a *descending* chamber. How do you get back up?"

Christian gave him a quizzical look as the room juddered to a stop. His cousin unlocked the door and they stepped out into a clerk's office, rather ordinary-looking but for the stone walls. Windowless, furnished with a desk, a lamp, and little else.

On the far side of the room stood a man about a foot and a half shorter than Stefan. A black greatcoat was draped over his arm, as if he had just come in from the cold. He looked like a frog dressed in a bank clerk's clothes. His brown tweed breeches were wide at the thigh and tapered down to flat, wide feet. His stiff white shirt was covered by a dark brown vest, and he had a pair of spectacles perched on his nose. His brown hair was turning mostly gray. In short, he was a somewhat disappointing, if appropriately sized, Napoleon.

"Young Drosselmeyer," he said.

Stefan started, but quickly realized the man was addressing his cousin.

Christian bowed. "You remembered, after all these years? Gullet, I'll start to think you've missed me."

Gullet squinted in disapproval and draped his coat on the chair behind the desk. "Ah, yes, Drosselmeyer. Smart as ever around the mouth." He sat down at the desk and pulled a ledger from the depths of his drawer, as if preparing to open an account for them. "Let's just hope the same is true for your head."

"Then you know why I'm here?" Christian asked.

"Of course," Gullet replied, not looking up. "When the mice started moving in Nuremberg, I assumed you were involved. We've received your reports over the years. Somehow, they never hold good news, do they?

"And now, toymakers are missing up and down the Rhine, the Danube, farther perhaps. They seem to be taken for days at a time, and then they turn up again with strange stories of darkened workshops and written instructions. Best we can tell, the captors are striving to build something, something that takes skill. If it's the mice, as it appears to be, then I was most certain it had to do with you."

Gullet scratched a note in his book. "The new apprentice?" he asked.

"Journeyman, sir. Stefan Drosselmeyer." Stefan introduced himself with a deep bow. This was his guild now. He needed to make a good first impression.

Gullet studied him with flat eyes. "No resemblance," he commented, and added another note in his ledger. "Welcome aboard, young man. Let's hope you'll fare better than your master." He gave Christian a pointed look.

Stefan approached the desk, hands clenched to stop them from shaking. "Herr Grüel said the missing toymakers were all journeymen and apprentices. But now my father is missing, and he is a master. Can you help us?"

Gullet regarded Stefan for a moment and closed the ledger. "With Boldavian mice?" He shook his head. "We will do what we can, but this is Nuremberg, not the Baltic. Far beyond our territory. I'm afraid it will be up to you. I'll have my men search the city, but I suspect if he can deliver the goods they're after, they will have taken him elsewhere. Nuremberg is too full of people for them to hide for long. My guess is they'll bring him back to Boldavia."

Stefan felt ill.

"Things have grown precarious in Nuremberg since you were last here," Gullet told Christian in the flat tones of a history professor. "Both in the Brotherhood, and in the city at large. It's as important to the rest of us as it is to you and your young friend here that what's begun in Boldavia is ended as soon as possible."

Christian stiffened. "Of course, but how?"

"Your hunt for the *krakatook* is legendary. Unfortunately, so is the nut, it would seem."

Stefan glanced at Christian—they had the nut, or so Christian thought. But his cousin shook his head very slightly and Stefan held his tongue.

"If King Pirliwig cannot be persuaded to act without first having a *krakatook*, I'm afraid there is little I can suggest," Gullet was saying. "Some things cannot be stopped, Christian. Only helped on their way. The mice will burn themselves out eventually. They always do."

He pulled a folded document from a drawer in the desk and spread it open on the table. "Mark this well, both of you." He waved them closer.

It was a hastily drawn map of . . .

"Nuremberg?" Stefan asked curiously, forgetting the rule of silence. The map was fascinating, for it had the shape of his city from above, but the streets were not streets he knew, and the river ran far wider than it should.

"Beneath the city, to be precise," his cousin explained. "These are the catacombs."

Gullet nodded. "Not all of them, but the ones that matter. The ones that lead to important places. He's your responsibility, Christian. Show him what he needs to know. When the time comes, he'll have use for it."

"For what?" Stefan asked.

Gullet frowned and pointed his chin at Christian. "He's your master now, boy. Learn from him."

Mouth shut, eyes open, Stefan admonished himself.

Gullet grunted. "Remember, Christian, the tide will rise from here, and here." He indicated two wide avenues on the map. "Those are the best points of entry to take the town."

With a sharp snap, Gullet refolded the map. "Our people have their eyes open. It's just this sort of overconfidence we must keep in check—in both mice and men," he said, giving Christian another meaningful look.

Stefan and Christian took a step back as Gullet rose from behind the desk. "If your father turns up, we will send word," he told Stefan.

"Thank you, sir," Stefan said.

"My duty is to the Brotherhood, first and foremost. But what are they without the city they hold?"

"Thank you, Gullet," Christian said sincerely.

"You can thank me by cleaning up the mess you've made," the little man replied. "Oh, by the way, the university clock tower chime is off."

Gullet's eyes crinkled slightly. Stefan guessed it was what passed for a smile.

"I'd noticed," Christian replied.

"That was your job to fix before you left, how many years ago? Sloppy of you, Christian. Really."

Stefan's eyebrows rose, but Christian smiled. "Don't look so shocked, Stefan. A clockmaker's work is his and his alone. Let that be a lesson to you. Once you start, you must see it through to the end. When it comes to clockery, a second set of hands might ruin the balance." He bowed to the clerk. "Fear not, Gullet. I'll see to it when we return."

"Be sure that you do." Gullet made his way to the moveable broom closet. "Behind the desk!" he called over his shoulder as he shut the door, leaving Christian and a bewildered Stefan to their work.

17

FLEETFOOT LED ERNST down a long flight of stairs and an equally long corridor with thick wooden doors set at intervals along each wall.

"We are deep in the bedrock now," the little gray explained. "Where it is easier to find chambers of this size."

Ernst was about to ask him to elaborate when they reached the end of the hallway. A scarred door no bigger than his escort stood before them. The mouse pulled a ring of keys from his belt, chose one, and unlocked it.

The rat had to duck to enter the room. On the other side, even straightened to his full height, he was dwarfed by the massive space. At least ten rats tall, the ceiling was shrouded in darkness. A walkway several feet overhead was lined with torches, illuminating a nightmare.

In the center of the chamber, stock-still and staring, was a life-size cat. Two times Ernst's full height, its metal body was intricately detailed down to the tufts of fur on its ears, and its glittering, bejeweled eyes. Ernst Listz had seen many things in his life, but none had brought bile to his throat the way this did.

"Good heavens," Ernst whispered, nearly choking. "Is it alive?"

The mouse shook his head and trembled despite the stillness of the beast. "It's a clockwork," he explained, leading the way into the chamber. "A toy. Silent, scentless, with no need to breathe. Impossible to hear coming. We call them the Breathless."

"*Them?* There's more than one? What monster considers this a toy?" Ernst wondered.

Fleetfoot whispered with a reverence born of fear, "Drosselmeyer."

The closer Ernst got, the more the cat-fear subsided, changing into fascination of the metal and cloth that replaced flesh and fur. "It's a *made* thing?"

"Devilish," the mouse acknowledged. "When the clockmaker first came to Boldavia, he made these for the King Above. The man is allergic to cats. One of the reasons we have done so well on the island. Few predators."

Ernst could only imagine life without the feline threat. How lucky to walk the streets of a city unafraid. He could leave his sword behind and feel safe as a mouse in a hole.

"How does it work?" he asked.

"Like a cat. Only faster. It swallows mice whole." Fleetfoot mounted a ladder that leaned against the side of the beast. "The belly here is a cage. Mice were held here. Some died in the crush. When the Breathless was full, it would go down to the ocean and sit beneath the waves. Machines have no need of air." The mouse mopped his forehead with a paw.

Ernst shuddered. A terrible name to describe both the killer and its victims. "They all drowned, trapped inside that thing?"

Fleetfoot nodded. "And then . . ." He reached out a finger and unfastened something on the underside of the construct's stomach.

A soft whir sounded from somewhere inside the cat, like a dreadful purr. From where he stood, Ernst could see a seam split apart the soft velvet underbelly and drop, swinging from two hinges. The floor of the cage was a trapdoor.

"It would dump the bodies, wash away any trace, and return to the castle to do it all over again." Fleetfoot fixed the rat with wide eyes. "The Breathless do not sleep, and they are always hungry."

Ernst shook his head in slow horror. "I have never heard of such a thing," he admitted. "This is a tale to be told across Rodentia."

"They're an atrocity that must never happen again," Fleetfoot squeaked. "The Queen's sons will save us. It has been foretold."

By the Queen herself, no doubt, Ernst thought. It was worse than he had imagined. Not a backward country Queen, but an insane one, with a monster in her house, and a litter of messiahs waiting to be born. Suddenly, starving quietly in Vienna seemed the simpler choice.

Fleetfoot climbed back down the ladder. "It cost many lives to subdue this beast. We have learned much from studying its workings. Just one of ten in all. Of the others, some were destroyed, and a few fell into disrepair after the clockmaker left Boldavia."

"Left?" Ernst gasped. "Why?"

The little mouse allowed himself a proud smile. "Our Queen. She poisoned the human princess and sent the clockmaker on a fool's errand for the cure. One small nut in all the kingdoms of flora and fauna. She has given us seven years of peace. And now she will give us seven princes to bring about a golden age."

Ernst gave Fleetfoot a respectful bow. "I had no idea, sir. The Piper was generations ago, but this, this is war."

Fleetfoot returned the bow. "And now you begin to understand, Herr Listz. Our kingdom has need of one who can teach her children about the world of Men. Languages, fencing. How they think, how they die. They will need to know all of this to scour the kingdom of mankind. You have lived with one paw in their realm for a long time, sir. You are a valuable asset."

Ernst gave the clockwork cat one last look; the emerald eyes danced in the firelight, far from real, but all the worse for it. "I'll do what I can," he promised.

He would teach the boys swordplay, strategy, diplomacy, and language, all useful things in warfare. But, looking at the clockmaker's creation, he wasn't sure if it would be enough.

18

GULLET WAS GONE. Stefan reached for the door to the descending chamber. "He's locked us in!" He tried to sound calm, but time was rushing away in a torrent. Christian and Gullet had been speaking in a code he could barely follow, and now they were stuck in this little room underground. Heartsick and terrified, he kicked the door. The wood did not seem to mind.

"Why didn't you tell him about the—" Stefan began.

Christian cut him off. "Now's not the time, Stefan. These days the walls could literally have ears."

Stefan bit his lip in consternation. The sooner they were aboveground, the better.

"We've got to get back to Samir," he insisted. "We've got to find my father."

"And we will, but first there are things you must see." Christian slid behind the desk and once again applied his master key to a section of the wall. He gave it a tap.

A panel swung open, a hidden door about three feet tall. Hardly big enough for a man stooping over, but a door nonetheless.

A trickle of anxiety crawled up Stefan's spine.

"A root cellar?" As he spoke, the map in his head suddenly clicked into place. "Oh."

Beyond the door was a narrow tunnel, barely lit by a single

torch. His cousin crouched and stepped through the doorway. Plucking the torch from its brazier, he held out a hand to Stefan.

"If you'll follow me, Herr Drosselmeyer, the mysteries of the clockmakers await."

Stefan edged his way inside.

A great grinding noise rumbled overhead. Stefan quickly raised his arms over his head, waiting for the cave-in that would bury them alive.

Instead, his cousin just laughed. "Look up."

Above his head turned a cog, the lowest part of a giant clockwork embedded into the ceiling of the cavern.

"What is this place?"

"Nuremberg," Christian said with a smile.

"What do you mean?"

His cousin thrust the torch higher and the shadows peeled back like dark curtains. "Remember the clock I showed you at the guildhouse?"

Stefan caught his breath. Above him, a massive set of gears hung like storm clouds in a cathedral.

The cavern itself was enormous. They were much farther underground than he had guessed. But, as high as the ceiling climbed, at least a hundred feet or more, the space felt close. Less than ten feet away, the lowest of the springs and spindles twined intricately, the bottommost workings of some great machine. The monk's clock on display at the museum had been a model. *This* was the real device. They were standing inside of a monstrous clock. Its casing was the very bedrock of Nuremberg.

The closest gear was at least five paces across. Stefan was no bigger than a church mouse crawling through the workings of a great organ. As he watched, a golden pendulum the size of a small moon drifted overhead on its long circuit to and fro. A cold breeze ruffled his hair, and beat like owl wings against his ears. He shivered.

For all the cold and damp of the cavern, the cogs above were well oiled, grinding slowly in the dark. High above, the gears were larger still, passing through the bedrock on which the city stood. This clock must be several miles long.

Stefan stood staring up at the shadowy device. The great gears made the hairs on the back of his neck stand up. Their sheer size made them horrible. And amazing.

"This is what the Brotherhood is, what the Brotherhood does," Christian said.

"I don't understand."

"I told you, clocks are the tools that run the world. Did you think that we only built timepieces for mantels and town squares? The Brotherhood is responsible for the cogs and springs of every great city. How many times have you used the expression 'ran like clockwork'? Well, everything in the world of men *does* run like clockwork, Stefan. Some say, even the human soul. What you see here above us is the Master Clock of Nuremberg. The Brotherhood uses it to keep the city running smoothly. Come on, keep up."

Stefan followed his cousin through the cavern. His thoughts had considerably more trouble keeping pace.

"How can a clock run a city?"

Christian threw him a curious look. "How can it not? For thousands of years, men struggled to merely survive. Then came the Renaissance and the Age of Reason. Suddenly, we were no longer sheep, but masters of our own destiny. Exploration, science, music, art. What changed?"

Stefan shrugged. Images of the Sistine Chapel, of Napoleon and Marco Polo danced through his head. "Great men were born."

"No," Christian corrected him. "Great *clocks* were made! Think. A farmer must know when to plant, when to harvest. If those dates change from year to year, how is he to plan ahead? He can't. He must sit and wait. All free time is lost in the waiting. But, set it to a reliable timepiece, and suddenly days are not lost, but gained. Only in measuring time can we use it more wisely.

"Now, what do you know about the sun and the moon?" he asked.

Stefan's mind stumbled, trying to keep up. "Um . . . The sun is a star and the planets move around it, and the moon moves around the earth." He had read a little about it in school, but helping his father build whirling models of the heavens was what had cemented the ideas in his head.

"How is that different from a clock?"

Stefan stared at his cousin's retreating back. "Very. A clock has cogs and gears and things that . . ." He spun his hands in the air, trying to show what he couldn't say.

"Things that turn and spin and move," Christian said. "Like planets."

"But, where are the gears?" Stefan asked, following once again.

Christian brandished a finger in the air. "Aha! And that is

the question. Perhaps one for philosophers and angels alone. But for those of us with both feet planted firmly on the ground, the gears are right here above us. When do you wake up in the morning?"

"When the sun rises?" Stefan hated that it came out as a question, but truly, he was no longer sure what to believe.

"How do you know the sun has risen?"

"It shines through the windows and wakes me."

"How can it shine through the windows if you have drawn the curtains and shuttered the glass?"

Stefan hesitated. "I . . . just feel it?" he stammered. "I can tell when the sun is up."

"Yes, you can!" Christian announced proudly. They had crossed the cavern into another rough-walled passageway. Christian bent his knees as the tunnel floor angled upward beneath their feet.

"But why? How?"

"What sound does a clock make?" the clockmaker asked over his shoulder.

"Tick-tock," Stefan replied, feeling silly.

"Put your hand on your chest."

Stefan did as he was told. He stopped walking to better feel the beating beneath his hand. His heart shuddered in his chest like a toy drum, *thump-thump, thump-thump, thump-thump.*

Overhead, the great gears shifted, *tick-tick, tick-tick, tick-tock.*

With a start, Stefan dropped his hand.

Christian turned back to face him. In the torchlight, his cousin's one good eye gleamed. "So you see? *Everything* in the world of men is clockwork. Everything can be wound up or run down. You simply need the key."

Stefan shivered, disturbed by this sudden knowledge.

"But who winds it?" he asked, afraid to hear the answer.

The eerie joy in Christian's eye faded to simple bemusement. He shrugged and moved up the tunnel again. Stefan hurried to follow.

"It doesn't matter, does it? As long as it keeps working. And the City Clock is a much smaller version of the universal one. You've heard of the keys to a city? Mayors and bürgermeisters give them out to dignitaries and important folk, but if you ever look, it's just one key. So why the plural? The *other* key is for the City Clock. The master key, which is given to no one outside of the clockmakers' guild." He patted his waistcoat pocket. "These little keys do more than open doors. They're the ones that keep the old girl steady." He waved a hand up at the ceiling, where the monstrous engine groaned. No matter how their path wound, it was always above them.

"It's synced to keep things moving. The milkman knows it's sunrise and delivers his milk on time, the shops open and close, the ships sail when they are meant to."

Stefan was beginning to understand. "That's why the university clock can be off sync for years? Because *that's* not the clock that matters. This one is."

"Correct. The City Clock is part of what makes Nuremberg great."

"And every city has one?"

"Only the best cities, Stefan. We are not everywhere. Not yet. The rest make do with what nature gave them."

Stefan frowned. "But wait. A moment ago you said 'everything in the world of men,' as if there could be another one."

Christian sighed. "There are *worlds*, Stefan. Kingdoms, I should say. More numerous than you can possibly imagine."

The chamber came to an end and Christian chose one of several narrow openings branching off into the distance. He ducked and stepped through into a long, sloping tunnel. Here, the clock of the city made the hewn walls hum.

"You've heard of the animal kingdom and the plant kingdom," Christian said. "Well, there are also subkingdoms, principalities of flora and fauna. It's why trees live forever and mayflies for just one day. Every beast, every plant, lives by its own schedule. Man cannot control them. That's nature's provenance. But, sometimes, the animal seeks to control nature. *That* is what the Brotherhood works against. The threat of the mice could be a major wrench in the works for the Brotherhood. That's why Gullet is helping us now, to avoid disaster later."

Stefan frowned. "Then what gives men the right to tell other animals what to do?"

"Mice, unfortunately, are not just any animal. They're vermin. They have no agriculture, no trade. They simply feed."

The clockmaker stopped in the middle of the tunnel, and Stefan leaned against the wall to catch his breath.

"Three hundred years ago, in Hameln, which is not far from our precious Nuremberg, the rats took rule of the town. They pillaged like pirates and ate like kings. The town's entire supply of grain should have lasted a year, but it was decimated in a day. The crops yet to be harvested, and the seeds for the new year's plantings . . . all gone by the end of a single week. Rats are not rulers, Stefan. They are scavengers. For fear of starvation, they'll feast until there is no more. If the Pied Piper hadn't come and washed them all away, the rats of Hameln would have fallen upon each other and eventually died from famine.

"As it is, Hameln was barren for a generation. That's how rats rule. And mice are no better. Boldavia has survived this long only because of commerce; most food is shipped in. But cut the ports off, and the humans would die as surely as the mice would crown themselves kings."

"And that's what will happen in Boldavia," Stefan said.

Christian continued in his long, swinging stride. "Because of me. Let that be another lesson for you. Pride. Be wary of it. That Advent calendar I told you about? The doors would have been twenty feet high, and opened up to reveal scenes from the Bible, each done in the finest clockwork. It was the kind of work a Brotherhood clockmaker should never have allowed—flashy, expensive, and overblown. But I was so sure of myself. One mistake, and the ripples run through the kingdoms of Man and Mouse to this day. Your father is only the latest in a long line of victims of my pride." He sounded heartbroken.

Christian Drosselmeyer was a master clockmaker, but even he was still learning, it would seem. Stefan wondered whether or not he would have made the same mistake.

They had come a long way, and the clamor of the City Clock was louder than ever.

Christian pressed a hand to the wall and muttered to himself. "It's too soon."

"Too soon for what?" Stefan asked.

"For your first lesson in High Clockworks. Unheard of for a journeyman, but it can't be helped." He took off down the tunnel again.

The grinding sound grew louder as they diverted to a sharply climbing path.

"What is that racket?" Stefan shouted over the noise.

They stopped in front of a high, wide wooden door banded with iron. "That is the Cogworks."

Christian reached into a pigeonhole set in the wall and pulled out a jar of what looked like sugarplum candies wrapped in wax paper. He held one up for examination. "We call them ear plugs," he said. "Beeswax wrapped in muslin." He took hold of his earlobe between thumb and forefinger, and twisted one of the plugs into each ear.

Stefan followed suit, and the grinding clatter became bearable. Christian swung open the door onto a large open space, bathed in buttery golden light. The floor beneath their feet was paved with stone cut from the bedrock. It formed a sort of patio or observation deck with a low wall at the far end. Beyond it lay darkness and the churning tick of clockery.

Stefan looked up into the light.

The source was as massive and brilliant as a captive sun. Hanging in the air above them was an exact replica of the Benedictine monk's golden clock.

Vertigo washed over him. From this vantage point, shining gears the size of carriage wheels whirred above him, connecting chains thicker than tree trunks. He felt like an ant peering up at the world. Beyond the gears, enormous cogs the size of buildings churned and spun in concert. Layer upon layer of clockery too dense to see through, an immense lacework of machinery that glowed a shimmering yellow gold.

Stefan opened his mouth to speak, but could not.

"It goes throughout the entire underbelly of the city," Christian said loudly. "The gears you saw out there are all a part of the City Clock, but the Cogworks are special."

Just then, the massive pendulum he'd seen in the outer caverns swung into the chamber, lifting Stefan's hair in its wake. In the light of the Cogworks, it shone like a slice of the sun.

"The pendulum," Christian shouted, "drives the movement."

Stefan followed the disk, wide-eyed.

As it passed, a man came scurrying toward them from farther down the observation deck. He wore large tinted goggles to shield his eyes from the constant glow, and a leather apron smeared with grease.

"Master Drosselmeyer, we've been expecting you!" the man shouted. "I'm Heinrick Waltz, master of the Nuremberg Clock. I was just an apprentice first-year when you left the city."

He pulled off his glove and held out his hand.

Christian shook it readily. "Cogsmaster, a pleasure. This is my journeyman, Stefan Drosselmeyer." The man's eyes widened. "Yes, there's more than one of us out there," Christian said in amusement. "He's here under my authority. We've come to see the cogs."

"Any one in particular?" Waltz asked with a nod. He led the way to a table and bookshelf opposite the abyss.

Eyes still locked on the clockery above, Stefan bumped into the table.

"Careful, son," the cogsmaster said.

"Sorry!" Stefan blushed.

The table held another replica of the golden clock.

"Think of it as a map," Christian told him. He turned to the cogsmaster and rattled off a series of numbers.

"That's my father's birthday. And my mother's," Stefan realized.

"Yes, and let's have yours, too, if you please," Christian said.

Stefan told the cogsmaster his birthday and watched the man jot it all down. The cogsmaster pulled a large leather binder from beneath the desk and flipped it open. Page after page of blueprint sped by.

"They're different layers of the clock!" Stefan blurted.

"Well done," Christian said. "The Cogworks are a complicated bit of machinery. For every man and woman who reaches adulthood, a cog is made and placed into the City Clock. We keep track by birthday and name. Your mother had a cog, and your father has one."

"Do I?"

"Almost," Christian said. "You'll get your cog when you do your masterwork. Children rarely earn a cog this early, unless some event makes them significant to the workings of Nuremberg."

Stefan watched as the cogsmaster flipped through the book. "What about my mother's cog?" he asked. "Can I see it?"

Christian grew solemn. "When someone dies, eventually their cog is removed from the clock to be melted down and recast into new cogs. It's a precious metal we use here, pure as gold and hard as iron, but difficult to come by. Especially as the city grows."

"Here we are, sir," Waltz said, pointing to the relevant blueprint. "Follow me."

He led them to a ladder bolted to the stone wall. They followed him up onto a giant scaffold built around the edge of the machinery.

At the second level, Waltz stopped. "Delicate work, this," the cogsmaster said. "You'll have to wait here."

He grabbed a long metal rod from a hook on the wall, which had a small mirror no bigger than Stefan's hand set on the far end at an angle. Waltz took a steadying breath. With great care, he inserted the rod between the layers of sandwiched gears. In one smooth movement, he slid it deeper, and tilted it slightly.

Stefan craned his neck to see the mechanisms at work, but the golden light cast by the clock made it difficult to distinguish the individual parts.

"Here we are. Zacharias Elias Drosselmeyer and Elise Drosselmeyer . . . I'm sorry for your loss, my boy."

Stefan's voice caught in his throat. "Is her . . . cog still there?"

Waltz withdrew the mirror. "Just a moment." He went to the wall and returned with a second tool in hand, this one hooked at the end, like a hex key. He set the shaft of this new tool against the scaffolding and clamped it into place. Once it was attached, Waltz peered down the length of it with one eye closed, and began to turn a crank on the handle, like a fancy fishing rod. Eventually, he cranked to a stop. Waltz manipulated his end of the rod again, and just as carefully withdrew it from the clockworks.

"Here you are, lad." On the end of the rod gleamed a tiny golden cog. Stefan plucked it from the hook and held it up to the light.

Elise Drosselmeyer was engraved on the metal in minuscule cursive. A black line of oxidation ran down the center of the golden wheel.

Stefan felt dizzy. "Thank you," he managed to say.

Christian remained uncustomarily silent.

He showed his cousin the darkened line. "What does this mean?" he asked.

"It means Elise's time is over. But your father's cog is still moving. So he's alive, Stefan. And that means we can find him, and we can save him."

Stefan closed his fingers over his mother's clockpiece. It was delicate as a butterfly. He held it out to Waltz.

"Are you sure?" the cogsmaster asked gently. "We can spare it, if you'd like to keep it."

The sliver of metal gleamed in his palm. "Can it be rewound? Is this her soul?"

Christian and Waltz exchanged a look.

"I'm afraid not," Christian said at last. "There are keys for unmaking in the clockmaker's kit, and keys to wind up or wind down. But the pendulum keeps the movement, Stefan. And once it has stopped, it is beyond our small skill to create again."

The air around him grew thick, making it harder to breathe. His eyes stung. "I understand," he said. "This is just a clock."

Christian closed his hand over Stefan's. "It's a bit of cold metal cleverly used. Nothing more."

Stefan pressed the cog into Christian's hand and started for the ladder. "Thank you, Herr Waltz," he murmured as he left. "Time's wasting. My father needs us."

THEY MOVED THROUGH the tunnels in silence after that, the ground continuing to rise beneath their feet. At last, the sound of the great clockworks faded until it might have been no more than the rush of blood in Stefan's ears.

His first day as a clockmaker had been overwhelming. The silence was only making it worse. "Why did you become a clockmaker, Christian?" he asked. After everything he'd seen that day, he wasn't sure he'd have made the same choice.

"Because I could count to one hundred." His cousin smiled. "And I needed to do something. I apprenticed with one of the Brotherhood's master clockmakers when I was very young. Gullet was his assistant at the time. And, much to my surprise, I found I was good at it. But not good enough to keep things running 'smoothly' in Boldavia. Now I'm in it for the long haul, or at least until I can set things right again."

"I'm not sure I can do this," Stefan confessed. "High clockery. It's . . ." He looked for the right word—Wizardry? Theology?—but found none.

Christian fell back beside him and put a hand on his shoulder. The stony walls of the tunnel gave off a damp chill. "It weighs heavily on you at first. Knowledge is often a burden. But each lesson is a tool, Stefan. The more you know about the truth behind the world, the better prepared you will be for what we face."

Stefan didn't respond. He wasn't sure he agreed.

Christian released him and picked up the pace. Beneath their feet, the rough floor gave way to a bricked path. "We're nearing your home." He stopped in front of another door that opened easily.

"Prepare yourself. This will be difficult."

Stefan took a breath, although he couldn't imagine anything harder than what he'd experienced already today. He stepped through the doorway and followed his cousin's torchlight up a narrow staircase. The walls grew closer until his shoulders rubbed the stonework on either side.

"It's like a coffin in here," he said. "Damp as the grave, too."

Christian remained silent.

They had reached the top of the stair. Overhead, the ceiling ended in a rectangular cupola. A chill crept down Stefan's spine.

"Hold this," Christian said, handing him the torch. Stefan took it with trembling hands. The heat of the firelight battled the chill of the stone. Christian reached up to the ceiling and pushed. The loud scraping drowned out all thought except for one.

Please, Stefan thought, *don't let this be the place.*

His cousin climbed out through the opening overhead and held his hand out for the torch. Stefan handed it up and clambered out of the deep stairwell.

They were in a small room lined with table-like crypts. Four stone boxes for four generations, two of them covered in dust. They had emerged from the third, which hid the staircase to the catacombs. A cloud of dust settled around them where Christian had disturbed it. At the front of the room stood the fourth crypt, newly polished and covered in fading yellow tulips.

Stefan's throat gave a strangled cry.

This was the place he feared. The family tomb. His mother's grave.

"Say your good-byes, Stefan," Christian said softly, "and we may leave without regrets. For who knows when we'll return?"

Stefan turned, red-faced with horror, shock, and shame. He opened his mouth to curse Christian, but all that came out was a sob. He fell to his knees beside the cold sarcophagus, placed a hand on the stone, fingers gripping the place where her name was carved deep, and wept.

He did not hear his cousin replace the lid to the staircase, nor did he see Christian press a gloved hand to the coffin, bow his own head in silent farewell, and quietly step outside.

THE ROYAL COURT of mice was boring. More boring than the weeks Ernst Listz had spent hitching rides on those strange subterranean rafts on his way to Boldavia. He had done as the Queen had asked—writing up documents, corresponding with Men. Paying them to do her bidding using coins pilfered from the counting rooms above. He had even eavesdropped in the human throne room and reported on various diplomatic visitors to ensure that King Pirliwig had not been soliciting help from the outer world.

And what did he have to show for it? Only the assurance that no one was importing a shipload of cats anytime soon.

Ridiculous waste of time, but it had solidified his position in the court. The Queen had grown used to seeing him as part of her council meetings. She smiled when he fed her compliments, and quivered with anticipation when he gave her any news. It was an easy, if uneventful, job.

He dealt himself another hand of solitaire. At least now the Queen's labor had begun. In a few days, he would be up to his whiskers in mouselings. He should have been glad of the peace and quiet the Queen's uncommonly long pregnancy had given him. But, then again, looking at the drab stone walls of his room, and the poor table made of twigs where he dined and played cards, he had to admit peace and quiet weren't everything.

A din sounded in the hallway. The rat rose from his game and stuck his nose out into the corridor. A young nurse was running toward him from the direction of the Queen's chambers. She was screaming hysterically.

"Young lady, dear lady!" Ernst exclaimed, catching the young mouse up in his arms before she could dash past. "Calm yourself, please. What is it?"

The mouse's wild eyes focused and she stopped screaming to catch her breath. "Oh sir, it's horrible. I've never seen such a babe before. I just . . ." She shuddered and hid her face in her paws. "It's magic of the blackest sort!"

Ernst patted the nurse on the back. That was the trouble with these uneducated mice. Any abnormalities, and superstition took hold. "The royal brood? Are they not well?"

The young mouse looked up from her sobbing. "That's just it, sir. There ain't no brood. Not a proper one at all."

"What do you mean?" Ernst was growing tired of the girl's roundabout talk. "Speak freely, and be direct about it."

"The Queen's had but one baby, sir."

"One? That's odd. Mouse broods are at least five, are they not?" Ernst's own mother had borne six along with him.

"A royal brood is seven, sir." The girl was calming down now. She took slow and steady breaths even as tears formed in her eyes.

"But it's not right, it's just not right. Old Marmade said the birthing was taking too long. She carried them way past term. And now . . ." She wrung her hands. "He's to be King, but it's just not natural, is it, sir? To have seven heads?"

ERNST PACED IN the antechamber outside of the Queen's suite, his tail lashing nervously with every step. Someone inside the room was singing. Snatches of the tune carried through the oak door. The small space, the heat of the torches, and the nearness of the birthing chamber were beginning to make Ernst feel light-headed. He stopped pacing and leaned against the cool stone wall.

Abruptly, the singing stopped. The midwife, a brown mouse with surprisingly large feet, stepped through the doorway and pulled two pieces of cotton out of her ears. This must be Old Marmade. If the old girl was disturbed by the delivery, she didn't show it. Likely the little nursemaid had merely been overwrought. New to the birthing chamber, perhaps. It could certainly be startling to witness a birth—that alarming shade of fuchsia, the sheer number of babes—but it could hardly be called *unnatural*.

"She'll see you now," the midwife said. "Mind she don't start singing with you standing there. If she does"—she held up the cotton—"there's more by the bedside. Or better yet, bow your excuses and go."

Ernst thanked her, although what backwater superstition the mouse was referring to, he had no idea. The Queen had summoned him shortly after the hysterical nursemaid had collapsed in his arms. There had been little time to wonder at her puzzling pronouncement. Now he would see the princes for himself.

He stepped into the chamber and bowed deeply. "Your Majesty," he intoned with all the dignity he could manage.

He did not look up until the Queen spoke. She sounded tired, as one would expect, but somehow even more so. As if her voice was starting to wear thin.

"Come, Herr Tutor. Meet your princes."

Ernst straightened from his bow, swept his tail behind him, and regarded the room. He was in a sizable parlor, comfortably outfitted with chairs and a fireplace. Beyond this first room, a set of double doors stood open to the Queen's sleeping chambers. It was from this room that she had spoken.

Her bed was a large, round, sumptuous-looking thing that made her look small. Beside the bed stood a bassinet draped in a matching deep purple velvet counterpane and creamy white linens. Gauzy purple fabric draped the bassinet in a canopy. The floor had been strewn with herbs in an attempt to freshen the stifling air. Sage and lavender tickled Ernst's nose, but did little to quell the meaty scent of blood.

He reached the foot of the bed, and bowed once more to the Queen. She nodded with a self-satisfied air.

Ernst pulled back the filmy drapes and looked into the bassinet.

A sound escaped his throat. He cleared it quickly. The nursemaid had been correct.

Tucked into the soft sheets, pink as scalded moles, the seven princes mewled blindly, as did every other mouse litter Ernst had ever witnessed.

Only, this was not a litter. This was . . .

A monstrosity. Seven heads perched on one small body, squashed from birth. Seven noses sluggishly pushed against the air, seeking their mother. Seven heads. Four paws. One tail. It would be a mercy to kill it now.

Ernst's tail lashed violently, betraying his horror. He blinked and sought something to say to the Queen.

Surely they would not live. Defects such as this . . . nature wouldn't allow it.

"Majesties," he managed to whisper at last, and dropped to one knee in a bow that showed humility to the Queen and her children, but also allowed him to hide his face until he had recovered.

"My Queen, you must rest. You have clearly labored long and hard. I . . . await the day, madam, when I can . . . serve your young."

He was going to be sick. The scents of lavender, copper, salt, and sage were stifling, the room too warm, the walls too close. He stood swiftly and backed out of the chamber with his head down before the Queen could say anything more. If she asked him to stay, he would not do it. If she asked him to stay, he would slay the beastly thing—things?—in its crib.

But she did not stop him.

Ernst reached the door and turned on his heel, escaping into the foyer. It seemed wide as a meadow compared to the chamber of horrors at his back. He paused only to close the door.

His last glimpse of the Queen showed her smiling fondly as she pulled the bassinet closer to her bed and, once again, began to sing.

BOOK II

The Prince of Mice

THE CREAKING OF WOOD and the sound of lapping water woke him, along with a faint, persistent scratching. Zacharias Drosselmeyer stretched and yawned. He'd been having such a pleasant dream. He was being rocked like a baby in a cradle, as that little princess, what was her name? Pirlipat. Funny name. Christian had told such a curious story about the little girl. Something about mice—

He came awake, as if a bucket of cold water had splashed him in the face. "Stefan!" he shouted, but the name came out as a croak.

"You're awake! That fool shouldn't have given you a second cup," a small voice said. A child's voice would have had more resonance than the one that addressed him now—but this was clearly an adult male. And not the man in scarlet.

"Where is my son?" Zacharias demanded. He tried to sit up, only to find that he was tied down to planks like a real-life Gulliver.

The voice came closer. "Safe in Nuremberg. For now. As long as you cooperate." There was that scratching again. The voice passed back and forth along his right ear. If it weren't pitch-black, Zacharias would have sworn the speaker was pacing close to the floor.

"Cooperate? This is preposterous. I'm your prisoner!"

"Regrettable," the little voice said. It had a strange accent he could not place. "But there is a remedy. You will answer a few questions."

"Where am I?" Zacharias demanded. His anger was the only thing keeping despair at bay. He clung to it like a shield.

"Far away from home. Where you are needed most."

For a wild moment, Zacharias imagined himself in the satchel of Krampus, the Christmas demon that took away bad boys and girls. Or, perhaps he was being delivered to Father Christmas, forced into service in his toy workshop . . .

Zacharias groaned. Whatever he'd consumed in those two thimblefuls of liquid, it was affecting his mind. He was in a boat, that much he was sure of. He could smell the river and hear the slap of water against the hull.

He slumped back against the ropes holding him to the floor. He would cooperate. He'd do anything to keep his son safe. "Tell me, what is it you want?"

A door opened. The scarlet man, now dressed in black, appeared and untied him. Zacharias stumbled on weak legs as the deck pitched gently beneath him. He was in a windowless ship's cabin, crowded with a large writing desk and stool. Sheaves of clean paper lay stacked beside an inkwell. The scarlet man hung a lantern above the desk without saying a word, then left, locking the door behind him.

Zacharias sat at the desk, unsure of what to do next.

From nowhere and everywhere, the small voice spoke to him. "Describe the following apparatus. Blueprints, please," it said.

Zacharias waited, listened to the description, pen poised

over the page. The words made no sense at first, and he asked the voice to repeat them.

"But what is this—"

"No questions!" the voice snapped. "Consider it an exercise."

"An exercise?" Zacharias muttered, flexing his fingers around the pen. With a sigh, he put nib to paper and began to draw.

21

THE WHEELS OF THE WAGON drummed against the cobblestones as the weatherworn carriage made its way out of the black forests and into the riverside streets of Regensberg. Stefan huddled in the corner of the backseat, using his coat as a blanket. He dozed in and out of sleep. His whole body was numb. He told himself it was from the jouncing of the coach, but that was a lie. His parents were gone. Better to be numb than afraid.

Their plan was simple. Samir and Christian had explained it to him as they hurried to meet the last coach of the night.

"If the mice have him, they will bring him to Boldavia," Christian said. "Under the castle . . . in the dark." A haunted look had crossed his face.

"But Herr Grüel said every toymaker that's disappeared has turned up a few days later. We should wait here," Stefan had insisted. Christian and Samir had not agreed.

"Believe me, Stefan, if I thought waiting was the best course of action, we would stay. But Zacharias is family—a Drosselmeyer. Whatever it is they wanted a toymaker for, they now have someone far more valuable. The Queen of Mice will want him brought to her."

"Is it a trap?" Stefan had asked. Was his father merely bait to lure Christian back to Boldavia? "Don't they know you'd return anyway, with the—"

Christian pressed a finger to his lips to stop him from speaking. "Please," he said in a hushed voice. "We are far from safe here. Seven years is a very long time to a mouse. The queen is ready for this to be over, as am I. It's time to pay the piper, as they say." He tapped his eye patch, beneath which lay the *krakatook*. "At least now we have the fee. When we cure the princess, the king will owe us a boon. What's more, he'll do anything to stop the mice from hurting his family again. With his soldiers beside us, we will sweep Boldavia clean. Your father will be found, Stefan, and the mice will be routed at last."

And so they had stolen to the edge of town by cover of darkness, and boarded the carriage to Regensberg.

"End of the line!" the coachman bellowed, and he jumped down from his perch, rocking the carriage. Stefan startled awake. They had come to a stop in front of an old, bedraggled alehouse.

"Quickly now," Christian urged. He rose, stretching like a cat beneath his coat, and ushered them toward the alehouse. "We can find a boat here. Most of the sailors take their leave inside."

Stefan shivered in anticipation. He had never been this far from home before. Now, he hoped every step away brought him closer to his father.

The river winds had weathered the alehouse to a sad brownish gray. Above the door was a sign showing a lady with a blue river for hair. *Die Donau*, the sign read. *The Danube*.

"I'll do the talking," Christian told them.

Inside, Die Donau was everything Stefan had imagined a wharfside tavern to be—dark, smoky, full of disreputable, rough men and harried barmaids. Their entrance brought a few stares—though far fewer than Stefan would have expected, for an Arab, a boy, and a one-eyed man. Stefan followed Samir to a table near the fireplace while Christian sauntered up to the bar, nodding a few hellos to people as he passed.

Stefan blinked in surprise. "He knows these people?"

Samir returned a wave from the barmaid. "Of course. We were here but a few days ago. And we have crossed paths with many sailors in our long years abroad. Perhaps you thought we'd only find cutthroats and thieves?"

"These are the wharves!" Stefan exclaimed. "They're notoriously dangerous, day or night."

"Yes," Samir agreed. "For some people. Look around you, Stefan. Look with both eyes, and tell me what you see."

Stefan scanned the room, trying not to make eye contact. "I see rough men with thick hands and scars." Stranglers and knife-wielding murderers, he imagined.

"Sailors," Samir said simply. "Their hands are rough from work, and the scars are from battling the rapids of the Danube, not tavern brawls. Well, not many."

Stefan took a third look. The man at the table closest to them was practicing knots. At another table, a man was making fishing lures.

The barmaid whisked by with a wink, depositing three large mugs of steaming broth on their table. "Take your order in a minute, Herr Samir," she said breezily.

Stefan sighed. "I'm sorry. I guess I'm seeing menace everywhere now."

"It's understandable," Samir said. "And at least you were being honest. But trust me, there are far worse places than Die Donau."

Stefan wrapped his cold hands gratefully around the mug, inhaling the scent of mutton and onions. He was starving.

"Little sips, it's hot," Christian said, coming over to them. He patted Stefan on the shoulder and sat down. "Georg knows of two barges headed south in the morning. One stops in Budapest, the other goes all the way to Silistra. With any luck, we can catch the Silistra-bound boat the rest of the way to Bulgaria."

"Not until morning?" Stefan asked. Worry fluttered in his belly.

"It's better than going by land," Samir replied, stretching his arms against the table. "No matter how smooth the horse or sturdy the boot."

"Provided we avoid the pirates," Christian agreed.

"Pirates?" Stefan said. "You're joking."

"I'm afraid not. Of course, there are bandits on horseback, too, and wandering soldiers, the war, et cetera. So one path's just as good as another."

Stefan almost dropped his mug. "You think *mice* can navigate my father safely through all of that?"

Christian frowned. "Not mice, Stefan. Men. You've taken commissions in your shop based solely on a letter, haven't you? More than one highwayman or pirate has done the dirty work for the kingdoms of Man and Animal alike."

Stefan had lost his appetite. He excused himself quickly from the table and strode out to the alehouse yard.

Outside, the air was fresh and damp. He bent over, resting his hands on his knees, and watched a speckled flock of hens scratch in the dirt. At his feet, a small purple flower struggled in the worn wagon treads and boot marks of passersby. Its delicate petals trembled in the wind. He was moved by a sudden urge to protect the little blossom, even if it meant plucking it. His mother would press it into a book, the way she had placed her wedding nosegay in the family Bible.

Stefan pulled a handkerchief from his pocket to wipe away the sudden tears that overcame him. The cloth scraped his cheek and he laughed involuntarily. It was Clara's handkerchief, complete with the crooked "S." Brown-eyed Clara, the embroiderer in the gardens. She was right; the linen was not so delicate after all.

Stefan rose. This was no time to daydream about clever girls with wry smiles and extra handkerchiefs. He was on a mission. Two missions, really, if you counted his father and the princess (a real princess!). He should force himself to eat something and get to bed. They'd be sailing with the dawn.

He returned the handkerchief to his breast pocket. He would wash it tonight and dry it by the fire. Maybe when all of this was over, he could return it to her, along with tales of all the places it had been. Regensburg was only the first.

22

THE QUEEN OF MICE was out of bed. She had recovered rather quickly, given the circumstances, Ernst noted. Childbirth had not been kind to her. Delivered of her burden, she was still ponderous and swollen. Her fur had taken on a coarser, wintry tint. It occurred to him she was much older than he had originally guessed. Regardless, here she was, holding court with much pomp and circumstance to present her true heir and only sons.

Ernst hung back at the farthest end of the throne room, unwilling to come closer to the royal bassinet. Around him, the mice of Boldavia were dressed in their finest clothes. They crowded forward, each wanting to be first in line to give their respects. Or to confirm the rumors.

The nursemaid hadn't stopped with Ernst, it turned out. From the the size of the crowd, it seemed she had run the entire length of the country crowing about the disfigured prince. Ernst pressed his back to the wall, allowing a pale mouse in a gown the color of autumn leaves to pass in front of him. She still managed to step on his left foot. The crush of mice would have been suffocating if Ernst was any shorter. But he was tall enough to see over everyone in the room, even the piebalds that guarded each entrance and ringed the back of the dais where the Queen and her bassinet stood on view. Blackspaw was there, along with Snitter, the old spy who'd recruited him in Vienna.

Snitter gave a nod of acknowledgment, which Ernst respectfully returned. He wondered what the old piebald thought of the new princes. Would the Queen's subjects remain loyal once they saw what they were kneeling to? Ernst supposed they might. Loyalty ran deep in Boldavia.

Three trumpeters in purple livery stepped forward, playing an impressive fanfare. A mouse in a ridiculous powdered wig and long, gold-trimmed coat strode up to the dais with a scroll in both paws. He unrolled it with great care, revealing the heavily calligraphed birth announcement.

"Her Royal Highness, the Queen of Boldavia presents to you the new royal highnesses, your sovereign princes—Arthur, Hannibal, Charlemagne, Alexander, Genghis, Roland, and Julius. Heirs to the thrones of Boldavia, above and below."

The crowd cheered. *Interesting,* Ernst thought. Not only had the beast, er, *beasts* survived, but the Queen had named them after royal conquerors from the world of Men. If they lived, he would do well to learn their names—and hide his own distaste. Seven or seven-in-one, they were his charges now.

The page droned on in his pronouncements and Ernst allowed his mind to wander, down into the depths of the castle, to the chamber where that terrible mechanical cat was kept. Perhaps it would take a monster to fight such monsters, he surmised.

And then the Queen was rising from her throne. As one, the mice in the throne room dropped to one knee. Ernst snapped his attention back to the present and quickly followed suit.

He had to admire the old cow's strength of will. She stood beside the royal bassinet, cooing over her creation. Dreamy-eyed and looking strangely tender, she hunched over the crib, the purple draperies blending in with her gown. Her royal crown perched daintily upon her head.

The Queen looked down at her subjects and smiled. "Thou may rise and see Our sons."

She reached into the bassinet and pulled out a wriggling bundle of linen and lace.

The audience rose. Whiskers quivered, noses quested, eyes strained to see the new brood.

The Queen raised her children into her arms. With a twitch, the linen and lace dropped away.

Seven heads turned to blink at their royal subjects, bleary-eyed and unfocused. Seven ruddy pink heads, seven quavering noses. Fourteen black eyes, lids sliding open and closed in unison. One pink, tiny tail twitching in the sudden chill. The otherwise perfect body trembled slightly, held aloft in its mother's arms.

"Are they not . . . perfection?" the Queen asked.

To their credit, not a single mouse squeaked, though some fainted—the pale mouse in the russet gown dropped like a leaf, narrowly missing Ernst's other foot. No one else moved.

Except for the little princes. They turned back toward their mother, her breath stirring their delicately folded ears. Two pink paws reached for her face, to grasp a whisker or stroke the warm gray fur. But those new eyes betrayed them. The hands spasmed (*Only two hands!* thought Ernst) and the blinking eyes slid out of sync. Another twitch, and the paws missed her cheek, tugging the crown from her head instead.

As with all infants, born knowing how to grasp but not how

to let go, the little paws gripped the crown tightly. It stayed clutched to the tiny mouse chest, rising and falling with the beating of a single heart. Some of the princely heads turned to see this new shiny thing; a few gazed in other directions. The one in the center, whose face was framed by the others like a jewel, only had eyes for his mother. Ernst had no doubt that one little boy would drop the crown in favor of her touch. If only his little hands knew how.

Hmm. Ernst had thought of him as a boy. Not a collective, but an individual. They were all boys, he realized. Trapped on one perch perhaps, but each face seemed to have its own will.

The Queen looked at her distorted brood and smiled.

"They reach for the crown! Thou seest?" she addressed the congregation. "They will be conquerors!"

As one, every mouse in the audience chamber, from piebald guard to noble guest, dropped to their knees and flattened themselves in obeisance.

The Queen looked out over their bowed heads at Ernst Listz, who stood, unable to move for all the mice crowded at his feet. The Queen crooned a few soft notes and the boys' ears twitched. A strange faintness swept over Ernst again, as it had outside the birthing room. Like the sound was drawing him away from his body. The feeling faded as the melody drifted away.

"Like the Piper tune of olden days, the melody binds them," the Queen said. "All the broods before these were weak. Born together, they died apart. Until one learns to bind them. Learns to keep them, link them, make them strong. Thus the Piper's magic becomes *my* magic. Thus the Piper's tune becomes our destiny!"

The mice swayed, enthralled by the might of their ruler. Ernst quailed. Had this country mouse been meddling in human magic? In Piper music? Was that the meaning of the strange tune that compelled, yet threatened to take him apart? No wonder she looked so ill. Black arts! And at the cost of her own vitality.

"Able, they will be," she continued. "Strong and able conquerors!" She grazed her nails against the nearest cheek. Tender skin blushed white and red. Tiny feet wriggled beneath her touch. The Queen clutched her brood to her bosom.

"King Above, beware!" she brayed. "My sons are born! And you shall see their greatness!"

Trembling like the newborn princes, Ernst bent over in an awkward bow, chilled to the bone. The mouselings were not the monstrosities he imagined after all. The real monster was the one who had made them.

23

GEORG THE BARMAN kept his promise and secured three bunks to Silistra on a shallow, unpainted barge called the *Gray Goose*. The captain was a blue-eyed, dark-haired man with the unwieldy name of Helmut Holige-Schwarzwasser. Helmut's bright eyes peered out from a bristly, bearded face. His grin appeared like the sun between black clouds.

"Welcome aboard," he boomed as Stefan's party clambered up the gangplank. The deck was long and wide, piled with stacked wooden crates tied down with thick rope. At the center of the barge, a long, low building served as quarters, mess, and wheelhouse in one.

A squeal sounded on the far side of the deck.

"Ah, our other guests," Helmut Holige-Schwarzwasser said. "We are carrying wine, pigs, and timber." He patted the barge's railing. "Fine company, if you can ignore the smell." His laugh was infectious. Stefan liked him instantly.

But the captain eyed him with a considering frown. "Ever been on a barge, boy?" he asked.

"No, sir." Stefan had never been on a boat in his life. "I'm a clockmaker in training," he added, as if that explained things.

"Then you won't mind a bit of work to keep you out of trouble. Come along, boy. Take your bags to your room and I'll show you a thing or two about sailing Die Donau. She's a shifty lady, but with respect, she'll treat you right."

"I'm afraid I can't," Stefan said, casting a glance at Christian. They had things to discuss—plans to make—if they were going to succeed in Boldavia. Besides, if he was going to learn about anything on this trip, it should be clocks, not barges.

But Christian had other ideas.

"He's all yours, Captain."

Stefan balked. "Shouldn't we . . . That is, I . . ." What he meant to say was, he should be learning his new trade. But the thought of poring over books right now was also maddening. What he really wanted to do was punch something. He was wound tight enough to snap.

"Mornings with the crew, afternoons with me," Christian said.

"Yes, sir." Stefan nodded and hurried after the sailor showing them to their room inside the deckhouse. Sailing wasn't the same as punching things, but maybe it would help.

Their cabin was small, with two bunks bolted to one wall, and a third cot lying alongside them. Stefan stowed their bags beneath the beds.

Samir sat down gratefully on the bottom bunk. "There will be no stars until evening, and even then, the trees on the banks will make for difficult viewing. I shall take my rest now and see what I may, come nightfall." With little ceremony, the astrologer lay back on the bunk and instantly fell into a deep, snoring sleep.

Christian sat back on the solitary cot and folded his hands behind his head. "Ah, Samir has the right of it." He rubbed his long fingers beneath the strap of his eye patch, closing his remaining eye with a sigh.

Stefan stood in the doorway and shifted from his right foot to his left.

Christian opened his eye. "Still here?" he asked. "Pacing the floor glaring at me won't make the time pass any faster."

Stefan pulled his sketchbook from his pocket and wrote *Is it safe to speak?* He handed the open book to his cousin, who shook his head slightly and waved for Stefan to follow him back out on deck.

The barge had shoved off from shore and was creeping slowly out into the current. Christian reached inside his coat.

"A beautiful day, isn't it?" Christian remarked. "I wonder what we'll have for supper." From his pocket, he produced a small penny whistle that looked like a piccolo, and pretended to play a few notes on it.

Stefan watched, baffled, as Christian's cheeks puffed and deflated. Out of the corner of his eye, he saw a ripple on the water, heading for shore. Several mice and rats had leapt into the river, fleeing the boat.

"Handy device," Christian commented, patting his pocket. "And now it's safe to speak. At least until the next port."

"What was that? I didn't hear anything."

"It's not meant for human ears, but mice seem to hate it. We'll have to make you one at some point. I have the materials in Boldavia—or at least I did seven years ago . . . Now, what did you want to tell me?"

"Why didn't you use that in Nuremberg? You could have chased that mouse right out of the kitchen before it heard anything!"

Christian looked embarrassed. "I had it made the next day while you were out on your *krakatook* quest. We really weren't expecting any trouble, Stefan, or I'd never have come. Now, you were saying?"

Stefan marveled at how quickly his cousin could switch subjects. His mind was like a busy port, ships full of ideas, coming and going. Stefan would have to train himself to be that way, if he wanted to learn all that Christian had to offer.

Now it was his turn to look embarrassed. "I should have told you before we left, but there wasn't time. It's about the *krakatook*. It can't be cracked."

"Of course it can. It's a nut. That's what they do—crack. It's how you eat them. Granted, I only know of one other fellow lucky enough to have done so, but he never mentioned it being a problem."

"May I see it?" Stefan held out his hand.

Christian shook his head. "It's far too valuable."

"Yes, it's worth my father's life," he agreed. "But only if we can open it."

Christian bit his lip in thought. "In the cabin, then."

Samir woke up when they entered.

"Our journeyman has presented us with a stumbling block," Christian explained. "He says the nut can't be cracked."

Stefan took a hammer from his tool bundle and placed the nut on a small wooden table. He held it as Professor Blume had done. "Step back, in case I lose my grip," he said.

"If we're going to extremes, let's be prepared," Samir said. He rummaged in his bag and produced a vial of amber glass. "We can keep the pieces in here if it works," he explained. "Nut oils can be potent. We must take care to retain their healing properties long enough to get to Boldavia."

"All right, then," Christian said. "Proceed."

Stefan brought the hammer down with a crash.

It bounced off the nut, digging it into the tabletop. One of the table's legs creaked. But the nut did not crack.

"Remarkable," Christian said. "May I?"

Stefan handed over the nut and the hammer. Christian studied them both. "You see, here along the seam where the two halves join? That's where we want to strike."

Stefan nodded innocently and took another step back.

Wham! The hammer rebounded and the nut flew across the room. Samir snatched it out of the sky before it could hit him in the face.

"Astonishing," Christian said, grinning. "What else have you tried?"

They used the table, a chair, Samir jumping up and down in his boots. But the nut remained unharmed.

"Huh," Christian said at last. "Well, the captain is waiting for you, Stefan. We'll deal with this."

"Fine," Stefan said. That nut was life or death for the princess and his father. It was certainly more important than busywork on deck. The little cabin was suddenly uncomfortable. He loosened his collar. His cousin wasn't treating him like a journeyman with something to offer. He was treating him like a child. Well, he refused to behave like one.

"I'll see you at lunch," he said, and went back up the narrow hallway of cabins to the deck for his first lesson in sailoring.

◆　◆　◆

SAILORING, IT TURNED OUT, was a very tedious affair.

Stefan's first afternoon was spent learning Captain Helmut's very precise method for coiling rope. "Hold one end, then gather it in loops like so," he instructed. The captain reached for another length of rope and pulled it to the loop hanging from his other hand. "And again." He created another loop, the coiled rope forming a perfect circle.

Eager to earn the captain's trust, Stefan spent the next several hours coiling and recoiling rope that seemed to be lying about, for no other reason than busywork. By lunchtime, all thoughts of princesses and magic nuts, pretty girls and missing fathers, had leached from him like poison from a snakebite. Stefan was bored as stiff as his aching fingers. He collapsed onto the deck near the makeshift pigpen and stared up at the sun filtering through the thick leaves.

They had reached a calm patch of the river. Stefan pulled his notebook out and began to write. It wasn't until he had finished that he realized it was a letter meant for Clara. His stomach did a little flip. It wasn't like he would ever send it to her. He put the book away.

The barge rolled downriver through sunshine and shade. Stefan sighed. The pigs made satisfied *snork*ing noises over the slosh of the water against the hull. Lying on the deck, blocked from the cool wind by the pigs, Stefan fell asleep.

"Ha!"

He started awake. Helmut Holige-Schwarzwasser stood over him, seven coils of rope running up the length of each arm. "Ha!" the barge captain shouted again. "Asleep with the pigs, are we?"

Stefan sat up, embarrassed. He quickly jumped to his feet, fighting the urge to rub the sleep from his eyes. "Sorry, sir!" A glance at the sun told him he'd slept through lunch! Christian would be waiting, and there was still rope strewn on deck.

Holige-Schwarzwasser gave him a stern frown. "Good sailors don't sleep on duty."

"It was my mistake," Stefan said hastily. "It won't happen again."

Holige-Schwarzwasser scowled. "It best not."

Stefan watched forlornly as the captain unraveled his rope down to the ground. "Now," he said gruffly, "there's rope to be coiled. We'll get the *Goose* in shape yet."

"Yes, sir." Stefan bent to pick up the first length of cord. By the time the captain had disappeared across the barge, Stefan had already finished two coils of rope.

24

ZACHARIAS WAS VERY COLD. Rough hands hauled him from his cabin, and lifted him from the heaving deck of his captors' boat and onto solid land. The men were clumsy and his coat got soaked in the process. Hands set to work peeling it off him.

"Don't want you to freeze to death," a voice smirked. Zacharias knew it now as that of the scarlet man.

But they did not lift the blindfold. Instead someone took his hands, which were bound in front of him, and led him to a roughhewn rock wall. The stone was cold and wet beneath his numb fingers.

"Climb," the scarlet man directed.

Zacharias felt forward with a foot, stubbing his toe against the first step. He waved his arms in front of him. There was a staircase carved into the side of the wall—with no railing, it seemed—and the rock was slick.

"I will fall," he whispered, hands clutched together as if in prayer. The scarlet man seemed to agree, for he pulled the blindfold from his eyes.

He found himself on a cliffside in the dark of a moonless night. Above him rose a mountain of black stone. Below and behind him, the lapping expanse of the sea. The waves reflected nothing, not even the stars.

"Where are we?" he asked in a panic. For all he knew, this could be hell and the man behind him the devil himself.

The scarlet man merely shoved him forward. Zacharias fell silent and climbed.

They were still far from the top of the cliff when the man stopped. Here, the rock face gave way to a broad ledge and the yawning black mouth of a cave.

"In here," said the man in scarlet.

Zacharias nearly fell to his knees with fright. He was shoved roughly into the cave. The stairs continued up the side of the cliff without them.

Under the mountain they went. The cold grew deeper. Wind sighed around them like a moist and clammy breath. Zacharias felt his way in the dark and found a rope tied to iron rings at intervals in the wall. His captor stalked at his heels, leather boots ringing out against the stone.

"Is this a dungeon? Am I to be imprisoned?" Zacharias asked through chattering teeth. He was only in his shirtsleeves and the work vest he'd worn the day he was kidnapped. Fortunately he had good shoes—Elise had made sure of that, and knitted him sturdy woolen socks as well.

"Congratulations," the scarlet man said. "You've passed the test. I had money on leaving you in a field like the rest of them."

There had been talk of missing apprentices in Germany, strange tales of kidnappings and mysterious tasks—like something out of a fairy tale. But this was no charmed fantasy. This was a nightmare.

If only he knew what was behind it. "Who do you work for?"

The scarlet man laughed. "Enough questions. We're to leave you here. The rest is up to them."

Them. Every task set to him was at the behest of a nameless *them* who clearly commanded fear in the hearts of their underlings. Or perhaps it was the sort of obedience bought with gold, and lots of it.

"At least tell me where we are," he pleaded, only to be cuffed in the back of the head. After that, he remained silent. But there were so many questions. Why didn't they use a lantern to light the corridor? Would they give him back his coat? Was there a warm room and a fire at the end of this march? Would there be more blueprints and plans, or some other cockeyed task for him to toil over?

The drawings had been absurd, of course. Standard toys fit for a young boy—but the size of them! Whomever his captors worked for, surely they were mad. A chilling thought, since he was at the mercy of those madmen.

At last the scarlet man called a halt. Zacharias had passed some unseen landmark. He leaned against the wall exhausted, and quickly recoiled from the damp. There was a fumbling of cloth, the jangle of keys, the tumble of a lock, and he was thrust forward into a room. The door boomed shut behind him.

He threw himself against it. Solid wood. Running his fingers along the length of it, he found a small barred window near the top. "Please . . ." he said through the iron bars.

"Better luck to you, then," the scarlet man muttered. His bootheels faded away into silence.

"Well," Zacharias said to no one but himself. "Here I am, and that's something. At least I am still alive."

He did not allow himself to wonder for how much longer.

25

ERNST LISTZ SAT DOZING in a chair by the fire, soothed by the sounds of thread through velvet. The royal seamstresses plied their trade close to the light of the flames. If he lowered his lids enough, the scene was almost idyllically domestic. At his feet, the young princes were wrestling with their tail. It kept getting in the way when they tried to grasp their mother's skirts. To be fair, the Queen was not exactly compliant. She swept up and down the threadbare carpets of her antechamber, tapping her long claws against her sharp, yellowed teeth.

They had not been yellowed when Ernst first came to Boldavia. Back then the Queen had been a little bland-faced thing, a bit long in the tooth, with a hard glint in her eye and a sharpish tongue, but still, pleasingly plump in a country kind of way. Now she was more than plump—bloated—as if the birth had left her with more inside than she could deliver. She grew with each passing day, and had lost her scent of hay and seeds. The Queen of Mice now smelled of swamps and rot.

Nursemaids whispered that it had something to do with the magic she was wielding.

It had been touch-and-go with the princes at first. Although they had arrived fully formed—or malformed—they had failed to rally after their naming day. It seemed as if they would die swiftly, the way so many other misshapen creatures did. But the Queen was determined. That song she had sung over their bassinet became an orchestra, a group of musicians playing night and day over her children's sickbed, their ears stuffed with beeswax and linen. It was a binding spell, the nursemaids said. Old magic, dark magic. The same that bound the rats of Hameln to the Piper and led them to their watery graves. Only, now it was wielded by a mad Queen intent on keeping the souls of her children firmly attached to their twisted flesh.

Ernst had visited the children daily, the Queen insisting they begin their education even as they lay possibly dying. Every day, he had descended the stairs to that dank chamber she called her suite and sat by their crib. Ears dulled with stuffing, he'd read to them from books he had procured and memorized, or rewritten in a more manageable size from the great tomes in the human libraries above. He had recounted the histories of their race, the wars, the victories. He told them mythologies of Mice, of the Piper, of gods, of Men. He spoke to them until they knew his voice better than their own mother's, his words droning loud in his own ears, overpowering the music in the chamber and the beating of his own heart. The boys would lean toward him, eyes staring, then slowly closing, as they fell into sleep.

One set of eyes never quite opened all the way. Julius, the runt of the litter, squashed to the side like a forgotten fruit at the bottom of a basket. Not dead exactly, but not quite alive, either.

After long days and nights of hedge witchery, at last, the brothers pulled through, rallied, and thrived. And now they were wrestling with their tail on the floor of the throne room.

Ernst encouraged this because it taught them coordination and how to each take a turn moving their hands. Arthur, the inquisitive young mouse in the center of his brethren, seemed best at it. As if his strength of will was greater, or perhaps he was the one meant to be born and all these others were simply mistakes.

The boys tumbled by. Arthur, giggling, waved a paw in greeting, and lost the grip on his tail. Ernst waved back, and pointed out his mistake. A look of determination entered the little face and he lunged once more for his tail.

Ernst chuckled. He was quite fond of Arthur. The others had their moments, too, but it was a relief to look into one set of eyes and see that his instruction had been understood. And so he had taken a favorite. But their mother, who had once favored them all so highly, no longer did so. She had turned inward, the old cow, and festered there. Perhaps she had used up the wealth of her own spirit buying her sons' lives.

The sewing stopped. The words that he had so painstakingly inscribed across the expanse of velvet had been stitched over in golden thread, emblazoning the bottom of the banner.

The Queen of Mice raised her nose into the air, as if scenting its completion. "Thee dost approve of it, rat?"

Ernst rose creakily and strode to the table where the three young mouse maids had plied their work. They each grabbed a corner and held the banner up for him to see.

Nearly a foot long and half again as wide, the bloodred cloth boasted seven golden crowns on seven stylized heads. Beneath them, in his own florid cursive, now raised and glittering in the firelight, read the motto: *E Pluribus Unum.*

"Out of many, one," Ernst translated. He bowed to the

seamstresses, who all blushed at the attention. "Beautifully done, my ladies." He bowed to the Queen. "Beautifully done, indeed."

The Queen nodded slightly and ran a claw through her whiskers, preening. Her sons were yet children, but she had made their armies a banner to fly in the face of war. She continued to pace, studying the banner and twitching her skirts away from the boys at her ankles. Impatient for her conquerors to come of age, Ernst realized, to rise up and take the castle by storm.

26

IT HAD BEEN days, and still they could not open the *krakatook*.

"When I was a boy, my grandfather showed me how to crack two nuts together in my bare hands," Samir said. So they had scoured the ship and found a sailor willing to share his stash of hazelnuts.

Samir placed them in his palm and squeezed with all his might. Blood would have come from a stone with that squeeze. Instead, the hazelnut was ground to powder. The *krakatook*, however, held firm.

From there, they tried knives. They used an awl and attempted to pry the shell apart. They tried bricks, a vise, and a variety of tools from the barge. They hoisted a crate on the deck and dropped it from as great a height as they dared.

The nut remained unharmed.

"Well, the good news is, we have the nut," Christian said brightly.

"The bad news is we cannot crack it," Samir added. "But, I've consulted the stars and it appears that *one* of us will figure it out. Eventually."

"But, will it be in time?" Stefan asked. Their whole plan to save his father hinged on opening the *krakatook*. Only then would King Pirliwig agree to use his army to help find his father.

Christian looked glum. "I'm working on it." He spread open his sketchbook, where he had drawn a plethora of new plans.

Stefan looked at them over his shoulder. "Waterwheels? Diamonds! Where are we going to get diamonds?"

"In Boldavia, of course," Christian said. "This is a *kingdom*, after all. I'm sure they can spare one or two medium-sized diamonds. We'll cut them to a thirty-five-degree angle and attach them to a dremel powered by a waterwheel. I'll need to make a few calculations, of course, and a model or two for a few practice runs—perhaps on test nuts made of granite or marble."

Stefan looked dubiously from the blueprints to his cousin's optimistic face. Granite could be crushed. Marble could be carved, as every Roman statue could attest. But nothing had cracked the *krakatook*.

"Maybe we can use the nut as more of a bargaining tool," Stefan suggested. "Ask for the king's help in exchange for it. Like you said, he's a king, with an entire kingdom at his command. Let *them* figure it out."

"Stefan," Christian said solemnly. "Samir did not lie when he said he was my jailer. There is a price on my head in Boldavia if I can't cure the princess. The king won't lift a finger until she's restored. But I swear to you, I'll do it. For you. For Zacharias. On my honor as a clockmaker, I will find a way to bring your father home again."

Stefan pushed away from the table and the sketchbook with its far-fetched plans. "Whatever it takes," he said. "I want my father back."

He walked away before any tears could escape, before he had to look at Christian's face clouding over with shame or Samir shifting uncomfortably beside him. A master clockmaker and a royal astrologer. They were the best the king had, and they had failed. And here he was, just a toymaker's apprentice . . . or rather, a clockmaker's journeyman in his very first week—what did he have to offer? They had no choice but to try Christian's fanciful plans, or the nut would remain uncracked forever.

Stefan slumped against the barge railing. Thoughts of his father threatened like rain clouds. Nuremberg had slipped away behind them, and with it, all sense of normalcy.

Everything was wrong.

Trees on the far shore dipped toward the water, heads heavy with leaves. The sky was blue and the weather mild. Sailors were napping on deck. There were no sails to trim, no booms to lower, or whatever things were done on ships. The river simply carried them on her wide back. The world didn't share Stefan's sense of urgency. Even barge travel was slow. And boring.

He drummed his fingers on the railing. He shifted and something in his pocket dug into his hip. He pulled out the little dove from his mother's funeral.

At last, this was something he could fix. Even if it was only a little thing. He set off in search of his tools and a piece of wood, determined to build a better bird.

HOURS LATER, STEFAN dropped his knife on the deck and wiggled his fingers, attempting to undo the curl they'd developed from wrapping too much rope.

He picked up the dove. This one was much more detailed than the one he'd released at his mother's funeral—it had a defined beak and individual feathers. There were plenty of birds on the Danube, swooping down for fish, insects, and handouts from the crew. Stefan watched them while he worked, pausing now and then to sketch the arch of a wing or the motion of a wingbeat.

This is what being a journeyman is all about, he told himself. Just him and his creation. He was literally carving a future for himself. As the bird took shape beneath his knife, he lost himself in the rhythm of the work. When he finished the second wing, he inserted it into the body of the bird. Inside, there was a tight coil of metal, salvaged from the first dove.

Being on the barge had served him better than he had hoped. He had a solution for the waterlogged wings now—pitch. The entire barge hull was painted with it, black pitch that kept the river from seeping into its planks. He used a thinned version to paint the joints of the bird. It wouldn't fare well underwater, but it would do for a rainy day. Or so he hoped.

Twisting the tail feather key of the dove, he held it aloft in his free hand and let go.

The wooden bird fluttered and hopped into the air, wings beating so fast they were a blur. It made a wide arc off the port bow of the barge, then circled back. Several sailors paused to see what this odd creature might be. Too late, Stefan realized it would not make it all the way back to him. He raced down the deck, dodging sailors and cargo, and leapt into the air to retrieve it. But he missed and the bird crashed into the river.

A second later, a net appeared over the water. Stefan turned to see his cousin retrieve the bird.

"Not bad," Christian said, pulling it from the braided netting. He held the dove up in his gloved hand. Gone was the solemn criminal—Christian was once again a dashing master clocksmith, in full control.

Stefan snapped to attention.

"A charming representation of a mourning dove," Christian said, wiggling the tail feather key and pumping the wings. "A straightforward spring design . . . taken from a mantel clock?" he asked.

Stefan cleared his throat. "A grandfather clock, trimmed to size. The mantel clock spring was too short to complete a full circle of flight."

"Very good," Christian muttered, peering between the joints. He held the bird up in the sunlight. "And what's this, pitch?"

"The wings of my last bird swelled in the rain, which meant shorter wingbeats, and a shorter arc. I thought maybe . . . But the pitch must have damaged the mechanism. Or else it would have . . . should have come back to me directly." His face was hot and his stomach fluttered like the wings of the wooden dove. This was the first time he'd displayed work in front of his new master, intentionally or not. He had no idea what Christian would think.

"I see," Christian said. He handed the bird back to Stefan.

Stefan waited for a response.

Light sparkled blindingly off the water. Around them, oak and ash trees slid by. The occasional oxcart ambled along on the shore. Stefan was sweating, even though the day was not overly warm.

Christian seemed to count every leaf and limb before he turned to Stefan again. "Promise me something," he said. "Promise me you won't quit."

Stefan had made progress on the bird—more than expected. He saw no reason to give up now.

"I promise," he said, befuddled.

"Well then, carry on," his master said, and wandered off across the deck.

Stefan released a breath. *Carry on . . . ? Is that a good thing, or a bad thing?*

The pitch he'd used had been too thick and scraped against the bird's wings. Peering inside at the mechanism, he saw that pitch shavings had wound themselves into the spring. *Carry on.* It was a good thing, he decided.

It was strange, given all that had happened. But here on this barge with his tools and his little dove, he felt more at peace than he had in a long time.

He'd found his father in their workshop the day after his mother died, sanding smooth the long sides of her coffin. How could he stand to build the casket that would take her away? It was too terrible for him to even consider. His father had been so absorbed in his work, he'd been unaware that his son was watching and getting angrier with every moment. Only now did Stefan realize that it hadn't been cold practicality he'd seen, but grief. His father was always happiest working with his hands. Maybe, alongside the sorrow, it had brought him a little peace.

Stefan hoped so. With a sigh, he went in search of oil to clean out the wings and start again.

27

"WHEN DO WE BEGIN strategy?" Hannibal demanded.

They were halfway through their history lesson for the day: the discovery of the New World and the reunion of mousekind with their cousins across the sea.

"Quiet, Hannibal," Arthur whispered. He was hard at work writing down answers to Ernst's questions. "Sorry, Herr Listz."

"It's all right," Ernst said. He patted the princes encouragingly on the back and stifled a sigh. It was a challenge, handling six personalities at once. Vacant Julius lolled to the side, while the others clustered around the central head, like petals on a furry flower—each with their own demands. In the end, he had found it best to focus on that center head, Arthur.

In Ernst's mind, Arthur alone was the prince. He was a sweet child, almost normal-looking, if one squinted. He had a head for books (and six others that weren't) and might have been quite the scholar one day, if his mother and brothers didn't have other ideas. Ernst liked Arthur, and perhaps the feeling was mutual.

It was the other boys who were problematic. Hannibal was the belligerent one, excellent at swordplay; Charlemagne had the qualities of a leader—insightful, decisive—but he lacked patience; Genghis could be a brute, but a careful one; Roland was demanding and had a tendency to whine, which grated on the nerves; and Alexander had a keen mind for chess . . . But perhaps that was Arthur, too.

In truth, Ernst suspected that most of the young mouse princes' skills belonged to Arthur alone. The other heads merely clamored to take credit for the boy's hard work.

Arthur put down his quill and sighed. "I think he's right, Herr Listz. I'm getting stiff with sitting. A little exercise might help clear our heads." Arthur smiled wryly at his joke.

Ernst returned the smile. It was hard to believe Arthur would one day lead armies into the castle above. But that was the Queen's wish, and Arthur was the kind of boy who obeyed, even feared, his mother.

"Fair enough," Ernst said aloud, dropping his quill to the desk. "Grab your foil and gear."

The Queen had been very clear on the schedule of instruction for her boys. Equal time was to be given to learning history, languages, strategy, and warfare. In the area of warfare, swordplay and hand-to-hand combat were taught. While Ernst was no genius in a fistfight, he did have a flair for fencing, and so those duties, in addition to history and human tongues, fell to him. The rest were handled by the piebald spies.

Strolling to the wall of the large royal classroom, Ernst selected a foil from the rack. Unlike the rapier blade he used in street fighting, the foil was longer, and needle-thin. Both were designed for thrusts and jabbing, but the foil had a protective tip for practicing. He watched with a morbid fascination as Arthur struggled to enclose his brothers in a specially made helmet—it wouldn't do for the tutor to accidentally blind one of the royal heirs. No such gear had been provided for Ernst.

"Ready?" Arthur asked, voice slightly muffled by the screen of their helmet. Ernst could hear Hannibal's low chuckle from inside the hood.

Taking a deep breath, the rat nodded. *"En garde!"*

Arthur—or was it Hannibal now?—pressed the attack, rather than taking the defensive, as Ernst had taught them. Ernst leapt back, annoyed at the boy's persistent assault. Riposte, parry . . . the young prince handled each maneuver with skill. And Ernst the rat was no longer so eager, or so young.

Ernst swished his tail to distract his charge. He had no wish to be nicked yet again by the royal sword. But the young princes were not swayed. They lunged with their foil and gave a sharp slap to the base of the rat's long pink tail.

Ernst dropped the tip of his sword and bowed. "Touché, my prince." A smile spread dutifully across his lips and he did not recoil when one of the other heads—not Arthur, but the fighter, Hannibal, sat straighter on the great stem of their neck and grinned slyly.

"We learn quickly, Herr Listz, do we not?"

Listz noted the appropriateness of the royal "we." He nodded and pressed his foil to his forehead again. *"En garde!"*

Ernst allowed the princes to attack again. He had learned that each personality merited a very different approach. Hannibal liked to win.

Ernst dodged for his life as the protective tip flew off his charge's foil. The prince, however did not stop. If Ernst wasn't careful, the little menace would draw blood. Again. Alas, Arthur

172

was never the one in control when there was real fighting to be done.

"Mother says we should learn strategy next," Hannibal announced, lunging toward his tutor.

Barbarian, Ernst thought. Out loud he said, "Your mother has mentioned that, yes. But first you must master languages. There are several texts on strategy that you should read for yourself—human books. Not that rubbish they teach mouselings in school."

Hannibal fell silent. He was not the intellectual of the group.

Arthur spoke up, eager to please, his boyish face a beam of light in the center of his brothers. "You're right, Herr Listz. I'll work harder on my languages and try to read the original texts. Mother would like that, don't you think?"

"Yes, my boy." Ernst's face softened.

The pinch-faced head next to Arthur spoke up. Ernst recognized Roland's whine instantly. "No, no, no! You are the royal translator—do your job! Translate the texts for us and we'll do the rest. We should begin strategy as soon as possible."

"Your Highness, you speak ahead of yourself," Ernst snapped, pricking Roland's nose with his foil.

Arthur looked ashamed, but Hannibal sprang back to life with a scowl, redoubling their attack.

The rat tutor found himself too hard pressed to chide them any further. Despite his friendship with Arthur, Ernst hoped he'd find a way out of this life soon.

28

STEFAN EXAMINED his handiwork. He'd taken his time testing different types of pitch. Now he had thinned the solution, painted his bird carefully, and tested the wings three times.

The sun was slipping behind the trees when he wound the bird. His stomach growled. It would be time for dinner soon, but he had to see if it would work this time. He lifted the dove into the air and let it go.

The bird rose, drumming its wings high over the dark river. Stefan watched with the net at his feet, ready to retrieve it from the water. The little dove soared.

"Ha!" Stefan exclaimed. "She's flying!" he shouted as it flew farther than ever, in a widening circle. It had worked! His idea with the pitch, his patience, his skill had all paid off. And now the bird was coming back toward him for a landing. Stefan held up his hand to catch her.

Whoosh! The air beat against his eardrums and a shadow swooped over the deck. Stefan ducked. He turned just in time to see his beautiful little dove carried off in the talons of a massive barn owl.

"No!" He waved his arms, but the owl had already disappeared into the trees.

"Imagine the bellyache *that* one will have in the morning," Samir said. The astrologer doubled over with laughter.

"Did you see that? That owl! It took my bird!"

"That owl *thought* it took a bird," Samir replied, still chuckling.

"There is no greater compliment," Christian agreed. "You fooled nature at her own game."

Stefan wondered how long they'd been standing there, watching. He broke into a grin. "I guess so."

"That, right there," Christian said sharply, stabbing a finger at Stefan's chest. "That feeling? Remember it, Stefan. It goeth before a fall."

Stefan stepped back in confusion and rubbed his chest. "Pride," the Bible said, "goeth before destruction, and an haughty spirit before a fall." But Stefan wasn't being haughty. He'd worked hard to get that bird perfect; he had a right to be proud of his work, didn't he? Over Christian's shoulder, Samir shook his head, cutting off Stefan's protest. Pride was a touchy subject with his cousin. That much was clear. "I'll remember," Stefan said. He lowered his eyes to hide his confusion. Pride might have been his cousin's downfall. But Stefan wasn't Christian. He was very sure of that.

AUSTRIA GAVE WAY to Hungary, its cliffs and hills melting into vineyards, and finally flat farmland. The sailors on board breathed a sigh of relief. Pirates, Stefan learned, had a much harder time hiding in the fields than they did in the craggy heights of the upper Danube.

Then the Western Carpathian Mountains rose up and the river headed sharply south, flowing through the heart of Hungary and on to Romania. Once more, the mountains hemmed them in, until the river became so narrow that Stefan could have easily swum from one bank to the other.

"Beautiful, isn't it?" Christian joined him at the rail, his black coat opened to the river breeze. The mountains were like nothing Stefan had ever seen. They made him feel small. He'd just finished saying as much in his latest umailed letter to Clara.

He tucked the notebook into his pocket and leaned against the railing to enjoy the view.

"Gentlemen," Captain Holige-Schwarzwasser announced, coming up beside them. "Welcome to the Iron Gate."

Up ahead, the "Gate" stretched out before them, a deep gorge cut into the rock by centuries of flowing water. The river dropped abruptly away from its smooth expanse, churning into a froth of white, choppy waves.

"Rapids?" Stefan involuntarily grabbed hold of the railing.

"Rapids," the captain confirmed. "Best hold on tight. Better yet, get inside. This is the worst of it." He broke into a grin. "I'm crazy to say it, but I think it's fun."

Stefan didn't agree. But Christian didn't seem concerned with going inside, so Stefan tightened his grip on the railing and wrapped a guard rope around his wrist. Now he understood what all of the rope on deck was for.

"Christian, hold on to something. It isn't safe."

His cousin seemed lost in thought. "No, it isn't safe at all, really." He smiled sheepishly. "Things never are around me."

With his free hand, Stefan checked to make sure his notebook was secured inside his pocket.

"Don't forget this," Christian said, handing him the *krakatook* in its silver casket.

Stefan snatched it. "Are you *mad*, bringing that out here?"

The river bucked and heaved beneath them as they passed the Iron Gate. Stefan's stomach dropped and rose. He sucked in a breath as it dropped again.

"Mad?" Christian asked in a distracted voice. "Perhaps I am. You look so much like your mother, Stefan. She would be proud of you. Now, remember your promise. And I'll keep mine." He smiled gently.

It was such an odd thing to say. Stefan opened his mouth to tell him so when the barge dropped, and kept dropping. Stefan was sure he would be sick.

A wave splashed over the hull like a grabbing hand. Water blinded him.

When it receded, Christian was gone.

Silence, but for the wash and spray of the rapids.

Stefan reached out belatedly, but his cousin was beyond help. Then a phrase clicked into place in his head like the winding key of a clock, dredged up from his memory of ships and sails and souls lost at sea.

"Man overboard!" he shouted frantically.

Instantly, the deck was alive with bargemen racing to the rail, towing ropes and nets and guiding poles.

"Where?" bellowed the captain. Stefan pointed to the place where the waves had claimed his cousin. How had it gotten so far behind them? There was the dead tree on the shore, the cluster of submerged rocks that looked like a cow wading in the river. Even as he pointed, the landmarks disappeared from view behind the frothing waves.

They trolled the water.

"He's light, faster than the *Goose*. He'll be ahead of us now, lad," the captain said, clamping a hand on Stefan's shoulder. It was hot against the cold weight of his wet shirt.

Stefan raced to the bow of the barge. "Christian! Christian!" He screamed his throat raw, desperate for a glimpse of the white hair, the black coat, any sign of his cousin.

But the rocks were black, the rapids white and gray, blowing back into his face as the river spat at him in contempt.

Samir stormed onto the deck, summoned by one of the sailors, or by the sixth sense that tells all jailers when their prisoner has disappeared. He raced from one end of the barge to the other, calling out each rock or piece of driftwood that might be a coat or an arm or face. But they were not.

The rapids churned, and Christian did not reappear.

Stefan was still screaming his cousin's name as they passed through the final rapids and the *Gray Goose* came to rest in a calm, still pool.

Flotsam and lost bits of cargo drifted in the silent water, circling as they rejoined the gentler flow of the river downstream.

Stefan gripped the railing with frozen fingers, staring into the water. "No," he murmured. If he took his eyes off the rail, if he looked away from the glassy surface, it would be true.

Christian would be gone.

Not gone. *Dead.* That place beyond the veil, where his mother had disappeared. There would be no miracle to bring him back.

"Here's where we find the bodies," a sailor muttered to Samir. "Not always," he quickly added. "It could take weeks if he's in the rocks."

Stefan gave the man a hateful glare. "Samir," he called, but the name turned into a sob. He turned to the astrologer expecting comfort, an embrace, assurances—all the things his father had offered when his mother died. Things Stefan had rejected. Trying instead to be brave, to be unaffected. He had shrugged off the warm hand, the sad smile that would have opened the door to shared loss.

But he wanted it now, all of it. He wanted the black wind blowing through his chest to stop; the cold empty curdling in his gut to cease. Everyone he loved had been taken from him. Was this part of the universe's design? Even now, another cog was being pulled from the clock in Nuremberg.

Christian Elias Drosselmeyer was dead.

29

"TWO INCHES, SEVEN EIGHTHS," Zacharias said aloud to himself. He had risen this morning (or this evening, it was impossible to tell) to discover that the table in his cell now held two candlesticks, a box of matches, and a sheaf of paper with ink and pen.

He lit the candles. His cell was every bit as awful as he had imagined. Even the door—a great solid thing, charred as if from a fire—was exactly as foreboding as he had imagined it would be.

He cleared the straw away from around the table, lest the candles catch it alight. And then he unrolled the paper. Here were his blueprints, drawn aboard the ship that had carried him here. And a note, written in fine cursive hand.

If you wish to see your son again, you will build what you have designed.

The note was unsigned.

Zacharias cleared his throat.

"You expect me to make toys without tools, I suppose!" he said aloud. If they were listening, perhaps he could engage them. If not, it was at least nice to hear a human voice again— even if it was only his own.

"I'll need an awl, for starters, and good wood . . ." He spoke a list of items required and wrote them on the back of the sheet of paper for good measure. Then, afraid to waste too much of the candles, he snuffed them out, and eventually fell asleep.

A scratching sound woke him. He sat up in his rickety chair and lit the candles once more.

There, by his straw bed, lay an awl, a small carving knife, and several large blocks of cured wood.

Like Beauty and the Beast, he thought to himself. But what unseen monster did he serve?

As there was little else to do, he began to carve.

30

HIDDEN WITHIN A CRACK in the stones of the castle, Arthur and his brothers pricked up their ears. They were eavesdropping on two mouselings gathering water from the trickling rain gutters above.

This particular rainspout was a vein of gossip the princes could mine without fear of being seen. The mice of Boldavia were chatty about their ruler, the Queen. But when the princes were about, they barely raised their eyes to them, let alone spoke in their presence.

Arthur sighed. He was tired of being a prince. Wouldn't it be more fun to swap stories with friends in the marketplace?

"They have one!" the first mouse said.

"One what?" asked the second.

The first mouse's voice trembled with a mixture of glee and awe. "They have a . . . Drosselmeyer!"

A shock ran through Arthur from tip to tail. He knocked heads with his brothers as each recoiled from the news. In silent agreement, Arthur and his brothers crept forward, all ears tuned to the conversation beyond the wall.

"Impossible!" said the second mouse. He was clearly older, his tone one of authority, his voice less squeaky. "There is only one Drosselmeyer and he was cast out of Boldavia."

"Not true!" the first mouse insisted. "The Drosselmeyer has

a family. There are more of them! I heard it from my mother's cousin in the Queen's guard. Well . . . my mother heard it from him. They didn't see me under the table while they were talking, or I'm sure they'd have never let me stay. They've got one and they've brought him here. *Here!* In the castle!"

Arthur gasped. A Drosselmeyer! The most dangerous of all things. And to bring him into their home?

"I think you're lying," the older mouseling sneered.

"Am not!"

Arthur withdrew into the chamber beyond his listening post, wringing his paws.

"It can't be true!" Genghis whined.

"Why not?" Charlemagne countered. "It's a brilliant move. We have a hostage now. Drosselmeyer will stay away or risk his kin's life."

"Or he'll come all the sooner," Alexander said. "To save him."

The princes fell silent at this sobering thought.

"Mother will kill the prisoner before Drosselmeyer has the chance," Roland decided. He looked side to side at his brothers for agreement.

Hannibal growled deep in their belly. "Revenge," he rumbled. "Then he'll come back for revenge."

Arthur felt sick. Their history lessons agreed with Hannibal. Nothing good could come of this. He wanted to sit down and be comforted, but by whom? His mother barely even stroked his ears, and the few times she had, it felt more like she was shopping for apples than showing tenderness. What would she want him to do?

"We need more information," he surmised.

"Yes, let's talk to Mother," Genghis agreed. "Or Herr Listz. He'll know what to do."

"If they wanted us to know, they would have told us themselves," Arthur said. He swallowed the lump of fear threatening to choke him. "No. We'll go and see the prisoner for ourselves."

The other princes fell silent. Arthur took a steadying breath and led the way to the damp dungeons.

THE PRINCE OF MICE peered out from their second hiding place of the day. Charlemagne snorted. He didn't think it seemly that the future ruler of Boldavia should skulk between walls, and said as much.

There was a general grumble of agreement.

Arthur shushed his brothers. "There's a spy hole in the wall," he said. "If you ever listened in our lessons, you would know that."

One of their mother's piebald spies had given them a quick education in espionage—spying—in the mouse world. Back when Boldavia was a rougher place, an ancient mouse king had ordered spy holes and hidden doors carved into every dungeon cell. Even then they knew that if they hoped to hold sway in the world above, they would need the help of men.

"Hands," they were called—humans who did the bidding of mice in the world of Men above. Before they had amassed enough gold to buy human assistance, they'd offered other things—comforts of food and blankets brought in by hidden ways. In exchange, the prisoners performed certain tasks upon being released. More than one wayward Boldavian had complied with their requests—drown a few kittens or unlock a granary door, wedge a window open in the scullery. By these means, cats grew scarce and mice more abundant over the years. King Pirliwig himself had done them a favor when his sneezing led him to banish cats from the kingdom entirely.

It was likely a gang of hands who had brought Drosselmeyer's kin to this cell, Arthur thought. He rested a paw against the stonework. A small panel slid aside, offering a wide view of the room from halfway up the wall. Pressing his face against the opening, he could see that the small damp chamber held an old table and chair, but little else. He waited for his eyes to adjust.

There. On the floor, strewn with old hay, a shape lay, its broad back to the room. Its shoulders quaked beneath a thin blanket, and it muttered softly to itself like a bedraggled old hen.

This was the Drosselmeyer.

"Let us see," hissed Roland. Arthur pulled away from the opening to give each brother a turn at the peephole. A sense of dread built in their stomach.

"He looks . . . small," Genghis said. It was the wrong word, but the brothers knew what he meant. After a lifetime of cautionary tales about the Mousekiller, here was his closest kin, huddled like an old maid. Neither fiery-eyed, nor breathing poison. He reminded Arthur of the aged deaf mouse that guarded the door to his mother's chambers when he was very young. A sad old creature, not made for the damp beneath the castle.

This Drosselmeyer was no monster to be feared.

Alexander was the first to smile. And then Hannibal. Then

Genghis and Roland and Charlemagne. A wave of relief washed over them. They had faced their enemy and survived.

"A dog with no teeth," Alexander said.

"A cat with no claws," Roland agreed.

"A victory," said Charlemagne.

And the Prince of Mice laughed.

Except for Arthur. He had listened well at the spy hole and knew that the Drosselmeyer in the chamber was calling for his son. Had his own mother ever done such a thing? Worried over him, maybe, but wept for him? And his father? He didn't even know the mouse who had helped give them life. The prince consort had died before they were born. A victim of the Drosselmeyer, some said, or the horrid mechanical cat he'd left behind.

For a moment, he leaned against the damp stone wall, disturbed in a way he could not define.

"What's the matter with you?" growled Hannibal.

"N-nothing," Arthur stammered. He knew what he was feeling was dangerous. *Pity*, for the man in the prison. Something he had only ever felt for himself.

31

BULGARIA MIGHT HAVE BEEN beautiful. It might have been vast, wild, and green, or drab, treeless, and gray. Stefan did not notice. He concentrated on putting one foot in front of the other, his cousin's bag slung across his back, his own bag swinging from his shoulder.

Samir carried the black cases along with his own luggage. The Arab hid his grief behind a wall of calm. Stefan had no such defenses.

They had left the river men to their work dismantling the *Gray Goose*, which was to be sold for her wood. The current of the Danube did not allow for a return trip. The captain and his crew would travel overland back to Germany, where they would build another barge and set sail again.

Stefan and Samir now followed a narrow road that wound its way through a scant forest. Stefan watched the ground, his boots taking one dusty step and then another. The rhythm was steady, plodding. It helped him stop thinking for a while. About his cousin, and the river, and his last glimpse of Christian's face.

His father standing by his mother's coffin in the rain. The empty toy shop, ransacked by man or mouse.

His coat was too warm, his feet sore, his legs weak from their days on the river. Still he walked, and the shade of the trees gave way to dappled sunlight. He could feel it on his neck, but he would not look up. Because then he would have to face the future. One in which he was alone.

When they were through the trees, Samir stopped and put the two cases on the mossy ground. Stefan dropped his bags and stretched. Walking might be peaceful, but it was impractical if they were to have any chance of saving his father.

"What are we going to do, Samir?"

The astrologer sat down on the grass and folded his legs in front of him. "I am ashamed to say I do not know. For too long, I've been led by the beard, following Christian, searching for the nut. It is as if I am looking up and seeing where I am for the first time." He gazed out at the peaceful countryside, empty but for the hum of insects and the sigh of the wind in the trees. "I am at a loss."

Stefan sat down beside the Arab and lay back on the grass. His head hurt. He tried not to think.

"There was a plan," Samir said at last. "We will follow the plan. Go to Boldavia, bring the nut to the king."

"But we can't open it," Stefan sighed.

"King Pirliwig has a kingdom of men, as you said. Men who might succeed where we have failed. We will trade it for help finding your father, and get you home to Nuremberg. That is what your cousin wanted. I promise to see it through to the end."

"Promises," Stefan repeated, remembering. "Just before . . . before Christian . . ." He swallowed and began again. "He told me to remember my promise and he said he would keep his."

"What did you promise him?" Samir asked.

Stefan sat up. "I don't know. Nothing that I can remember.

He said I looked like my mother, and she'd be proud of me. It was strange."

"Anything else?" Samir asked intently, as if there were clues in the memory.

"Nothing. He said it was a beautiful day." He collapsed back to the ground and sighed. "Christian was the master clockmaker. *He* was the one with the plan. I'm just . . . a toymaker's apprentice." Without a master, he could no longer be a journeyman. He'd been orphaned yet again.

"And I am no longer a jailer," Samir said. "So, what can an astrologer and a toymaker's apprentice do?"

Stefan recalled the blueprints of the City Clock, layer upon layer. Even the smallest cog fit somehow to make the whole mechanism work. When one cog was removed, another took its place. But he was too young to fill the gap his cousin had left behind.

"'Promise me you won't quit,'" Stefan whispered. There was something else Christian had said days ago, after their argument about cracking the nut.

"What's that?" Samir asked.

Stefan sat up and dusted himself off. "Did you know that too many clockmakers can spoil a clock?"

"What nonsense is that?" The Arab's patience had worn thin. He rose and began fiddling with his bags.

"It's true. Christian told me. Once a clockmaker has begun work, only he can finish it. Another hand might throw off the rhythm."

"What's that to do with us?" Samir demanded.

"Don't you see? Christian was my master, but he's gone. The work is unfinished. Unless I finish it for him."

Samir stopped his fiddling and gave Stefan a confused look.

Stefan rose to his feet. "Christian said he knew of someone who'd eaten a *krakatook*. Who was he?"

A vague look crossed Samir's face. "Allah be praised. He must have meant the Pater."

"We have to go see him. He's our only hope."

Samir shook his head. "Not in this instance, I am sorry to say. The Pater is a squirrel."

"A squirrel."

"A wise squirrel. But the *krakatook* is a religion to such creatures. Like your Holy Grail. If he knew we had it . . . No, we must find some other way."

"There is no other way!" Stefan cried. "We have to go to the squirrels."

"Did you not hear me? They will *take* the nut from you."

"They'll *try*. But I won't let them—" Like a lens throwing everything into focus, the wheels of his brain were starting to turn, making his path clear. "If the mice succeed and spread out into the world, men will rise up to stop them. Then where will the squirrels be? Hunted alongside the mice, maybe, or driven to starvation by their excess. Professor Blume said the *krakatook* imparts longevity and wisdom. If there is a squirrel who has eaten one, he'll see I'm right. He'll be sensible where kings and queens might not. Please take me to the squirrels. For my father's sake."

Samir regarded him for a long moment. He reached for the satchel that held his telescope and star charts. He spread the charts on the grass, weighing the corners down with rocks, and read the strange series of circles and lines.

"How can star charts possibly—?"

The Arab held up a finger for silence. Stefan paced impatiently, but Samir paid him no heed. Instead, he muttered under his breath, pulled out a small instrument, and made some measurements. Using a tiny pencil, he jotted a few notes, nodded, and stared at the result.

Stefan stared too, clueless.

At last, the astrologer slowly rolled up his charts. He carefully packed away his instruments and closed his bag. "All right."

Stefan scrambled to his feet. "All right? You'll take me there?"

Samir shrugged. "Yes. It seems I am fated to travel with one Drosselmeyer or another. I cannot argue with the stars."

Stefan took a deep breath, filling himself with purpose. "Right. Then we'll have to get horses," he said. "I don't see us carrying all of this for more than a mile or two."

Samir knelt beside his case. "Well, these are yours now. It's time you learned how to use them."

He opened the first case. It collapsed into two neat rectangles. "Help me with the legs," the astrologer said.

Stefan stared at the box. "Legs? We've been carrying around picnic tables?"

"Not that kind of leg," Samir said, and unfolded a section of the box. It was sleek, black, and curved, and ended in a hoof.

"What the devil is that?" Stefan asked.

Samir scowled. "Pay attention. Legs!"

He bent to the task of unfolding two more legs while Stefan, a bit belatedly, addressed the fourth.

"There. Now help me turn her over." Squatting to get their fingers beneath the rest of the box, they gently rotated the whole affair so that it sat on top of the hooves, looking for all the world like a tall, unattractive desk.

"Oh." The puzzle clicked into place. Stefan shook his head in admiration. "Very clever."

"'Magnificent' was the word I used when I first saw them," Samir said. He helped Stefan open the second box. When both "tables" were set up, Samir pulled a winding key from along the inside of the box, adorned with a long plume of horsehair.

"If you would?" He indicated Stefan do the same. Stefan hurried to the end of the second box and found his own plumed key. "Insert here and twist like so . . ." Samir demonstrated.

Stefan pushed the key into a waiting slot and gave it a twist. The crank of gears increasing in tension greeted him and he grinned. It was like his little wind-up bird, on a much grander scale.

The "tabletops" accordioned upward, like a bellows filling with air.

"Now counterclockwise," Samir said. Stefan followed along, twisting the key three times in the opposite direction. "Now, step back."

Stefan did as he was told.

The cases bloomed into horses. The tails, for that is what the keys resembled, unwound slowly and a series of hydraulics and hidden gears lifted each box, plumping it up into the shape of a body. A head cleverly unfolded from the front of each case and flipped itself forward onto a neck that extended to the correct length and height. The mane fell over the neck in a cascade of black. The horses appeared to breathe as the bellows that opened them filled out the lines creased into their sides from

192

storage. Each animal snorted a fine puff of dust and stamped experimentally on four metal hooves before coming to a rest.

Two black stallions, as real to the eye as any horse, stood before him. Their unnatural stillness was the only sign that they were not real.

"Incredible," Stefan said. He circled the horses. "And they run on . . . steam?"

"Perpetual motion and winding. Christian can . . ." Samir faltered and cleared his throat. "Could have . . . explained it to you better than I."

Stefan's eyes stung as he blinked away sudden tears. "Well, I'll have to teach myself. I hope I do as well with my own inventions someday."

He secured his bags across the back of the nearest horse and mounted. He smiled as the stallion gave slightly beneath his weight. It was soft but firm, like sitting on a cushion of air.

Samir beamed back. "You did not think we could ride the world for seven years without *some* comforts, after all?"

Small comforts were all they had left.

Stefan settled gratefully into the saddle and experimentally kicked his heels. The horse responded as naturally as a real one might, striding forward at his touch. The beast was guided by slight pressures on the reins and withers.

Samir assured him they could go at greater speeds than the best horses, as long as their gears were maintained.

"In that case, lead on, with all speed." Another click of his heels, and they were on their way, to seek fortune or ruin among the squirrels.

32

THE QUEEN WAS IN BED. "Come closer," she said, her voice so worn that it was nearly unrecognizable.

Arthur and his brothers edged closer. Every week, they were brought before Her Majesty, for inspection and a progress report. There was war waiting to be waged on the King Above. When would they be ready?

The Queen of Mice looked her brood up and down through tiny pince-nez glasses, her gaze lingering on Julius. Disappointment creased her face, making Arthur feel self-conscious. Not all of her sons had thrived. She made Arthur feel as if it was somehow his fault.

"Tutor, what dost thee think?" she asked.

Ernst Listz snapped to attention. "They acquit themselves well, Majesty. Languages, history, tactics, philosophy—"

"Yes, yes," she said, testily cutting off the list of accomplishments. She pounded her small fist on the coverlet. "But will they *fight*?"

Arthur winced. A ripple of fear ran through his brothers, adrenaline pumped by one anxious heart. He had worked so hard to please her. They all had.

Unbidden, the sound of the Drosselmeyer's misery for his own son echoed in Arthur's mind. Was this the difference between mice and men, or mothers and fathers? Or royalty, even? Did his mother simply not know how to love?

"We will fight, Mother," they said in unison, filled with a brief rush of solidarity. For the first time, Arthur was glad to have brothers around him.

Stuffed in against the cushions, their mother quirked a small smile that quickly faded. She was in such poor health these days, bloated as an overripe plum.

The midwives no longer whispered of unwholesome dark magic. Most mice thought her sorceries had been well worth the cost. But guilt rattled through Arthur's heart over her diminished state. He wanted to stay by her side and hold her paw. But her only comfort was in seeing her mouselings become fierce mice.

"Regard thy mother well, young ones," the Queen seethed. "All of this is for you. Kingdoms await . . . kingdoms." Her yellowed eyes rolled in her head, then closed, and she slipped into sleep.

The brothers stood for a moment, unsure if she was still awake. Unwilling to leave if she was. Arthur wondered—not for the first time—how she could make him feel so precious and yet so afraid.

The captive Drosselmeyer had been in the dungeons for weeks, drawing up plans, carrying out the orders of his mother and her generals. Arthur had stayed away, disturbed by the smell of the man, a tang of fear and sorrow. But no longer. He would do something to make her proud.

Fighting Charlemagne's urge to pull back, Arthur leaned over his mother and pressed his cheek to hers, forcing his brothers to do the same. Hannibal whispered warlike promises into her ear. Arthur hummed a little tune—something his mother used to sing when they were young.

The Queen's eyelids fluttered open. She smiled up at them, warming Arthur from nose to tail.

"My beautiful sons," the Queen said. "My beautiful boys."

"SHE'S DYING," ARTHUR DECLARED when they reached the study room.

Ernst Listz shrugged eloquently. "We all have our season, I'm afraid."

The princes were silent for a long moment.

"And the siege engine?" Charlemagne asked. "We must move sooner."

"Not ready just yet," Ernst said. "This 'Drosselmeyer'"—he said the word as if it were a foreign taste on his tongue—"is not motivated by our schedule. He works, and then stops."

"Stops to do what?" Hannibal asked.

"Nothing, as far as we can tell."

"Perhaps he is afraid," Alexander surmised. "He fears for his life."

"Good!" That was Genghis, crowing triumphantly. "Let the man fear us! He can spread the word to his kind that we are not to be ignored."

"Very clever," Charlemagne snapped. "Set him free to *warn* them. Have you not listened to anything Herr Listz has taught us? The tsars of Russia knew best—blind him, so he may never see to draw these plans again. Cut out his tongue, so he may not speak of it. Maim him so he may not write what he has seen."

"Why not just kill him?" Hannibal asked. "We can figure the rest out ourselves."

Each of them knew it was a lie. Mice were experts in plunder, not construction.

Arthur ignored his brothers. He studied a set of copied blueprints, identical to the Drosselmeyer's larger ones. Yes, the man was afraid. But there was something more.

"I think he's lonely," Arthur ventured.

He had to say it twice before Hannibal and Genghis stopped their bickering.

"He's what?" Hannibal snapped. "That's ridiculous. He's our prisoner! What do we care if he is *lonely?*"

Arthur put the paper down and lifted the hand mirror they'd begun wearing on a chain around their neck, so he could look his brothers in the eye. They quieted, as they always did when one of them used the mirror, appalled into silence at the sight of their own deformity. It was easy to imagine themselves normal, if a little crowded, until they saw all those eyes, all those mouths, gaping back at them.

"It matters because the beast that despairs does not work. It dies. It's common among birds—swans and eagles perish when they lose their mates. We've separated him from his young, and intelligence tells us his mate is dead. He's lonely . . ." Arthur faced himself in the mirror, greeted the stares and glares of his brothers straight on. He sighed audibly. As usual, they did not follow his way of thinking. "Which means . . . he will *die*. And *almost* finished is not the same as being done."

"Yes . . . of course," Charlemagne acknowledged slowly. "But . . . what can we do about it?"

Their reflection blinked back in bewilderment.

Arthur dropped the mirror and turned to his tutor.

"I imagine none of you has ever felt alone," Ernst said. He glanced at Arthur and hesitated. "Most of you, that is," he amended.

Arthur smiled, pleased to be understood, if only a little.

"I'd suggest . . . some reconnaissance," the tutor continued. "Get to know the toymaker. Learn what he pines for. And then, if we are able, give him what he wants."

Arthur nodded before his brothers could protest. "Yes. *We* will speak to him. I'll attempt to befriend him. The rest of you can observe," he quickly added, "and learn his weaknesses. They may be of use in facing his cousin."

Arthur bit his tongue. He'd almost given away his sympathies for the toymaker, but his brothers were too self-absorbed to notice.

SMOOTH AS THE clockwork horses were, between riding all day and sleeping on the ground at night, Stefan was so bruised and stiff by the end of the week he was sure his bones would break. And yet, he would not let it stop him. While the sun shone, he rode as if the devil were at his back. At night, he slept the sleep of the dead. That in itself was a blessing, for it kept bad dreams away.

"We'll stop here for the night," Samir announced early one evening. "Here" was a hilltop above a rolling meadow. The sun was fading behind a crest of trees that gave shelter, if not warmth. Stefan spread out his bedroll, and after a simple supper of hard bread and cheese, quickly fell asleep.

It wasn't until hours later, when nature called, that he woke to find Samir with his telescope out. But this time, instead of having it pointed up at the stars, he was looking out across the landscape.

Stefan's heart somersaulted into his throat. "What's wrong?"

"Come and see for yourself." The astrologer waved him over.

Stefan put his eye to the glass.

In the meadow below, two armies were locked in battle.

"Is that . . . ?"

"The Prussian army," Samir confirmed.

Stefan pulled away from the spyglass, tilted by the same

sense of vertigo he'd felt beneath the gears of the City Clock. How had he forgotten the world of men was still at war?

From this distance, they looked like toy soldiers on a felt-top table, laid out in the same geometric formations Stefan and his father used in their mock battles. But this was different.

A soft snapping sound filled the night. "What was that?" Stefan asked, breathless.

"Gunfire. They're using muskets. Rifles. Cannon, too, no doubt. Only those mountains keep the sound from being deafening," the astrologer said.

Stefan could just make out the shapes of the Prussian soldiers' shakos—tall, black felt hats with short visors. He steadied himself and once again pressed the cold brass to his eye. Through the spyglass he could see the gold braid, the brass buttons on their uniforms, twinkling in the moonlight. Stefan had painted countless such rows down the tin jackets of soldiers in his father's shop.

"And to the south . . ." He turned the spyglass as he spoke. Strange silhouettes resolved into wide pantaloons and a variety of oddly peaked soft caps.

"The Turks," Samir confirmed.

"The Ottoman Empire?" Stefan could hardly believe it. Such skirmishes had been going on for longer than he'd been alive—the Serbians fought the Turks for independence; the Austro-Hungarian Empire fought for land. The deposed Emperor Napoleon had fought to rule all of Europe and failed.

The coffeehouses and biergartens of Nuremberg were full of talk. About the war, about the Treaty of Vienna. Local newspapers doggedly followed the latest strife. But it had always been so distant to Stefan, just stories and tin men on the table in the toyshop. Now it was in front of him—screaming horses, shouting men, and the stench of gunpowder in the air. Tiny men fell in puffs of smoke and did not rise again. This was war.

"Will they come close to us?" Stefan's voice was small.

"No. We were wise to keep to the trees." Samir took back the spyglass. "This is merely a skirmish. With luck, they will be gone by tomorrow, since our path lies on the far side, beyond those hills."

It was one thing to read about battlefields, quite another to walk through one like a carrion crow sifting through the dead.

Samir grimaced. "Perhaps you should not have seen this. One is never old enough to see war." He placed the glass back in its case. "The stars will tell me nothing more tonight. We should both get some rest."

Reluctantly, Stefan agreed. He did not think he would be able to sleep, but his lids grew heavy swiftly and he did.

IN THE MORNING, the armies were gone, but their dead remained.

"Will they come back for them?" Stefan asked.

"Yes, with wagons," Samir replied. They picked their way along the edge of the battleground. "We must make it into the foothills before then."

The mechanical horses moved steadily along the edge of the battleground, weaving a path through the fallen soldiers and abandoned guns. High in his saddle, Stefan stared at the carnage on the field. To his left, a boy not much older than him lay faceup beside his bayonet, the red uniform like a second terrible wound on his pale, cold skin.

"Father never gives them wounds," Stefan said, wiping his eyes. Tin soldiers might break, but they never died.

"We'd best be gone before either side returns," Samir suggested. They kicked in their heels and did not look back.

34

"HERR DROSSELMEYER?" said a tremulous voice.

Zacharias sat up with a start. He reached for his carving knife to defend himself, and strained his ears.

The ridiculous toy he'd been creating sat abandoned in the middle of his cell. Work was no longer a solace. His captors had made no attempt to engage him, and they had told him nothing of Stefan. He'd laid down his tools in protest, but defiance had turned to despair. Now his voice was hoarse and rusty with disuse.

"Who's there?" he croaked.

"Don't be afraid," the small voice said in perfect German. It was a child's, perhaps, for it was soft and high, and came from somewhere mid-height along the far wall.

"Why shouldn't I be?" Zacharias asked. "I am kept here against my will with no knowledge of my son. I am very much afraid."

"Then, don't be afraid of me," the voice said.

"Who are you? Show yourself."

"I cannot. But you may call me Arthur."

Zacharias closed his eyes. It was so good to hear a human voice. He'd half feared he'd gone deaf, so profound had been the silence of his cell.

"Hello, Arthur. How do you know my name?"

"That doesn't matter, does it?"

"It does to me," Zacharias said. He had to keep the boy talking. Maybe he could persuade him to open the door. Suddenly, a horrible thought struck him. "Are you a prisoner here, too?"

The voice hesitated. "Of a sort."

"You live here, then?"

"Yes."

"I see," Zacharias said softly. "Not a very nice place for a child to grow up."

"What do you know?" the voice spat. Zacharias recoiled. It sounded like the same voice, but not the same tone. Had the boy brought a friend?

"I'm sorry, I meant no offense," Zacharias said quickly. "Only, I've seen nothing more than this cell."

There was scuffling and then a long silence.

"Arthur? Are you still there?" Another long silence.

"Yes."

"It's nice to talk to someone. It's one of the things I miss down here. Work—even work you love—is not enough to keep a person alive," he said sadly. But there was also something sad about an unfinished toy, even in these circumstances. Like the boy on the other side of this prison wall, a life not given the chance to truly live.

"What are you working on?" Arthur asked.

"I'm not sure, to tell you the truth. A toy soldier, but he's much too large for any child's play." He pulled himself to his feet, his joints popping as he stretched his limbs; it was the most he'd moved in days.

"I suspect it's by royal request." In the silence of his cell,

Zacharias had thought a great deal about his captivity. The long trip and the dungeon had at last convinced him. He must be in Boldavia. The king had kidnapped and imprisoned him, perhaps to punish Christian.

"Why?" Arthur asked.

Zacharias shrugged. "I only half understand the circumstances. But normal houses do not have dungeons, Arthur. Who else would live in a castle, but a king?"

"A queen," Arthur said, but his voice was bigger somehow, as if more than one person had spoken. Zacharias put a finger in his ear and jiggled it. The cold must be getting to him, or the sound was affected by the thickness of the stones.

"Why didn't you finish?" Arthur demanded. Or, perhaps this was no longer Arthur. Zacharias felt his forehead. Did he have a fever? His hands were too cold to tell.

"Because toys should be made out of joy, or there will be no joy in playing with them. I am too sad."

"Why are you sad?"

Zacharias sat at the desk again. The blueprints looked back at him accusingly, unfulfilled. "Because I have a son, Arthur, a little older than you, by the sound of it. I don't know where he is, and he doesn't know where I am. My wife . . . his mother, she passed away recently. A boy shouldn't have to face that alone." He fell silent, sinking again into despair. He'd left his son all alone. "I'm sorry, Arthur. I don't feel like talking much anymore. Perhaps you will come again?"

There was some whispering. The boy was definitely not alone.

"Arthur, who's with you? Don't get yourself in trouble by talking to me."

"I won't," the boy said. "But . . . Herr Drosselmeyer?"

Zacharias's head was beginning to hurt, and the straw bed was calling to him, telling him to lie down and never get up again. "Yes?" he managed to say.

"I like toys," Arthur whispered. "I'd very much like to see what you've made."

The construct was little more than a framework now, the bones of a person, weighted pulleys at the joints, cables running down the spine. It would take a clever puppeteer to manipulate it, but one day the soldier would walk and even hold a sword.

"I confess I'm curious to see it myself," Zacharias admitted at last. His sorrow receded just a little. Just enough.

"Will you finish it?" Arthur asked. "Please?"

Maybe because the boy reminded him of Stefan, or maybe it was simply that a child was asking, but Zacharias nodded. "Will you come back to visit me? If it is safe?"

Only a slight hesitation, then, "Yes."

Zacharias smiled, lifted on a strange wave of relief.

"Then I will build it," he agreed.

"Thank you," Arthur whispered.

In the silence that followed, Zacharias knew he was gone. He rose and pressed his ear against the wall, searching it with both candlelight and fingers for the crevice that allowed the boy to speak to him. He found nothing. Both heartened and disturbed, he returned to his desk. Picking up his carving knife, he went back to work.

35

STEFAN FOLLOWED SAMIR across a wide, flat grassland, like a tundra in summertime, but the rain was coming down, hard, wet, and cold. As far as he could tell, they were lost. They had passed no towns or villages for almost a fortnight.

By evening, the rain had lightened into a mist. There was no wood to make a fire, but Stefan doubted it would have stayed lit anyway. Samir helped him drape waxed canvas over the horses—standing still in the rain caused more damage to the clockworks than when they were in motion.

Stefan patted his pockets. He could feel the casket containing the nut, his notebook, parts of a new wooden dove, and Clara's handkerchief deep inside. They were all he had left in the world. He crawled under the belly of his mechanical horse. The canvas formed a tent that made things almost comfortable. At least he was out of the weather. He quickly fell asleep.

HE WAS HOME AGAIN, in his own soft bed in the loft above the shop on Kleinestrasse. Shadows played in the eaves above his head. He could hear them. Breathing.

Stefan threw back the covers. The shadows lunged. He screamed. Darkness reached out and grabbed him, tugging at his sleeve.

Stefan tugged back. There it was again—tug, tug. Annoyed, he yanked his arm across his chest and rolled over.

"Tsk, tsk, tsk," someone said.

Stefan sat up so fast, he hit his head on the bottom of his horse. Something was standing next to him. *Mice!*

Stefan shrieked and scooted out of his makeshift tent, backpedaling with the heels of his boots and hands.

The sun had not yet risen, but there was light enough to see by.

"What's happened?" Samir crawled out from under his own horse-tent, turban half wrapped, eyes wide.

"Mouse! Mouse!" Stefan pointed wildly at his horse. It had been tugging at his sleeve! He patted his arm, but he was unbitten. What if it had gone through his pockets?

The canvas brushed aside and a small reddish squirrel with giant tufted ears emerged from beneath the horse. Stefan froze, his heart thudding madly.

The squirrel looked at him, then Samir. It raised its delicate black nose to sniff the air, then turned toward Stefan. And charged.

Stefan screamed, an embarrassingly high-pitched squeal as he fell backward, struggling to get away from the attacking ball of fur.

"He's looking for the nut!" Samir cried.

Stefan batted at the squirrel on his chest, terrified of those long, sharp teeth. Equally afraid the little beast would burrow into his pockets and find the *krakatook*.

"Stop!" Samir thundered. He stood up and barked three sharp, high yelps.

He's been bitten, Stefan thought. Samir had gone rabid.

But the squirrel stopped. It chittered at Samir. Samir chittered back, no longer yelling.

The squirrel looked at Stefan, who hesitated unsteadily on his palms and heels like an awkward crab. Abashedly, the squirrel straightened Stefan's collar before climbing off him.

Samir let out an explosive sigh.

"Stefan. This is—" he made a *snicking* sound around the side of his tongue. "He apologizes for the attack. It appears the scent of the *krakatook* drew him here."

"That's impossible," Stefan said. "It's sealed in its box." He patted his pockets and pulled out the silver casket. The latch had slipped, probably from sleeping on top of it. The *krakatook* had rolled out of the case and into his rain-damp pocket.

"Oh, no."

The squirrel's eyes bulged at the sight of the nut.

"Stefan, put it away!" Samir thundered.

Stefan shoved the nut back into its case. The squirrel quivered, but relaxed.

Stefan eyed him dubiously. "You speak his language?"

"I've been a guest of the squirrels more than once over the years. I'm hardly fluent, though. It's a branch of High Rodentia," he explained. "The way French and Italian share Latin roots. Come." He helped Stefan to his feet. "He will escort us the rest of the way."

Stefan began to dust himself off, only to realize that the dust had turned to mud in the rain. "Maybe I was wrong about the squirrels, Samir. How can we trust him? Did you see those teeth!"

"I did," Samir said. "And I tried to warn you this might not be a good idea. But I've invoked the name of the Pater. We have safe passage for the time being. Let's not try our luck."

Stefan went through the saddlebags until he found the stick of sealing wax Christian used to seal his letters. Striking a flint to a fairly dry piece of tinder, he was finally able to melt the end of the wax stick and use it to seal the nut's casket shut. He hoped it would be enough to keep other rodents away.

They broke their meager camp and mounted the horses. The squirrel opted to stay on foot. He disappeared over the grassland, rising up every once in a while to look back and wait for them to catch up.

"We're not far now," Samir said confidently. "Just remember what Christian told you. 'Keep your eyes opened and your mouth closed.' As you've seen, our hosts will be rather skittish. We must be respectful."

They rode the rest of the way in silence. Stefan struggled to remember the argument he had constructed, the clever way he would induce the squirrels to help them. But all he could see were those sharp yellow teeth and bright black eyes. As if the dreams he'd been having weren't bad enough.

The gray day turned into a dim evening. At last, their guide mounted the top of a rise, chittered in an authoritative way, and scampered off over the hill.

A small forest rose above the plain. The squirrel led them into the woods, which grew deeper and taller with each passing moment.

When they finally stopped, they were confronted with a ring of trees. Stefan glimpsed a clearing up ahead. The squirrel scampered up to Samir's horse, chittering rapidly.

"We'll leave the horses here," the astrologer announced. He

unrolled the waxed canvas again, and covered the steed from the worst of the rain.

Bewildered, Stefan dismounted and draped his horse, too.

Following the squirrel into the clearing, it felt like they were entering a town, or a small city. But it was neither.

"The Pagoda Tree," Samir said with satisfaction.

It was a giant tree, shaped by the wind into a towering Asiatic palace, as if an entire city had grown upward instead of out. Little lights shone in the hollows of the tree, and every gnarled branch was planed smooth by a wide avenue of activity, sheltered by broad leaves, and teeming with life. With squirrels.

"The Pater is waiting," Samir said.

Ignoring the astrologer's advice, Stefan entered the squirrel city with both his eyes and his mouth wide open. He resisted the urge to feel for the silver box inside his coat. The wax seal seemed to have helped. At least no other squirrels had attacked him. Yet.

Stefan was surprised to find that he didn't need to bend down to pass through the main door, which was nearly twice his height, and cleverly concealed within the rough bark of the tree. The passageway inside was almost as high.

"They have a variety of guests here," Samir explained. "This tree was once merely an outpost for trade with the squirrels of Asia. But, as you can see, it has grown into a renowned center of knowledge for scholars worldwide."

Stefan doubted anyone at the University of Nuremberg knew about this place. He turned the corner, and was met with a wall of tapestries—four woven portraits of the Pagoda Tree hung from branches grafted high along the inner walls.

"The four seasons," Samir explained. "A gift from the King of Dates."

Stefan balked. "He's a talking fruit?"

"Not at all," Samir laughed. "He is as human as you or me. His kingdom is in Persia, between the Tigris and Euphrates."

"Ah, I see," Stefan said, hiding his embarrassment. There was so much he didn't know about the world. When this was all over, he would buy himself a map.

They followed the curved wall, Stefan craning his neck to admire each panel. The summer weaving was a fury of greens against a bright blue sky, the tree in full leaf, like a colorful cloud. The autumn hanging shone beside it, the tree deep green against a forest of copper and gold. The winter tapestry was done in silver, brown, and white, as snow gilded every leaf and branch.

"Does it never lose its leaves?" Stefan asked.

"Ah, you've noticed. It does, but never without another one taking its place. The new shoots literally push the old ones off the branch. Eternal youth, and yet"—he tapped the strong brown trunk in the last tapestry—"the wisdom of the ages."

The final hanging, spring, showed the clearing around the tree awash in yellow and red tulips like great strokes of a paintbrush.

Stefan's heart twinged at the sight. "My mother would have loved this," he said, brushing his fingers along the flowers. They were so vibrant, he half expected to smell their green, growing scent. "Clara, too," he said without thinking.

"Clara?" Samir asked.

Stefan shook his head. "Just a girl I met back home." What would she make of the industrious squirrels and the smooth yellow walls of living wood? He decided to draw a sketch of each wall hanging to share with her when he returned.

Little torches lined the corridor, lighting the inside of the main hall with a buttery glow. On closer inspection, Stefan realized they were not candles, as they had first appeared, but fireflies, darting among the tender leafy shoots growing out of the walls.

The Pagoda Tree was alive in every sense of the word. The hall was flooded with traffic, squirrels carrying nuts and rolls of dried-leaf parchment, barely giving the humans a second glance as they scurried by. Stefan imagined it was like a human government office, with couriers and clerks racing back and forth. Doorways of varying sizes branched off from the main hallway, which Stefan now realized was curving upward. At each new level appeared several passageways so low that Stefan had to stoop to look down them. These tunnels led out into the open air—the limbs of the tree held the treetop highways Stefan had seen from outside.

"The human quarters are down here, in the larger trunk of the tree." Samir pointed to man-sized doors as they passed.

"Humans live here?" Stefan was amazed.

"Certainly," Samir replied. "They come to study, or to trade. The squirrels do a healthy business with nuts. The commerce gives them the tools they need to deal with the outside world."

Stefan's head spun. "But, who would do business with

squirrels?" He imagined a young squirrel coming to buy nut-crackers from his father's shop.

"The man who can get us in to see the Pater, among others," Samir replied. "Almande. The King of Almonds."

"First a king of dates, and now an almond king?" Stefan said wryly.

"Not *an* almond king, *the* Almond King," Samir corrected him. "From the country of Morocco, on the northern coast of Africa. I've known him for many years. Our guide tells me Almande is here on his annual trade route. By the season, I'd say we've just missed Al'a Palmir, the King of Dates. I have a nephew who lives in his court," Samir said proudly. "Lovely country, plenty of shade. Without Almande's help, we would have to wait weeks or longer to see the Pater, who is very busy and does not interrupt his studies often."

"And the Pater can tell us how——"

Samir waved him to silence. "Squirrels have very good ears," the astrologer whispered.

Their guide squirrel had led them to a great set of double doors and was watching them curiously. Stefan remembered his cousin's request—mouth closed, eyes open—and complied.

The squirrel turned to Samir and chattered hurriedly. "Ah," Samir said, "we're in luck. The king's entertainment is about to begin in the audience chamber."

As if on cue, the doors swung open onto a hollow in the heart of the tree.

Stefan caught his breath. The room before him was as large as a barn, and shaped like a giant round bowl of honey-colored wood. Glowworm lights hung in clusters from vines dangling from the ceiling, like natural chandeliers. A bole in the tree—a natural hole in the wood—had been shellacked over in amber tree sap to form a giant window. Starlight gently illuminated the rest of the room. Along the floor, the wood rose in ridges, forming benches. On each tier sat rows of squirrels, resting their fretful elbows on the wood.

Their guide led them to empty seating toward the middle of the hall, where the wooden resting ledges had been coaxed to human height. Pressing his paws together, the red squirrel gave a little bow, and departed.

Following Samir's lead, Stefan lowered himself, cross-legged, to the floor. He opened his mouth to speak, but suddenly a drum sounded, like a great thunderclap. In the center of the room stood a large, broad-chested man. His skin was darker than Samir's, from sun or from birth, Stefan couldn't tell. This must be a true Moor.

The man smiled broadly at his audience, white teeth like pearls in the coffee expanse of his face. On his head he wore a shimmering turban, like Samir's, but made of a gorgeous striped cloth of many colors: gold, pale red, pine green, purple, and peacock blue. He wore pantaloons to match, curled-toed slippers, and a gold-trimmed vest.

"Is this the king?" Stefan asked.

Samir chuckled. "No. Only a performer. The king is over there. And that is the Pater beside him." The astrologer pointed to the left of the stage, where an ancient squirrel rested on a cushion beside another human, not as darkly handsome as the man on the floor, yet more regal-looking in a pure white turban and kaftan. His legs were all but invisible beneath the drape of his cloak. His dark hands were bedecked with golden rings, and his beard was carefully trimmed to a point that curled slightly, like the performer's slippers.

King Almande scanned the audience. Catching sight of Samir and Stefan's wide-eyed stare, he smiled and tilted his head, his hand making a series of waterfall movements from the forehead downward. Samir repeated the gesture.

"What does that mean, Samir?" Stefan whispered.

"It is a blessing, asking God to grant you peace."

Stefan rested back against the bench. He was torn between wanting to lie down and sleep for a year, and getting quickly on their way to Boldavia. Here he was in a court of wonders and all he could think of was being home again with his father and a cup of Miss Prue's elderflower tonic.

His eyes prickled. He rubbed the sensation away. The Pagoda Tree was fascinating, but he hadn't come here for a show. How long would they be expected to wait before he could speak to the Pater and get some answers?

A cluster of human musicians were seated near the floor. They began to play thin, reedy music on an instrument that Samir called a sitar. A pipe joined in, the thin cry of a lonely crane at the end of summer. Then chimes, a hundred silver bells. The Moor in the rainbow turban clapped his hands once, twice, three times, and began to dance.

Stefan had never seen anything like it. It was like watching a djinn, an Arabian genie, come to life. The music grew wild, a storm of bells and thunder and screaming winds, and the Moor whirled and whirled like a top, spinning in joyful circles around the room. The squirrels watched serenely, as if they had trapped a storm under glass for observation.

Stefan's heart beat faster. Suddenly, the man leapt into the air, turning an impossible arabesque. A second leap, and he pulled his knees into a wide crouch, then sprang sideways and continued along in a circle of crouching spins. The whirling reminded Stefan of the City Clock, a complex spiral of motion.

In spite of himself, Stefan began to clap in time to the music, oblivious to the incredible calm of the squirrel audience, to anything but the stunning display of acrobatics. The man spun round and round, a circular metronome. Stefan could hear his own breath in counterpoint to the music, the beat of his heart thumping the rhythm. Was there a City Clock under the Pagoda Tree? he wondered. Whatever the case, Stefan knew that he had been pulled into synchronicity with *something*.

With a crash of bells, the music ended, and the dancer landed on his knees, forehead pressed to the ground before his king and host. The ancient squirrel, the Pater, clapped his tiny forepaws politely, and bowed to King Almande.

Stefan was breathless. "How do they do it?"

"King Almande's dancers train for many years," Samir told him.

"Not the dancer. The squirrels. They're so . . . calm. I feel like I've run a race, and they look like they're having tea."

"These squirrels are an enlightened group. They study, they observe, but they do not participate. Squirrels have one of two goals in life—to find a *krakatook* to bring them longevity and insight, or to be invited to study at the Pagoda Tree. A longer path to wisdom, but a more likely one."

Stefan frowned. "Enlightenment looks boring."

Samir shrugged. "After all those years frantically looking for nuts—they deserve a little peace and quiet, don't you think?"

A soft breeze rose in the hall as doors around the room opened. Samir rose to his feet. "Perhaps now we can gain an audience with King Almande."

36

THE TOYMAKER WAS NOT at all what Arthur had expected. As promised, he and his brothers had returned several times, and each time there was progress on the toy soldier, as the Drosselmeyer called it.

But these visits had disturbed something deep inside Arthur. After all, the princes had never known their father. There were rumors, of course—one of the palace guards, a piebald, or other such scandals. And worse. There was talk of dark magic. Whatever the truth, Arthur found himself longing for what he'd never had.

It was a weakness. One he was trying to amend. Each visit should have strengthened his resolve, but it had the opposite effect. He *liked* Zacharias Drosselmeyer. And that was the highest treason.

This morning, after their mother's daily inspection and Ernst's lessons, Arthur took a book and candle down to the river that ran beneath the city. It was a good, quiet place to read where his mother's piebalds rarely sent for him, and his brothers would often grow bored and fall asleep, leaving him in peace.

Already the others snored softly, crowding around him, lulled by the rush of the river. Arthur wanted to talk. But to whom? His mother would call him weak. The court advisers would read it as a sign, and his brothers refused to speak about it: Arthur was having bad dreams.

He was the only one of the brothers to suffer from them, as far as he could tell. Ever since the toymaker had come to Boldavia, he'd been wracked with restless nights. Only now, having spoken with the captive Drosselmeyer, did he start to understand his nightmares. He would like to share the insight with his tutor. The old rat had seen much of the world. Maybe he could make sense of it, or at least disperse Arthur's fears. But, after today's fencing lesson, the rat had requested time away to heal his wounds. Arthur knew that he and his brothers would not be welcome, at least for now.

Arthur shuddered, thinking about the darkness of his dreams, and immediately felt sheepish. He held his small candle up to play along the walls of the cavern. Here he was, sitting in a gloomy old cave by choice, and now he was afraid of the dark? But the dark in his dreams was different. It wasn't empty. Something, or someone, was there. If only he had a candle to hold in his dreams to see for himself.

A snort pulled Arthur out of his reverie.

Hannibal had woken up. "Daydreaming again?" he sneered.

"Thinking," Arthur said defensively. "One of us has to."

Hannibal made a face and yawned. "Some of us think *too* much. Action. That's all we need."

"Action," Arthur repeated, bemused. That was his mother talking. Hannibal knew her speeches by heart. Act. Lead. Triumph. The world of Men was theirs for the taking. And Arthur, young Prince Arthur and his brothers, were the ones to do the job.

The thought terrified him. Arthur had only glimpsed the humans from hiding places in the castle above. As the crown princes, they'd been told time and again that their life was not to be risked by gallivanting aboveground. The few men he had seen were enormous, like walking trees, while Arthur and his brothers were so very small. For all of Hannibal's bluster and Roland's demands, Arthur was still just one insignificant mouse.

How different life could have been if he were separate from his brothers! He might have chosen to be a scholar, not forced to read quickly so his brothers didn't get bored. Or to travel! To see the sun shine rather than stay hidden in the walls until some future date known only to his mother and her plans. Had he been born separate, one of the others could have been King and Arthur could have just been . . . Arthur. But he was not.

Hannibal had fallen asleep again, his head nodding off to the side. Now Arthur was getting tired, too. He could feel himself being pulled in by his brothers' slumber. The candle flickered in a light breeze, sputtered for a moment, then shone brighter than ever. The glow gleamed off the rocks and the white rush of the river down below.

It really was quite beautiful, Arthur realized. *Nothing to fear.*

He repeated the thought to himself, humming the refrain to his mother's old lullaby as he lowered the candle and let sleep take him. With sleep, again came the dreams.

37

THE KING OF ALMONDS swept out of the audience chamber with his entourage and stopped in front of Samir and Stefan. The two men greeted one another, standing like rocks in a river, as the squirrels streamed around them in a flood of red, white, black, and brown.

A few brushed up against Stefan as they passed and hesitated, delicate noses twitching, then shook their heads and moved on. Before he could worry about it, Samir was introducing him to his first king.

"Your Majesty," he said, and bowed deeply.

"Another Drosselmeyer?" the king said with amusement. The king had a deep, rich voice that reminded Stefan of an organ at a fair.

"Yes, I am Stefan," he said, rising.

The king came forward and offered his own courtly bow. "Samir tells me Christian is no longer with us. You have my condolences. He was an interesting man to know."

Stefan fumbled for a response, but a sudden surge of grief made him mute. He could only nod.

"But now is not the time for mourning," King Almande continued, not unkindly. "I hear you've made a discovery!"

It took all of Stefan's willpower not to pat his inner pocket, where the *krakatook* lay hidden inside its case.

"You think you can keep such things secret here for long?"

The king laughed. "My nose may not be so keen, but the Pater will smell it on you."

"He needn't guess," Stefan said. "I will tell him myself."

"You have the confidence of a lion." King Almande laughed. "If it's real, what makes you think he'll let you keep it?"

"I'll do my best to convince him." Stefan shrugged. "Then again, if he can open the blasted thing, maybe he deserves it."

The king smiled. "Come join me, young Drosselmeyer, and we shall see."

Almande led his entourage up a long winding pathway that climbed the inner trunk of the tree. His robes flapped behind him in a silken ripple that reminded Stefan of a flying carpet.

Stefan and Samir fell back, allowing the king's people to lead them. From their place at the end of the line, Stefan drank in the sight—women draped in pale, sheer veils of silk, guards bearing scimitars at their sides. It was like a page from his book *Arabian Nights*. He half expected a genie to rise out of one of the glow-worm lamps and offer to grant him a wish. As eager as he was to get to Boldavia, he hoped he would have time to sketch later. Certainly his father would be amazed, and Clara would admire the fine embroidery that edged the women's veils.

As they continued to climb, the number of side tunnels grew smaller. The tree branch highways became narrower until they were almost at the top of the tree.

"Where did the other squirrels go?" Stefan asked Samir.

"They are outside. They climb the trunk of the tree far more swiftly than they could travel these human walkways."

Rounding the last spiral, they came to a dark wooden door, planed smooth and polished to a deep shine. The king's entourage lined either side of the hallway. Stefan and Samir moved forward to stand directly behind the king as he bowed to a little black squirrel that stood outside the door. The squirrel returned the bow and pulled a thin rope beside the door.

A gong sounded overhead. The squirrel bowed again and scampered back down the walkway.

Stefan was sweating, uncomfortably aware of his wet coat and matted hair.

Samir adjusted his turban as if having the same self-conscious thoughts. He gave Stefan a reassuring nod just as the great door before them swung open.

A delicious, spicy scent wafted toward them, warm and inviting. Involuntarily, Stefan took a step forward. He could have kicked himself for stepping in front of the king, until he realized that both Almande and Samir had been drawn forward by the smell, too.

"Sandalwood," Samir murmured, taking a deep breath. "Wonderful."

This was the pinnacle of the Pagoda Tree. The ceiling soared high above them; windows sat high in the crown of the room, revealing small tatters of rain clouds and stars. The windows here were also of hardened tree sap, applied in many layers, yet clear enough to see through.

Despite the lofty ceiling, the room itself was inviting and cozy. The walls and floor were covered in gorgeous crimson and cream oriental rugs. In the center of the room, curled up on a pile of sumptuous pillows, sat the wizened squirrel from the audience hall. His fur was gray as much from age as from natural coloring.

"*Pater* is Latin for 'father,'" Samir whispered to Stefan. "It is the highest office a squirrel can hold."

The Pater began to chitter, his small body quivering beneath the yellow cloth wrapped around his shoulders. Stefan watched as King Almande and Samir bowed deeply to the aged squirrel and quickly followed suit. The Pater nodded and gestured for them to sit.

He turned to King Almande and chittered. The king nodded gravely and chattered back in a close approximation of the squirrel's language. After a moment, the Pater turned his keen brown eyes on Stefan.

"Herr Drosselmeyer," the squirrel said in flawless German. "Is it true, Christian Drosselmeyer is dead?"

Stefan blinked, taken aback both by the novelty of a squirrel speaking German, and by the question. He would never get used to talking animals. "It's true, sir." The aching hollow in his stomach returned. Saying it out loud gave Christian's death more weight.

"A pity. Life was always interesting with that one."

"So I've heard," Stefan replied.

"He will be missed, most certainly," the Pater soothed. "In no small part because where Christian went, the dramatic was sure to follow."

"I can't deny that," Stefan agreed. "I was a toymaker's apprentice when I met my cousin, and now I sit here with Paters and kings."

The Pater laughed, a chittering sound not unlike the squirrels Stefan was used to hearing before all of this began.

The Pater wiped his eyes with the back of a paw. "Even when

the storm has stopped, it does not mean the leaf has landed. For better or worse, we will all feel the effects of Christian Drosselmeyer, perhaps for years to come. Unless things can be set right."

The Pater gave Stefan a curious look. "You have a *krakatook*. But what do you intend to do with it? Eat it yourself? Your years would be greatly extended. Or perhaps you intend to barter with it? What do I have that is worth such a price?"

Stefan cleared his throat.

"The nut is for the Boldavian princess, but I need your help to administer it."

The Pater's shrewd eyes shone in the lamplight. "What cures the child does not cure the nation, young Drosselmeyer. Give the girl the nut, and what is to prevent the Queen from biting her again? You must not think so small," he admonished with a pointed claw.

"Cure the princess, and we'll weaken the Queen's hold on Boldavia," Stefan said. "King Pirlipat hasn't fought back because he's afraid a second bite will kill his daughter. If we cure her, maybe even get her away from Boldavia, he'll turn his army against the mice. He has to!"

"You give the old king too much credit," the Pater said. "Had he been a wise man, he would have seen the threat to his nation long ago."

Stefan stumbled. He'd forgotten that he'd had a similar impression of King Pirliwig from Christian's story. The man couldn't rock his child to sleep; how could he save an entire kingdom?

But he wouldn't worry about that now. Stefan needed to

open the nut. He needed the king's help. Which meant he needed the squirrel. *Think, Stefan, think!*

The Pater clapped his paws and a red squirrel appeared with a tray of tiny clay cups resembling acorns. The ancient squirrel accepted one, removed the cap-like lid, and a scent like sun-dried oak leaves rose to tickle Stefan's nose.

The old squirrel drank deeply, then offered the tray to his guests. Stefan carefully took a cup between two fingers. It was no larger than a thimble, the tea inside barely more than a splash on his tongue, but it tasted of autumn and he was glad when the Pater offered him more. If nothing else, it gave him time to think.

Then the obvious solution came to him.

"Come with us," Stefan said excitedly. "*You* could open the nut and save the princess."

The Pater shook his head sadly. "If I were to open it, I would eat it. It is a compulsion no squirrel can ignore." For a moment, the old squirrel's eyes shimmered. "Two *krakatooks* in one lifetime! Such power is not meant to be." He shuddered, and Stefan finally realized what a huge chance he had taken in coming here. King Almande and Samir had been right. He only kept the nut now because the Pater allowed it.

"I did not realize," he admitted.

The old squirrel sighed. "One cannot balance the world by throwing another kingdom out of place. I could never show myself to the king—what would happen if more men learned of talking squirrels? How safe would we be in our trees if they believed we were hoarding *krakatooks*?"

Stefan's shoulders slumped. He could only imagine the treasure hunt that would ensue—men seeking the mythical cure for everything.

"If the mice found out we squirrels had interfered, the battle would not end, but shift. It might leave the realm of Men for a time, but believe me, you do not wish to see all of Rodentia at war. To put it in terms you might understand, you must learn to see the whole clock and not just the cog," the ancient squirrel explained.

"But they have my father," Stefan said, his voice catching in his throat.

The Pater clucked his tongue, a very squirrel-like sound. "All the more reason to take my advice," he said sorrowfully. "They will not stop, and if they already know you exist, nothing you hold dear is safe."

But Stefan had nothing left that death or the mice hadn't already taken. Then he thought of Clara and her amused smile. His father's workshop, the streets of Nuremberg after a rain. His mother's grave. He imagined it all overrun by mice in a plague of the blackest proportions.

"But if the mice take over, what would happen to squirrels?" Stefan asked. "When men hunt vermin in earnest, they will not care about the shape of their tails. Too many mice means famine for man and beast alike, doesn't it? Or having eaten a *krakatook*, do you no longer require food?"

"Stefan, I must protest—" King Almande began.

But the Pater had not taken offense. He raised a paw for silence.

Stefan held his glittering gaze.

The Pater nodded. While he didn't smile, he did appear to be amused.

"Another Drosselmeyer, indeed. The *krakatook* is a fulcrum. Let us see if we can use it to shift the balance of the world back into place. How may I help?"

Stefan should have been relieved. He was lucky the Pater hadn't already taken the nut, let alone put up with his insolence. But an idea had taken root.

"Squirrels can't smile," he observed.

Samir's patience broke. "Stefan, what nonsense is this?"

"Why can't you smile?" He directed the question to the Pater.

The old squirrel shrugged, his face an inscrutable blank of gray fur and piercing eyes. "Perhaps it does not seem like it to you, but I am smiling even now."

Samir looked astonished. King Almande was clearly confused.

Stefan took out his notebook. "Do you have any nuts?" he asked.

Samir coughed nervously. The Pater blinked. "Certainly." He signaled for the little red squirrel, and a bowl was brought out, full of hazelnuts, acorns, walnuts, and almonds.

Stefan popped a walnut into his mouth and squeezed his jaws tight.

The nut wobbled between his teeth. A thin trickle of drool ran down his chin. He wiped his mouth with Clara's handkerchief and spat the mess out.

He turned to the Pater. "Would you please open one?" he asked.

"Surely this is not necessary," Samir protested.

"I wouldn't do it to waste his time," Stefan said, and immediately winced. He sounded so sure of himself. So much like Christian. "That is, I think this is important." He turned back to the Pater. "You see, we have been unable to open the nut, and I suspect it has something to do with our not being squirrels. Our mouths are not built the same."

The Pater chittered in amusement and selected a walnut. "Do you propose to watch me crack the whole bowl?"

"And sketch your movements—if I may?" he said, producing a pencil.

The Pater nodded and opened his jaws, placing the golden nut squarely between his small teeth. With barely a shudder, he closed his mouth a fraction, and the nut's halves fell neatly into his lap.

Stefan produced a pencil. "Again, please."

The Pater obliged. Eventually, all of the nuts were open. Their meats lay cleanly in the bowl, so unlike the pasty messes they'd made pounding test nuts on the *Gray Goose*.

"Anything else?" the Pater asked.

Stefan regarded the gray squirrel's jaws. Like the mechanics of the wooden dove, he strove to see the clockwork beneath the skin. His hands twitched. "May I . . ." He flushed. "May I touch your jaw, and ask you to open your mouth?"

The attendant squirrel squealed in dismay. "Sire, this is beyond the pale, surely," he chittered in German, so Stefan would understand.

"Stefan, we have taken enough of our host's time. Let us find another way," Samir pleaded.

"No!" Stefan said urgently. "This is the only way. I've thought of little else since Christian fell. We must crack this nut. And the answer is here, Samir. Only a man can cure the princess, but only a squirrel can open the nut. Unless . . . unless we make the world different than it is." He turned to the Pater. "If not you, then maybe one of the others? I merely need a model—" He stopped in midsentence. The Pater was looking at his notebook where it lay open in his lap.

"Do I truly look like this?" he asked.

It was a fair likeness of the hoary-furred creature, except his cheeks were removed in the drawings, showing the inner workings of tooth and tongue. Stefan had already begun sketching a second study, laying in the gears and levers that would replace bone and sinew, but it was guesswork unless the squirrel would give him a closer look.

"I imagine so," he replied. "But we need more than my imagination if we're going to succeed."

The squirrel rose from his cushions and came around to Stefan's side. Studying the images before him, he tilted his head for the best light, and opened his pink mouth wide.

"Thank you, thank you," Stefan murmured. His pencil flew across the page. The little red squirrel buried his face in his paws.

Stefan might have been rude and uncouth—he was clearly breaking protocol according to the squirrels—but an idea was taking shape in his head and he was sure it would succeed.

If a squirrel's mouth was best suited to opening nuts, then he would make himself a new set of teeth. He would become a squirrel.

38

THE TOY SOLDIER was finished. Zacharias examined it in the dull glow of his lantern. The smell of paint still hung in the air. Blue, black, white, and gold, the soldier's uniform gleamed wetly in the light. He sat down at the desk and put his head in his hands.

"Herr Drosselmeyer?"

Like clockwork, the boy had returned.

Zacharais rubbed his eyes and tried to sound jolly. "Ah! There you are, my boy."

"How is the work today?"

Zacharias was glad Arthur could not see his haggard face. "Do you know the story of Ulysses?"

"The Greek myth?" Arthur asked.

Not for the first time, Zacharias marveled at the depth of education given to this jailer's son. "Yes. Ulysses set sail for Troy and fought a ten-year war. It took him another ten years to find his way back home. In the meantime, his wife, Penelope, stayed true to him."

"She knew he was alive?"

"No, but she had hope. There were suitors lining up to marry her, but she put them off. She told the men she was weaving a marriage blanket, and only when it was finished would she choose a new husband. But, secretly, each night, she would un-ravel some of the work she had done during the day, and so she wove for ten long years without finish, and thus held off her fate until her husband returned."

Arthur was not like other boys his age, demanding to hear the heroic adventures of Ulysses and his men. Instead he said, "And you are Penelope?"

Zacharias chuckled. "I'm not so clever, my boy. The soldier is done. I fear my fate must soon arrive. And Ulysses is still lost at sea."

39

"HOW IS IT COMING ALONG?" Samir asked one morning.

Three days ago they'd left the miraculous Pagoda Tree with the Pater's blessing and ridden south for Boldavia. Necessity and nightmares drove Stefan in equal measure. Something was haunting his sleep. In daylight, he could recall nothing. But at night, his dreams swallowed him whole. And so he concentrated on the problem of the nut.

In another four days, they'd be at the enemy stronghold. Stefan had set his horse at a smooth gait that allowed him to work on his new invention as they traveled.

Squirrel teeth, he called them, or *dentata*. Samir called them a nutcracker.

Stefan held up the teeth, carved from a piece of ash tree that he'd hardened with fire. They were oversized, two U-shaped plates with channels inside to make room for Stefan's own teeth. Once fitted to the upper and lower jaw, the sharp incisors carved into the front appeared close to natural—for a squirrel, at least. The two long teeth acted as both vise and tiny chisel to pry the seam of the nut open.

He pulled out his handkerchief and opened his mouth, popping the false teeth in. There were small gears inside that he had culled from the clockmaking kit he found in Christian's bag. Each time he opened his mouth, a piston would shift, clicking over into a new gear, increasing the pressure of his bite.

The "teeth" had additional pads carved into them that lined up along the seam of the test walnuts (a gift from the Pater), to place added pressure on the nut's weak spot.

Stefan had learned from his session with the Pater that a squirrel jaw was much narrower than a human's and exerted more than fifty times the pressure in each bite. To achieve the same power, Stefan gnashed his "teeth" five or six times, as if he were priming a pump to bring water to the surface.

He grinned at Samir, gnashing his teeth.

"A ghastly sight," the astrologer said. "But quite clever. Christian, himself, might never have thought of such a thing."

Stefan pulled the teeth out with the help of the handkerchief—it was very slobbery work—and allowed himself a real smile.

"I left the nuts in the bottom of my saddlebag. We'll have another test run tonight."

"Very good. You are handling this quite well, Stefan. I daresay your family would be proud."

Stefan shook his head as he folded away the teeth and his tools into a convenient pocket. "To tell the truth, Samir, I wouldn't know what else to do anyway."

They rode in silence for a while.

At last, Samir spoke. "It seems like something is troubling you. Beyond . . ."

Stefan laughed. "Beyond everything? I'm not troubled, I'm curious. There's so much I don't know about the world."

"Such as?"

"If mice and squirrels are self-aware, what about the other animal kingdoms?"

Samir shrugged. "We are all God's creatures. In these ways we are the same."

"But, we ride horses and we use oxen for field work. And we hunt deer—rabbits, too. Why don't they rebel?"

Samir shrugged again. "The best and worst answer is simply: that is the way of the natural world. Humans and horses have a good working relationship, food and shelter in exchange for transportation. And the deer and rabbits . . . well, to them, Man is just another predator, like the fox or the wolf."

Stefan frowned, less sure on this point. "But—"

Samir interrupted him. "I had many of the same questions when I first came to understand the trouble in Boldavia. It was Christian who told me, 'Consider the life of a rodent, and you will see why they hate us.' They are dependent on our crops and stores for food, but we set traps and poison them. In fact, most nations set out to kill rodents brutally. It is solely in India that they are treated with any reverence. And then, only in one corner of the country. Rodents owe us no love."

Stefan recalled the way some boys back home would trap rats in sacks and drown them in the river. "But then what about the squirrels—" Before he finished asking the question, he knew the answer—old women in the parks making kissing noises and scattering nuts. Rats were vermin, but squirrels were beloved like pets.

"Squirrels are a more philosophical species," Samir said. "They are scholars, thinkers. Their only concern with the world is food and study."

"But, what are they studying?" Stefan wanted to know.

"The mysteries of this world and the next. Secrets guarded

as closely as those of your own guild, no doubt. A squirrel may scrabble for nuts for many years before he is called to study at the Pagoda Tree. But once there, that is where they remain. Two goals in an entire lifetime make for a peaceful life."

A peaceful life. That was what Stefan had once had in Nuremberg—his toys and his family were all that had mattered. Now, his mother was dead, and his father was missing. Stefan wondered if there would ever be such a thing as peace in his life again.

ON THE FOURTH DAY, Stefan noticed a change in the countryside. The steppes gave way to farmlands and ran out toward the sea. Around them, gardens lay fallow, vines bare where there should have been squash and pumpkins, bushes stripped raw of autumn berries.

"What happened here?" he asked.

Samir grimaced. "Mice."

The farms were reduced to fields of stubble where oats and wheat once grew. On the last cliff overlooking the sea, the golden stalks were gnawed to the ground. The stiff, coarse grass that remained was rustling. But there was no wind.

Mice. The broken fields writhed with unseen vermin stretching along the bluff in all directions.

"There she is." Samir pointed south, past the cliffs, along a man-made causeway that stretched out to sea. A city rose up, carved from the bedrock of the island, like a castle made from a mountain, emerging from the sea. Stefan's breath caught in his throat.

Boldavia.

40

NEWS OF THE siege engine's completion spread quickly. It had been taken from the Drosselmeyer's cell while he slept, and moved into the chamber that housed the diabolical cat. The Queen even rose from her bed to see it for herself. Decked in their finest, the entire royal court turned out for the unveiling.

Ernst wore a particularly fetching coat of midnight blue. It set off the gray of his fur quite nicely, bringing out the silver highlights. As ludicrous as the circumstances were, he was still a fan of pomp.

Having lingered in front of his mirror, he was among the last of the subjects to crowd into the great chamber, where the Breathless stood poised in awful memoriam. If the Queen had given a speech, he had missed it. Instead, he was greeted by the jubilant roar of the crowd. Alongside the mechanical cat towered a scaffold built around the thing the Drosselmeyer had created. Ernst's back prickled at the sight. It was easily five feet tall.

A toy soldier. Of the sort he used to see in the shop windows of Vienna in wintertime. Glossy black cap, blue coat, white breeches, a sword sheathed at its side. The flat black eyes stared blindly into space, far above the heads of the mice congregating below. Even so, the face was incredibly human.

"Magnificent!" a noblemouse standing next to Ernst said. He used a monocle—clearly an affectation—to peer up at the towering manikin, and patted his own plump belly in self-congratulation. "We'll surely rout those devils from over our heads now!"

Ernst doubted that. "Undoubtedly," he lied.

He waited for a demonstration, a sign of movement, or evidence of martial skill. The toy soldier merely stood, not even at attention. Ernst wondered if the scaffolding was the only thing keeping it from tipping over.

On a grandstand built knee-high to the soldier, the Queen observed her engine of war. What she saw in it, Ernst couldn't imagine. How a toy—even a very large one—could hope to defeat a living man was beyond him. But the Queen seemed pleased.

Indeed, the sight seemed to invigorate her. She rose from the chair she had been carried in on and bestowed seven kisses on the foreheads of her monstrous sons.

Even from here, Ernst could see Arthur's nose twitch in delight. The boy deserved to be fêted for his work in persuading the Drosselmeyer to complete the task. Ernst had accepted his share of the accolades (in the form of his new coat, a gift from the Queen) for teaching the boys diplomacy and the art of persuasion. But, in truth, the rat knew he had nothing to do with it. Arthur had a fascination with the captive toymaker that Ernst did not understand.

They were all mad, these Boldavian mice. From the Queen on down. Still, the toy soldier was very large. And that was impressive. Ernst had built a career with that talent alone. Perhaps an impression was all the royal mouse army needed to make.

239

41

IN THE EARLY MORNING, they rode into Boldavia across its causeway, jutting out into the Black Sea. The city nation was whimsical, turreted, peaked, and steepled, like a city created by gingerbread bakers. But it was also full of mice. Along the gutters and alleyways, even between the cobblestones, mice scurried, skittered, and ran.

Stefan and Samir reined their horses in to a slow, high-stepping walk, trying their best to avoid the wave of pests. Stefan's stomach turned. Like ants at a picnic, the mice of Boldavia swarmed throughout the city. He had never imagined it could be this bad. Boldavia was overwhelmed.

They passed a bakery, the display window empty of all food. On view was a large safe with a sign on its door saying *Fresh Bread Inside.*

"Food is scarce here," Samir told him. "You will only find fish and preserved vegetables in most places. It's impossible to maintain a garden, let alone a farm, without seeing it destroyed by morning. Only the wealthy can afford fruit or fresh vegetables, and those must be brought in by sea."

Stefan observed the Boldavians as they passed. They were all thin and sallow. Even the smallest children wore boots. Infants were carried high on their parents' shoulders. And the women, to Stefan's shock, wore their full skirts tied close to the ankle with ribbon, making them look like onion bulbs. They juddered down the streets in tiny steps, struggling to keep their balance. Some had gone so far as to don hats shaped like tall green stalks or, even stranger, like upside-down baskets.

"Bubble skirts," Samir explained. "Modeled after onions and hot air balloons."

"Which explains the hats, anyway," Stefan said.

"Since the princess fell ill, there has been a dreadful fear of mouse bites, but breeches would be immodest. And so—"

"Ridiculous skirts. But, don't they worry about falling over?" Stefan exclaimed, watching one elderly woman attempt to navigate the curb. From nowhere, an urchin in high sturdy boots rushed forward and offered his arm. The old woman leaned heavily on the child and gave him a coin for his trouble. The boy ran back to a group of bedraggled children who all clutched brooms made from bundled twigs.

"Commerce in the face of adversity," Samir said. "Remarkably adaptable, the Boldavians. This is an improvement. In the first days . . . well, I shudder to remember how terrible things were. The people underestimated the mice. And, newly risen, the creatures were hungry and dangerous indeed. Babes with milk on their breath were overwhelmed in their cribs. The tiniest tots could not be left unattended for a moment, lest they be bitten. And of course, there is always the fear of plague."

Stefan shivered at the thought. Europe had seen more than its share of the scourge known as bubonic plague. It had all but destroyed Barvaria a hundred years ago, and torn through Russia when his father was just a child. And everyone knew the harbingers of plague were rodents. "The Four Horsemen," he murmured.

"What's that?"

"In the Bible. The Four Horsemen are the heralds of the Apocalypse. War, Famine, Pestilence, and Death."

"We have wars," Samir agreed, "and famine. Let us hope we quell this invasion before the other gentlemen arrive in force."

They had barely made it to the end of the block when two of the older boys on the corner approached Samir.

"Beat a path through the mice for you, sir?" asked the taller of the two. He was maybe a year younger than Stefan and looked him over with interest. This was what happened to boys without apprenticeships, Stefan knew. Left to make their way in the world with only their wits and their muscles.

"Headed to the castle, are you?" queried the smaller one. They were both lean and rangy as alley cats.

"Thank you, gentlemen," Samir said. "That would be most kind." He tossed a coin to the taller boy, and the two set about slapping the road in front of the clockwork stallions.

Mice scurried as the cobbles were swept clean, only to flood back again in their wake.

"The little beasts get into every crevice here," Samir said. "Easier to pay them than clean the hooves off later."

"But where are the cats? And dogs, for that matter? I knew a baker who used a rat terrier to keep the storeroom free of pests."

"Remember, cats are illegal—the king is allergic and banned them long ago. As for dogs, they are not native to Boldavia. It has proven hard to import enough of them to make a difference. Now, they would welcome any mousers—cats and dogs alike— but you'll find both animals steer clear of the city entirely."

Looking around, Stefan could see why.

The two boys moved as fast as their brooms would allow. They were indeed making better time through the streets with their help. A soaring wall of dark brick rose ahead of them, above which Stefan could just make out the peaks and turrets of Castle Boldavia.

As they approached the castle wall, Stefan saw a line of doleful young men, each with a well-guarded nut to try their hand at curing the princess. Stefan rode grimly past, glad of the silver casket around his *krakatook*. Given the plague of mice, it was a wonder there were any nuts left in Boldavia at all.

When at last they reached the castle gates, their escort-sweepers accepted another coin and disappeared back into the city. Samir showed his credentials to the surprised guards (who had not seen him in seven years) and they were directed across the courtyard—swept clear of mice by a row of diligent gardeners wielding brooms—and into the royal stables.

Samir handed the reins to an attentive groom.

"We will keep the horses standing by, just in case," the astrologer murmured quietly.

Now that he was here, Stefan was ready. Excited, even. He was in the heart of the enemy's territory, yet not a single mouse had paid him the least bit of attention. He was invisible to them. No one credited a toymaker's-apprentice-turned-clockmaker's-journeyman as a threat. He would show them how wrong they were. For taking his father. For turning Christian into a criminal. "Drosselmeyer is an old name," Christian had once said. Stefan would make sure it was remembered well.

Speed was of the utmost importance. He would cure the

princess in exchange for the king's help in finding his father. Once he was safe, Stefan would ask for the use of Christian's old shop. He would build a better mousetrap. He would succeed where his cousin had failed. He would rid Boldavia of its rodents once and for all.

It never occurred to him that this was the sort of arrogance that had gotten Christian into trouble in the first place.

Stefan scraped his boots by the servants' entrance and followed Samir into the castle.

They moved through back passageways, brushing past servants and tripping over mice. The interior was cold, the sort of chill that settled into masonry and rarely left, even in the heat of summer. They climbed a narrow staircase in tight spirals almost to the top. At the landing, Samir fumbled with a long key.

"These are Christian's rooms. I lived . . . I *live* above," he pointed to where the stone steps became wooden. "A small observatory," he said with shy pride. He pushed open Christian's door.

Stefan hadn't known what to expect. Something miraculous, like a wizard's laboratory, maybe? Mechanical dolls, tables covered in gears and tools, towering creations, small scuttling apparatuses, whimsical whirligigs. At least a clock.

"It's like a monk's cell!" he exclaimed, taking in the pie-shaped room. It held a black-curtained alcove with a partially concealed bed. A long table, a bench. Dust swirled in the sunbeams pouring through high windows at the top of the room. A large rug was the only sign of comfort.

They dropped their bags in the middle of the room.

"It was not always like this," Samir said apologetically. "But once the princess was stricken, Christian became very single-minded."

At the moment, Stefan didn't care. He sat down on the bench, knowing the bed would be too hard a temptation to resist. He removed his boots and recoiled from the smell. "I need a bath," he said. "And a change of clothes. Then I'll be ready."

Samir pointed him to the facilities. "We have running water, hot and cold."

It was more like running rust. Stefan let it flow until it was clear and filled the claw-foot tub as high as he dared. He stripped off his clothes and sank into the water while Samir headed to his own chambers to do the same.

Every muscle ached, and his hair was full of sand for some reason. He ducked under the water. The *krakatook* lay sealed in its case, now on a chain around his neck. Waiting to be opened.

"HOW DO I LOOK?" Stefan asked.

Samir had returned in fresh robes, a newly wrapped turban around his head. His clothes were brilliant peacock, scarlet, and gold. A far cry from the drab things he'd worn on the road. He looked like a prince.

Stefan, on the other hand, looked ridiculous. The pants were at least an inch too short, though his boots covered the gap. His sleeves were another story.

"Perhaps if you undo the cuffs?" Samir suggested.

"I did," he replied, shrugging. It seemed he'd grown since leaving Nuremberg, and his clothes, unfortunately, had not.

"What about gloves?"

Gloves. Was that why Christian wore them, to hide the fact that his sleeves were too short? Stefan doubted it. A royal clockmaker could afford newly tailored clothes. A masterless journeyman would have to manage without. "No. This will have to do." He ran his fingers through his damp hair, smoothed his black waistcoat and tan breeches.

Samir arranged his tie. "There," he said at last.

They looked each other over, the astrologer and the clockmaker. Suddenly, Stefan jumped as a cacophony of chimes, cuckoos, bells, and clacking rose from the castle to strike the hour.

"Ah. Another of your cousin's legacies," Samir said wryly.

Stefan allowed himself a small smile. "I guess that means it's time we got on with it."

Together, they descended the stairs to the audience chamber. And prayed that it would go well, for all their sakes.

42

THEY WERE COMING to kill him. Zacharias could hear a mighty roar, even through the walls of his cell. He had finished their diabolical toy, and now his time was up.

He pulled a sheet of half-used parchment from beneath his sleeping pallet. They had left his pen and ink, and half a candle. Zacharias sat at the worktable and scratched out a letter of farewell to his son.

It was not eloquent, but it was all he could do. Even now footsteps were drawing nearer. At the behest of the dreaded "them," the man in scarlet was returning to finish the job.

Zacharias hefted the pen. He could try to stab the man and escape. But he was no killer.

Instead, he signed the letter and addressed a note to Arthur on the outside of the folded paper. He hoped the boy would find it once he was gone and get it to Stefan, somehow.

Hope. It was laughable that even now he felt it.

The candle guttered out and all went dark.

The moment hung in silence.

Bang! The cell door jounced on its hinges. Another powerful bang, and the door gave way. Bloody red light flooded the room. A monster stood in the open doorway—tall and black with a glowing red eye.

Zacharias jumped up, pen in hand, finding himself more ready to fight than he'd thought.

"Zacharias?"

The pen dropped.

The red lantern flipped up and a human eye looked out from the darkness.

"Christian?"

"Thank the heavens!" Christian said, and reached for his hand. "Quickly. While the mice are away and everyone still thinks I am dead."

43

THE THRONE ROOM of Boldavia was massive, with a soaring ceiling that could hold a block of houses stacked three high. The walls were made of stone and were covered in rich red and orange tapestries. A long carpet ran the length of the room to a dais at the far end, where the King of Boldavia sat on his throne like a bored schoolboy. He was just as Stefan imagined he would be. A huge man with an even huger waist, he wore white breeches, buckle shoes, and a white tunic belted with a rope of gold. Over that, he wore a crimson robe trimmed with white fur. A large gold medallion hung from the king's neck, and a golden crown perched on his fire-red hair. He looked like Father Christmas in the off-season. His scepter dangled idly in one hand, while the other twirled his auburn beard. A row of young pages in livery circled the edges of the room with long-handled brooms, sweeping at the corners and along the walls.

The king sighed audibly over their constant swishing. He didn't even look up when another page led in his latest guests.

"May I present the Royal Astrologer, Reader of the Stars, Samir abd al-Malik, servant to the king," the page announced. "And . . . Stefan Drosselmeyer . . . Journeyman," he added, unimpressed.

The king's yawn turned into an apoplectic fit of coughing.

"Good gracious! Samir!" he bellowed. "Seven years we've

waited for you! Pirlipat's almost a grown woman, or would be, if it weren't for her condition. What's taken you so long?"

Samir bowed extravagantly, touching his hand to his forehead in the same waterfall movement he'd exchanged with King Almande. He rose and spread his fingers in a calming gesture. "Forgive me, sire," he said. "The road has been . . . difficult. But fruitful, at last."

"We'll see," the king sputtered. "Do you know how many fools have been here with haycorns and peanuts, hoping to win my daughter's hand? You'd better do it right, or I'll have that clockmaker's head. Speaking of which, where is the rascal? Too afraid to show his face in my court, eh?"

Samir stepped slightly aside, leaving Stefan in full view of the king.

"Your . . . Your Majesty," Stefan said, with an awkward bow. This was not like meeting King Almande, a royal who stood on the same ground as he did. King Pirliwig was propped up in a throne on a dais in the largest room Stefan had ever been in outside of a cathedral. The effect was impressive, and humbling.

But I am a Drosselmeyer, he reminded himself. That had to count for something.

"That 'clockmaker' was my cousin, and he is dead. As his journeyman, it falls to me to dispatch his last duty to you and the princess."

"Dead? What deviltry is this? How dare he die in my service? I didn't order it. Did I? That was a mistake! That scoundrel must see this through to the very end!"

Stefan dropped his eyes, afraid the swell of anger in his chest would show. All around him, the brooms kept time—swish, swish, swish. Like the rush of blood inside him. With every sweep, shadows in the crevices trembled. Stefan's anger turned to ash and he shivered. Even here, there were mice.

"I'll have to get a new clockmaker now," the king said. He sighed. "Well, what are you—*who* are you again?"

Stefan bowed and repeated the page's introduction.

"Journeyman? How can a journeyman succeed where the master has failed?"

Stefan took a deep breath. "I'll show you. But first . . . I need your help."

The king grumbled. "Of course you do. No one ever just does their job anymore. It's always 'What's in it for me?' Well, spit it out."

Stefan paused. This was not going as he had imagined. And each mouse the room-sweepers missed would be a spy for the Queen below. How he proceeded could affect his father's captivity before Stefan even had a chance to act. If only he had his own silver whistle, like the one Christian had used to clear the barge . . . but it had been lost over the side with its owner.

"Sire," he began, giving a significant look at the corners of the room, "may I approach the throne?"

King Pirliwig sighed. "Yes, yes, of course. Be quick about it. We haven't got all day." He laughed, short and loud. "Well, we do, but we'd rather not spend it all here. Well then, boy, what's so hush-hush we can't share it with the mice?" he asked in a reasonable whisper for a man his size.

Stefan stood a step below the king and leaned in. "Sire, in

the course of serving this court, my father was kidnapped. My cousin had reason to believe he is being held prisoner beneath the castle by mice. I must ask for your help in rescuing him."

King Pirliwig regarded him shrewdly. His eyebrows rose and lowered, one at a time, like the scales of justice.

"*If* you can restore my Pirlipat," he said at last, "you shall have all the men you see at your disposal, and more. I will happily help you rid my land of this scourge once and for all. Can you do it, Sir Journeyman?"

Stefan bowed deeply. "I can, and I will. Your Majesty." He backed away from the dais, keeping his head down until he could see Samir's boots beside his own.

The king harrumphed and turned to his attendants. "Get the queen!" he hollered, and a servant scurried to do his bidding.

The king hopped up from his throne, gesturing wildly. "Well, open the gates, start the ceremonies."

"Ceremonies?" Stefan asked.

"Every day seventeen suitors are admitted to attempt to cure the princess," Samir explained.

"That line of men outside?"

"Mostly boys now. In seven years, it has become something of a fool's errand."

"You don't mean we have to wait—" Stefan began, but was interrupted as a plump pink woman in a shockingly pink gown came screaming into the room like a winter storm.

"Saints be praised!" the queen shrieked, howling so loudly that her blessing sounded like a curse. Weeping, she threw herself at Samir, who held her sheepishly and said, "Madam, please. All will be well."

"Yes, of course, of course." The queen brushed her dress smooth and wiped the tears from her eyes. "It's just been dreadful here since you left, dear Samir. And where is Christian?"

"He's dead, Your Majesty."

"Dead?! Terrible, terrible! Such a tragedy!" She dabbed a sleeve at her eyes and nose. "We've all had tragedies, my dear. You know, Pirlipat is—" Her eyes darted left to right, searching the corners of the room. Regaining her train of thought, the poor woman sniffed, smiled bravely, and said, "Well, do what needs to be done and we shall have our sweet Pirly back soon enough."

"Yes, Your Majesty," Samir agreed.

"Well then," the king bellowed, "plant your boy in the middle, will you, Samir, to make it seem fair? Good lad. We don't want to have to sit through more than we must."

"Sire." Samir bowed and pushed Stefan toward the door to find his place amongst the suitors.

"Wait! This is ridiculous," Stefan whispered. "I've got the only nut! Why not get on with it?"

Samir shushed him, but King Pirliwig had turned a deep and serious shade of red. "We are *royalty*, young sir. Protocols must be observed!"

Samir ushered him away before Stefan could say anything else.

At the far end of the great hall, on a dais exactly opposite the thrones, sat a small four-poster bed. Its posts were wrapped in pale blue silk and the canopy hung open above a mound of pillows. From where he stood, Stefan could see no sign of the princess.

A page below the first step of the dais unraveled a scroll and announced in a booming voice: "On this, the two thousand, six hundred and forty-sixth day of our beloved Princess Pirlipat's affliction, we invite all eligible suitors for a chance to cure the future queen and reap their rich and just rewards." He cleared his throat dramatically. "Let the first suitor approach!"

A boy a few years older than Stefan, who looked like he'd just been dragged out of bed, stumbled forward with a walnut in his hands. He glanced uncertainly toward his parents—a plump, well-dressed man and his wife—who stood at the side of the hall.

"You can do it, Johan," his mother urged, waving at him.

Johan gave an awkward bow, climbed the dais, and shoved the nut to the back of his mouth. He chomped down.

Something cracked. But it was not the nut.

The boy howled in pain, and spat the nut—and part of a tooth—into his hand. Still howling, he chucked the walnut across the room.

A servant scurried to collect it.

Clutching his mouth, Johan stumbled off the dais. His disappointed parents shook their heads and led him away.

Stefan patted his pocket. His squirrel tooth device clacked comfortingly against his leg.

"Dentists must make a fortune here," he whispered to Samir.

"Yes, I have a cousin who is a dentist. Very comfortable work," he agreed.

So the line went on, one unhappy boy after the next, each failing to crack open their nuts.

Stefan found his hands sweating as his turn approached. The *dentata* should work, but what if it didn't?

Finally it was his turn. The page leaned forward. "Remember, in order for the ceremony to be complete, the nut must be opened and presented to the princess, and then you will back down the three steps, bowing three times."

Stefan gave the page a blank look.

The page frowned.

"Fine. Um . . . thank you?" Stefan said, wondering at this latest royal nonsense.

As he climbed the dais, the rim of the bed gave way to a smooth expanse of rich silk brocade comforter and velvet pillows. In the center of the bed, where the princess should have been, lay a wooden doll. Even Stefan's father would have been impressed by the design, so lifelike, every hair individually carved. Each finger had been given delicate joints, as had the jaw and limbs. He had no doubt that this doll could be made to sit, stand, and even dance, with a few strings. Perhaps someone had made the marionette as a stand-in, the real princess being sick of this ridiculous ceremony.

Then the wooden eyelids blinked and the doll frowned up at him. "Well, hurry up, clod. We haven't got all day."

Stefan started. This was no doll.

"Yes, yes, it's shocking. I'm a hideous little manikin. You can laugh and tell all your friends later. Now go on, break a tooth and be done with it."

"Your Highness," Stefan stammered, "I don't find you to be hideous at all."

The doll's painted eyes widened. "No?"

"Not even close," he said, seeing her strange, angular movements, so unlike a real girl, so similar to Christian's mechanical

255

horses. Her neck joint was flawless. "Actually, you're really well made."

The princess's painted cheeks grew redder in two perfectly round spots. "Well made? Well made! I am not a MADE THING! I AM A PRINCESS! YOU STUPID, STUPID CLOD!"

Stefan blinked. "Sorry. I'm sorry!" Across the hall, Samir was glaring at him.

"Who are *you* supposed to be, anyway? Another Drosselmeyer, did they say? When I am queen, Drosselmeyers will be banned from Boldavia. Nothing but trouble, the lot of you."

At that, Stefan smiled, opening his jaws, and popped the squirrel *dentata* inside. The gears and pulleys that delivered the compression were as small as the pieces of a pocket watch, and yet they dug into his cheeks and forced his mouth wide. The teeth themselves slid onto his own like a sleeve. The gears and pulleys aligned so that, as he gnashed his own teeth, the *dentata* gnashed too.

The girl shrieked, high and shrill. "Papa! He's going to bite me!" she exclaimed.

Stefan thought it more likely he was about to drool on her.

The guards rushed forward and he could hear Samir pleading with them to let him finish the job. It was best to be quick about it.

Stefan withdrew the little casket on its chain from his neck, thumbed the lock, and extracted the *krakatook*.

"That's just a walnut. It's a walnut!" she called out to the assembled crowd, and began to laugh.

He turned the nut slowly in his fingers until she could read the unmistakable script flowing across the shell. The princess fell gratifyingly silent.

Opening his jaws wide, he placed the nut between his teeth, slowly squeezed them shut, and nibbled at the seam.

He tasted lemons, sawdust, cedar, and sunlight. The slightest hint of the nutmeat flooded his tongue. He opened his mouth and the *krakatook* fell, neatly halved, into his hand. The nutmeat remained whole.

Princess Pirlipat sat up in her bed and snatched it from his fingers. She fell upon it ravenously, devouring every last piece. Each time her jaws snapped shut and open again, they lost a little more of their mechanized look.

Stefan removed the squirrel *dentata* and massaged his aching face.

The princess was doing much the same, slapping her cheeks and pinching her legs with dexterous little hands. But while blood flowed back into Stefan's cheeks, *life* flowed into hers.

He had succeeded where so many had failed—he'd finished his master's quest. It had cost him his father and his cousin, but Princess Pirlipat of Boldavia was flesh and bone once more. With each passing moment, her skin grew smoother, softer, until it was dimpled and pink and very much alive. The terrible rigor mortis melted from her body, revealing a beautiful young woman of fourteen years, with deep blue eyes, perfect ringlet curls, red cheeks, and a mouth perhaps still a bit too wide.

Pirlipat didn't bother to thank him. She reached for a mirror beneath her pillow and began to primp.

The room was dead silent. As if, after seven years, the kingdom was afraid to believe that its trial had come to an end. Then the princess stretched from her years-long confinement, and rose from her bed.

Everyone in the crowded audience chamber gasped. Their princess had been restored! There was a collective sigh of relief and admiration.

But not from Stefan, who couldn't have cared less about the beautiful girl with the sharp tongue.

For over her shoulder, propped up in a doorway, stood his father and *Christian*.

Alive.

Both of them. Crumpled, haggard, filthy, but alive.

Stefan's heart threatened to break his ribs, his smile to crack his cheeks.

"Finish the ceremony!" the page hissed.

Stefan bowed quickly and stepped away from the bed. He bowed, stepped down, bowed again, and reached back his boot to take the final step.

"Interloper!" a voice squealed.

Stefan's hands flew to his ears. The voice was like a knife of ice.

The pages froze at their stations, their brooms silenced. And the shadows that had kept to the corners of the room flooded forward—just as they had in Stefan's nightmares. Mice spilled into the crowd.

Behind him stood a bloated parody of a Queen. A mouse dressed in royal purple wearing a tiny golden crown.

She pointed a sharp claw at Stefan. "With all my might, and

that of my sons, I curse thee!" she shrieked. Throwing herself forward, she sank her long, wicked teeth into his leg.

"Mother!" someone cried. It might have been Christian, or Samir, or even his own voice. Stefan couldn't tell. Everyone was screaming, the princess begging to be saved, her parents trying to calm her, servants rushing around, stamping at the mice.

The world blurred. In slow motion, Stefan fell to the ground as the Queen's venom took effect.

His joints stiffened and he hit the floor with a sickening crunch. *I've broken something,* he thought.

But he was wood, solid and unbreakably hard. His limbs were too heavy to move, and his jaw had clamped shut in a terrible rictus. It was as though he had retreated from his body to some small room at the back of his mind. Terror beat at the door, and hysteria begged to come in, but he did not heed them any more than the great oak heeds the summer wind.

The last few weeks of grief, yearning, and urgency disappeared with that one bite, locked out of the little room in his mind, as surely as he was locked in.

He had been cursed. And, with a distant understanding, he realized he had crushed the rodent Queen.

She lay beneath him, her tiny form half-crumpled underneath his wooden leg. Her wicked eyes gleamed. "My sons shall avenge me!" she hissed in her strangely accented German.

And then she died.

Stefan was not so lucky.

44

"MOTHER!" ARTHUR AND his brothers roared.

The human throne room sprawled out before them, walls towering like trees, greater than the subterranean caverns beneath the city.

"To the Queen!" Hannibal bellowed. But the battle cry was diminished, dwarfed by the scale of the room. A room full of *men*.

They were so *huge*! And so many. The flaw in his mother's secretive designs became clear. She had hidden her sons from the world of Men. All of their studies had little prepared them for the hulking reality.

"Majesty!" Several mouse soldiers had reached the edge of the throne room and blocked the prince from rushing across the floor after the Queen. Here was the danger, as if it was always meant to be, the nightmare from Arthur's dreams.

But they surged forward. Roland and Hannibal and Charlemagne gnashed their teeth. Genghis, Alexander, and Julius—even Julius!—rolled their eyes and screamed, twinning their voices to the echo of their mother's death curse.

"Sire, it is too late!" the mouse soldiers cried.

The Drosselmeyer boy had turned to wood and fallen. So very hard.

Hands held the princes back. Arthur looked away. He and his brothers fell to their knees.

In the giant throne room, the humans were moving. Scooping

up the boy, grabbing the princess and her ridiculous bassinet, until all that was left was the small, broken figure in a tattered purple dress.

"The clockmaker!" someone hissed beside Arthur. It was Tail-itch, the spy lieutenant, pointing across the room.

"Drosselmeyer." All seven brothers said the word with venom, curiosity, hatred, and fear.

He was tall, lanky of limb, with milky white hair tousled above a long face. Drosselmeyer strode swiftly toward the door. A black patch covered one eye. *Like a piebald,* Arthur thought. In his arms was the boy who had murdered their mother.

Arthur knew he should do something. But he no longer had the will to move. He knelt with his brothers on the cold flag-stones, unable to act. He had lost her.

A hand pressed into his shoulder.

"Come, sires. You must stand up." It was the rat, Ernst Listz.

The tutor's words rang hollow. After a moment, Arthur pulled himself to one knee, and stood.

"The Queen is dead," Tailitch announced. "Long live the King!"

Arthur had known this day was coming, hadn't he? All along, the dreams had been preparing him for this moment, just as all of his studies were meant to prepare him for what came next.

Arthur searched the tutor's face, his heart breaking. "I can't," he said.

Seven heads shook in disbelief. "We can't."

"I'm sorry, son, but you must." Ernst turned to the retinue of mice. "Give them a moment," he said, and the mice turned their backs so no one would see the King's pain.

"We should be hunting him; kill him before he leaves the castle!" Hannibal said.

"We should ask for guidance," Charlemagne fretted. "Snitter or Tailitch will know what to do."

"We need to prepare our mother's burial," Alexander said reasonably.

"Our mother," Roland echoed. As if a plug had been pulled from a drain, their grief swirled and threatened to pull them under.

Hannibal fought it. "Vengeance, brothers! We must have revenge!" His spittle flew as he called them to battle.

Revenge. Arthur closed his eyes against the bloodlust raging through his brother, the fear and confusion in each of them. Seven heads, and one shattered little heart. But this was not the time for self-pity.

"Mother meant for us to continue," Arthur said. "With clear heads." His brothers might succumb to baser instincts, but he would be the son she had asked for. He would make her proud.

"Together, now," he said. "Together." It was not encouragement. It was an imperial command.

His brothers reacted, holding their heads a little straighter. Not by choice, but by Arthur's will.

Arthur turned to Tailitch. "Fetch the Queen's body. And bring me the crown."

Tailitch bowed deeply, nose to the floor, and swept the soldiers around him into service. The Queen was gathered on the shoulders of her soldiers and carried through the tunnels to her chambers down below. The mice followed her final descent into the castle.

262

Except for Arthur. He stood in the shadows of the throne room, taking in the breadth and width of the space before him.

"You said the world was big, Ernst. This is but an inch on the map, is it not?"

A respectful two steps behind him, the tutor replied, "Less than that, I'm afraid."

Arthur exhaled slowly and nodded.

"She had large ambitions, your mother," the rat noted. He looked older than Arthur remembered. Then again, Arthur had aged a lifetime in the last few minutes.

"Tailitch," Arthur said. The piebald emerged from the shadows with a deferential nod and held out his mother's golden crown. It had been smashed by the falling boy, several tines now dented and the rim crushed flat. Arthur pulled it into shape, recalling the many days and nights when it had been their plaything. The one gift their mother had given them. It was more than a crown; it was her soul.

Once he'd repaired it as best he could, Arthur bowed, pausing to screw his courage to the sticking place. They would need more of these, he thought, and he placed the crown on his head. He looked down his nose at the piebald, the rat, and the few soldiers that had remained to guard him where they had failed to guard the Queen. They all fell to their knees, bowing to their new monarch.

"Our mother is dead," Arthur proclaimed. "Now, we are King."

BOOK III
The Nutcracker

45

"WAKE UP, STEFAN. *Wake up, my beautiful boy. It's Christ-mastime. Don't you want to go to the Kindlesmarkt?"*

A cool hand patted his cheek. Warm fingers touched his brow. Stefan opened his eyes. He was in his own warm bed in the loft above the workshop at home. The room smelled of baking bread and his mother smelled of flowers.

"No," he moaned into the sheets. "I want to stay here. I want to stay with you."

He'd been so cold and afraid just a little while ago. But he couldn't remember why. This was better. Much better than before.

Stefan's mother smiled, her gray eyes crinkling in amusement. "Then you may stay, just for a little while. And then you must get up!"

Stefan tried to nod, but he could not will himself to move.

"SOMETHING IS WRONG. It wasn't like this with Pirlipat," Christian said. "There was the same stiffness of limb, but within a day or two, she was awake and moving. I don't understand."

The three men sat watch over the boy who lay, stiff as a Nativity baby, in the bow of the fishing boat they had hastily commandeered. Zacharias sat beside Stefan, holding his son's hand. The toymaker's face was gray as ash. Stefan's own skin was pale and hard, the softness turned angular as if chiseled rather than alive. The venomous bite had robbed him of his newfound height, as well. Stefan was now less than five feet tall. The captain, a stout Boldavian man, kept his own counsel, his hand on the tiller. They were a long way from Boldavia, as the mouse ran—a full day's sail up the coast—but still not far enough to be safe.

Christian sighed. He'd seen the streets of the city emptied of mice, as they fled with Stefan, a block of ice, in his arms. They'd all disappeared suddenly, called away by the death of their Queen. If they were to rally, the wave of destruction would be formidable. Certainly more than a catatonic boy and three men could face alone.

It was remarkable how small Stefan had become—he'd been condensed by the Mouse Queen's venom into a solid, hardened doll, so different from the rangy young man Christian last saw on the deck of the *Gray Goose*. Stefan's spirit, if not his actual life, seemed to have been taken from him, along with the softness of his skin. And it was all Christian's fault.

"The boy has lost his will to live," Samir said. "He has suffered more these past weeks than that spoiled princess has in her entire life. Yet, his heart still beats, there is breath in his chest. He will wake when he is ready."

"You don't know that!" Christian said with anger born of frustration.

Samir merely shrugged. "We've all had our share of suffering. I am familiar with its effects."

"I'm sorry for the charade, Samir. I had to play dead to reach Zacharias. The mice were watching us too closely. Pirliwig would have left him to his fate."

"No doubt," Samir agreed. "I see your logic. But it was difficult. Especially for the boy."

Christian gripped the side of the boat. "At least it worked. I had the solution, a trick up my sleeve. But now?" He waved his hand in the air. "I'm not accustomed to being so helpless."

"I should think seven years was plenty of practice," Samir said under his breath, almost—but not quite—extracting a smile.

"Do you know what time of year it is?" Zacharias asked suddenly. A strange smile played across his lips. "It's Christmastime. Nuremberg will be alight with the season. The Kindlesmarkt . . . I haven't missed one in thirty years. We should be there, Stefan. Even without toys to sell."

He had told Christian of the task the mice had set him to. It made little sense to either of them. A single toy soldier, whatever its size, was of no use that they could see.

"A Trojan horse?" Zacharias had suggested. But the soldier he'd made could not hold enough mice to cause any real damage.

In the end, Christian feared that all the mice had managed to do was sully his cousin's love for making toys. It might be gone for good. Like Elise, and now perhaps Stefan, too.

"Take us home, Christian," Zacharias pleaded.

"I will," Christian promised. "And I'll find a way to save your son."

46

IT WOULD HAVE BEEN INSPIRING, if it hadn't been so misguided. Ernst stood on a rocky ledge overlooking the main cavern beneath the Boldavian capital. For a quarter mile in each direction stretched rank upon rank of mice. Soldiers bred to fight ever since the caverns opened up beneath Boldavia and the old Queen first squeaked of rebellion. So what if their parents had been scrabblers and thieves? *They* would be heroes.

Ernst snorted delicately at the thought. During the Rat Insurrection of Hameln, the soldiers had come from a line of warriors that stretched back to the days of ancient Babylon. They had fought like true rats and died like them. They were nothing like the rabble that stood before him now in poor mimicry of a human army.

"Are we not extraordinary?" It was Hannibal, speaking again in that new, disturbingly diplomatic voice, made even more unnerving by the use of the royal "we."

Ernst steeled himself and bowed. "Indeed, sire. The siege engines are quite astounding."

This much, at least, was true. There had been industry in secret. While the captive Drosselmeyer had made the first of the soldiers, the mice had been making copies.

Beyond the mouse army, he could see the engines of war packed, end over end, on low, wheeled platforms. Unfolded and assembled to their full height, they wouldn't fit in this cavern. And so they were strapped down for the long journey to Nuremberg, where the new King of Mice would confront his mother's killer. If they were looking to make an impression, it would be done.

"Every wounded animal returns to its den," Hannibal had told Ernst. "You taught us that."

Hannibal was learning how to take control, Ernst noted. The other boys spoke less and less, while he spoke more. He was a natural tyrant, unlike Arthur, who hadn't spoken for hours. It was as if his brothers had used Arthur to woo the tutor and learn their lessons, and then took over with the knowledge he had brought them. Or perhaps the boy let them take over. If it was war they were waging, Hannibal was the most warlike of the bunch.

The rat tutor frowned. Fond as he was of Arthur, a word came to mind more frequently these days: "abomination."

If the fiercest rat warriors could not overtake humanity, then certainly the monster beside him would fail. Most likely before they even reached Nuremberg. Ernst had seen the plans laid out in the war room. The army would sail upstream via a series of subterranean rivers. Days without light or fresh air on rafts that could be taken apart, carried through tunnels or over open land as needed. There, the danger was greatest. Hawk and owl attacks had decimated more than one rodent tribe before. This army would be no different.

"Citizens! Soldiers!" The voice of the Mouse King roared from five mouths at once.

Ernst jumped in his red velvet coat, his lace cuffs trembling. Arthur remained quiet, a hard stare on the young face. And

271

of course, Julius merely lolled to the side, dull-eyed and oblivious to his brothers.

"The death of our mother is a wound to us all." The King indicated the crowd of soldiers and advisers, as well as his other heads. "A wound that will be avenged!"

The army roared.

Ernst applauded politely and wondered what the weather would be like in Germany.

"The enemy has a face," the King crowed. "A human named Stefan Drosselmeyer."

The name "Drosselmeyer" rippled around the room, whispered by a thousand awed tongues. Drosselmeyer, ever the enemy of mice.

"He murdered our Queen! And it's no wonder. He is kin to the Master of Mousetraps, the villain who created the Breathless! But now, we will use their tricks against them! We will destroy their entire line! And then we shall take our rightful place in the world above. No man can stand in our way!"

The crowd roared again.

Hannibal nodded at a mouse to his right, a tattered-looking piebald in a worn blue coat. Ernst recognized the mouse's significance—another spy.

The little spy whispered into the King's ears. Hannibal's eyes narrowed. He dismissed the mouse with a flick of his paw and the piebald disappeared down a side corridor. A host of small shadows detached from the wall and followed him into the cave. The King's spies were abroad.

A moment of silence hung in the expectant air. And the King roared with the might of a raging storm. "To Nuremberg!"

Throughout the cavern, horns sounded a brassy call to arms, and the entire host of mice snapped to attention. A hoary-furred general in full regalia, his uniform gleaming with gold braid and medals, climbed atop the first siege engine. He bellowed an order and the army surged forward into the deep tunnels, to the river and the first battle of the new insurrection.

47

STEFAN GRABBED HIS HAT off the peg by the door.

"Don't forget your coat," his mother said. Her cheeks were pink from the heat of the kitchen and her apron was dusted in sugar.

"I won't," he promised.

"Sugarplums," she announced, happily displaying a tray of treats. "It's Christmas again. Your father will be very busy, Stefan. He needs you. Don't forget that."

He looked out the window. "Who is that?"

His mother turned around. Now there were flowers in her hands instead of sweets. Yellow tulips, Chinese peonies. Her apron was dusted with potting soil from the window box she was filling. "That's your cousin Christian. That rascal. I thought you said he was coming to visit me, not stand in the yard plotting with your father."

Stefan moved to the window; it was cold and frosted with ice. He pressed his hand against the glass to wipe it clean. Suddenly, the pane was clear, warmed by spring sunshine.

Outside, his father looked worried. Christian hung his head.

"What are they plotting?" he asked. If he listened very hard, he could hear them.

"Join them," his mother said. But Stefan could not find the door.

48

AT THE EDGE of the Iron Gate—where Christian had sup-
posedly drowned—they were forced to go on foot. Christian
flagged down a farmer bringing a load of turnips north and, for
a few coins, purchased a ride back up the river.

The oxen leaned slowly into the added weight, and soon they
were off, the men's boots dangling from the back of the cart.
Stefan lay on his coat amidst the turnips. It was early afternoon,
but the December sun was already sinking behind the trees.
There had been too many sleepless nights, and only Christian
seemed unaffected by the constant wakefulness. Within a mile,
Zacharias and Samir had nodded off.

The countryside was peaceful—broad-leafed trees and the
steady rumble of the cartwheels, as rhythmic as a metronome.
The sun to the west was a golden pendulum that swung in time
to the gears of the planets and the stars.

A low shadow swooped overhead in a whoosh of wings.
Christian ducked. There was a rustle in the trees. An early owl.
That was good. The mice could not be far off, he knew, and
with the hunters in the sky, they would keep low for now. If
only the oxen could be coaxed to move faster. But one thing
every clockmaker knew was that things tended to happen in
their own good time.

Another rustling in the trees. Christian peered into the
hedges lining the road.

Scuffle, scuffle.

His blood froze.

Skitter, scuffle.

There! In the ditch a mere ten feet behind him was a solitary black-and-white mouse.

Christian tapped Samir awake. Without moving his lips, he said, "We are being watched."

Samir stiffened.

"Don't wake Zacharias," Christian said. "Not yet. We can't outrun them with Stefan in this state. My kingdom for a windup horse, eh?" In the melee, they had left their steeds behind with only one thought in mind: to flee as fast as possible. The fisherman's boat had saved their lives.

"Shall we set fire to the brush?"

"Not a bad idea, but our farmer here might disagree. Especially when the wind rises and the flames sweep across his fields."

"You're right, sunset is nigh," Samir agreed. The wind always rose with the setting of the sun, as if a great doorway was sliding open to admit its passage.

"Samir, can you reach Stefan's coat pocket?"

The astrologer shifted and a turnip tumbled to the ground. "I can."

"Feel around for something the size of your fist. Do you have it?"

Samir rummaged in one pocket, then the other, and emerged triumphant. "A wooden bird?"

"Good lad!" Christian proclaimed. "He stuck with it after all.

Don't look so disappointed, Samir. This is not just any wooden bird. It is a decoy, the best one I've seen of late."

He wound the tail feathers carefully, holding tight so the bird would fly far.

"Now, if you were an army of mice, which direction would you come from?"

Samir watched the road winding along the riverbank. "Away from the water, I'd imagine. The ground here would be too muddy for such short limbs. Across the fields beyond those hedges?"

In the ditch, the little mouse hopped forward, keeping pace with the cart, but never coming too close. It was disturbing to see the small animal moving toward them with such purpose. Christian removed a glove with his teeth. He licked a finger, held it to the wind, and did a calculation in his head.

"Let's see if you're right," he said, and let the bird go.

Stefan's gray dove rose up into the early evening sky, a pale spot against the purpling clouds. She soared out over the road, past the trees, and over the distant fields out of their sight.

In the road, the piebald mouse paused, inquisitive eyes following the path of the wooden bird.

A shadow swooped overhead. And another. The mouse dove for the ditch, scurrying beneath piles of drifted leaves.

From the trees rose three great owls. On mighty wings, they beat the air and silently sailed after the dove.

"Good hunting," Christian called softly. With luck, they had bought themselves another night. But they were going to need a better plan.

"Zacharias," he called. Samir nudged the toymaker awake.

"Yes? Is it safe?" the sleep-befuddled toymaker asked.

"Not as safe as I'd like," Christian replied. "We're being followed."

Zacharias stared fearfully down the dwindling road.

"Once we reach the far side of the rapids, there will be boats to hire. We'll do our best to outrun them. But, when we reach Nuremberg, we must be ready. I suggest we give them more than one place to look."

"What did you have in mind?" Zacharias asked.

"We'll need supplies. We can get them outside of Vienna. And then, get ready to carve, toymaker. This will be your greatest work yet."

49

IT BEGAN WITH a single bird, gliding over the winter fields, a small gray dove with strangeness in its flight, pursued by a silent shadow. Then two. Then many.

Cold dread seized Arthur's chest. His back crawled like a wound infested by maggots. His brothers trembled. Birdsign.

"To ground!" came the cry from the infantry.

"Hold fast," Alexander whispered. "Hold fast!" he cried, and Arthur cried with him. The King of Mice pulled themselves together and stood tall while around them their soldiers cowered in fear.

"Sires, to ground!" the piebald Snitter begged. The King's guard had already begun digging a trench. Was he expected to lie down in it until the danger had passed? His mother never lay down. She fought. Like ice shattering on the surface of a pond, Arthur came awake. The numbness that had settled over him since their declaration of war had finally melted away. Hannibal was the fighter, but he was only one-seventh of their might. It would take all of them to win this war. Alexander, Charlemagne, Genghis, Roland, even Julius. They were each a part of one whole. The King of Boldavia. The King of Mice. He would not cower any longer.

"They are only birds," Arthur said as an owl dove toward him. "We are hunters of men." He pulled his sword. And felt his mother's love.

But the piebald guards knew their duty. Snitter deftly pushed his sovereign leader into the freshly dug trench. He dove in after, covering Arthur and his brothers with his own small body. Over the piebald's shoulder, mice dug in, their spears butted into the earth to form a crown of thorns to protect their King.

The owl screamed, a sound that could flay the fur off an honest mouse. Arthur smelt the chalky stench of owl feathers and droppings, the foul, hot breath of an entrail eater. The great yellow claws stretched down, only to be thwarted by the bristling spears.

One shaft broke. The rest held.

Angered, the owl screamed, and with a thunderous burst of wings, pulled up into the sky.

Around them, more birds came swarming from the north. The sun had set, and the scent of mice had risen in the wind, waking the night raptors. Above them, the enraged owl cut an arc across the heavens and swooped, skimming its claws across the stubbled field.

It was more than some mice could take. Three soldiers broke and ran, chased by the curses of their fellows. The great bird raked the deserters with its talons, tearing them to pieces. With a shrill cry, it rose into the sky again, its sharp gaze on the greatest prize. The largest mouse it had ever seen.

Within the circle, the King of Mice rose to his feet. "Release me!" his voices bellowed as one.

The mouse guard trembled and obeyed. They stepped back, spears to the sky, a sparse ring around their leader.

Hannibal hefted their sword. Arthur and his brothers looked into the yellow eyes of death.

And they struck with the force of seven kings.

The owl cried out as the sword pierced its breast. "Attack!" Arthur bellowed.

"Attack!" his brothers joined in.

The King's guard sucked in their collective breaths. A mouse of Boldavia had stood alone against an owl, and won.

"To the King!" they cried, and struck in a rush of pride and fury. The owl fell beneath their weapons, their teeth, and their claws.

Rising above the fray, Arthur and his brothers watched their army attacked and harried from above. Here and there, a mouse was taken, screaming a high shrill death cry.

Arthur wanted to weep from exhaustion and fear, but his pride would not let him. Hannibal and Charlemagne wanted to continue to fight. But the remaining piebald guard was determined to keep their King alive.

"We've found a moleway, sire," Snitter muttered into Arthur's ear. "We can get Your Majesty underground. Half your soldiers are under way already. We'll lose some, but save more. Come, sire. Let us flee before nightfall. We've no chance against more owls."

"No!" Hannibal snarled. "We have our sword!"

A cold stillness surrounded Arthur, despite the flickering shadows from above, despite the owl-darkening skies. They had felled one raptor, it was true. And, following his lead, the rest of the army had brought down three more. But that was not the reason they had left Boldavia.

"Birds are not our quarry," he reminded them. "We hunt men. Lead on, Snitter. Our mother must be avenged."

Pressed close to the earth, hidden by dirt and winter wheat, Arthur and his guard made their way across the frost-chilled field. One of his guards was lost in the process, twenty-seven mice in all. But his army counted in the thousands. Nothing could stand in their way for long.

50

"WHAT A RACKET THEY MAKE!" Stefan's mother said.

They sat perched on the roof of their townhome. Her apron pockets were full of broken gingerbread that she hurled into the air.

Stefan laughed as seagulls swooped down to snatch the pieces out of the sky. "And so far inland!" he exclaimed.

"They come in whenever there's a storm, dear." His mother wrapped an arm around his shoulders. "It's getting cold. Come inside and we can have some cocoa."

"Look how they catch the air," Stefan said, pointing at the arc of a gull wing, cupped on a gust of wind.

"Yes, amazing," his mother said. "A pity your father doesn't make birds. What child wouldn't want a toy that could fly?"

"I would," Stefan agreed.

His mother was in the kitchen, pouring cocoa. "You would what, dear?"

"Like to make birds," he said. "Like on the roof."

She smiled her brilliant smile—the one that pulled smiles from all other lips—and handed him a tray with four mugs. "That's a wonderful thought, Stefan. When you figure it out, I'd love to have a little gray dove."

Hadn't he made her one already? Stefan accepted the heavy tray. The warm, sweet steam of chocolate and milk curled about his face.

His mother patted his cheek. "Go, beautiful boy. Don't keep your papa waiting."

Through the window, he could see his father and two other men. "Look! It's Cousin Christian," Stefan said. "And . . . Samir."

Their heads were together, discussing . . . something. He heard them say his name. Christian drew plans in the air. Stefan listened closely. He wanted to join them, but could not find the door.

51

THEY ARRIVED IN NUREMBERG on Christmas Eve, like three premature wise men—Christian, Zacharias, and Samir. On each of their backs was an identical bundle, wrapped in brown paper and tied with string. They joined the latecomers to the Nuremberg Kindlesmarkt, no more unusual than the other traveling peddlers toting their wares. Once through the gates of the old city, Christian went right, Samir turned left, and Zacharias went straight ahead with the crowd into the heart of the Christmas Market.

"Mein Gott," Zacharias muttered as he entered the main square. The sun had gone down and the sky had turned deep blue. In the glow of lamp- and torchlight, the pride of Nuremberg spread out before him—music, people, and market stalls.

The Kindlesmarkt—a three-hundred-year-old Christmas tradition to which the entire city flocked in the days leading up to Christmas. This year was no different. Every toymaker, clockmaker, craftsman, and baker for miles around had set up shop in neat little rows beneath the central clock tower.

Above it all, from the clock's cloth-of-gold-draped balcony, ruled the benevolent golden-ringleted Christkind, or Christ Child. Usually a young girl chosen for her father's standing in the town government, the Christkind wore white robes, a long blond wig, and a golden crown. She also carried a scepter with which she blessed the proceedings each year.

The rich scents of gingerbread and roasted nuts wafted through the air, making Zacharias's mouth water. Cold wind bit the tip of his nose and melting snow sloshed over his boots as he made his way through the jostling crowd. A group of children sang carols at the intersection of two rows of booths. A little boy dressed as an elf laughed, a bell-like sound that almost brought tears to the toymaker's eyes.

He continued on, running through Christian's plan in his mind. It was mad, of course. Life had offered nothing but madness since the day he buried Elise. All he could do was press on.

Zacharias shifted his grip on the bundle and pushed through the crowd to the judging stage. Here, the toymakers' guild accepted the finest craftwork of every eligible master toymaker in Nuremberg and the surrounding area.

"Zacharias Drosselmeyer, of Kleinestrasse," he presented himself at the small sign-in table. A platform had been built, as it was every year, with tables that showcased the prize pieces of the market.

"Zacharias, you're here!" the guildmaster cried. Herr Grüel tugged at his red hair where it peeked out from beneath his hat. "Are you all right? We've not heard from you since the day that boy of yours feared you'd been kidnapped! By mice, was it? I should have known you were merely working in secret on your Kindlesmarkt toy. And thank heavens for that! It was a bit frightening, but all our guildsmen are accounted for since that day. You make the last." He tittered with relief. "Now, what great work have you brought for the judging?"

Zacharias slid the bundle gingerly to the ground and bent to peel away the loosely wrapped paper.

"Wonderful! Rather a portrait of the original, eh?" the guild-master exclaimed. "The limbs are moveable?"

"Most lifelike, indeed," Zacharias said, mopping his damp brow.

"Table twelve, to the left," the guildmaster directed him, making a note in his ledger.

Zacharias lifted the bundle into place and removed the rest of the wrappings.

It was a wooden soldier. Not so different from the one he'd made in Boldavia, it was nearly life-size, standing four and a half feet tall. This one had red coattails, white breeches, black boots, and brass buttons, a shiny black cap, and startlingly life-like gray eyes that were exactly like Stefan's.

Zacharias sat the doll in place more tenderly than one might have expected. He adjusted the soldier's cap and made sure the coat was secure on the body.

"There we are, in plain sight," he muttered. The mice had spies in the crowded marketplace, he knew, but none could reach him up on the platform here.

Overhead, the Christkind stood on the balcony of the cathedral with her entourage of angels, smiling down at the crowd. Zacharias said a short prayer for his son and settled in to wait.

"HOLD YOUR horrible horses!" Professor Blume shouted.

Someone was pounding at the door hard enough to bring the house down. He'd given the staff the night off to visit the Kindlesmarkt. He preferred to stay home and soak up the warmth of his greenhouse over a nice book rather than brave the cold for roasted chestnuts and gewgaws. He clapped a hand over his fez to keep it from flying off as he sped down the stairs, jamming his feet into his slippers every third step. Out of breath and nearly as red as his velvet housecoat, he threw open the door.

"Yes, what is—?" The rest of his exhortation fell away. Perhaps he was dreaming after too much roast beef and potatoes. Nothing else could explain why one of the three wise men was standing on his doorstep the night before Christmas.

"Professor Blume?" the Arab asked rather unexpectedly.

"Uh . . . yes?" The professor was very aware that his fez was remarkably out of place in front of such an awe-inspiring turban. The little gold tassel on his hat jostled belatedly to a stop in front of his right eye. He brushed it out of the way.

"Samir abd al-Malik at your service. Might I come in?"

Blume stammered for a proper response to the florid bow the Arab presented. He stepped aside before any words came to mind.

Shutting the door, he tried to gather his composure while his unexpected visitor lowered a bundled package to the ground and paused to rub the warmth back into his hands.

"Is that for me?" Blume asked, eyeing the package.

Samir followed the man's gaze. "If you like. Perhaps we can effect a trade. The nutcracker in exchange for a nut."

The professor's eyes glided across Samir's whole being, before settling on his face. "Would you . . . fancy a cup of tea?"

Samir grinned, white teeth startlingly bright against his dark face. "Very much so, but I'm afraid my business is pressing. I seek the *krakatook*. Have you another?"

Blume, who had rather begun to enjoy the idea of such a bizarre Christmas Eve, blinked twice, reeling to catch up. "The *krakatook*? My dear fellow, why would I want two of the useless things?"

The Arab's face fell into a thunderous scowl. "So you only had the one?" he asked.

The despair in his visitor's voice was deeply affecting. He patted the big man's shoulder. "I am afraid so. And unfortunately I can't tell you where to find another." He shrugged. "There was a boy here some weeks ago, but I haven't heard from him since. Had the loveliest ideas for my bonsai trees—"

"I come on his behalf," Samir said. "These are bad tidings, indeed."

Professor Blume hovered for a moment, twiddling his fingers anxiously. "Bad tidings? Hardly. He was playing a prank of some sort. Now, are you sure you wouldn't like some tea?"

The Arab took a deep breath and seemed to regain some of his height and strength. "Another time, perhaps. For now, lock your doors and sleep soundly. This is not a night for being abroad."

He threw open the door and left just as quickly as he had come.

"You forgot your—" Professor Blume let yet another sentence hang unfinished in the cold air.

The Arab had left his package, the paper torn across the top. Staring out from the brown wrapping was a beautifully polished wooden nutcracker with the face of the boy to whom he'd given the *krakatook*.

"Will wonders never cease?" he asked the empty foyer, and carried his sole Christmas present into the greenhouse to study it someplace warm.

52

THE BROWN-AND-GRAY PIEBALD twitched his whiskers in an effort to look less suspicious. Of course, his target hadn't seen him—he was too well trained a spy for that. But other humans passing by might notice him, and a scurrying mouse drew less attention than one that was standing still.

The clockmaker and the boy assassin had arrived in the city, just as intelligence suspected. But they had been clever and divided their party. Each man carried a bundle. One of them, undoubtedly, concealed the Queenkiller, but which one?

Tailitch had been forced to split up his band of scouts to follow the astrologer and the boy's father as they fled into the city. He chose to follow the clockmaker himself. At this time of year, it would be difficult to follow them through the wide avenues and rolling cart wheels, but not impossible. Tailitch had been chosen for his ability to move about this city, his hometown.

He would not fail like the last Nuremberg spy. Caught by the enemy! Tailitch twitched his tail in indignation. No, he would not fail.

His only real concern was not being able to send word back to his superiors, if he chose to follow his subject now. But humans were foolish. Now that they had reached the city, they likely thought themselves safe, and would no longer be moving at night. Confident in this realization, Tailitch sent one last missive down the tunnels. There it would be picked up by the hourly courier, carried through the massive network of tunnels beneath the city to the paws of his superior, and eventually to the ears of the Mouse King himself.

Tailitch twitched with pride. He had seen the King in action at the Battle of Owl Run. Four owls had been felled that day! And the King had taken one single-handedly! Aye, the Mouse King was a force to inspire awe even in a soldier as weathered as he.

Taking a final bead on his target, Tailitch gathered himself and leapt forward into the whirling street after his prey.

53

NUREMBERG, ERNST LISTZ said to himself.

It sounded rich. Not as rich as Austria or Paris, but it would do. Anything was better than the terrors of the open country-side with its death strikes from above, and the moldy stench of damp tunnels. They had marched hard all the way from Boldavia, using log barges on underground streams when possible. They kept up their speed, even racing through tunnels and under mountains, knowing their enemy must travel the longer way.

A mouse could run twice as fast as a man could walk, if necessary. For this journey, the King of Mice had deemed it very necessary indeed. And so they had run and sailed, to the point of exhaustion.

For Ernst, anyway. These Boldavian mice never seemed to tire. Fanatics rarely did. Ernst had hoped Arthur and his brothers would eventually forget him, caught up in the tides of war. He was beginning to fear he would never be free.

A paw clutched him from behind. The paw of the Mouse King.

Ernst used every ounce of self-control he possessed to not jump out of his skin. "Sire."

As the army approached Nuremberg, Arthur's brothers had grown more agitated. The owl attack outside Vienna had only made matters worse. The rodent army had been forced to flee underground. For the first time in this ridiculous campaign, the mice had been frightened. What's more, their spies in the city had lost sight of the clockmaker's boy, which had only served to feed the anger of their King. The bloodlust in Hannibal's eyes had become more apparent with each step as he gnashed his teeth, drunk on power and the promise of vengeance.

And now, per Arthur's orders, each head wore its own golden crown.

When Ernst turned to face his King this time—not *his* king, he had to remind himself, merely an upstart rabble-rouser of lesser Rodentia—it was not Hannibal he saw, but Arthur. One of those odd eclipse-like times when the other heads were asleep and the boy seemed like himself again.

"Ernst, may I speak with you?" Arthur's voice sounded hollow and young even though his body had grown to adulthood.

Pity wrapped around Ernst's jangled nerves. Why did he stay, if not for this boy? Perhaps because Arthur was the only creature to treat him with real respect in all of the years since Ernst's family's decline.

"Of course, dear boy," Ernst replied softly, not wanting to wake the other brothers. It seemed to be Arthur's gift, to stay awake while the others slept. But it made the boy seem even lonelier than usual.

Ernst kept his voice soft and light, but he was afraid. For Arthur and for himself.

"Ernst, I've been having dreams again." Arthur tucked his arm around his tutor's elbow and they began to stroll. They were camped beneath the roots of a great oak tree in one of the parks outside Nuremberg. Intelligence had scouted it as the perfect headquarters. In fact, the chamber here was so large, it had allowed them to begin the curious work of assembling the siege machines.

"What kind of dreams, Majesty?" Ernst asked in real concern. Nightmares had begun to wrack all of the Mouse King's heads in the past few weeks, but Arthur was the only one willing to talk about it.

"I see *him* in my dreams," Arthur confided. The young face paled beneath the silvery fur. "Mother's killer. I can't face him, Ernst. I could barely stand up to my own mother. She was a sorceress, she had such power. What on earth could snuff her out?"

"You haven't actually seen the assassin, then?" Ernst asked. Even he had caught a glimpse of the human boy, through a chink in the wall as he fled the Boldavian throne room. Ernst had been attempting to escape.

"I have. On that terrible day, and every night, in my dreams," Arthur said softly. "He's a monster. My brothers think we are invincible, that we will triumph by divine right. Not even the hawks have swayed them. But Mother reaped what she sowed, don't you think? What hope have we against one man, let alone an entire race of them? I fear we will all perish."

Ernst gripped the younger mouse by his shoulders. At last, a lick of sense in the entire escapade! "Then stop it, Arthur. You are the King—*you* are! If you can see your mother's legacy as the idiocy it is, then call an end to it!"

"I can't," Arthur cried forlornly.

"Why not? Your brothers? Will you let them bully you into the grave?"

"If that's what it takes."

Ernst's heart skipped a beat. The voice was not Arthur's. Hannibal was awake, leering at the rat through slitted yellow eyes. Ernst let go of the King's jacket and stepped back. The other heads were awake, as well.

"I told you the rat was not loyal to us," Genghis said.

"And you were right." Hannibal frowned. "Herr Listz, you disappoint us."

"Treachery!" Charlemagne hissed.

The other heads echoed the word. "Treachery."

Ernst was bewildered. Arthur would not look him in the eye.

"Seize the rat. Lock him up!" Hannibal called out.

Two armed guards stepped from the shadows to follow their King's command.

"Arthur?" Ernst's voice cracked.

"I'm sorry, Ernst. We had to know if you were with us or against us," he said in a voice Ernst hardly recognized. "You must understand. She was our mother. *My* mother."

With a start, Ernst realized Arthur had truly loved her. She who had only ever seen him as a means to an end. Who had made him into this unnatural form. In spite of all that, Arthur loved her fiercely, and would follow her into the grave. Ernst's last slivers of hope began to fade.

"Enough, Arthur," Charlemagne snapped. "Visit him in the dungeon if you must."

"The enemy has been spotted in Nuremberg," Hannibal said. "We have work to do."

So the Drosselmeyer was here. The war would begin by nightfall, if Hannibal had his way. All Ernst could hope to do was save himself.

"You can't imprison me! You need me!" the rat called out as his escort dragged him from the chamber. Hannibal snorted. The little upstart would suffer for that, one day, Ernst swore.

His last sight was of the Mouse King laughing from all of his mouths but two. Ernst closed his eyes. Julius had been blank as ever, but the look on Arthur's face was all too clear. Nothing would stop him from having his revenge.

54

CHRISTIAN HURRIED UP the steps, the cloth-wrapped figure solid and unyielding, but distressingly light in his arms. They didn't have much time. Once they reached the city, the mice could move quickly through the sewers and catacombs. They could be everywhere, anywhere, at once.

Behind him, the expanse of Englestrasse Square made his back itch. But much worse was the grinding ache in his bones. Something was out of step. The City Clock of Nuremberg was losing time. He could feel it with each stuttered beat of his heart, as if he, and not the city, had somehow slipped out of rhythm.

He paused at the top of the stairs and swallowed a wave of nausea. Unlike the neglected university clock, very few things could knock a City Clock off-kilter—an act of sabotage (unheard of in his lifetime), an immense natural disaster, or a shift in the balance of the world. Without seeing the movement himself, he knew it was the latter of the three. The mice had reached Boldavia, and there was a real chance that they would win the day.

A subtle shift, for now, sure to go unnoticed by the shoppers celebrating at the Kindlesmarkt. Birds and animals were more sensitive, of course, which might have been why the streets were empty of dogs and cats. And clockmakers. Every clockmaker in the city would be able to feel the damage being done. They would rally to the Brotherhood, do their best to guard the

Cogworks. Other than that, it would be as he'd told Stefan so long ago. Every clockmaker is responsible for his own work. A second set of hands might ruin the timing.

This crisis was of Christian's own making. He could rely on the Brotherhood only so far. But, in the end, he'd have to solve it on his own.

He paused a moment longer to take a deep breath, and another, gauging the rise and fall of his chest until each inhalation was as long as his exhalation. He could not adjust the movement of the city all at once, but he could certainly rebalance himself. An unsteady clockmaker did unsteady work.

Through the heavy oaken door, he could hear the sound of the little piano in the corner of the parlor. That would be Lisle Stahlbaum, who'd had quite a career as a pianist in her youth. Christian allowed himself a small, nostalgic smile, then forced it wider as he hefted the brass knocker and announced his arrival.

"Uncle Drosselmeyer!" came a rousing chorus as he swept into the foyer, the chill night air wafting from his great coat.

"Merry Christmas, meine kinder!" he bellowed. He gently lowered his package to the floor beside the resplendent Christmas tree and was accepted into the house of his foster family.

The scents of pine, woodsmoke, and mulled wine assailed him. The Stahlbaums were famous for their Christmas Eve parties. Half the neighborhood was here—a good sign. There was safety in numbers for people this night.

He scanned the grand parlor, heavy with garlands and the scent of clove-studded oranges. A fire crackled in the marble hearth that took up the better part of the far wall. He would see to closing the flue the moment the fire died. There was his foster brother, Franz, with his young son, Fritz, Franz's wife, Lisle, and his goddaughter, Marie. Here were the Gerstenfelds from across the road, and the Pfeffers, and Mrs. Walden from the kitchens, and their maid, Clara, serving hot mulled wine. He accepted a glass of the spiced drink gratefully and turned to his foster brother.

"Christian, we've heard so little from you after you wrote about your royal position, and now, two visits in the same year?" Lisle exclaimed. "We'll begin to think you miss us."

"Of course I've missed you," Christian replied. "All of you. The past few years have been difficult. I tried to send word when I could."

He scanned the room and spied a large box in the corner.

"Ah, my packages have arrived," he noted with satisfaction.

"As they do every year," Lisle assured him, gently placing a hand on his arm. There was a strange tugging in his chest that he recognized as longing. The Master Clockmaker of Boldavia was homesick.

"Well, don't just stand there," Franz said. "The children have been desperate with anticipation for days!"

The tugging in his chest grew stronger.

"Very well." For a few moments, Christian Drosselmeyer allowed himself to be at home. He played with his young foster nieces and nephews, congratulated the older ones on their accomplishments. He pried open the crate sent so many months ago out of foreign ports of call, and unpacked his gifts.

A ballerina unfolded from the crate and rose to her full five-foot height and danced delicately before the cluster of children and adults. Then there came the jester, and then a

Moor, mimicking the whirling dance of one of King Almande's entertainers.

The children laughed and clapped, and the adults congratulated him, while Marie, his favorite, sat in the corner reading quietly and offering her applause when called for.

At last, the furor moved on without him and he went to Marie's side.

"Ah, so now you see me," she said, her brown eyes sparkling merrily in the firelight.

Christian kissed her hand. "Young lady, I hardly recognized you, so beautiful have you become."

She swatted him with her book. "Come, Uncle, the only thing that's grown here is your nose. What is the corpse in the winding sheet over there? What have you brought into our house?"

Christian scowled. "You are too bright by far, Marie. It's something that deserves tender care and safekeeping."

"Then you'd best bring it here. Fritz is knocking it to the floor."

Christian rushed to save Stefan from a fate worse than he'd already suffered, but he was too late. The veil slipped, and the beautifully carved soldier fell facedown onto the floor.

Fritz jumped back. "Sorry, Uncle Christian! It slipped!"

His mother gasped. "Fritz Stahlbaum, you little terror!"

Only Christian noticed the split lip.

"I am so sorry, Christian. Has he broken one of your manikins?" Lisle asked. She was so like her daughter, Marie, but a harmless honeybee, where Marie could sting.

"He'll be fine. I . . ." Christian picked up his cousin.

"So lifelike," Franz exclaimed.

300

"Indeed." Christian touched the split lip. It came away reddened with—

"Sap? How freshly you carve your wood!" his foster brother said.

"Father, really," Marie said, pushing through the cluster of guests. "Your son has destroyed my gift. I'll take him from you, Uncle," she said gently, and lifted the doll in her arms.

"What a clever nutcracker he is," she said, and carried her prize up the stairs.

MARIE STAHLBAUM'S ROOM would be the envy of collectors everywhere. The walls were lined with neatly kept cupboards, each containing row upon row of clever, beautiful dolls. They watched with silent glass or painted eyes as she entered the room with her latest acquisition.

Laying the nutcracker on the counterpane of her four-poster bed, she examined the lip. "Curious, indeed." She cast about for a napkin or handkerchief to blot the sap with, and found the corner of one sticking out of the toy soldier's pocket.

"Thank you," she said, and tugged it free. She shook the linen open and nearly dropped it—a small handkerchief embroidered with the letter "S" in pale blue.

"Impossible!" she exclaimed, and looked into the toy soldier's wooden gray eyes.

It *was* impossible. But evidently true.

55

"THE ASSASSIN. Where is he?" the King of Mice demanded. He paced the hard-packed floor as his piebalds scrambled to answer.

One tough-looking mouse stood to attention while the others conferred behind him. "Sires, we have followed the clockmaker and his companions to three locations. The main market, the gardens, and a private home off a residential square. Our spies are attempting to infiltrate. We should know which of the three harbors the assassin within the hour."

"An hour is a lifetime," Roland said.

"Too long!" Genghis spat. "We should attack them all. Teach these men to fear us! Take the city, and our mother's killer will also fall."

Charlemagne hissed through curled lips, balling their paw into a fist. "The city. We'll crush it as we did Boldavia. For mousedom."

"For Mother!" Arthur said. He turned his brothers away from the gathering of spies until they faced one of the soaring cavern walls. The underbelly of Nuremberg was unlike anything they had ever seen. The constant roar of the river above- and belowground was similar enough to the susurration of Boldavia's shoreline, but there was another sound. A grinding, as if the bones of the very earth were breaking. It made Arthur uneasy.

The wheels of the world were turning. At any moment he could be crushed.

But not before he took the life of the boy that killed his mother. Let his brothers become emperors and rulers of Men. Arthur no longer cared. His mother was dead, and with her his last hope of love. He had no heart for conquest, but he would have his revenge. As long as he lived up to one-seventh of her expectations. Let his brothers do the rest.

He turned to his spies. "Take them."

The piebalds looked up from their plans, like pigeons scrounging for feed in a park.

"Sire?" the tough one said apologetically.

"Three targets. Take them all. We will not wait a moment longer. Vengeance is at hand."

The piebald hesitated. "The townhouse and the villa, yes, but sire . . . the marketplace? It is what the men call a holiday. The square is unmanageably large and packed with them. I am afraid it is strategically impossible."

"Impossible?" the King said coldly, his voices harmonizing in a way that made even Arthur's fur crawl. "*We* are impossible. Yet, Boldavia is ours. *You* are ours. If it costs us your life, we will spend it gladly. For the honor of our fallen Queen."

The piebald blanched, a strange effect behind his mottled fur. "Sire." He dropped to one knee and bowed until his whiskers brushed the ground.

56

"WAKE UP, BEAUTIFUL BOY. Wake up!"

A cool hand slapped his cheek. Stefan blinked his eyes open. "Mother?"

"I should hope not," a wry voice replied.

"What?" Stefan rubbed his eyes with stiff wooden hands. His lids rasped over the hardened orbs. His body creaked when he moved, like an old ship bobbing at sea. But his arms and legs seemed to obey his commands. He looked at his wrist. A well-carved ball-and-socket joint allowed his hand to swivel, almost like a real wrist. It loosened up as he worked it round, becoming more natural with each revolution. Next, he cracked his fingers. They clacked open and closed, each joint as well made as the most poseable of his father's toys. He sighed and blinked.

A girl was standing over him.

"Clara!"

She smiled. "Not exactly."

He sat up, his waist bending oddly at what he realized was now a hinge. His heart beat furiously in its frozen cage. "Beautiful?"

"Thank you," she said with a little curtsy.

"No, not you—"

"Oh. I see."

"No! I mean, of course you. You're beautiful. But you called *me* beautiful. It's not dark enough in here to make that mistake."

Clara's smile returned. She dropped down to sit beside him.

He was in a bedroom, he realized. A rather nice one, with a soft mattress and walls full of books and well-made dolls. Carefully, he pulled himself up farther and rested his back against the pillows.

His knuckles had seams and little carved joints. They didn't feel quite like his own, nor did the rest of his body. He felt like a marionette, but one that he could control with his mind. Like he'd told Princess Pirlipat, he appeared to be well made. He touched his face with a clack of wooden fingertip on wooden skin. Well made, but ugly.

"Of course you're beautiful, Stefan," Clara said. "Any boy who has gone through what you've obviously suffered and still kept this next to his heart"—she held up the folded square of linen—"is beautiful indeed."

Stefan felt himself blush, his wooden cheeks flushing with sap. At least that part of himself still worked normally. "I told you I'd keep it with me," he replied.

"Of course you did. It's what all young men say, but not what most of them do." Her smile faded into a gentle look of tenderness. She dropped the handkerchief to his chest and patted it. "And I owe you an apology. I did what young women do. I lied about my name."

"It isn't Clara?"

"Clara's our maid."

"But why?"

"Because proper young ladies don't hide in the arboretum with their toes in the dirt when they're meant to be home learning to be dull. If Arno had known I was more than a simple maid, he'd have thrown me out long ago. Imagine the scandal, a groundskeeper alone with the unescorted daughter of a respectable family. It would be in all the papers, and give my mother a heart attack! As would a talking nutcracker, I suppose. But you won't turn me in, will you?"

"I . . . no, never." He struggled to keep up with the quickness of her tongue.

"Good. Then, my real name is Marie. Marie Stahlbaum."

Her eyes dropped significantly to the handkerchief with its neatly embroidered "S."

"Of course." Had he still been made of flesh, his already red face would have also gone hot. Humiliation on top of humiliation.

Why had Christian brought him here, of all places?

"But that changes nothing else," she said. "A rose by any other name, and all that. Though I prefer tulips, and seem to be more of a dandelion, personality-wise."

Clara, now Marie, was just as he remembered her. The warm brown eyes, the shining braids. She had been in his thoughts since the day they met.

Stefan groaned and she gripped his hand. "What is it?"

"I've just realized, I've written an awful lot of letters to your maid."

"Then let's hope the mail is slow." Marie smiled and her eyes danced.

Stefan struggled to form a grin, but could not. "Worse. I forgot to mail them."

"Never mind the letters, my poor nutcracker," Marie said,

smoothing his cheeks with her hand. "It seems you've had quite an adventure. Sit up now, and tell me all."

Like poison leeched from a wound, the story came out.

The death of his mother, his flight from Nuremberg. Losing Christian. The Pagoda Tree. The teeth, the princess, the nut. The Queen of Mice.

"That old wolf has gotten you into more trouble than either of you can handle," Marie surmised at the end. "My godfather is many things, but uncomplicated isn't one of them."

"Christian's your godfather?"

"I'm afraid so. More like an uncle, really. You know he was orphaned and raised by my father's family?"

Stefan laughed a short, harsh bark. "I know nothing about him. He showed up on the worst day of my life, shook the world upside down, and—"

Something flickered in the corner of the room. The same sort of flicker he had seen in the throne room of Boldavia. The vermin couldn't possibly have reached Nuremberg so quickly.

But they had.

The mouse came into full view and headed straight for Marie.

"No! Leave her alone!" Stefan cried, and leapt up from the bed to throw himself at the creature.

The mouse squealed as Stefan came down, pounding his wooden fist.

Marie leapt up onto the bed. "Kinyata!" she cried.

A great orange cat with yellow eyes emerged from the hallway, pressing the door open with her huge weight. Glancing curiously at the wooden boy on the floor, and the mottled brown mouse in his grasp, the cat decided on the familiar, and went after the mouse.

Stefan pulled away as the cat batted its prey. The mouse let out a high-pitched squeal that made even Stefan's sap turn cold. A moment later, there was a crunch. A pink tail twitched in the corner of the cat's mouth, and was gone.

Kinyata smiled, prowled the perimeter of the room, and then, seemingly satisfied, left again.

Stefan and Marie stared at each other. The silence was broken when Christian burst through the door in his robe.

"Marie!" He shut the door behind him. This was not something for the rest of the household to hear. "Gods, Stefan, you're awake! Have you frightened this girl?"

Stefan's jaw worked, but no sound came out.

Before he found his voice, Marie stepped in. "No, Uncle, in fact he saved me. From a mouse," she said, climbing down to sit on the settee.

Christian's face turned gray. He helped Stefan up from the floor. "They've found us, then."

"No," Stefan replied, with a glance toward Marie. "I caught the mouse. But her cat—"

"Kinyata," Marie said, nodding.

"Kinyata . . . finished him off. They might not have word yet."

"I see." Christian sighed and joined his niece on the settee. "Marie, this is Stefan Drosselmeyer. My cousin's son."

"We've met," Marie said.

Not as recently as he probably believes, Stefan thought.

Christian nodded. "He lives on the other side of town. I feared he wouldn't be safe there, so I brought him here."

"Is anyone hungry?" Marie asked.

"Actually, I'm starving," Stefan said.

"Me too. I'll get you some soup so you don't try your jaw." She fixed her uncle with a stern look.

Stefan was surprised to see Christian blanch under that glare.

"And when I return, Uncle, you'll tell us how you plan on fixing this mess."

57

GULLET HURRIED THROUGH the tunnels as quickly as his feet would carry him. On his head he wore a miner's helmet with a red lantern affixed to the center. It made him look like a crimson-eyed cyclops. Between his lips, he held a small silver pipe that he blew into every so often. It could not be heard by human ears, but it was certain to keep all rodents away.

Most of the Brotherhood was spread out across the city aboveground. While the City Clock lay in the catacombs, the city's *clocks* perched in church steeples and towers far above the madding crowds made for good lookout points. An advantage when your city was under siege, and as safe a location as any when the enemy came swarming from underground. But there was one place where the clockmakers still held sway beneath the city.

A position to be maintained at all cost.

Within minutes, Gullet had reached the Cogworks. Pausing to insert some ear plugs, he cranked the door wide and sealed it shut behind him. Within the great room, the shimmering gears of the City Clock moaned as if in pain. Gullet had lived long enough to witness a shift in the clock once before, years ago. When the Black Plague spread through Barvaria, thousands of shining cogs had shifted and fallen away. So many deaths had devastated the clock movement, and it hurt his bones as deeply then as it did now.

But Gullet was not a sentimental man. It had taken years for all of the fallen cogs to be replaced with new ones. But it had happened, and balance had been regained. So it would be again, in due time.

Gullet waved a short arm over his head at the cogsmen on shift. Brühl and Waltz waved back, but only Brühl clambered down from the scaffolding. The man wore goggles and ear plugs, and a belt over his leather apron. The belt held a jar of grease for the gears and a variety of wrenches and keys for fine-tuning the clock. They often had to adjust for drag on the pendulum caused by moisture in the atmosphere. The job of the cogsmen was to keep the City Clock running accurately. Which often meant clearing debris and, quite literally, bugs. The insect kingdom was one of the few that proved near impossible to regulate by city clockery.

"How's she holding?" Gullet asked when Brühl was close enough to hear him over the churning of the machinery.

He was a lanky fellow with a tendency to shrug. He did so now, almost apologetically. "She'll hold, but she's shifting and there's not much we can do to stop it."

Gullet nodded and led the cogsman over to the desk-size replica of the Cogworks. He pointed to the rod of the pendulum, where it was anchored onto a large gear.

The movement of the entire mechanism was managed with weights that hung from chains looped over the teeth of a series of gears—each weight controlled the hour, the minute, the second, the chime, like any pendulum clock. But this was a City Clock, and far more complex.

There were weights for all the kingdoms of Man and Animal,

for the planets, the seasons, and any other measurable unit of time. The weight assigned to the Kingdom of Mice had been shifting ever since the mouse army turned its head toward Nuremberg. Soon, the pendulum would swing to a different beat.

"We can't stop it from here, but we can slow things down a bit."

"Sir?" Brühl asked. "You mean . . . tamper with the weights?" It was interference of the highest order, and something no self-respecting member of the Brotherhood would ever attempt to do.

"Don't be ridiculous, Brühl. Just lower the pendulum. We can't shift the balance, but we *can* slow down time. The world will take its course either way, just not as fast as it might like." He jotted a few names and dates on a scrap of paper and thrust it at the cogsman. "Here. When we're finished, adjust the cogs for these names, along with those of the Brotherhood. We'll need agents afoot during this madness."

Unlocking a cabinet against the wall, Gullet revealed a series of keys and wrenches hanging from hooks. He removed the largest of these, a socket wrench the size of his leg, and hefted it over his shoulder. "Can you manage the basket, or shall I?"

Brühl glanced about nervously. "I . . . uh . . ."

Gullet rolled his eyes. "Just the basket, Brühl. This is my task to complete. Be quick. And set the organ playing," he added, holding up his silver pipe. "We need to keep this room clear." A self-playing organ had been installed in the cavern years ago, tuned to deter various sorts of vermin as needed. It would not play forever, but wound properly, the mice would steer clear of the Cogworks for a while. "Buck up, now. I'll be back soon."

The cogsman sighed with relief, took the wrench from Gullet, and scurried to set up the basket.

Gullet craned his neck. The pendulum swung through this chamber every thirty-seven minutes. It would hover overhead for less than twenty seconds. At the end of the great golden disc was a small hexagonal nut, the size of a man's fist, made of the same shining metal and bolted to the base of the rod. This was the adjusting nut for which the socket wrench had been designed.

Time was slipping away. The gears of the great clock clamored in tiny increments. Gullet checked his pocket watch out of habit. He clapped the brass casing open and closed, ticking off the seconds.

"Sir, ready when you are," the cogsman said. A breeze lifted the hair off the top of his head. The pendulum was swinging nigh.

Brühl operated the pulley system to raise Gullet in a basket usually reserved for hoisting cleaning crews into the works. Moments later, the great disc swung into view. Brühl threw his weight against the levers, keeping the basket beneath the gliding saucer. Gullet took a steadying breath, slipped the socket wrench onto the pendulum, and gave the adjustment nut a counterclockwise quarter-turn twist.

Nuts, Gullet thought bitterly a few moments later, shutting the door to the Cogworks behind him. He blew on his silver pipe and adjusted the wick on his lantern. This whole Boldavian misadventure came down to a handful of nuts.

At least this one would buy Christian some time. He hoped that it would be enough.

58

ZACHARIAS HAD BITTEN his nails to the quick. Sitting on the judging stage beside his giant nutcracker soldier, he watched his neighbors and friends carry on normally while his son hid for his life across the city.

This was lonely work. People swirled around him like colorful snowflakes in the wind. Girls in their winter coats clustered together, laughing and whispering like conspiratorial hens. Young men in new hats strutted by like peacocks. Babies bounced in daddies' arms. Mothers herded their children past the toy display, clucking at naughty little ones who certainly could *not* have yet *another* toy before morning. It was a veritable farmyard of humanity. Wonderful, but utterly alien to him tonight.

Samir had shared Stefan's analogy of the Horsemen of the Apocalypse with Zacharias. Now, all he could see was how many of these good people would fall to the famine and pestilence of mice.

"Come, Zacharias. You act as if this is your first Kindlesmarkt!" Tobias Muller said, thumping him on the back. Tobias was a woodmaker like Zacharias, but where they might have been rivals, they were friends.

"Of course, this will be the hardest time of year, with Elise gone now. You always were a nervous one in competition. She knew how to handle you just so," Tobias said kindly. "This piece of yours, though. It's wonderful. A perfect blend of truth and whimsy. I thought it was Stefan himself when you first arrived. It's sure to do well tonight. It's one of a kind."

In fact, it's three of a kind, Zacharias thought. Smiling, he allowed himself to be cajoled into drinking a cup of hot cider. As the warmth of cinnamon and apples filled his mouth, the taste of fear and the chill of the Boldavian dungeons began to wash away. He was safe for the first time in many weeks.

And then the screaming began.

SAMIR HAD BARELY REACHED the street when the enemy appeared. The road before Professor Blume's house was teeming with mice.

Samir turned and ran. Down the walkway, through the rows of carefully tended flowering shrubs, the annuals, the perennials, the evergreens. His boots slapped the flagstones as he bounded up the front steps. He raised his fist and banged on the door.

Professor Blume blinked out into the night air. "Yes?"

Samir broke into a relieved grin. "I'll have that tea after all, if you don't mind."

The old botanist stepped back and let the Arab inside. He did not appear to notice that the underbrush in his garden was moving.

Samir pulled him away from the door, throwing the bolt.

"I say, it looked a bit breezy out there," the professor said.

"Indeed, that is what chased me back," Samir lied. He peered out into the night from behind a heavily draped curtain. "Must be a storm coming," he murmured less boisterously.

For on the lawn and in the trees, the eyes of a hundred mice looked back at him.

59

IT WAS MARIE'S IDEA TO send Kinyata out for more information.

Stefan watched, impressed, as the girl knelt by the cat and whispered the task into her ear.

"Find us another mouseling, Kinyata. But don't hurt it. Bring it to us. Uncle Drosselmeyer wants to talk to it."

"You speak Catish?" Stefan asked.

Marie shook her head, eyes still on her pet. "I haven't a clue. But Kinyata understands me."

The cat blinked her yellow eyes slowly. With a soft *mrrowl*, she padded to the window and leapt out onto the open ledge.

"She climbs down the tree next door. Scared me half to death coming home one night, scratching at the window. I must've closed it not knowing she was gone. But now, no matter the weather, I keep it open just enough for her."

Christian frowned. "If a cat can get out, a mouse can get in. When Kinyata returns, we'll have to find a better way of securing your room. It's not safe here until we do."

"It will be if I leave," Stefan said. "I can't stay here if they know where I am. I won't put anyone else in danger."

"They don't know where you are yet," Christian said. "And, quite frankly, I don't know where else to go. Let's not make decisions until we have our stool pigeon. And then we'll know where we stand."

A knock at the door announced the light supper Marie had ordered.

Stefan froze into the perfect likeness of a doll as Marie opened the door.

A gray-haired woman entered with a tray.

"Thank you, *Clara*," Marie said with emphasis.

Stefan stifled a chuckle.

"Now don't leave a mess, Miss Marie. We don't want to draw any nasty pests," the maid admonished. Clearly, she had once been Marie's nurse. "Merry Christmas, Miss, Herr Drosselmeyer." Clara dipped a curtsy and left them to their snack.

Half an hour later, Kinyata returned, her fur damp from prowling the misty night. In her mouth was a motionless gray-and-white mouse.

"She's killed it," Stefan said.

"No, she hasn't," Marie replied. She picked the mouse up from Kinyata's delicate grip. "It's fainted." Her mouth pursed in concern. "How do you revive a mouse?"

Efficient as an army nurse, Marie laid her patient on the dressing table. After a moment's thought, she reached for a small bottle, and waved the stopper beneath the mouse's nose.

"Rose water," she explained.

It seemed to work. The mouse's nostrils twitched, and then its eyelids fluttered, revealing pink, albino eyes.

"BE CALM, WE WON'T hurt you," the human growled.

Dusker forced himself to squirm the way a mouse would be expected to. But his mind was not clouded by fear. He assessed the situation the way he was trained to.

The smell of the cat that had caught him was fading, but a sniff told him the beast was still in the room. *Stupid*, being caught like that. He'd be demoted if he ever survived this encounter. It would be no less than he deserved.

Dusker had been on reconnaissance for the chief of intelligence himself, having just left the presence of his commander and a glimpse of the wondrous King. It was the sight of the King that had set Dusker's head whirling off the task at hand. He had to concentrate to deal with the situation. *Ponder the wonders of the universe later,* he told himself. *For now, survive.*

Dusker squealed incomprehensibly, in a convincing imitation of dumb terror. The human frowned at him. It was a male. From the description Dusker had been given, he supposed it was the clockmaker himself, the one who had thwarted the Queen's curse in Boldavia with that despicable nut.

Dusker scented the air. Perhaps the boy was here, too. The piebald shuddered for real this time, but in pleasure, not fear. To bring the new King this prize would establish him forever in the intelligence branch.

"Don't kill me, don't kill me!" Dusker cried in his best country accent. He doubted the human was familiar with mouse dialects, but it was always best to be thorough when undercover.

A second human, the one with the rose water, appeared distressed by his cries. *Good. A sympathizer.*

The cat was still in the room. It leapt up onto the table to peer at him with murderous interest.

Dusker cursed himself for a fool. Best to get this scene over with, discover how much the humans knew.

"What do you want?" He spoke more clearly, dropping the country act.

The clockmaker's lips parted in a vicious smile. "Ah," he said in passable Mouseish, "you know who I am?"

There was no use lying. Honesty brought answers more quickly. He nodded once, yes.

The girl beside the clockmaker seemed anxious, or curious. Dusker wished he had a better grasp of human languages.

"Have you reported our location yet?" the clockmaker asked.

Dusker hesitated. If he said yes, the humans might kill him now, with nothing else to lose. If he said no, they still might kill him, or they might keep him for later.

Dusker shook his head, no.

"When do they expect to hear from you next?" The human seemed to have all the right questions.

"At dawn," Dusker lied. In for a nibble, in for a bite—dawn was as good a time as any to die, if it came to that. There were too many mice out to even consider a periodic report from each of them. Instead, each scout had been given one command— report when you find the clockmaker and his boy, or do not come back. The King's intelligence had spies out in every quarter, scouring the city for the clockmaker. Dusker had found him only by misfortune.

The clockmaker nodded, and exchanged some words with the girl, who'd been watching with great interest. She produced a small cage and ushered him inside. The lock was simple, a latch he could easily throw with a paw. But, he would not do it. Even when the girl took the extra step of covering the cage with a thick towel, dampening sounds and blocking his sight, Dusker merely smiled.

It was difficult enough to be a piebald in this day and age, but being albino was worse. Dusker would have been lucky to make sergeant. But, his luck had changed. He had the clockmaker, one way or another, which meant a promotion. He'd be a hero to the crown. Not to mention warm and dry until sunrise. His comrades in the sewers and streets of Nuremberg would not be so lucky tonight.

"WE'RE SAFE UNTIL DAWN, at least. That gives us some time," Christian told them.

"That was Mouseish? Such a painful-sounding language," Marie said.

"I'm sure German sounds quite clunky to them," Christian replied.

"Where is my father?" Stefan wanted to know.

"Safe for the moment at the Kindlesmarkt." Christian pulled a watch from his pocket. "Which lasts for another hour. Time to put on our thinking caps. By then we'll need a plan."

"What about the cats?" Marie asked. "Can't they do something against an army of mice?"

Christian shrugged. "If they wanted to, I suppose. But, aside from your friendship with Kinyata, diplomacy is difficult in the language of cats. Furthermore, what the politics are between other animal kingdoms, I can't say. Let's not forget our history. In Boldavia, and in Hameln years ago, cats were nowhere to be found. We've no reason to think Nuremberg will be any different."

320

"Well, that hardly seems fair." Marie frowned and flounced down on the edge of her bed. "Let's rouse the mouse again and ask him about his army. Kinyata will make him tell the truth."

"Marie, my dear, we already know the truth. The King is here. His soldiers are beneath the city—" Christian broke off, thinking.

Stefan's own mind had wandered, flowing beneath Nuremberg, following paths they had walked just weeks ago. "The catacombs of the Brotherhood!" he exclaimed. "If the mice are here, wouldn't your friend Gullet know where?"

"Without a doubt." Christian nodded. "It's time for a little reconnaissance mission of our own. Keep an eye on our guest, you two. Rest, if you can. And Stefan, watch over Marie."

She gave him a look.

Christian cleared his throat. "I mean . . . look after each *other*. If I'm not back by morning, send for Samir. He and Zacharias are supposed to meet me at the clock tower at midnight. Send for them there. Samir will make sure you are all safe. But then, God help us all."

60

THEY CAME FROM UNDERGROUND. First at the edges of the Kindlesmarkt, then from the drains and sewers that dotted the cobblestone square. From beneath the carts and stands with their fresh gingerbread, their candles and soaps, their trinkets and dolls.

The mice rose.

"Aieeeee!" A woman screamed and tried to jump onto the counter of her cart. It toppled under her weight, sending delicate ceramic mugs shattering to the ground.

Around her, women dragged shrieking children into their arms. Men stamped the cobblestones with hobnail boots. Girls fainted, boys laughed, until it became clear that this was no prank. The Kindlesmarkt was under attack.

A brigade of piebalds led the march; swarming through legs that could crush and maim, they ran with the fearlessness that gives rise to legends. Passing the nut vendors, the cake sellers, the sweetmeat men, they ran until they reached the stage of the toymakers' guild, guarded by a figure in red coat and black boots. A nutcracker. The boy that killed their Queen.

A man shouted hoarsely as the figurine was pulled into the vortex of mice. Teeth, eyes, claws flashed, and suddenly, as if sharing an exhalation, the mice stopped and pulled away.

The piebalds conferred and gave out orders. It had been

a ruse, a manikin of the young Drosselmeyer hiding in plain sight. That left the garden villa and the townhouse across the city.

As quickly as they had come, the mice retreated, leaving stunned revelers clinging to the booths and carts of the Kindlesmarkt like driftwood abandoned by the tide.

From the safety of the Christkind's balcony, pulled there by the quick-thinking Tobias, Zacharias Drosselmeyer watched the enemy take a trophy before the last of the army left.

They severed the head of the nutcracker and carried it away.

On the balcony, crushed into the press of hysterical women and men, the golden girl in her Christkind costume took Zacharias's hand and held it as the toymaker stifled a sob.

"THE DOLL, WHERE IS IT?" Samir asked.

Professor Blume was barely able to catch his guest's teacup as it toppled from the serving tray. "Goodness, it's right here. In my study."

Samir looked around him.

"No, no, my study. The greenhouse. It's a sunroom. A wonderful thing for someone used to warmer climates, such as yourself, I would imagine."

He led the way with a dawning awareness that something was agitating the Arab at his heels.

"Right through—oh . . ." The professor stopped in his tracks, face pressed to the glass door.

Samir swore softly.

A whirlwind had reaped the greenery. Plants lay in shreds,

roots exposed, bulbs eaten away. Mice were everywhere. And destruction followed in their path.

The professor's jaw worked as he tried to speak, and failed.

Samir placed a firm hand on the man's shoulder and pulled him aside. "Oh, Stefan," he murmured, and his heart fell.

In the middle of the once lush room, spread-eagled like a fallen scarecrow, lay the nutcracker doll. Torn, chewed, and battered. The mice had taken its head. There would be no mercy for Stefan, if he was discovered. The mice would not hesitate to kill. Samir could only hope Christian had hidden him well.

"My beautiful plants," Professor Blume moaned. "My lovely *Aspidistra campanulata . . .*" His fingers trailed down the windowpanes in the door. "Wait! Where are you going?" he cried.

But Samir was already gone.

61

ERNST SAT IN his damp cell—a cage of roots guarded by two piebald mice. If he had any hope of outrunning his captors, he would have chewed through the roots an hour ago. But the mouse army of Boldavia was as wide as an inland sea, and he was but a tiny raindrop.

You're a fool, Ernst, he told himself. He had seen madness in the Queen's eye, and used it to feed himself, to cloak himself in glory. But now it was time to pay the Piper. He laughed bitterly. The Queen had been right. Hameln was a failure for ratkind alone. Soon, Nuremberg would belong to the mice. And then what use would there be for a washed-up rat?

"Captain to see the prisoner!"

The piebalds guarding his cage snapped to attention.

Ernst peered through the root bars with interest. Even bad news meant new opportunities, and he'd rather not waste the whole night in jail. He rose and straightened his coat and tail.

The captain was none other than Snitter, the hoary-furred piebald who'd hired him so long ago.

"Not so different from that tavern in Vienna, is it?" Snitter asked in his rough voice.

Ernst wrinkled his nose. "No, I suppose not. Except a warm stove would be welcome right about now."

"No doubt," the old soldier said. "I see you served our Queen well. Her boys have come a long way under your tutelage."

"Under her spell, is more like it," Ernst said before he could stop himself. Bitterness never won allies. "The Queen was a formidable mouse."

"The Queen, in my opinion, was mad," Snitter said without compunction. Beside him, the guards' ears twitched. Such remarks were treason, and traitors belonged on Ernst's side of the cage. "But perhaps madness is divine after all," Snitter added smoothly.

The guards shared a glance and shrugged.

"What brings you my way?" Ernst asked. "Small talk is a fine art, but it can be managed just as well outside of a prison cell."

Snitter laughed. "Patience, Herr Tutor. The King might have need of you yet. I just came by for a little company. You and I are alone here, Listz. Never mind the guards. They'll do as they're told. But tell me. My mice will follow their King to the very shores of death on faith alone. Is it well founded? You helped raise these boys. I need to know—can they do it? Can they topple a city like Nuremberg? If so, we'll back the King to the very end. Or should we . . . cut our losses, when the time comes? Let the madness end with the King?"

Ernst peered at Snitter through the roots. The mouse was getting on in seasons. This would likely be his last campaign. The outcome mattered little for him, then—unless he was the sort of leader who cared about his troops. Would he be willing to let his King commit suicide rather than see his foot soldiers' lives dashed uselessly upon the rocks of vanity?

Ernst made a decision. One that he hoped would get him out of this cage and back into the game.

"Yes," he said. "They can."

Snitter whistled a low breath, and a weight seemed to lift from his shoulders.

"With guidance, that is," Ernst added quickly. "From those of us who have more experience."

The old mouse gave Ernst a strange look. "Very clever. Now, if I leave you here and we lose, it'll be my fault. If I let you out and we lose, none of us will live to regret it. But, if we win . . ." At last, Snitter waved a paw for the guards to open the cage door. "You're crafty, rat. I'll give you that. And we'll need craftiness on top of numbers to win this war. You're reinstated. Come with me."

62

CHRISTIAN HURRIED HEEDLESSLY through the streets of the city. After the first few stealthy blocks, he no longer cared about Boldavian spies. It would confuse the mice to see him alone. His coattails flapped in the wind as he ate up the distance in long, loping strides.

The streets were empty of both man and beast. The people, of course, were at the Kindlesmarkt or in their own homes. But that did not explain the lack of mice.

The university clock chimed ten. Christian checked his pocket watch. It was a quarter past. He would have to fix that clock, someday. Heaven willing there *was* a someday.

Using his master key, Christian slipped through the rear entrance to the clockmakers' guild. Once inside the descending chamber, he patted his pockets and withdrew a red headlamp. It had led him safely through the dungeons of Boldavia—mice could not see red light—and he knew he would need it here. While the streets of Nuremberg may have been empty, he was sure the cellars would be a different story.

The door to the little office opened. "Gullet?" Christian called. A light shone at the desk, but the room itself was unoccupied. Christian crossed the room to the hidden door behind the desk, and hesitated. It was no different than searching the dungeons for Zacharias. Except now the mice were expecting him. "For Stefan," he muttered.

Lowering his headlamp, he went through the door and into the catacombs.

It was deathly quiet in the dark tunnels. The rush of the river and the groaning of the City Clock were both drowned out by the beating of his own heart. Christian followed the path of ruddy light cast from his headlamp. He hadn't gone far when a rocketing figure bowled him over. His headlamp fell over his eye and went out.

"God's sake!" a voice bellowed.

"Gullet?"

Christian fumbled for his flint again, but his assailant beat him to it, opening the shutters on the lamp he wore, bathing them both in a deep ruby light.

"Good, it's you, then," Gullet said by way of reply. He reached down a thick hand and helped haul Christian to his feet. "You should have better sense than to be down here, but I've been looking for you, so it saves me a trip."

"I've been looking for you, too."

"Really?" Gullet said dryly, with a glance around the cavern. "The mess you've made, Drosselmeyer, it astounds me. The Kindlesmarkt's been overrun, then some house near the botanical gardens. And now you've gone pale, so I assume you know the reason."

"We gave them decoys," Christian said in a broken voice. "But I didn't think they would act so boldly—or so quickly."

Gullet frowned. "Yes, well, you're not the only rash youngster

329

in town, it would seem. The mice have a new leader. A persuasive one, from the sound of it."

"I need to get back to my cousin. He killed their Queen. He's in danger."

"We're *all* in danger, Christian. It's the one thing you seem to keep forgetting about clockery. Gears upon gears, one move affects the others. We'd best get a handle on this quickly, before Nuremberg is lost."

Gullet turned and led Christian back the way he had come.

"The catacombs are difficult to travel tonight with our new tenants in town." If the Kindlesmarkt and Herr Blume's house had been attacked simultaneously, Christian could only begin to imagine what size army he faced. "Boldavia was overrun, it's true. But this is Nuremberg. It's seven times Boldavia's size. How many mice are we dealing with?"

Gullet granted Christian a sidelong glance of pity. "Better to ask how many drops of water in the sea, boy. They're vermin. And they're not just Boldavian. They've joined forces, these mice— we've gotten reports from the Netherlands to the Black Sea. If we aren't careful, the scales will tip and the world will belong to Rodentia."

Christian balled his gloved hand into a fist. "I'll stop them," he swore through clenched teeth. "Mice are nothing without a strong leader. Like the hydra, cut off the head and the body dies." Christian wished he was as certain as he sounded.

"The analogy is more apropos than you realize, Drosselmeyer. The trick will be in guessing which head to take. Our hydra, we're told, has seven."

Christian stopped in his tracks. He braced himself against

the damp wall of the cave, his glove sinking into the mossy slime. The gears and cogs of the city groaned like old men.

"The spy we captured said the King was divine. I took it as fanaticism. Not fact."

"One leads to the other, eventually," Gullet commented. He stopped at an alcove that contained a plain wooden door, and produced a ring of skeleton keys. "In here. There are some things you'll be needing. And then I'll show you the devils' lair."

The door swung open to reveal a room full of chests.

"Ho, Gullet. This room is new," Christian said.

"Not new, just off-limits to the likes of you," Gullet replied. "Some clockworks are not for everyone to toy with. You, of all people, should know that."

"What does that mean?" Christian asked. He had studied all the levels of clockwork there were—mechanical, celestial, mundane . . .

Fishing in his pocket, Gullet produced a small brass key and unlocked a wardrobe against the back wall. The cabinet swung open in the soft light of Gullet's torch.

Christian's mouth fell open, his pulse quickening. "An unwinding key . . ." He shook his head in wonder. "I thought they no longer existed."

"Nor should they," Gullet grunted. All clockmakers had pondered it, much the way alchemists had striven to turn lead into gold: a key to unwind a living soul. Could a human even begin to divine the clockworks of the immortal soul? For most of the Brotherhood, the search had proven to be a fool's errand. But not for all of them, it seemed.

Christian frowned. It would not do to be careless with such a tool.

"A drastic measure. But, I suspect you'll find a use for it, somehow," Gullet said, placing the key in a narrow sack. He handed the bag to Christian, who stood there, torn between the need for haste and a new, unexpected fear. "Now, let me take you closer to home."

Christian came back to himself. He had gotten the help he'd come for. Now he needed to find Samir and Zacharias. "The university clock tower. My companions will be there. But first . . ."

Gullet read his mind. "Reconnaissance? On the way. Believe me, you'll want to keep moving once you see the force they've got on their side."

Gullet sealed the room behind them, and led the way deeper into the catacombs.

Above their heads, the city clockworks ticked with purpose. It had been lifetimes since Christian had delved this deeply into the tunnels beneath the city. The slow roaring sound that steadily built over their heads told him they had reached the place where the river ran above them, through the very heart of Nuremberg. The walls grew wet with spray as they followed the course of the river. Their red lamplight flickered in the moist air.

When the river was its loudest, Gullet turned away down a side tunnel that narrowed until Christian was forced into a crouch. The roar of the river fell away behind them, and a new sound poured out of the tunnel in front. Gullet slowed and edged forward. Raising a hand in warning, he shuttered his lamp.

Christian stifled a protest. It was pitch-black, too dark for human eyes. Until he realized he could see.

They were in the mouth of a tunnel that spilled out into a large cavern below. Above him, Christian could see the roots of ancient trees woven into the ceiling of the cave. Below was the source of the new sound. His heart stopped at the sight.

Beneath them seethed, not a river, but an ocean.

An ocean of mice.

Gullet opened his headlamp and brushed past him, turning back the way they'd come. Christian stumbled after him. Only when they reached the wider tunnel beneath the river did he swear under his breath. "Gods, Gullet. Boldavia was just the beginning."

The clerk shrugged his broad shoulders and took off down the tunnel. "That's mice, though. For every one you see, seven in the walls."

Christian nodded. But there hadn't been *seven* for every *one*. There had been thousands.

"And that's little more than half of them," Gullet added as they came to the university cellar door. "They're on the move. After your nephew, I'd say. Go. We've begun fixing the city clockwork to keep the streets free for a time. Internal rhythms are a bit tricky, especially with the children, but most everyone should sleep through the night, present company and relevant parties excluded. Have done with this by cock's crow and, with the exception of a rather nasty end to the Kindlesmarkt, Nuremberg need be none the wiser. If not . . . then I fear for us all."

Christian nodded and took the older man's hand. "Thank you, Gullet."

"Good luck, Drosselmeyer," the clerk said, and disappeared back into the catacombs.

Christian stood for a moment, alone in the basement of the university, his face as pale as his milk-white hair. What he had seen was unimaginable. And his responsibility, alone. Christian had opened the gates to a flood of biblical size. Looking down at the sack in his hands, the weapon seemed inadequate, and yet it was their only hope.

He stormed up the cellar steps and prayed that Samir and Zacharias were safe and waiting. If he was to live through the night, Stefan would need them all.

63

STEFAN ROCKED FITFULLY in his sleep. Fatigue had overcome him at last.

In Marie's room, he was as safe as he could be, considering. And well fed. And warm. His dreams were another matter.

In his mind's eye, a specter rose up through the gloomy night. Seven heads, each one towering over the next to form an impossibly tall foe, dwarfing Stefan in its shadow. A sound like a clock, like a heartbeat, drummed faster and faster. Fourteen eyes glowed demon red . . .

Stefan came awake with a start.

"What is it?" Marie sat up in her chair across the room. She had been watching over him.

Stefan shook his head and pulled himself into a sitting position on the divan that had become his makeshift bed. The room (or was it the world?) tilted, slipping out of balance. He could feel it, like a dizzy spell washing over him. He steadied himself. "Nothing. Sorry I fell asleep."

"Nonsense," Marie said. "You've been literally petrified for days. You must be exhausted. What? Am I wrong?"

Stefan shook his head. "No. You're . . ." Wonderful? Amazing? The words came to mind, but he could not say them. Instead, he blushed furiously, the deep rosy tint rising to his wooden cheeks once again.

Marie smiled and tactfully pretended not to see him blush.

Much the way she'd pretended not to see his tears that day in the garden, he realized. He swallowed his embarrassment.

"Now that you're awake, tell me what kept you tossing," she said. "Was it a bad dream?"

"I started having them at the Pagoda Tree." The chill of his dreams receded as he recounted what he'd seen, and how he'd thought Marie would have loved to see the place. "It's a university, a place of great learning. Hundreds of squirrels run along the branches of the biggest tree you've ever seen."

Marie held up the handkerchief she'd rescued from his coat pocket. "Just think of the things my linen has seen!"

Stefan smiled wryly. "As promised."

They looked at each other and he felt unaccountably warm inside.

"Go on," she urged.

"I don't know why. Maybe because we were so close to Boldavia, to the Mouse King. I think it has something to do with him. I see him—in my dreams. Sometimes he's just a young mouse. And then there are nights where there are two, or three—"

"Two or three what?"

He swallowed hard. "Heads. One is a warrior. One . . . one is dead, I think. Its eyes are glassy and never blink."

"Heads?" she said softly. There was horror in the hush of her voice. "How many did you see tonight?"

Stefan bit his lip. "Seven."

Marie gasped. "If it's as you say and the dreams increase with proximity, then the King must be near. We have to warn Uncle Drosselmeyer. And prepare the house."

She ran to the window to check the lock. "Stefan," she said in a strangled voice. "Something is out there."

In an instant he was at her side.

"Oh, no. Marie," he breathed her name like a prayer.

Outside the house, in the public square, soldiers were moving, walking awkwardly, to congregate on the far side of the fountain. Their blue coats and brass buttons caught the light. So close to Stefan's own uniform, it gave him a chill.

"Uncle Drosselmeyer sent the city guard?"

Stefan peered closer through the glass. "Those aren't people, Marie. Look closer. They're made of wood. Like me."

Marie huffed. "Marionettes. Toys. Not like you at all. But very clever, just the same."

The toy soldiers lurched forward, ten of them in all. The ground flowed around them as they moved to encircle the entrance of the house. *A masterwork*, Stefan thought with a shiver. At least the motive for kidnapping was now clear.

"So they can fight on our level," he realized.

Marie shivered, pointing. "Look, the streets are flooded."

"That's not water," said Stefan. "We're surrounded. By mice."

He drew away from the glass, unable to think.

"I'll be right back!" Marie disappeared and returned with a short, curved sword. She pressed it into his hands. "You've played at swords before?"

"Of course; I'm a toymaker's son." Stefan accepted the weapon. The curve of the handle was surprisingly familiar.

"This is from my father's shop!" he exclaimed. Knowing his father had carved it made Stefan feel stronger.

"I took it from Fritz, the little horror. Uncle Christian sent it to him two Christmases ago. It's not much, but it's the best we can do until he returns."

Stefan took her hand. "Thank you, Marie."

She squeezed his palm. "You're to watch over me, remember? And I over you."

"Should we wake your parents?"

"I tried to, but it's like something out of a fairy tale. I couldn't rouse them." Marie settled her robe around her and curled up in the window seat to keep watch. Stefan was suddenly filled with the urge to protect her at all cost. Another wave of vertigo washed over him.

"Hurry, Christian," he whispered, and drew the curtains shut.

64

SAMIR AND ZACHARIAS found each other at the base of the university clock tower just as it struck eleven o'clock.

"The marketplace," Zacharias gasped, trying to catch his breath. "Overrun." He leaned against the round stone base of the clock tower.

Samir's turban was askew. He paused to straighten it. "Professor Blume's as well." He checked the clock, high in its tower. "We must wait for Christian, but I fear anything we do will not be enough."

Zacharias scowled in frustration. "I won't let my son be taken. There is still time to prepare."

He charged off into the darkened city.

Samir didn't give chase. He had waited seven years for something to happen. It was a hard thing to do, but he would wait for Christian to appear.

Time ticked by slowly. The moon showed her face through scudding clouds that scraped across the sky, pushed by a damp and tattered wind. Samir crouched before the clock tower and listened. A small yellow dog wandered down the street. It sniffed at the gutter, whined plaintively, and was gone.

In the buildings around the university square, what few lights were still on turned down until they went out.

Samir waited.

And then, footsteps echoed from the depths of the clock

tower. He stepped back from the door in its base, the one used by clockmakers to keep the clock running smoothly.

Silence. A click. And the door swung open just a crack.

"Samir?" Christian's voice was barely above a breath.

"Christian," he said in his deep bass.

"Thank the heavens." Christian emerged from his hiding place, with a long bag hung at his side. "Gullet told me what happened. We must—" He went pale. "Where is Zacharias?"

Before Samir could answer, the clock struck the half hour and Zacharias came scuttling across the cobblestones. The large sack slung over his shoulder made him look like a bedraggled Father Christmas.

"Sorry, sorry!" Zacharias whispered. "I had to grab a few things. To help. Now, quickly, take me to my son."

The three men slipped silently into the night.

Christian traveled with Gullet's sack slung securely across his shoulders. It weighed no more than a pound or so. The key within was about the length and size of a clarinet. And yet, to Christian, the contents of the bag were heavy indeed.

Zacharias hauled his own bag of tricks without complaint. They took front streets, as the alleys were more likely to be filled with mice. But a few blocks from their goal, it no longer mattered. Every path before them was flooded with vermin—a sea of fur, claws, and black eyes, all swarming toward the same goal.

"Mein Gott!" Zacharias exclaimed. "How will we get through them?"

Samir pointed up. The moon had sunk behind a bank of clouds, but the rooftops stood out quite clearly. "The other day when I was up on your roof, I noticed your houses are built very closely together. It's like a second highway up there." A slanted, treacherous highway perhaps, but a better idea than the flooded streets in front of them.

"Up we go," Christian agreed.

They mounted the stairs of a nearby church steeple and began to pick their way across the building tops toward the Stahlbaums' house on Englestrasse.

65

THE MICE WERE GATHERING.

Stefan's heart had sunk lower than he thought possible. "He won't get back in time." His breath steamed the glass, momentarily obscuring his view.

The ten clockwork soldiers stood at attention, bayonets raised in challenge. *Pointing to this very window,* thought Stefan. *To me.*

Marie made a small cry.

"What is it?" he asked. She had handled everything so matter-of-factly to this point, he was afraid to see what could have startled her.

She stamped her foot angrily and pointed across the room where, a moment before, the draped cage had held the piebald mouse spy. "He's gone."

The towel was awry, the lock tossed easily open.

"We've underestimated them," Stefan said softly. He stumped to the empty cage and uselessly closed the door again. "Marie."

She stood before him in her dressing gown, her cheeks flaming with anger.

He took her hand. "I wish we'd met a year ago."

"What difference would that—" she began.

"I need to go. Stay here. You'll be safer."

"Go? Out to them? You can't!"

"I have to," he said. "I killed their Queen. Christian made a mistake once that led to this. What will my mistake lead to?"

"It was an *accident*." She squeezed his wooden hand between her own soft palms. "Please, Stefan. I won't let you go alone."

He bent low and kissed her hand, wishing his lips were not made of wood.

She quickly planted a kiss on his cheek. "All right," she said. "I'll stay here, but I'll be watching you."

An odd sense of peace filled him and he let go of her hand. "Thank you."

He slid the wooden sword into his belt and straightened his coattails.

It was time to go.

66

ARTHUR SHIVERED IN HIS CHARIOT. The four albino mice pulled it dutifully to a stop before a makeshift tent at the base of the square's decorative fountain. It would be comforting to be back inside again. Perhaps because of his mother's protectiveness, or the recent memory of owls, Arthur found he did not like open places and, above all, he did not trust the stars. They winked down at him now, like the many heads of his ancestors enjoying a private laugh, and he was the butt of the joke.

The chief of intelligence, a severe older piebald with an unnervingly calm voice, ushered Arthur out of the coach along with his tutor, the rat, Ernst Listz. Ernst had been brought along in chains for his usefulness as a translator. Use him now, they had decided, and punish him later.

They emerged from the chariot in silence. Arthur hurried toward the safety of the tent, but the rat stood on his haunches and sniffed the open air wistfully.

Hannibal scowled. "We've a battle to command," he hissed.

The small party proceeded inside.

"My liege," the head of intelligence was saying. Arthur couldn't remember his name. He'd had difficulty focusing since leaving Boldavia. His nightmares now came in droves, night after night. He was being consumed by a beast that he could not escape. A terrifying voice called to him from beyond. It offered help, but also—something else. Arthur did not know what. All he knew for sure was that trying to escape the beast would mean his death.

His brothers, of course, said nothing of these dreams. They hardly slept anymore, so eager were they to lead Mother's army into war. And if the dreams did leak over into his brothers' minds, they saw it as an omen. Rodentia was a ferocious warrior and they stood at its beating heart.

It made Arthur sick.

"—just escaped, Your Majesty," the piebald was saying. He was pointing to another piebald, a filthy thing mottled amber instead of black, with shrewd red eyes.

The albino bowed deeply, graceful despite his appearance. "Agent Dusker, sire. I have cornered your enemy for you, up-stairs in the house across the square."

"Why didn't you report back earlier?" Hannibal hissed. "We have had to rely on others for your information."

The albino faltered. He was having trouble deciding which head to speak to.

Hannibal solved that for him by hissing again.

"I . . . uh . . . I wanted to watch his moves closely, sire. The as-sassin is unarmed but for a toy sword. He had two companions, the clockmaker and a young girl. The rest of the house sleeps. I confer him to you."

"Confer?" This was Ernst, speaking in the contemptuous tones Arthur had heard him use toward so many others, but never to Arthur himself. "You can hardly confer that which you do not possess."

The rat turned to Arthur and his brothers. "You have a field army, sirs, not a guerilla band. City mice survive by hiding. But your army is designed to be bold. Your mother trained them to meet the enemy in open spaces, not townhomes. Too many men in close quarters"—the rat shuddered—"and the tramp of feet alone could defeat you. What were your losses in the market square?" He did not wait for an answer. It was many, they all knew. "And then there is the furniture. Enter the house, and your army will be scattered, every chair and sofa an obstacle. I would not send them in without first getting the full lay of the land. And even then . . ." He let doubt hang in the air for a heartbeat.

Arthur frowned.

"Those siege engines of yours are useless beyond that front door," Ernst continued. "I doubt they could even climb the steps. You must fight one of two ways—on your own territory by issuing a challenge, or inside the house, alone."

"Alone?" Arthur piped up before his brothers could stop him. "That's impossible! We have no chance against that monster on our own!"

"It's true," Roland agreed. Hannibal started to protest, but Roland continued. "Shut it, Hannibal, we're not all as tough as you. Besides, that monster killed Mummy, and she was tough as nails. Why risk it? Call the monkey out into the field."

"Yes!" Arthur concurred. Although, why on earth the human boy would come out to them, he did not know. "We'll draw him out. Taunt him. Scare him into running straight onto our sword."

"Sires." It was the chief of intelligence again. Snitter—that was his name.

The old piebald's whiskers twitched in distaste. *He disapproves of us,* Arthur realized. *No. He disapproves of bickering.*

"You won't have to," Snitter said. "It appears our enemy has come to the gate on his own."

A cold wave of fear washed over Arthur. This was it. Trapped in the belly of the beast, with no one else to save him.

And then a voice the size of the ocean called out across their ranks. "Where is your King?"

67

STEFAN STOOD ON THE STEPS of the townhouse, an astonishing sight in his bright doll's uniform. He had judged correctly. The mice would take time to swarm the steps, and the soldiers, while clever and dangerous at close range, hadn't the proper joints to carry them up to meet him.

"Where is your King?" His voice quaked, but it was loud and it carried. He hoped the mice would not notice his fear.

Maybe they wouldn't understand him at all. He recalled the horrible, high-pitched noises Christian had made. He had no hope of imitating them.

Silence reigned across the square. He waited.

From the far side of the fountain there was a ripple of movement. A path split open in the ranks, and a litter was carried forward by four liveried mice. To a child in an attic window, this would look magical. But there were no little children to witness the event, only Marie's pale face above him. Stefan suspected Marie was right. The square, perhaps all of Nuremberg, had indeed fallen into an enchanted sleep.

It must be the City Clock, he realized. Christian had found Gullet after all.

The litter came to a stop a few yards away and a great, lean rat stepped out. He was dressed like a gentleman, almost foppish in a long, pale blue overcoat with lace at his cuffs and collar.

Stefan blinked. He should have been surprised. But the lump of ice in his stomach prevented it.

"Good evening, sir," the rat said in flawless German. "I am Ernst Listz, emissary to the King. Our terms are as follows. Your life, sir, as the murderer of our beloved Queen, is forfeit. Surrender yourself and the clockmaker, and the lives of your friends and family will be spared. However, should you refuse to lay down your arms, they will be given no quarter in the coming revolution. I'm afraid you will simply be the first of them to fall."

Stefan stifled a nervous laugh. "I'm no master of diplomacy," he told the rat. "And I'm afraid I haven't the authority to speak for anyone but myself. Your King may have his chance at me. But when I fight, it's for the city and its entire population. Your 'revolution,' as you call it, must come to an end."

The rat fixed him with glistening black eyes. "Our King knew your father, and showed him mercy."

Stefan clenched his wooden jaw. "You mean he kidnapped my father and held him captive."

"That was the Queen's doing. His majesties were rather taken with your parent, and he with them—or so I believe."

Stefan swallowed. His father *had* survived his ordeal. Did the Mouse King have any part in that? "Tell your King to leave now, and we won't follow. The clock that turns this world is out of balance. Doesn't he see that?"

The rat shrugged eloquently, and Stefan wondered if the King simply didn't care.

"He has my condolences, for his mother," Stefan said hesitantly. "Her death was not my intent."

"But your death is his, I'm afraid. A life for a life. Those are the terms." The rat bowed and returned down the stairs to his palanquin.

The litter flowed back through the crowd to the far side of the fountain.

After a moment's silence, a bugle call sounded, small and tinny in the cold night air. As one, the mouse army surged forward.

68

STEFAN HELD HIS GROUND.

The mice gained the first step, then the second. Still he did not move. The third step, and he could feel, rather than see, Marie in the window, hands pressed against the glass.

The heat and the dry, musky scent of a thousand mice rose into the air. He gripped the pommel of his wooden sword.

The mice reached the top step.

"Kinyata," Stefan called softly.

The cat appeared like a shadow at his side. She blinked at him with her yellow eyes, and leapt into the ranks.

Rodent foot soldiers were tossed aside like toys.

And Marie's cat had brought friends. *Good,* Stefan thought. Let the cats deal with the mice. He would handle the soldiers.

The disarray on the battlefield had caused two of the soldiers to sway and topple on their own. They lay prone on the cobblestones, mice swarming over their useless forms, unable to lift them again. Stefan approached the nearest of the remaining eight, and drew his sword.

The toy soldier was taller than him by half a foot, but on the steps, Stefan held the higher ground.

"*En garde,*" he said, touching his own blade to his forehead. With a small skip of his heart, he realized that his opponent's sword was gleaming metal and all too real. He would have to risk shattering his own wooden blade or disarm the manikin and take the weapon for himself.

The toy soldier moved with alarming speed.

Stefan jumped back to avoid the first swing of its blade. Reaching out with his left hand, he grabbed the soldier's mechanical wrist and slashed back down the arm with his sword.

For an instant he could see through the skeleton work of the soldier, to the shining eyes of the rodent controllers within. Their faces were alien—whether they were frightened or angry, Stefan could not tell. He closed his eyes and completed his stroke, at the weak part of the neck joints, where his father always took extra care. It required patience and an eye for balance. Not a skill that could be performed well alone, in the dark.

The blow rang true and the head of the toy soldier toppled from the body, the wooden sword lodged in its neck.

As the head dropped away, the mice inside panicked. The soldier's sword hand loosened its grip.

Stefan grabbed the hilt, wresting it from the manikin's grasp.

A squeal of dismay rose from inside the soldier carcass. The arms and legs were independent of the head, and the mice inside had eyes enough to continue the fight. But they hesitated, and Stefan took his opening.

Hacking with the sharp end of his new sword, he severed the arms of the wooden soldier at the shoulders. The machine lost its balance. Stefan slapped it in the chest and it toppled backward, mice leaping from its cavities as it fell to crush or scatter the army that followed in its wake.

Three more soldiers approached.

Stefan was sweating. He wondered if it would stain his wooden skin. The army seemed demoralized by the loss of their first three siege engines, but the other mechanical soldiers pressed forward through the fray, and Stefan stepped up to meet them.

69

CHRISTIAN PAUSED on the rooftop across the square and caught his breath at the sight.

"So many soldiers!" Zacharias exclaimed. "I only ever made the one, I swear it!"

"Stefan's done well, though," Samir noted. Three of the life-size mechanical soldiers lay broken in a half-circle in front of Stefan.

The mouse army milled about in confusion, worsened by a fury of cats, who were clawing their way through the ranks—playing more than fighting, Christian realized. Their cruelty appalled him, even though it worked in his favor. Kinyata was at their head.

Looking up at the Stahlbaums' house, Christian caught a glimpse of his niece. Whether or not the girl spoke true Catish, her pet seemed to have understood her quite well.

Samir laid a hand on Christian's shoulder. "My friends, the boy is strong, but he tires. Seven soldiers, even manikins, are too much for anyone."

Zacharias lowered the sack from his shoulder and pulled out the first of his makeshift weapons. "Lend a hand," he said.

"Zacharias, you're a genius," Christian exclaimed. "Stefan, ahoy!" he bellowed from the roof to the plaza below.

Stefan pulled back from the fray long enough to look up. He

had no time to do more than nod before the next soldier was upon him.

"Into the house, Stefan!" Christian shouted. Stefan did not respond.

Christian waited, heart thumping.

The boy slammed his sword into the inner workings of an attacking soldier and wrenched it free, shattering the soldier's skeletal chest. In the chaos that followed the soldier's crashing demise, Stefan leapt backward up the stairs and into the house.

STEFAN MADE THE LAST STEP and slammed the door shut behind him. His toy clothes were stained by sweat and shredded by sword slices. Shuddering, he stomped the floor in case any mice had found their way inside. A small part of his brain was amazed that the rest of the household—that all of the houses in the square—could sleep through this.

He ran upstairs as swiftly and quietly as he could.

Marie opened the door to her room and beckoned him inside. "To the window, quickly. It looks like Uncle has a plan after all."

Stefan entered in time to see his father hoist a huge Roman candle firework onto his shoulder, take aim, and fire.

A colorful fireball shot from the tube, arced across the side of the square, and collided with the fifth toy soldier as it attempted to climb the stairs.

A sigh of wonder spread through the army of mice. Even the cats paused in their butchery to watch the small comet light up the square.

And then the soldier frizzled; sparks shot from where its heart would be. The entire frame went up like the Roman candle that had destroyed it.

Five more fireballs from the far rooftop, and five more columns of flame burst to life in the square.

Stefan stifled a cheer.

Marie hugged him tightly. She smelled of vanilla and lily of the valley. "You're very brave," she said.

"So are you."

Something thumped against the window.

"Kinyata?" Marie called. But the cat was still leading the assault below.

Instead, a rope ladder bumped against the sash. Marie opened it and a moment later, Christian, Samir, and Zacharias descended from the roof and climbed into the room.

Stefan hurled himself into his father's waiting arms.

"Well," Christian said, surveying their handiwork through the window. "That worked like a charm."

70

THE SEVEN-HEADED MOUSE KING roared and cuffed his intelligence chief on the side of the head.

The piebald did not wince, just bowed and stepped out of arm's reach.

"Be reasonable," Ernst said, stifling a snort of contempt. By the piebald's report, all ten soldiers, the full complement of the Mouse King's siege engines, had been waylaid by a mere boy and a few fireworks. It served the little upstarts right to think they could succeed against humans where rats had failed. He had half a mind to abandon ship now while the attention of his captors was elsewhere.

The Mouse King turned on him, five of the seven heads snarling in fury.

Ernst jumped, taken aback. Even Arthur was angry. No, not angry, Ernst realized. Terrified. All of the brothers—perhaps even dull-eyed Julius—were scared beyond reason.

"Advise us!" Hannibal demanded.

"Yes, tutor, give counsel." Roland nodded readily.

Six sets of eyes peered at him keenly.

Ernst resisted the urge to preen his whiskers. They were asking for his help. He could be a prince of the new republic, if he led the Mouse King to victory. For a moment the idea rose, sweet and delicious in his mind's eye. But the fact of his imprisonment could not be forgotten. Or the foolhardiness of their plans. The specter of Hameln loomed too large. Even if they won tonight, the victory could not last. The clockmaker's boy was right. A balance must be struck.

The rat sighed dramatically. They had given him the rope. All he had to do was let them hang themselves. Then, at least, he would be free.

"The quarry has merely gone to ground," Ernst said robustly. "And when hunting a shrew in its den, what's the best way to roust it?"

"Burn the den down," snarled Genghis.

"Smoke it out," Arthur said dully.

Poor boy. He'd nearly come unhinged at last. But sympathy was too expensive a gift these days. *Good-bye, Arthur,* Ernst said silently. He could not save the lad from his brothers, but at least he would try his best to end this current madness. If the King did not survive the battle, then so be it.

"Think, boys, think!" Ernst urged them. "You are all but defeated, your armies demoralized. And this against one boy! A handful of humans, at best. And yet, you still believe you can lay claim to their entire city?" The rat shook his gray head. "Not today, not today."

The Mouse King stared at him, eyes fixed, watching the rat's every move.

Ernst smiled to himself. He was a brilliant orator and he knew it. "You have to woo your army back, sire. Show them who you are—the chosen ones, destined to lead them to victory. You must give them glory." Ernst pointed through the tent flap at the townhouse across the square. "We have an enemy here, made of wood. Fire will simply keep him inside. And what glory is there if he merely burns to death? You are leaders!"

He grabbed the Mouse King by the paw, raising it in the air. "You are kings! Lure the others out, then go yourself into the lion's den. Remember—you turned the tide at Owl Run. Let your people know that you single-handedly laid your mother's killer low. Then they will follow you, against the humans, against the gates of Heaven itself."

A sharp sigh sounded throughout the tent as the brothers sucked in their breath. "Yes," they hissed.

Hannibal bowed his head slightly toward the rat, his eyes glinting bloodred. He snapped his fingers once.

The intelligence chief nodded and sent for the mouse that had been held captive by the clockmaker's boy.

71

ZACHARIAS'S BEAR HUG threatened to turn Stefan into sawdust. But he did not care. "Father!"

"You're awake!" his father cried. He released his son, taking in how much Stefan had grown. "And very brave, besides. Your mother would be—"

"Horrified," Stefan said. "She hated mice."

Zacharias laughed and brushed the sweat-dampened hair from his son's forehead. "She would be very proud."

They clambered downstairs with the others to take stock of their situation in the living room before the great Christmas tree.

Stefan inhaled the scent of crushed pine needles and sought that same calm that had allowed him to confront the enemy.

"Wait. What's that smell?" he asked.

Christian sniffed the air. "Take this." He thrust a sack into Stefan's arms. "This is your weapon."

Stefan raced after him to the foyer. Smoke came seeping under the front door, and with it, the glow of orange flame.

"For God's sake, Stefan, stay back. Tell Marie we need buckets. They're setting us on fire."

72

TO ARTHUR, it was like moving in a dream—in a nightmare.

The bodies of the wooden soldiers had been gathered and placed along the base of the townhouse. The makeshift bonfires burned brightly beneath a top layer of freshly gathered leaves. The foliage sparked as it burned, sending smoke swirling high above the square to block out the stars. The smoke smelled sweet—oak leaves and pine—like the incense his mother used to burn when he and his brothers were newborn and only half-made. It was making Arthur light-headed, clouding his vision.

But the fires had worked. The humans had come to the front door.

Arthur and his brothers mounted the steps, each one thirsty for the blood of the boy within.

They would face him in the parlor, Hannibal had said, brandishing his sword with his brothers behind him.

The King of Mice would kill this killer, and then, with the strength gained from that victory, he would resurrect his army of manikins and conquer all of Nuremberg. Tonight the bad dreams would end.

The door opened and the clockmaker came running out, a bucket of water in each hand. Two other men followed. The smoke was thick. They didn't see the Mouse King on the stairs. Lunging forward, Arthur and his brothers darted into the pitch-black parlor, swallowed into the very depths of the beast.

73

STEFAN RETREATED to the parlor, towing the sack behind him. Fire was instant death to a boy made of wood.

Marie took point, slogging buckets of water from the kitchen to the front door. She lined them up and refilled them as quickly as she could.

In the Stahlbaums' family parlor, Christmas waited to begin. The great evergreen tree towered over the center of the room while the fireplace burned low, giving off heat and a flickering light. The debris of Christmas Eve gift-giving littered the floor—colorful paper, boxes, cloth wrappings. There was even a bit of orange peel from the treats stuffed in the stockings above the mantel.

Stefan tugged at the strings of his cousin's bag. Christian had said there was something besides fireworks inside. A weapon. He fumbled to undo the ties, but his fingers were stiff and tired from the battle.

A breeze stirred the wrapping paper littering the floor.

Marie emerged from the kitchen with yet another bucket of water. She smiled bravely at Stefan. "We're beating it back," she announced, and carried on.

The paper rustled again. This time, from behind the Christmas tree.

Stefan frowned. What breeze could do that? The windows

were shut, the only gusts coming from the front door each time Marie opened it.

An icy chill ran up Stefan's spine to his scalp, where it froze in a lump of dread.

Something was inside the house.

Stefan's hand went to his scabbard, but his sword was no longer there. He edged away until his back was against the wall opposite the tree. To his left, the room opened onto the foyer where Marie labored. To his right, a great mirror hung the length of the wall, reflecting the fireplace. It gave the impression of a much larger room with two trees, two sofas, many scattered chairs, and two strangely carved young men.

"Show yourself!" Stefan said.

The rustling stopped. He could hear small footsteps beneath the furniture.

He struggled again to open the sack, but the bag would not yield. Frustrated, he grabbed an unlit candlestick from a side table and hefted the pewter base in his hands.

He could hear breathing across the room, close to the fire. He waded through the wrapping paper, edging toward the sound.

"Ah!" Something sliced at him below the knee. His pant leg tore. He stumbled backward, swinging the candlestick toward the ground, hitting only the floor.

"Marie!" he called out, his back against the tree.

Snickt! A flash of blade and tassel fell away from his shoulder, and a dull ache stabbed the small of his back. They were in the tree!

Stefan spun, eyes darting from star to garland to cross-shaped base, seeking the enemy. He could see nothing but the gleam of ornaments and shadowy branches.

He backed away again, coming close to the fireplace. Too close.

The paper on the floor rustled again, and a high-pitched keening rose up around him.

A shadow grew along the far wall, spreading upward to touch the ceiling.

It's not a mouse, Stefan thought. It couldn't be. For the shadow towering over him was bigger than a man, taller than the tree. And it wore seven crowns.

"Thee hast killed our mother," seven voices spoke at once in smooth, archaic German. A shadow sword flickered at its side. "Now, boy, thee shalt pay."

74

IT WAS A MISTAKE. Arthur knew it as soon as they entered the house.

The Drosselmeyer they faced may have been a child by Man's standards, shrunken further by their mother's curse. But he was a giant in the view of mice.

"Mother was wrong," he told his brothers. She had taught them to fight as if they, too, were men. But now, barely able to see above the floor, cleverly blocked by great wads of paper that made stealth impossible, Arthur could see they would not win in a direct fight.

"They have a *tree*," he told his brothers. "What beast cuts down trees just to watch them die?"

"Coward!" Genghis accused. "If you will not fight, stand aside and let your brothers do their work."

"I'll fight," Arthur hissed back. "But not like a fool, out in the open. We are outmatched!"

"We have killed owls," Charlemagne reminded him. "What threat is this boy compared to a raptor's claws? He doesn't even have a sword!"

"And we don't have our guards about us, either," Arthur insisted. "To avenge Mother, we must fight like mice."

There would have been more squabbling, but the Drosselmeyer called out, "Show yourself!"

The sound of that voice alone—as booming and hollow as a fallen tree—silenced his brothers.

Arthur took charge. He rushed across the papered floor and struck again and again from the depths of the tree. "He is wood!" he told his brothers. "We must drive him into the fire!"

75

STEFAN FROZE. His mind struggled to understand what he was seeing. His nightmares. A beast with seven heads. Echoes of the priest's words at his mother's graveside. The book of Revelation. A chill wind blew through him. The Beast had risen.

He needed a weapon. He found the sack again and tore at it desperately.

"Stefan?" Marie stood in the doorway of the parlor. Water sloshed over the edge of her bucket.

He followed her gaze. Something—or someone—stood in the middle of the carpet, outlined by the smoky firelight. He had the impression that a pack of vermin was inching toward him.

And then the front door burst open as Stefan's father reached inside for the next bucket. The door slammed shut just as quickly, but in that burst of light, Stefan's heart leapt into his mouth and Marie screamed.

The ties on the sack finally fell away.

"Stand back!" Stefan cried. He rose from beside the sofa, shaking the weapon free from the bag. Suddenly everything became clear as day.

In his hands was a giant golden key worked with scrolls and fine, spidery script. A small bellows was seated inside the handle. Stefan waved it in the air. Dozens of tiny holes along the length of the key sighed. The King of Mice cocked his fourteen ears at the sound.

"What is this?" the mouse asked. He hoisted his sword with a flourish, signaling his attack.

Stefan leapt into the air.

The King stopped short, jabbing upward, stabbing the sole of Stefan's foot.

The sword stuck in the surface of the leather.

The King yanked his weapon free, dancing backward.

Stefan climbed onto the sofa, buying time to study this new weapon. How it was meant to work, only his uncle knew for sure. But it had a handle and length to it. A clumsy sword, but a serviceable one.

He swiped down toward the King, but the beast was gone.

Again, a rustling in the papers.

"He's beneath you!" Marie cried.

Stefan clambered to the top of the sofa, balancing with one foot on the arm, and waited.

The room wavered in the firelight. The very walls were alive.

A china figurine shifted on the mantel and fell. Stefan turned. The Mouse King leapt from the shelf.

Sskit! He slashed at Stefan's face, the blade singing through the air.

If he had still been made of flesh and bone, Stefan might have bled. Instead, his curse protected him.

He flailed, tumbling sofa and all, into the fire.

"Stefan!" Marie cried out.

He scrambled away from the flames, his coat and hat already alight.

"Hold still!" she demanded. "You'll burn down the house!"

He collapsed on the hearth and she doused him with her bucket of water. The flames on his clothing hissed and died. Water sloshed everywhere, soaking his back like sweat.

All around him, wrapping paper collapsed into sodden lumps. Panic sat on his chest. He fought it back, struggling to catch his breath.

He clenched his hands. They closed around nothing. In falling, he had lost the key.

"Revenge!" the Mouse King roared, and ran from the shadows across the muck-covered floor, driving his sword toward Stefan's eye—

"Look out!" Marie shrieked, and hurled her slipper.

76

TIME FROZE. Stefan's nightmares hovered before him. Seven heads, seven mouths, seven curses on their lips.

And then Marie's slipper slammed into the King with a loud crack.

The heads wailed in pain.

"Charlemagne!" the center head cried.

One of the heads lolled to the side, spilling its crown like a coin.

"She broke his neck," another of the voices moaned. "He's dead."

Bile rose in Stefan's throat.

Five faces roared. The Mouse King threw himself at Marie, teeth bared.

Stefan moved. Sweeping his leg across the floor, he kicked out at the mouse and pulled himself up to a sitting position.

Marie fled into the kitchen, blocking the attack with a heavy wooden door.

"Stay in there, Marie!" Stefan shouted.

The Mouse King turned back toward Stefan. They faced each other in the sputtering firelight. And then the beast darted into the shadows once more.

Stefan backed away from the fireplace. Away from the Christmas tree. The damp floor no longer rustled. He couldn't see or hear a thing. Worse, he couldn't find the golden key.

"Murderer!" The many voices echoed from everywhere at once. "You killed our brother!"

Sskit! A blade sliced the buckle from his left boot. Stefan stumbled. He kicked out with a foot and connected.

The Mouse King gasped and was gone. "No!" a thin voice cried. "Alexander!"

Then panting, and moans of pain.

"He is killing us!" a single voice whined. "Do something, Arthur! Hannibal! Or we will die!"

"Then we shall die well," a gruff voice replied.

A fresh wave of terror pushed Stefan to move. Where was Christian's weapon? In the mirror on the wall, he caught a gleam of metal by the fire.

There, beneath the fallen sofa. He raced past the hearth to retrieve the golden key.

The wet smack of boots on sodden paper rushed toward him from behind. A voice bellowed with strength beyond its size.

"For. Our. Mother!" The Mouse King dove forward.

Stefan swung his weapon around.

King and key collided in the smoke-filled air.

He buried the metal shaft into the monster's chest.

The room grew still.

The bellowing heads sagged and the Mouse King grasped the key in two paws, struggling to free himself.

Stefan did the only thing he could think to do. With a sharp twist, he wound the key.

A thin wail rose from the body of the Mouse King as the unwinding key sang with his breath. A simple tune, played backward. Something a mother might hum to her newborn baby.

"Treachery," one of the heads whispered.

The music played louder.

"No," another head sighed.

In a slow spiral, each head grew still until only the one in the center remained, staring unblinkingly into Stefan's eyes.

With small paws he felt the stem of the key where it had entered his chest. "I tried, Mother," he said wearily.

Stefan was mortified. This was not what he had expected. "I'm so sorry," he said, and sank to his knees, lowering the King to the ground.

The mouse shrugged his back, arching in pain. "Ah . . . My brothers . . . are gone. I must follow. Please . . . tell your father. I would have liked . . . to have been . . . his friend." He sighed, and the bellows inside the handle of the key expanded. The holes in the stem wailed like reeds in the wind. "I forgive you," he whispered to Stefan. "I . . . release you. I release us all . . ."

The last echo of his voice played back through the key.

The air in the room shimmered around them as the Queen's royal curse was torn asunder.

Arthur was dead.

77

THE BODY DROPPED from the end of the unwinding key.

Stefan released it quickly, frightened by what he had done. He staggered to his feet, eyes still on the strange corpse on the floor.

Marie had emerged from the kitchen. She touched his arm.

Their eyes locked. "Stefan, you're changing."

He could feel it, like sap running through his veins. His wooden skin was melting back into flesh.

Suddenly, the front door burst open. "We need more water!" Christian shouted. "The fire is almost out!"

Marie ran for another bucket.

Stefan turned to the clockmaker. "Christian?" His voice was pained.

Christian came forward and stopped short at the sight of the Mouse King and the unwinding key. His blue eye glinted in the firelight. "God in heaven. You're cured!"

He strode forward and clasped his cousin by the arms. "Stefan, my dear boy, you've done it. You've broken the curse—" He looked at the fallen figure of the Mouse King. "Somehow . . . Now come, take the body. Show the mice what you have done. We can end this war."

Stefan shook his head, his newly thawed limbs suddenly cold. "I can't," he said softly. "I don't want to touch him."

The murdered King lay where he had fallen, all seven heads tossed brokenly to the side.

Stefan picked up the key. He turned on his cousin in disgust. "What sort of key is this? It didn't just kill him, it *drained* him. It was terrible."

Christian gently drew the device from his hands. "It's a soul sieve. An unwinding key. A rare clockmaker's tool for unmaking. The Brotherhood wouldn't have given it to us if it hadn't been our last hope." The filigreed scrollwork on either side of the key was now darkened with blood. Christian pulled a handkerchief from his pocket and wiped the key down before putting it back in its sack. "It is a difficult thing, the unmaking of souls."

Stefan shuddered. "What have I done?"

"What needed doing." Christian placed a gloved hand on his shoulder. "The work of a clockmaster and a brave man."

"I should have stuck with toys."

"Buckets, gentlemen!" Marie broke the moment, entering with another sloshing pail for the fires outside.

"Right away." Christian turned toward the kitchen, then paused. "Stefan, you must show them what you've done."

Stefan hesitated. Then, with hands of flesh and a wooden heart, he knelt beside the fallen Mouse King. *This is the enemy,* he thought. But all he could see was the one young face in the center of them all.

He had forgiven Stefan with his last breath. But Stefan doubted he'd ever be able to forgive himself.

Lifting the body gently, he carried it outside.

On the steps to the townhouse, his father and Samir were dousing the last of the flames.

"Stefan, you're cured!" his father called to him.

Coming toward him, he saw the body in his son's arms.

"Papa." Stefan stepped to the edge of the stairs. "Did you know him? He asked me to tell you he would have liked to have been your friend."

Zacharias stared. "My friend? I . . . Mein Gott." His face went pale. He dropped his bucket to the ground. "Arthur? Little Arthur?"

Stefan's face crumpled, watching his father, the kindest, best man he knew, in mourning yet again. It made him feel very young, and very old at the same time. But, there was still so much to do.

The square was a wasteland of mice and ash. The remnants of the wooden soldiers lay piled in charred, steaming heaps. What mice remained were hard-pressed by Kinyata's band of cats. Still, the small encampment on the far side of the fountain remained.

Stefan and Zacharias descended the steps and carried the broken body across the battlefield. Mouse and cat alike stepped aside as they passed. All were aware of the body in their hands.

"Mouse lords!" Stefan called out in a heavy voice.

There was a scuffle inside the tent. At last, the rat emissary that had addressed him appeared, flanked by a white-and-black mouse in a drab brown coat.

"I bring you your King." Stefan laid his burden on the ground at their feet.

For a moment, he was eye level with the rat. A breath of sadness passed across the creature's face. "Make them stop, rat. This war can do no good."

The rat said nothing. He nodded to the piebald, who was already signaling for a litter to carry the King's body.

A small horn sounded, and the mouse army broke. Chased by cats and the loss of their King, they fled down into the sewers of Nuremberg. The tent was abandoned, the King carried away by his brethren.

Mice flowed into gutters and cracks in the street. After a moment, the rat followed the body of his King, and the square was empty once more.

Months of fatigue settled on Stefan in an instant. With a tired sigh, he turned and walked slowly back to the townhouse.

His father clasped him to his chest, and Christian patted him on the back.

"Let the boy rest," Samir said. "We will watch over him."

Marie stood in the doorway, watching him with concern. She grasped Stefan's hand and tried to lead him to the sofa.

"No." Stefan pulled away gently. "It's not over yet. Is it?" he asked.

All eyes turned to Christian. The clockmaker rubbed his forehead and sighed. "No. It's not. The King fought like a human. The rest will fight like mice. If we are to spare the city from famine, there is still work to be done. Go home, Stefan. You've done your part. Now the Brotherhood and I will do ours." Shouldering the sack with the Brotherhood's key inside, the clockmaker took his leave, grimly striding into the night.

"Where is he going?" Marie asked.

"Beneath the city," Stefan said. "The mice have gone underground. If he opens the walls to the river, their army will be washed away."

"Drowned, you mean," Marie said disapprovingly.

Stefan stayed silent. It was, after all, a war.

"And then, will it be finished?" his father asked quietly.

Samir shrugged, placing a hand on the toymaker's shoulder.
"Let us hope so."

78

CHRISTMAS DAWNED BRIGHT and cold over a strangely sleeping Nuremberg. A fresh snow had fallen in those deepest hours between midnight and sunrise, blanketing the city in a sheet of sparkling white.

As the sun rose, households came awake, fires were stoked, and children ran downstairs to tell their parents of the strange dreams that had visited them in the night. The parents, however, had slept dreamlessly, the most restful sleep they'd had since they were very young.

Smoke curlicued from chimney stacks, joining puffy clouds in the sky.

A small gray dove made an arc through the air over the cobblestoned squares of the city. Above the black trees, it flew over the iron gate of the cemetery, where a sad-faced man laid bright tulips at the door of a crypt. Had the dove been given more than paint for eyes, it would have seen that the flowers had been carved from the coats of wooden soldiers. Their only perfume was faint smoke. But the dove flew on. Smooth wingbeats carried it skimming over rooftops, brushing wingtips against the winter-barren trees, its shadow gliding over the pristine snow. It was as if the city had been erased in the night and redrawn with only houses and the barest outlines of the natural world.

Onward the dove glided, past a squat man in a heavy coat, one of a very few people running errands this early on Christmas morning. Over the empty stalls of the Kindlesmarkt, above the silent steps of the great university with its stone clock tower it flew, and on to the square at Englestrasse, where the fine houses and lawns slept peacefully beneath their frosted quilt.

Here it passed the squat man again, entering the back of a house on the square, ushered in through the servants' door by a man with hair nearly as white as the snow.

The dove completed its arc smoothly, swooping down to the house on Englestrasse to land in the hands of a young man standing on the roof.

Stefan caught the dove with cold fingers and examined the seals on its wings. Wooden wings, but fingers of flesh and bone. He could not decide which was more remarkable. The dove had flown well this time. Even better than the version he'd set aloft on the Danube. The wintry air hadn't compromised the clockworks inside. And yet, he was worried. Why had Gullet just slipped in through the Stahlbaums' back door?

Unlike his own home, the Stahlbaums' roof had a terrace for taking the sun in summer. He could imagine Marie's family sipping lemonade and looking down on the square below.

Stefan put the dove back in his coat pocket and stood for a moment, looking out onto the sea of white-capped roofs. His father had gone to visit his mother's grave. This view above the city was his own way of remembering her.

The air was crisp and sharp. He breathed it in, feeling older and tired, but very much alive.

Behind him, the door opened.

"I thought there was something odd about that bird," Marie said, coming out onto the landing. She was dressed for the day and bundled in her father's greatcoat. "Merry Christmas, Stefan. May I join you?"

"Please."

She stepped up to the wrought-iron railing beside him and shoved her hands into her drooping sleeves. The coat was much too big for her, but she wore it like it was her own. Stefan's own coat fit him perfectly, at last.

"Strange," she said. "How normal everything looks in daylight."

The snow had covered much of the night's damage. Samir and Zacharias had cleared the street of debris. The scorched pavement left by the burning toy soldiers and the war-ravaged lawn in the square center would have been apparent, however, if not for this fortuitous snowfall.

"I'm sure the Brotherhood had something to do with it," Stefan said. He pulled the dove from his pocket again and began to fiddle with it. "Do you know why Gullet is here?"

Marie shrugged. "Is that the toad of a man who's come to visit Uncle Christian? I gather he wanted to get a look at me."

"At you? Why?" Stefan said.

Marie shoved against him with her shoulder. "Again with the flattery. Honestly, Stefan, it takes an army of mice for you to say anything a girl might want to hear."

Stefan cringed, but found he was smiling. "Sorry. You know what I meant."

She gave him an arch look. "Well, Herr Gullet is interested in my role in last night's affair. It seems no one has been able to talk to the cats in quite some time."

"But you didn't really—" he began.

She shrugged, smiling like the proverbial cat with tail feathers already in its mouth. "Apparently, I did. And it's earned me some sort of scholarship."

Stefan put the dove away one more time. "What are you saying?"

Marie broke into a grin and grabbed his hands. "I'm going to the Pagoda Tree! To study animals and kingdoms and cats and everything. I don't know how Herr Gullet did it, but he's impressed my father. And Christian . . . well, he's working on Mother as we speak. But he'll convince her, I know it. I'm going to be a part of your world!"

Stefan allowed her to swing him around, a happy circle that stopped suddenly when he dropped her hands. "Marie. This world, it's not as wonderful as it might sound. Last night we did horrible things."

Marie grew serious. "Stefan Drosselmeyer, you dolt. *Why* do you think we did horrible things? Because we didn't *know* any better. Ignorance is the refuge of the . . . ignorant. Imagine if we had ambassadors to the other kingdoms. What conflicts we could avoid. All of this might have been resolved by negotiation long ago. Before pride and accidents got in the way. Honestly, I finally meet a boy and he's dumb as a stump."

"Hey," Stefan snapped back. "No tree jokes."

Marie's glare was hot enough to melt snow. And then she laughed.

He couldn't help but laugh, too. They collapsed against each other until they sighed and stopped, Marie's cheek pressed against his chest.

His arm went around her waist as if it was the most natural thing in the world. "The Pagoda Tree," he said softly.

"Yes." Her glossy brown hair smelled of orange blossoms. "If the universe truly is a clock, perhaps knowledge is the key that winds it."

Stefan buried his nose in her hair, breathing in the scent of spring on Christmas Day. "Thank you," he said.

Marie's impish face was mere inches from his own. "For what?"

"For this."

He leaned in and kissed her, and she kissed him back, and Christmas, and the world, went on for a little while without them.

Epilogue

THE RAT SAT in the corner of the tavern, his back to the broken chimney pipe that warmed the room. It was his habit every night to sit by the fire, as if drying out from the flood that drowned the ancient world. He despised water, avoided rivers and the shore. When asked, he would say death lived in the waves.

He worked for his supper, writing letters, sharing news. And sometimes, if he was in the mood, he would sing.

"Give us the one about the Piper," an old rat called from the far side of the room, where he sat with his cronies from the docks.

Ernst Listz shook his head. "Not tonight," he said.

A few of the rougher wharf rats jeered. The mice in the room looked at him curiously.

"Something else, then?" the barkeeper asked, knowing that songs kept his clients in their seats longer, buying rounds of ale and supper. "How about something new?"

Ernst took a breath and dropped his heavy coat to stand before them in his own gray fur, streaked prematurely white. A grizzled specimen that had seen better days. "I have a song for you. It's about a boy with six brothers, who comes to grief in a city called Nuremberg."

The room shifted. The rats stared into their cups and the mice sighed collectively as they turned to face him. They knew this story. Many had lost family to the making of the tale.

Ernst had suffered as well. Like the rat in the ballad of Hameln, he was last to the river that Christmas Day, the river that ran beneath the city. He had walked beside the body of his King, seen him laid to rest beneath the roots of a weeping willow tree. And by the time he reached the tail end of the fleeing army, every last mouse from Boldavia had been drowned and swept away.

Ernst hung his head. Took a deep breath. Then lifted his voice, and sang.

Appendix

The Ballad of Hameln Town

I travel the long way home
Although it leads nowhere
O'er track and field and stone
Through cold and bitter air

Hameln town is a long way down, a long way down

The sky grows dark and threatens me
The ground bites at my feet
The wind beats back my whiskers
With rain and snow and sleet

Still I go on
Through field and farm
To where my darlings lie
'Twas only the weight of bitter Fate
I lived while they did die

Hameln town is a long way down, a long way down

*They say that day the sun shone bright
And bellies were well filled
When the sweetest sound
Broke the hush
And beckoned down the hill

*Young lads they heard their true love call
Old mothers heard their young
And children heeded their families
Begging them to run

*And so they came
Unaware of the game
To frolic at the shore
Of the river wide and blue that sighed
Of summer green and pure

Family by family
Cousin, sister, son
They leapt in by the hundred
And drowned
Every last one

Except for me
And Woe is she
My constant companion still
For I was away from Hameln town
The day that tune played ill

And now I'm home
The rest have gone
Beneath the river black
I'm going too
Through bracken and rue
To the shore that took them back

From Hameln town.
It's a long way down. A long way down.

*Rare verses

Lament for the King of Mice

A boy with six bound brothers, in a kingdom by the sea—
No joy, no love, no sunlight is fated there for thee.

The clockmaker, Scourge of Mousedom,
He dug too far and deep,
Cracked the sky beneath Boldavia
And caused the world to weep.

The Queen of Mice, she sacrificed
To magicks dark and wild.
"Avenge my kin, my kingdom,
By giving me a child!"

A boy with six bound brothers, in a kingdom by the sea—
No joy, no love, no sunlight is fated there for thee.

The spell was cast, seven souls lashed
To the body of one wee babe.
Crushed 'neath the heel of a Drosselmeyer
Their mother they could not save.

"Follow me, lads," the orphan kings howled
In a voice like the seven seas.
"The clockmaker's life is forfeit.
We'll press him to his knees!"

A boy with six bound brothers, in a kingdom by the sea—
No joy, no love, no sunlight is fated there for thee.

Onward to cursed Nuremberg,
Beneath the earth and above,
To the den of the Drosselmeyer,
All for a mother's love.

Hannibal, he led the charge;
Oh, how he fought and died!
Julius, Genghis, Charlemagne,
Hard-pressed and side by side.

A boy with six bound brothers, in a kingdom by the sea—
No joy, no love, no sunlight is fated there for thee.

Roland, then Alexander fell,
Crushed by boot and blade.
Until one mouse stood alone:
Arthur, true and staid.

"Oh, Mother, we are sorely pressed;
My brothers leave me at last.
Would that I were the king you bore,
But I fear my time has passed.

"A boy with six bound brothers, in a kingdom by the sea—
No joy, no love, no sunlight is fated there for me."

Golden sword and golden crown,
The King fell and lay still.
No longer above, but far below.
Was this his mother's will?

Where now your bright promise, Boldavia, your kings beneath one
  crown?
Where lies the glory of Mousedom, seven fathoms down?

All is lost in shadow. Seven kings lie in one grave.
Unavenged, their mother and the kingdom they failed to save.

The Piper has been paid his due, the clockmaker his fee.
Who will harvest summer now, in that land beside the sea?

Author's Note

IN 1816, E. T. A. Hoffmann (1776–1822) published a strange story called *The Nutcracker and the Mouse King*. In it, he spun the tale of a wooden princess, a sorcerer-like godfather, a young girl named Marie, and her beloved nutcracker prince. The story inspired Alexandre Dumas's retelling, *The Nutcracker*, which in turn inspired Pyotr Illyich Tchaikovsky's ballet. *The Nutcracker* ballet was first performed in Saint Petersburg, Russia, in 1892. It went on to become a holiday favorite and one of the most popular ballets of all time.

When I was a little girl, my mother took me to see the great Mikhail Baryshnikov dance the role of the Nutcracker. Alexander Minz performed the role of my beloved Christian Drosselmeyer, and Gelsey Kirkland danced the part of Clara. I can still see them on stage together—the Nutcracker transformed into a handsome prince, the beautiful young lady in her white nightgown, and the dashing, mysterious man in black.

For some reason, when Dumas wrote his version of the Nutcracker, he changed Marie's name to Clara, and the name stuck in the ballet. In fact, in the original story, Clara is the maid, which is why I have used both names here. A change in my own version is the spelling of "Drosselmeyer." I have seen it spelled with both a "y" and with an "i"—"Drosselmeier." I have opted to use the "y" spelling because it seems to lead to less mispronunciation.

Hoffmann never gave the Nutcracker a name. In the book, he is Christian Elias Drosselmeyer's cousin, son of the toymaker Zacharias Elias Drosselmeyer. In the ballet, he is also known as the Prince. I have named him Stefan after my high school German teacher. Can you guess where some of the other names in the book come from? (Hint: What do the "E" and the "A" stand for in E. T. A. Hoffmann?)

I loved Godpapa Drosselmeyer as a little girl. And when I discovered Hoffmann's original story (tucked between the sofa and the wall at my piano teacher's house when I was in elementary school), I knew it was only a matter of time before I would build on his story.

Hoffmann had a wild imagination. I hope I have done it justice. His original work, along with Tchaikovsky's music, and Baryshnikov's dancing, inspired this story. I hope my book, like Hoffmann's and the ballet, will also be a favorite for generations to come.

Sherri L. Smith

Los Angeles, 2015